THE WOMAN WAS BORN TO MAKE TROUBLE; HE KNEW IT FROM THE MOMENT THEY MET . . .

The beautiful redhead glaring at him from the cell's narrow cot was the latest in a seemingly endless succession of shocks. As pretty as she was, she wasn't the woman they'd put in that cell. Her unexplained appearance had sent a geyser of alarm through several law enforcement agencies. Joe had been dispatched to find out what the blazes was going on.

It couldn't be true. That had been his first, stunned reaction. People didn't just materialize and dematerialize inside locked jail cells. But he couldn't deny the proof his own eyes provided. There was no sign of the prisoner who was supposed to be occupying that cell. And while the mystery woman's presence—or more to the point, her specific location—might turn out to be a mistake, she was conspicuously, vibrantly real.

She was the most stunning women he'd ever seen. The bolt of sexual awareness that slammed through him unnerved Joe as much as anything that had happened in the last tense, stressful day and a half. But it also angered him, which, thankfully, allowed him to maintain his austere facade.

"You have some explaining to do, miss."

"FBI?" she asked, as casually as if she were asking him to pass the salt. "Come on, 'fess up. It's written all over you. Nice stare, by the way—intimidating, but not overly hostile."

"You don't seem to realize how serious your situation is." He pulled a gold fountain pen from his pocket and unscrewed the pen's cap.

"Oh? My name is Samantha Cook. I have no idea how I got here. I'm twenty-eight, single, and self-employed. Several hours ago I woke up here, on this cot. This is all I was wearing." She stood up and held the blanket covering her open for half a second, long enough to let the man see but not ogle.

For a moment, Joe Mercer forgot to breathe.

Praise for Lynn Turner's previous work:
". . . A wonderful tale of cat and mouse. With expert pacing and wonderful romance, Lynn Turner pens a keeper!"
—*Romantic Times* on *The Woman in the Mirror*

LYNN TURNER

RACE AGAINST TIME

PINNACLE BOOKS
KENSINGTON PUBLISHING CORP.

PINNACLE BOOKS are published by

Kensington Publishing Corp.
850 Third Avenue
New York, NY 10022

The P logo Reg. U.S. Pat. & TM Off. Pinnacle is a trade-
mark of Kensington Publishing Corp.

First Printing: July, 1995

Printed in the United States of America

One

Of the several hundred people who noticed the four derelicts huddled in front of the Trailways terminal, few spared them more than a passing thought. In Washington, vagrants and undocumented aliens were as commonplace as cherry blossoms in April.

All four men were inadequately dressed, and the way three of them hunkered into their thin jackets, now and then stamping their feet or slapping their arms, suggested they were accustomed to a much warmer climate. The fourth man stood slightly apart, shoulders hunched against the cold and hands buried in the pockets of his worn pea coat. He kept a watchful eye on the intersections to the left and right while the others conducted a frantic conference.

Nicolai couldn't understand a word of their gibberish, but he suspected they were discussing his deteriorating health. He was worried, too. Under the knit seaman's cap his hair was falling out by the fistful. It had been three days since he'd been able to keep anything down, and the slightest movement caused his joints to scream in agony. His alarming physical decline wasn't the source of his anxiety, though, nor was the knowledge that he was going to get much worse, very quickly. He was worried because, should he become completely incapacitated, none of the others was qualified to take over his part of the mission. He was prepared to die, was in fact looking forward to it, but he didn't want his death to be for nothing.

His impatient gaze drifted to his companions, who were apparently oblivious to the possibility that four men standing around in this bitter cold might eventually attract attention. He reflected grimly that it was a miracle they'd made it this far.

Strange to think that less than three months had passed since Rashad first appeared in his village to present their mad, desperate plan and solicit his help. At first Nicolai had been shocked and alarmed, then contemptuous, convinced Rashad's hatred had driven him insane. He must be, to believe that four men could do what he was proposing.

But Rashad had stayed in the village for two days and two nights, hammering at his skepticism with a combination of rational arguments and impassioned appeals, until finally he convinced Nicolai that it *could* be done. The most difficult part, of course, would be getting the device into the United States, but Rashad assured him that "friends" were already orchestrating a plan to accomplish that. Once on American soil, though, Rashad promised that the very openness of a free society would work in their favor.

So far Rashad had been right, about everything. Less than thirty minutes ago the two of them had arrived in America's capital, precisely on schedule, in a Ford Escort they'd rented yesterday in New York.

Nicolai was still amazed at how easy it had been. Once they left the airport, no one had expressed the slightest interest in their identities or their destination. In fact, if not for the atlas Rashad had purchased and the large roadside "Welcome to" signs, he was sure they wouldn't have known when they left one state and entered another. Still, he was glad for the semiautomatic pistol resting in the deep right pocket of his coat. The gun had been waiting in a locker at JFK. As requested, it had no safety mechanisms, and Nicolai had pumped a round into the chamber before placing it in his pocket. Not that he didn't trust Rashad or his associates, but the mission was too important to leave anything to chance.

Deciding that their incomprehensible jabbering had gone on long enough, he caught Rashad's eye and jerked his head in the direction of 12th Street. Rashad nodded, said a few terse words to the other two, and moved to his side.

"There is a problem," Rashad murmured. His breath streamed from his mouth like cigarette smoke. "The maps were misleading."

Nicolai straightened in alarm, grimacing as the sudden movement set off an avalanche of pain. "Are you saying we're lost?"

Rashad hastened to reassure him. "No, no, we're directly north of the Mall, just as we intended. But it's farther away than I thought. Perhaps we should go back and collect the car."

Nicolai vetoed the suggestion with a curt shake of his head. They had abandoned the vehicle several blocks from the rendezvous point to eliminate the potential difficulties of traffic and parking. By now someone might have discovered it, reported it to the authorities.

"Let me see the maps."

He sifted through a stack of glossy tourist maps the other two men produced until he found one that provided the routes for the Metrorail subway system.

"What are you looking for?" The anxious query came from Kahlil, the youngest and least experienced member of the team. "We cannot alter the plans."

"Or the schedule," Amir added. Both his tone and the stare he leveled at Nicolai were hard, uncompromising. "The statement will be released within the hour."

Nicolai refolded the map and pointed to a circle centered over parallel orange and blue lines. "Exactly. Which is why we'll have to use the underground railway."

Amir started to object but Nicolai cut him off, his voice sharp with impatience. "The military probably detected our presence as soon as we removed the device from the special case. This section of the city will be swarming with NEST teams before we can reach the target on foot."

Kahlil and Amir exchanged an uncertain look. "What are NEST teams?" Amir asked suspiciously.

"Nuclear Emergency Search Teams— nuclear intelligence specialists who are trained to locate radioactive material."

Nicolai turned the map so they could follow as he explained. "These circles are subway stations. We can reach this one— the one labeled Federal Triangle— in ten minutes or so, and then get off here, at the Smithsonian station on the south side of the Mall. They won't be able to track our movements once we are underground."

"This station is closer," Rashad pointed out, indicating a circle a couple of blocks south of their present position.

Nicolai shook his head. "It's the central station, the place where all the lines intersect. We could be separated, or take the wrong train."

He could see that Kahlil and Amir didn't like this sudden change in plans, but evidently he had convinced them it was necessary. Neither man objected when Rashad hefted the faded khaki duffel bag from the sidewalk and slung it over his shoulder. The bag weighed less than thirty pounds, but Nicolai was in no shape to carry it five feet, much less all the way to Pennsylvania Avenue.

Samantha Cook was finishing her complimentary continental breakfast when the phone rang. She downed the last half ounce of reconstituted orange juice on the way to pick it up. The voice that answered her greeting caused her full, sensual mouth to curve in pleased surprise.

"Mornin', gorgeous. Did you sleep well?"

"Like a log," Sam replied as she sank down on the bed. She deposited the empty juice glass on the bedside table and picked up the TV's remote control, punching the mute button to silence the morning newscast just as a graphic commemorating Pearl Harbor Day appeared over the perky young reporter's left shoulder. "You know me—I could sleep through the Second Coming."

"Rub it in, why don't you," Lucas replied, his rich baritone rumbling in her ear.

"Hey, it's not my fault you have chronic insomnia. If you didn't read those dumb books right before you go to bed—"

His indignant protest came on cue. "Science fiction isn't dumb! In fact, I find it intellectually stimulating."

"Then why don't you read it first thing in the morning? Save the Congressional Record or the *Post* Op-Ed page for bedtime."

There was a moment's silence, followed by a wry chuckle. "You'd think by now I'd know better than to match wits with you before noon."

"You'd think," Sam concurred. She picked up a pale blue conference brochure next to the phone and scanned the printed agenda. "You're in luck, ace— lunch is at 12:30. Your ol' gray Delco should be fully charged by then."

"Yeah, well . . . that's what I called about."

Samantha frowned and replaced the brochure on the table.

"Much as I was looking forward to lunch with you and a couple hundred cops, I have to cancel."

"Dammit, Lucas," she complained. "I haven't seen you in four days."

His sigh came through as clearly as if he'd been sitting next to her. "I'm sorry. Really. I'll make it up to you, promise."

"Dinner at Blackie's," she said without missing a beat. "Tomorrow night."

"It's a date."

Mollified by the prospect of a medium rare filet mignon, Sam shoved a pillow against the headboard and scooted back to recline against it. "So what's up? Is something about to break?"

Lucas's slight hesitation was an answer in itself. "Maybe. It'll probably turn out to be a false alarm, but I think I should stay at the station just in case."

Sam twirled the telephone cord around an index finger, her eyes narrowing speculatively. Such circumspection, coming from dyed-in-the-wool news hound Lucas Davenport, was a sure sign that something big was in the air. "C'mon, Lucas," she coaxed. "In case it's slipped your mind, I have a Level 3 security clearance."

There was another, longer pause. "Give me your word you won't say anything till you've checked with me."

Sam rolled her eyes and reminded herself that all the journalists she knew were neurotic; it seemed to come with the territory. "You have my word— I promise not to leak the story to your competition."

"Or to any of the cops at the conference, or your FBI contacts," Lucas insisted.

"Them either," she said in exasperation. "What's going on?"

"There's been a flurry of communications between the Nuclear Regulatory Commission and the Pentagon this morning, and a few minutes ago we got a tip that several NEST teams have been activated. It may be just an exercise, but none of our sources were aware one was scheduled."

Sam sat up and swung her long legs off the bed. "The NRC? Why would they be in touch with the Pentagon, unless— oh, God, you think— ?"

"I don't think anything yet," Lucas interrupted. "Like I said, it'll probably turn out to be a false alarm."

"Yeah, right," she muttered.

"But just in case . . ."

"What?"

"Stay at the hotel till we know for sure."

A sudden chill lifted the hair at Samantha's nape. The opened drapes at her third-floor window framed a pewter sky that threatened more snow, traffic streaming by on I-495 and, beyond, the Alexandria suburbs. It appeared to be a typical December morning along the Potomac. Except that evidently some people in Washington had reason to suspect there might be a stray nuclear bomb in the vicinity.

"Christ, Lucas," she said softly.

"Look, I didn't mean to scare you. It's just that I'll feel better knowing where you are. I'll be in touch as soon as I find out what's going on. Meanwhile, go ahead with your plans— make your speech and then network till you drop. Just please don't give your phone number to any more John Law types. The competition's intimidating as hell already."

His attempt to lighten the mood failed utterly. Her presentation about advances in DNA matching had suddenly dropped to dead last on Samantha's list of priorities.

"You're staying in Silver Spring, right?" she demanded. "You haven't got some wild idea about going into D.C. to check this out?"

"I'm not going anywhere," Lucas assured her. "We've got a half dozen people out digging for leads, from the Pentagon to the White House and Langley. I have to be here to piece everything together for the noon newscast— assuming, of course, that there's a story to piece together."

After she hung up, Sam continued to stare out the window for a couple of minutes before she got up and carried her breakfast tray to the hall. Lucas was right, she told herself; there was no point getting spooked over a few exchanges between the NRC and the Pentagon and the activation of a couple of NEST teams. This was Washington, D.C., after all. There were how many— close to a dozen?— military facilities within a hundred miles or so. Readiness drills and exercises were everyday occurrences.

Unfortunately the pep talk didn't get rid of the knot that had formed in her stomach or the goose-bumps covering her arms. She absently rubbed them through the sleeves of her robe as she restored the television's audio. She stayed glued to the set for several minutes, in case the Alexandria station had also picked up on the story, but they seemed to be devoting the entire segment to Pearl Harbor Day coverage.

Her mouth twisting in frustration, Sam turned the television off and headed for the bathroom to shower. Damn, she wished Lucas hadn't even called. She'd have been pissed when he didn't show up for lunch, but he'd have charmed her out of it, like he always did.

A few minutes later, as she tugged a slip into place over her still-damp body, she suddenly froze, the silky fabric bunched around her hips. Pearl Harbor Day. The timing couldn't be coincidental . . . could it? Surely the army wouldn't conduct a nuclear readiness exercise today, of all days.

By the time they reached H Street, Nicolai knew he wasn't going to make it, even with Kahlil and Amir virtually carrying him. He struggled to hold despair and anger at bay; he must think clearly, conceive an alternate plan while he was still lucid.

They would have to use the Metro Center station, just ahead at 12th and G Streets. There was no other choice. He would arm and enable the weapon after they entered the subway, and leave it to Rashad to throw the firing switch when he and the others reached the target.

The knowledge that he wouldn't be with them when they detonated the device left a bitter taste in his mouth. *He* was the expert, the one essential member of the team. These ignorant fools knew nothing about nuclear weapons, nor did they possess even a rudimentary understanding of the struggles taking place beyond their small, godforsaken corner of the world.

Forcing himself to swallow his resentment, he muttered a hoarse request to stop. Kahlil and Amir halted in the middle of the sidewalk and immediately took advantage of the opportunity to shift their grip on his arms and back and redistribute his weight. Nicolai clenched his teeth against the pain their manhandling caused. Rashad, walking a few feet ahead, stopped and turned toward them with a questioning frown. Before Nicolai could speak, the piercing shriek of a siren rent the air and a large white van swerved to the curb half a block to the north.

Several pedestrians glanced around, more curious than alarmed, but no one else stopped until a half-dozen soldiers in full combat gear, their rifles unslung, scrambled from the van and an amplified voice began blaring instructions.

"Attention, please! Will anyone carrying a briefcase, attaché case, or any package of that approximate size or larger immediately stop and step to the curb."

The message was repeated in several languages, including Russian and Farsi. Amir's grip on his arm became excruciating, but Nicolai scarcely registered the pain. An identical white van had appeared farther down 12th Street, and the same orders were being broadcast to pedestrians approaching from the south.

"They've found us!" Kahlil said in a harsh, panic-stricken whisper.

"The subway," Rashad barked. "Across the street, quickly!"

Nicolai clutched Amir's arm. "Take the pistol," he said hoarsely. "In my right pocket."

The first NEST team member lumbered from the rear of the van, moving slowly and awkwardly in his antiradiation suit, as Amir released Nicolai and withdrew the gun. Rashad was halfway to the subway entrance by the time Kahlil lunged off the curb and into the 12th Street traffic. Half carrying, half dragging Nicolai, he shrieked frenzied curses at the oncoming vehicles as he navigated an erratic course between them. One of the soldiers shouted an order to stop.

Through a haze of pain Nicolai saw Rashad reach the sidewalk, then hesitate for a moment, pivoting to look back over his shoulder. He opened his mouth to speak— probably to exhort Kahlil to hurry— but whatever he intended to say was lost in a burst of automatic weapons fire. His body jerked convulsively as the bullets ripped through him, and then the firing suddenly stopped and he collapsed to the pavement, his eyes and mouth opened wide in astonishment. He landed on his back, on top of the duffel.

The squeal of brakes and screams of terror replaced the sound of gunfire. Kahlil stumbled to a horrified halt several feet shy of the curb. More shots rang out, directly behind them. Nicolai recognized the difference in the reports and knew they came from Amir's pistol. His fingers closed like talons on Kahlil's wrist.

"*Go!*" he said in a guttural snarl.

Either the command or his grip penetrated the young Palestinian's terror. They staggered over the curbside mound of snow and slush together and Nicolai threw himself to the pavement beside Rashad's body, shoving at him to move him off the duffel.

"Help me!" he rasped. "We can still make it."

Kahlil dragged the duffel free, while Amir fired several more rounds as cover. Nicolai stumbled toward the subway entrance. Three men and two well-dressed women cowered on the steps just below street level. He lurched past them, leaning on the handrail for support. There was another volley of automatic fire from the street. In his haste to get down the stairs Kahlil shoved one of the women hard against the wall. She whimpered softly, too frightened to cry out.

Nicolai's legs gave way as he tottered off the last step. He fell hard onto his hands and knees, his breath coming in ragged, anguished gasps. Kahlil clattered down the last few steps and knelt beside him.

"Amir . . ."

Nicolai moved his head in a blunt negative. Clutching Kahlil's shoulder, he levered himself to his feet. "They'll be coming after us. Quickly, bring the bag."

Samantha fastened the safety clasp of the Daniel Mink gold watch that had been a birthday present from Lucas, absently noting that the time was 7:55 as she turned away from the dresser mirror. A tailored bronze gabardine suit and cream silk blouse lay on the bed. For a few moments she stopped worrying and wondering when Lucas would call. She even allowed herself a small smile of satisfaction as she reached for the blouse.

She'd spent a considerable amount of time putting together today's ensemble, down to the tiger's-eye brooch and earrings that subtly drew attention to her fair complexion, deep green eyes and lustrous, shoulder-length auburn hair. She'd set out to create the image of a professional who took herself and her work seriously. She wanted a look that was knowledgeable, competent, yet feminine. Too mannish, and this group would immediately label her a ball-breaking dyke with designs on their turf; too ladylike and they'd categorize her as a "girl" who didn't know beans from buttermilk about forensic science. Samantha preferred to define herself. For today at least, she knew she'd succeeded.

The phone rang just as she slipped her fingers inside the collar of the blouse. Her entire body jerked in startled reaction. Dropping the blouse, she spun around and snatched up the handset.

"Lucas?"

"Thank God I caught you." He sounded harried, stressed out. "I was afraid you might already have gone down."

"I don't speak until 9:15. What have you found out?"

"Enough to put me in touch with my own mortality. Apparently it's a full-scale alert. Not, I repeat, *not* a drill."

Samantha dropped onto the bed. She didn't notice that she was crumpling her freshly pressed suit.

"Are you saying there's actually a nuclear threat? Here? In *Washington, D.C.*, for God's sake?"

"All I know for sure is that for the past fifteen

minutes or so NEST teams and army antiterrorist units have been scaring the bejesus out of commuters from the Potomac to RFK Stadium." An excited clamor erupted in the background. Lucas muttered a terse, "Hold on. Something's coming in from the remote unit I sent to the FBI Building."

Samantha waited, unconsciously gripping the phone with both hands as she listened to the largely incoherent, chaotic sounds coming from Lucas's end of the line. The newsroom could never be described as peaceful or even particularly organized, but this morning the staff seemed to be setting a new standard of deranged pandemonium.

"Oh, God," Lucas said in her ear. His tone, more than the words, brought Samantha to her feet. Miles of fiber optics transmitted his alarm and the dread underlying it with perfect clarity.

"What?! Lucas, dammit, what's going on?"

He didn't respond, but someone near him muttered a shaken, "Christ."

Sam suppressed an urge to scream into the mouthpiece. "Lucas, please . . . what's *happening?*"

He barked an order to "Go to the RPU!" and then finally answered her, his words clipped as he relayed the live feed coming into the control room. "Something's going down at the Metro Center station— a NEST team, two antiterrorist teams . . . an exchange of gunfire between the army and four men . . ."

Sam grabbed the remote control. A couple of seconds later the live remote broadcast appeared on the television screen.

"I've got it," she said. "I'm watching."

A nervous but excited young male voice described the mayhem being captured by a minicam's lens.

"— was carrying some kind of satchel, which two of the remaining three men have now retrieved. As you can see, they're moving toward the subway entrance, apparently attempting to escape. Two civilians and one NEST team member have been wounded, in addition to the suspected terrorist who was killed—and let me emphasize that 'suspected.' We have no confirmation as to the four men's identities or their intentions . . ."

The minicam had zoomed in on a swarthy man backing across the street. He moved slowly, almost leisurely, insolent defiance in every line of his body. He neither crouched to make a smaller target of himself nor took evasive action, though he could easily have dodged behind any of several vehicles which contained potential hostages. As Samantha watched, mesmerized, he raised a pistol and pointed it at someone out of camera range.

The ratcheting pop of automatic gunfire punctuated the young reporter's narrative and the swarthy man's head suddenly disappeared in a red mist. The picture wavered for a second or two, as if the cameraman had flinched, then quickly refocused on the body sprawled in the dirty gray slush at the edge of 12th Street.

"Shit!" squawked from the speaker before the reporter collected himself. "Excuse me, I apologize. But as you just witnessed, another of the four suspected terrorists has been killed by army fire. The remaining two men have entered the subway station. It looks like one of the antiterrorist teams is going after them . . ."

"Sam!"

She jumped as Lucas's voice cracked like a whip

in her ear. "Jesus, Lucas," she said in a shaken whisper. "Did you see—"

"Listen to me! Get into the bathroom, *now*, into the tub!"

Sam shook her head in confusion. "What?"

"Just do it, goddammit!"

And then she understood. She only took time to murmur a choked, "Lucas . . ." before she dropped the phone and scuttled across the bed. She was several steps short of the bathroom door when the room's large plate glass window imploded and a shock wave of intense heat knocked her off her feet.

Two

The American Airlines 727 had begun its final approach to National Airport when Nicolai threw the firing switch. Within seconds the plane plunged from the sky like a dart, nosing into a shopping center adjacent to the hotel where 207 law enforcement officers had convened to learn about recent advances in forensic science. One wing clipped a third-floor balcony at the southern end of the hotel, sending several thousand gallons of aircraft fuel and a river of flame into the corridor beyond.

Fortunately the fire was contained on the third floor and quickly extinguished, and many of the hotel guests had gone down to the main dining room for breakfast. However, by the time rescue workers reached the charred and bowed door of Samantha Cook's room, the death toll exceeded twenty. A volunteer firefighter and a hotel employee carefully lifted the slender young woman they found lying face-down on the singed beige carpet and carried her to the nearest stairwell. From there, waiting paramedics transferred her to the triage area that had been hastily assembled in a cafeteria at the far end of the shopping center. Though she was unconscious and had sustained first-degree burns, her vital signs were strong and

she wasn't in shock. She received emergency first
aid and was moved to the Cajun restaurant next
door, along with a dozen other victims who could,
and therefore would, wait for further treatment.

In that first frenetic hour, several people who
came in contact with the young woman remarked
on how lucky she'd been to escape with such minor
injuries, but none of them had time to spare more
than a fleeting gratitude and relief for her miraculous good fortune.

Public communications had been knocked out,
though no one could say whether the plane crash
or the horrendous explosion across the river was
responsible. For the time being at least there was
no telephone service, no radio or television reception. Some wireless transmitters worked; others
didn't. A teenager who'd shown up with four sets
of Radio Shack walkie-talkies was temporarily put
in charge of dispatching the emergency vehicles
that were still operational.

Gradually reports began to filter in as more vol-
unteers arrived and people stopped to pass on
scraps of information. It was true, most affirmed
in stunned tones that said they were having trouble
believing it themselves: a nuclear weapon had been
detonated inside Washington. Several people said
the bomb had gone off in a subway tunnel not far
from the White House. Others claimed the Capitol
Building had been ground zero. Still others con-
tended that it couldn't have been a nuke, because
soldiers with equipment that measured radiation
had been sent to Bethesda and Arlington, and
their gauges and meters weren't picking up anything.

For almost two hours the young woman who'd
been carried from the third floor of the hotel lay

on a sleeping bag someone had appropriated from a sporting goods store in the shopping center, oblivious to the tumult surrounding her. Eventually she was put aboard an ambulance and taken to a hospital emergency room, where her burns were treated and she was subjected to a battery of tests and x-rays, none of which yielded an explanation for her failure to regain consciousness. She lay on a gurney in a crowded corridor until early evening, when an exhausted resident signed the order to transport her to one of the few facilities in the area with available beds— a nursing home between Alexandria and Virginia Hills. In the confusion of that long day, no one had taken time to obtain her name from the hotel register. The middle-aged woman on duty at the ElderCare admitting desk wasn't fazed by this oversight. She simply assigned the young woman to a private room at the end of the east wing and recorded the name Jane Doe on the necessary forms.

Lucas finally got a call through to the hotel at 6:40 that evening. The connection was poor to begin with and kept dissolving into crackling static, but eventually he comprehended that everyone who'd been injured in the fire had been evacuated to area hospitals, and that a temporary morgue had been set up at a nearby community center.

The assistant manager on the other end of the line gave him directions to the community center to pass on to the station's audience, then asked him to urge anyone in the Alexandria area attempting to locate relatives or friends who'd been at the hotel to go there, since several bodies hadn't yet been identified.

Lucas closed his eyes in reaction to that last piece of information. *Please, God, no,* he prayed silently as the woman droned on. Red Cross personnel had taken charge of the hotel's registration records, she said, and would have an updated list of casualties at the community center morgue.

He thanked her and hung up, then immediately dialed the number she'd provided. Of course the lines were jammed. Or maybe melted. He swore in frustration. Even if he could have justified leaving the station in the midst of a bona fide national emergency, the army had closed the interstates as well as all major routes through or around D.C., and the streets that were still open were choked with stalled vehicles and panic-stricken citizens trying to escape before somebody set off another bomb.

So far six terrorist groups— including a couple nobody had ever heard of— had claimed credit for the bombing, and three of them had promised further unspecified "acts of retribution." During the past hour, since partial phone service was restored, the newsroom had received a dozen unconfirmed reports that military roadblocks were turning people back into the city. Lucas didn't doubt that it was true. According to a source at the Defense Intelligence Agency, anyone who'd been within a mile of ground zero was probably contaminated immediately. The source referred to those who'd been above ground, of course. Most of the explosive force, and most of the radiation, had been confined to the Metrorail tunnels. Anyone who'd had the bad luck to be down there had been atomized or burned to a cinder within seconds. But thousands on the surface had survived the blast, for the time being at least. They couldn't be allowed to just drive off in their radioactive cars and minivans.

Lucas tried the community center number a couple more times before things got so hectic that he had to abandon the effort. It was after nine when he finally got through. The good news was that Samantha Cook wasn't on the list of fatalities. The bad news was that she wasn't listed among the survivors who'd been admitted to local hospitals, either. A Red Cross official explained what that meant in the professionally benevolent voice of an undertaker, as if Lucas hadn't already figured it out for himself.

"Either she's been admitted somewhere under the wrong name— or possibly as a Jane Doe— or she's one of the deceased who still haven't been identified."

"How many of them are women?" Lucas asked tautly.

The man consulted his list. "Three, for sure. A few of the . . ." He floundered, his poise momentarily deserting him. ". . . the bodies are so badly burned that a medical examiner will have to determine their sex."

The picture that flashed into Lucas's mind was so hideous that he flinched in reaction. "Ms. Cook is a 28-year-old Caucasian. She's tall— five-ten— and slim, like a model. She has shoulder-length dark red hair and green eyes." He paused, trying to hold her image and at the same time maintain the precarious balance between hope and dread. "She'd be wearing a gold watch, and a square-cut emerald ring on her right hand."

The Red Cross man hemmed and hawed, unwilling to commit to even a tentative identification on the basis of a telephone conversation. His obduracy nudged Lucas past the limits of his self-control.

"For crissake, man!" he exploded. "I'm way the hell up in Silver Spring! In case you hadn't heard, Washington got nuked today. It's a fucking war zone inside the beltway. Not much is working and *nothing* is moving, in any direction. God knows when I'll be able to get down there."

His vehemence convinced the man to hie himself to the unheated storage room where the corpses had been laid out and repeat Lucas's description to whomever had been drafted to serve as morgue attendant. When he returned six minutes later, he reported that two of the three unidentified female corpses were black and the third was a middle-aged woman "of Hispanic extraction." Lucas stayed on the line long enough to get a list of hospitals that had received the survivors, then went in search of an Alexandria phone book.

Levander Grisham's big hands were gentle as he tucked the sheet around the pale young woman. Levander was always gentle with his patients, which came as a surprise to most of them. Usually they took one look at his six-foot, four-inch, two hundred-plus-pound frame, and expected to be flung around like bags of fertilizer. It showed on their faces. They almost always winced the first time he reached to help them out of bed or turn them or assist them onto a bedpan. Levander understood that it was an involuntary reflex and was never offended.

His patients were all old, and sick, and tired. Their bones were porous and brittle and their arthritic joints hurt and their dentures didn't fit right anymore and their hearing and eyesight and memory were starting to go, or had already departed, leaving them imprisoned in frail, disintegrating bodies. Some of them required as much care as newborn babies. Others' fear and loneliness made them querulous and mean. Levander treated them all with the same patience and respect. He understood, and he sympathized. They were approaching the end, with nothing now to look forward to but a series of interminable, monotonous days and nights that all blurred together after awhile.

Except for this one.

He gazed down at her pensively, wondering who she was and why no one had come to claim her. She was a pretty girl, or had been. The bandages camouflaged but couldn't conceal the delicacy of her features—both high, aristocratic cheekbones were visible, as well as a small straight nose and her innocent yet surprisingly sensual mouth. Her ringless hands were small and elegant, the unpolished nails trimmed short. Whoever she was, those soft, perfectly proportioned hands had never scrubbed floors, or probably dishes either.

Refined. That's how she looked to Levander: a lady. He might be wrong, but he didn't think her silky wheat-colored hair had come from a bottle. He couldn't be sure because her eyelashes had been singed and the gauze wrapped around her head covered her brows. Levander wished she would open her eyes. He'd bet cash money they were the blue of a rain-washed sky.

Who was she? Where had she come from, before the hotel? People must be out looking for someone as special as her. Lots of people, probably; people with money and influence. 'Course, the mess

things were in right now, it might be weeks before
her people could trace her to this small private
nursing home. Levander would gladly have contacted them, if he'd known who and where they
were. But until she opened her eyes and spoke,
gave him a name or an address or a phone number, all he could do was take care of her and wait.

Samantha floated in the pleasantly nebulous
zone between sleep and waking, unwilling to completely surface and unable to slip back into the
dark cradle of oblivion. She was vaguely aware that
something wasn't quite right. That something was,
in fact, seriously wrong. Sooner or later she would
have to open her eyes and face whatever it was,
but not just yet. First a preliminary audit was
called for; a little information-processing to stimulate her brain cells . . .

Item one: she wasn't in her own bed. The mattress was thin and lumpy, and the feather pillow
beneath her cheek had a fusty smell that triggered
memories of the summer camp she'd attended as
a child. Item two: her ribs hurt— not badly but
with a muted ache that eventually got her attention— and her back and arms felt sunburned.
Which was, of course, impossible. She hadn't been
outdoors without a sweater or jacket since October.
She cautiously extended her right arm. Her fingers made contact with item three: a cool masonry
wall. Rough stone, or possibly cinder block. Powdery surface. Chalk? Mildew?

Sam's forehead crinkled in a puzzled frown. But
a moment later her bewilderment was forgotten as
a procession of surreal vignettes suddenly flooded
her mind— murky, out-of-focus images, each ap-

pearing for hardly more than an instant before dissolving into the next. She saw herself, smiling as she turned away from a mirror . . . grabbing the phone . . . jumping as Lucas barked her name . . . diving across the bed, racing for the bathroom. And then the images were eclipsed by physical sensations and vivid, piercing emotion— the nubby carpet under her feet . . . the sound of glass shattering behind her . . . a horrible moment of realization, followed by stunned, *this-can't-be-happening* disbelief and, finally, a headlong rush into blind terror as a giant hand seemed to lift her and hurl her forward . . .

Her eyes snapped open and she scrabbled to her knees, her movements clumsy with haste. She was trembling. Her breath came in sharp, shallow gasps and her heart knocked against her ribs, as if she'd abruptly woken in the middle of a nightmare. But if it had been a nightmare, Sam thought dazedly as she took in her surroundings, she must still be asleep. She was kneeling on a narrow cot shoved against one wall of a dreary eight-by-eight foot cell.

A jail cell, if the floor-to-ceiling bars in front of her were any indication.

A Third World jail cell, judging by the furnishings, which in addition to the cot consisted of an old-fashioned wall-mounted porcelain basin and a toilet, sans lid, wedged into the far corner. Equally unnerving, she belatedly realized that her wardrobe was as scanty as the accommodations: panties and a slip.

"Whoa," she muttered. And then, trying to convince herself there was no need to panic, "Okay, take it easy. You've had stranger dreams than this."

Which was certainly true. The trouble was that,

while her dreams were often so graphic that she emerged from them feeling slightly disoriented— unsure whether the images swirling out of her consciousness like water down a drain were wisps of fantasy or authentic, half-forgotten memories— she didn't recall ever being aware that she was dreaming *while* she was dreaming.

Did that mean she *wasn't* dreaming? That all this was *real?*

"Uh-uh, no way," she assured herself, but with more bravado than conviction.

She closed her eyes and inhaled several deep, cleansing breaths, then pinched her arm, hard, for good measure. She felt the pinch, in fact it hurt like the devil, but otherwise nothing changed. Her ribs still ached, her knees still communicated the presence of flat wire mesh beneath the lumpy mattress, and the staleness of the air still saturated every breath.

Terrific, she thought, opening her eyes and sitting back on her heels. *So much for Plan A. All right, Sammy, you're a scientist. Observe, analyze, deduce.*

Despite the evidence confronting her, reason and every law of physics that had ever been drummed into her decreed that she hadn't actually been whisked from a comfortable hotel room to a musty jail cell in some Third World hellhole. Ergo, she *must* be dreaming. Which meant there'd been no phone calls from Lucas, no bomb . . . maybe even no law enforcement seminar. She wasn't here— wherever "here" was— she was in her own bed in Rockville, snuggled under the comforter she'd bought last year at Penney's white sale.

All of which would have been a hell of a lot easier to believe if she didn't keep flashing on the image of a man's head being blown apart.

Fear nibbled at her with sharp, pointed little teeth. Her hand shook as she reached out and gingerly brushed her fingers against the wall. It felt real enough— cool, rough, definitely solid. But despite the mild throbbing in her arms, the skin didn't appear to have been burned, either by the sun or nuclear radiation. God, was she losing it? If a nuke *had* gone off in D.C., might she be experiencing some kind of radiation-induced delirium? An atomic psychosis, or something?

"Get a grip, Samantha," she muttered impatiently.

Delusion, dream, or nightmarish reality? One thing was for sure— she wasn't going to come up with any answers sitting on her butt. She climbed off the cot and went to shove her face against the bars.

"Hey! Is anybody out there? I know my rights, dammit! I'm entitled to a phone call."

There was no response, not even a crabby "Shaddup!" from a neighboring cell. The faint, far-off sound of music wafted down a gloomy corridor that stretched away to the left. It was a bouncy, spirited tune, the kind it was impossible to listen to and not tap your foot. Sam tried to remember where she'd heard it before, and eventually realized it was from one of her grandfather's collection of big band LPs. She thought it was a Benny Goodman number or maybe Glenn Miller— "String of Pearls," or "Something Stomp."

"Weirder and weirder," she murmured. If all this was a hallucination, it had to rank right up there with the top ten most original of all time. So far she'd survived a nuclear detonation, woken up in a jail cell wearing nothing but her underwear— though she didn't care to contemplate what abstruse Freudian meaning *that* detail might signify— and now she was hearing music straight out of the 1930s.

She couldn't wait to see what would happen next.

Lucas had been running on adrenaline for almost thirty hours. His last meal had been his usual breakfast of a high-carb, high-fiber breakfast bar, a couple of vitamin capsules and a cup of herbal tea, yesterday morning. At least he thought it had been yesterday. He longed for a shower and shave, a clean shirt, a hot meal. He desperately needed to crash for a couple of hours. Unfortunately none of those things was a realistic short term goal.

He was cleaning his glasses with a tissue when assistant producer and jill-of-all-trades Cassie McGregor entered his office. She didn't bother to knock first and Lucas didn't bother to comment on the lapse. Protocol, never a high priority with the news staff, tended to be the first casualty in times of crisis. He slipped the glasses on and lifted bloodshot eyes to her in question. Cassie looked even more rumpled than usual. A clipboard and a padded mailing envelope were tucked under her left arm, and she held a pink telephone message slip in her right hand. She waved the slip at him.

"Dave just checked in. He got as far as Chevy Chase before the army stopped him and turned him back. He says there are two dozen cases of radiation sickness at Bethesda. Can we include it in the next update?"

"Has he verified the numbers?"

Cassie nodded. "They came from a navy surgeon, but we can't use his name."

No, of course not. Considering the security crackdown, Lucas was surprised a naval surgeon had been willing to talk to a member of the media.

"Okay, use it. If he's willing to risk his career by feeding us the information, the least we can do is get it out."

"While we can," Cassie muttered. "This item might earn us that visit from Big Brother everybody's been expecting."

Lucas shared her concern. The broadcast grapevine was buzzing with reports that subtle and not so subtle intimidation was being brought to bear to keep news departments from communicating information of a "sensitive" nature. So far no security types had paid them a visit, but Lucas suspected that was only because, for the time being at least, they were too newsworthy themselves. As the only station that had had a remote unit on site when the bomb was detonated, they'd received worldwide coverage, as well as a flood of requests to use the tape of Andy's live report.

"If we're lucky we'll have a couple days' grace," he murmured, sinking back against his chair in exhaustion. "Assuming, of course, that nobody nukes the Pentagon or the Lincoln Memorial this afternoon. Christ, I never want to live through another twenty-four hours like this."

"It could've been worse," Cassie observed.

The comment provoked a cynical bark of laughter. "Worse?"

"The President's out in California rubbing elbows with movie stars, and Congress is in recess," she pointed out. "And apparently our terrorists weren't aware that a lot of government offices would be closed to commemorate Pearl Harbor Day."

"And they were considerate enough to use a clean nuke," Lucas added derisively. "I'd like to meet the idiot who comes up with these labels. How in God's name can *any* nuclear weapon be considered *clean?*"

"If we're talking morality, of course you're right," Cassie agreed. "But from a military perspective they're different kinds of weapons, so they have to have different designations. Whether a nuke is 'clean' or 'dirty' boils down to the degree and type of damage it causes— does it mostly take out buildings, or people?"

Lucas flicked one hand in a dismissive gesture. "Somehow I doubt that anybody who was within a mile of ground zero yesterday would appreciate the distinction."

"No," she murmured somberly. "I didn't mean to sound callous. It's just that it's easier to focus on the abstracts. If I let myself think about all those *people* . . ." She trailed off with an involuntary shudder. "This may not be the best time to ask, but has there been any word on Samantha?"

He shook his head and slipped his thumb and forefinger under his glasses to massage the bridge of his nose. "There are two hospitals left on the list. If she doesn't turn up in either of them— "

"All it'll mean is that she didn't require medical treatment," Cassie said firmly. "Think positive." She gave him an encouraging smile and started to leave, then stopped and turned back.

"Almost forgot." She plucked the mailing envelope from under her arm and deposited it on his desk. "This was left for you at reception."

Lucas picked it up. Judging by the size and weight, it contained a videotape cassette. "By whom?"

"A foreign-looking man, according to Yolanda, about a half hour ago. Probably a civilian responding to our call for eyewitness tapes."

About to jab the five-inch blade of a stainless steel letter opener into one end of the envelope, Lucas suddenly froze. " 'A foreign-looking man'?"

"That's what she said. But you know Yolanda—to her, Tom Cruise is foreign-looking. What's the matter?" she asked in amusement when he just sat and stared at the package. "Afraid it might be a letter bomb?"

He frowned at her over the top of his glasses but didn't reply.

"Come on, Lucas, who'd send you a bomb? Other than your ex wife, I mean."

"Her attorney," he muttered, and thrust the tip of the letter opener through a layer of dense padding. He was relieved, and a little embarrassed, when nothing happened. Blaming the stress of the past couple of days for his uncustomary jitters, he laid the letter opener aside and ripped the envelope open. As he'd guessed when he first picked it up, it held an ordinary half-inch VHS cassette.

"Now don't you feel silly?" Cassie said as she headed for the door.

"Extremely," Lucas replied a second after it closed behind her.

He got up and crossed the room to insert the cassette in a VCR that was connected to a brand new high-definition television. Standard procedure was to pass civilian tapes on to one of the assistant producers for screening. But right now Cassie was no doubt regaling her co-workers with an exaggerated account of his reaction to the "letter bomb." He'd prefer to find out firsthand if the tape was a video record of somebody's bar mitzvah or golden wedding anniversary.

He picked up the remote control and settled himself in an armchair in front of the TV. The set was one of the new rectangular models, with the same 16-to-9 width-to-height ratio as a movie screen. Aside from a much sharper image, the major improvement over the old format was that the sides of the picture didn't get lopped off. Lucas appreciated both the technological and aesthetic advantages, but he didn't think he'd ever get used to watching a rectangular television.

The screen was blank for fifteen seconds or so, and then the heads and torsos of four men appeared. They stood shoulder-to-shoulder in front of a scarred and pockmarked wall that looked like whitewashed adobe, or maybe rough plaster. Definitely not a basement rec room in suburban Virginia.

A row of jagged craters in the upper left corner of the screen caught Lucas's eye. He leaned forward for a closer look. Anxiety began to percolate in the pit of his stomach. He'd seen marks like that before, on graffiti-covered walls in Chicago, D.C., and South Central L.A. And the second man from the right— there was something unsettlingly familiar about him. Before Lucas could connect his face to a place or event, the man on the far right began to talk.

"By the time you receive this message, most of the city of Washington, D.C. will have been destroyed by a nuclear weapon."

Lucas suddenly remembered where he'd seen the man standing next to the speaker.

"Oh, Christ," he breathed.

Yesterday morning, on a monitor displaying

Andy's remote feed. He'd been backing across 12th Street, toward the entrance to the Metro Central station. The hatred and resolve on his face were clearly visible for several seconds, before army antiterrorist fire blew his head to smithereens. The two men on the left of the screen had been there, too, kneeling on the sidewalk on the far side of the street. Beside the body of a fourth man.

Four. There'd been four terrorists.

The fourth man's face hadn't been visible yesterday, but Lucas knew with a chilling certainty that he was looking at him now, listening to him speak.

He shot out of the chair and lunged for the door, yelling for the station manager in a voice made hoarse by exhilaration and fear.

Three

"I am Rashad. *Allahu Akhbar!*"

"I am Amir. *Allahu Akhbar!* Death to unbelievers and blasphemers!"

A dozen people, only half of them news staff, had gathered in the control room to watch the videotaped message.

"I am Kahlil," the third and youngest of the four declared solemnly. "We represent the oppressed people of Gaza. *Allahu Akhbar!*"

A muttered, "Palestinian?" was answered by a sibilant chorus of *shush!*

Station manager Vernon Marshall swiveled his considerable bulk to deliver a glare and a short-tempered "Quiet!" as the fourth man— the one on the far left of the screen— began to speak.

"I am Nicolai. I represent the millions who have been persecuted and the tens of thousands more who have been slaughtered while waiting for assistance from the West. Specifically, I represent the Republic of Kazakhstan and their brothers and sisters in Bosnia and Herzegovina."

"He sticks out like a sore thumb," Lucas remarked. "How did Nicolai from Kazakhstan end up with a bunch of what appear to be Middle Eastern terrorists?"

Vernon paused the tape, his interest caught by the question.

Lucas nodded absently. "Kazakhstan."

"Yeah," Cassie muttered. "Rings a bell, doesn't it?"

"What?" Vernon asked. "A news story?"

Cassie shook her head in frustration. "Probably, but damned if I can remember when or what it was about."

"Let's see the rest of the tape," Lucas suggested. "Maybe it'll jog our memories."

Vernon thumbed the pause button and the frozen quartet twitched to life. Apparently the one on the right— Rashad, he'd called himself— was the designated spokesman. He began their spiel as soon as Nicolai finished introducing himself.

"For more than forty years the infidel government of the United States has provided the financial and military aid which allows our enemies to carry out their criminal policies. We have been systematically robbed of our homeland and rights, while America continues to supply its allies with the means to make war on their peace-loving Arab neighbors.

"Despite all their efforts no one has accomplished the total subjugation of my people. We now fear that our enemies intend to cut off the water supply to Arab farmers in the Gaza Strip, even though Jewish settlers there consume thirty times more water per capita than the Arab majority, and to divert Lebanon's Litani River for their own use."

"Is he telling the truth?" one of the secretaries asked.

Cassie nodded and whispered, "Yes and no. Only the most obsessive fanatic would believe Israel intends to commit genocide. But it's a hard fact of life in the Middle East that before long there won't be enough water to go around."

"Since the United States has refused to intervene to prevent the implementation of this policy," Rashad continued grimly, "it will be held accountable. The detonation of a nuclear weapon in Washington on the seventh of December was both a punishment and a warning. Unless our demands are met, further retribution will be delivered. *Allahu Akhbar!*"

All four men repeated the phrase in unison and Rashad belatedly provided a translation for their audience— "God is great!"—before he moved on to the demands.

First, within one week the United States was to present a resolution to the United Nations Security Council recognizing the State of Palestine and renouncing all Zionist claims to both territory and statehood. Second, the United States was to negotiate the release of several political prisoners, both in the states and abroad, listed by name.

"This concludes our list of demands," Rashad announced. He stared straight into the camcorder's lens, his expression hard and implacable. "One copy of this tape will be delivered to an American television station in the Washington area. One copy will be delivered to the headquarters of the BBC. And in case the American and British governments decide to keep our message from the public, a third copy will be delivered to the offices of the Information Ministry of the Islamic Republic of Iran."

He barely got the last word out before the monitor screen went blank.

One of the lighting technicians muttered "Holy shit," into the strained silence, which effectively broke the tension. Suddenly everyone started talking at once.

"You think they're serious?"

"Where've you been the last two days, Einstein? I'd say a nuclear bomb is pretty fucking serious."

"No, I think he means about the demands. They can't actually expect— "

"Of course not. The United States would never betray Israel— "

"Screw Israel. I want to know who the hell these guys are."

"*Were*, Frank. Past tense. Anyway, what does it matter who they were?"

"It matters because they were working for somebody. Those terrorist groups all have sponsors— Iran, Syria, Libya. Whoever sent these four has to pay."

"Damn straight!"

"So what are you suggesting, that we ask the Pentagon to nuke Teheran, or maybe Baghdad?"

"Either one'd be a good place to start, if you ask me."

Lucas stared at the blank screen, deliberately tuning out the furor surrounding him. Nerves were stretched taut, and the tape had provided a much needed release for the staff's emotions. Virtually everybody in the room knew someone who'd been in D.C. yesterday morning; now they finally had a target for their collective rage, frustration and fear.

Suddenly he turned from the monitor and grabbed Vernon Marshall's arm.

"One copy, he said— *one copy* of the tape to a television station in the Washington area."

Vernon didn't react for a second or two. Then he swore under his breath, snatched the cassette out of the machine and headed for the editing bay. Lucas stayed with him.

"Will four be enough, you think?"

"Better make it five," Lucas said. "Once we've aired it, the suits will be all over us." He turned and yelled to be heard above the increasing din. "Cassie!"

She reluctantly disengaged from a heated argument with the engineer named Frank and trotted over to join them.

"Are you still seeing that guy with CNN's Washington bureau?" Lucas asked.

"Avery? Uh-uh, he turned out to be a manipulative jerk. Why?"

"But could you get in touch with him, pass something to him?"

"Sure, I guess so, but why would I— Oh, no, Lucas. Don't tell me. Dammit, you can't hand that tape over to CNN!"

He clasped her shoulders and turned her away from the people wrangling on the far side of the control room. "Think of it as insurance," he murmured. "There wouldn't be much point in shutting us down if we'd already delivered copies to CNN and the networks, now would there?"

She cast an uneasy glance at Vernon, who was setting up blank tapes for dubbing. "I guess not," she allowed, but without much enthusiasm. "You really think they might force us off the air if we broadcast this?"

"As strung out as everybody in the government is right now— yeah, I think they might. Paranoia is contagious, Cassie. It's already infected the Pentagon and the FBI. Who's to say the FCC won't be next."

She gnawed on her lower lip, scowled, then gave

in with a nod. "Okay. I'll see if I can get hold of Avery."

Lucas squeezed her shoulders. "Atta girl. Make the call from an outside phone, though, and don't tell him what's on the tape. Insinuate all you want, but don't *tell* him."

"You're right," Cassie muttered. "Paranoia is contagious."

She was either going to go stark raving mad—assuming she hadn't already, which, all things considered, was a pretty big assumption— or expire of boredom. Samantha thought it was a toss-up which would happen first.

According to her watch, a little more than three hours had elapsed since she woke up, or came to, whichever. Of course she couldn't be sure her watch was keeping accurate time. Real time, that was, as opposed to dream time, which she assumed would be distorted.

Another assumption. Sam ground her teeth in frustration. She instinctively distrusted assumptions, especially her own. She much preferred to arrive at logical, rational conclusions.

Certainty. Unconditional conviction. That's what she liked, felt comfortable with. Not wishy-washy, I-can't-say-for-sure-so-I'll-just-take-a-wild-guess *assumptions*.

The trouble here was that in order to be sure of her conclusions, she had to be sure of the evidence that had led her to them. And the evidence she had to work with was, to say the least, highly questionable.

She'd had ample opportunity to inspect her accommodations. Several times, in fact. Each circuit left her more frustrated and depressed. The only access to the cell was via a door made of iron bars welded to a heavy frame. Each bar was as thick as her wrist. The frame was held in place by two large hinges and a lock that looked solid enough to withstand a direct mortar hit. There was no window, so she had no idea whether it was day or night. A dim, fly-specked bulb on the ceiling was imprisoned in its own wire cage, presumably to prevent her from leaping up and smashing it with her bare hand.

The cot, which was bolted to the floor, had been furnished with a rough, coarsely woven wool blanket. She'd cocooned herself in the blanket, partly for warmth (after her initial shock wore off she discovered that the cell was freezing) and partly for the sake of modesty. After wasting close to half an hour yelling herself hoarse, she'd pretty much abandoned the hope that her anonymous jailers would respond to her demands for attention. But just in case . . . Hallucination or not, she didn't care to confront some potentially hostile stranger in her underwear.

The powdery coating on the wall had turned out to be yellow chalk, the kind teachers write on blackboards with. Some previous occupant had killed whatever time he'd spent here adorning most of the wall above the cot with a dozen or so lavishly detailed illustrations. Sam envied him; at least he'd had a box of chalk to keep himself occupied, not to mention a lively if decidedly lecherous imagination. That the artist had been a "he" was one assumption she felt completely comfortable with; no woman would have burdened a sister human with breasts the size of beach balls.

She was on her knees, studying an especially inventive drawing, when she heard the screech of hinges in need of a lube job and then approaching footsteps. She scrambled off the cot just as a hefty woman wearing, predictably, a dowdy prison-guard-gray shirtwaist dress and ugly black oxfords stopped in front of the cell door.

"They want you in interrogation," the woman said in a stolid monotone.

"It's about time," Sam replied.

The matron looked up in surprise as she inserted a key in the lock, then froze, then blinked a couple of times, fast, as if to clear her vision. Her chins— all three of them— dropped, pulling her thin, bloodless lips apart.

The blanket slipped off Sam's left shoulder, exposing the strap of her silky champagne slip. She hitched the rough fabric back into place as she padded across the cell to confront the matron through the bars. "Well, c'mon," she said impatiently. "What're you waiting for?"

The woman gaped at her as if she'd just that instant appeared in a puff of smoke. Sam stared back, her toes clenched against the freezing floor. The matron was so close that she could have reached through the bars and grabbed the key from the woman's pudgy hand.

The matron must have had the same thought. She suddenly took a giant step back. The key went with her.

"Who are you?" she demanded.

Now here was an interesting twist, Samantha thought wryly. Was the woman retarded? Deranged? Experiencing her own psychotic episode?

What the hell, she might as well play along. She didn't exactly have a wealth of options, after all. It had taken three hours for the Gray Lady to show up. God knew when somebody else might come strolling down that corridor. Sam lifted her left eyebrow a sardonic centimeter.

"You don't know who I am? I thought somebody sent you to collect me."

The matron's head bobbed in agreement, setting her chins to wagging. "That's right. They did. But— " She stopped, her heavy salt and pepper brows pushing together, almost meeting over her broad nose as she reconsidered. "No," she said firmly, contradicting herself. "I wasn't sent for *you.*"

Sam digested the response in silence. The Gray Lady was obviously flustered and suspicious as hell, but she didn't appear to be congenitally stupid or crazy. Could it be possible. . . . This was really nuts, but what if she was standing here having a conversation with her own subconscious?

"You're not who you're supposed to be," the matron informed her. She made it an accusation.

Something weird happened inside Sam's head. Nothing so dramatic as a clanging bell or flashing light; it was more like a muted *aha!* Her psych professor had claimed that adopted children often harbor idealized fantasies about how much more wonderful their lives would be, if only they'd been raised by their "real" parents. Personally, she'd always discounted such pop theories as garbage. The loving couple who'd raised her, sat up with her when she had chicken pox, paid for her orthodontia and flute lessons, comforted her when Eddy Hoskins dumped her for Melissa Wolford in tenth grade, put her through college— *they* were her parents, period.

But if the Gray Lady *was* her subconscious . . .

"If you say so," she murmured. She made an

effort to be polite, even a little obsequious. "But if you don't mind my asking, exactly who am I supposed to be?"

Obviously she hadn't carried off obsequious. The matron stiffened as if she and all her ancestors had been grievously insulted, pivoted smartly on her thick rubber soles, and quickstepped off down the corridor, all before Sam could react. She let go of the blanket to grab the bars.

"Hey! Wait!" she yelled at the matron's wide gray back. "Forget I asked, okay? It's not important, really."

The woman marched out of her line of vision and once more she heard the squeal of rusty hinges. Sam dropped her forehead against the cell door and muttered a disgusted, "Shit."

This delusion or nightmare, or whatever the hell it was, was turning out to be a real bummer. Oh sure, it had started off with a bang, but the past few hours had been a colossal waste of time.

What was Lucas doing, she wondered, while she languished in this imaginary cell? Had he tried to get in touch with her? Was he leaving a message on her answering machine this very minute?

"Some newsman," she grumbled as she collected the blanket and slouched back to the cot. "Your girlfriend's doing time in the twilight zone and you're probably having a two-martini lunch with some jerk from OSHA."

Lucas tapped a pen against his desk blotter while he waited on hold. He'd been ready to explode with frustration when, miraculously, the last hospital on his list turned up an ER nurse who remembered assisting with the treatment of a young

woman from the hotel the airplane had crashed
into. To Lucas's immense relief, she also recalled
that the patient was unconscious but uninjured except for minor burns on her head and arms. Just
this morning the Red Cross had notified the hospital that her name was Samantha Cook. Not that
the information wasn't appreciated, the nurse said,
but they could have used it yesterday, *before* the
patient was transferred to another facility.

Lucas's right foot began tapping in time with
the pen as he waited with barely contained impatience for the nurse to track down Sam's chart.

"Got it," she suddenly said in his ear. He
stopped tapping and grabbed a memo pad. "We
transferred her to the ElderCare home outside
Virginia Hills."

He jotted down the name of the place and the
phone number. "You sent a 28-year-old woman to
a nursing home?"

"It was one of the few places left with empty
beds," the nurse explained. "All the hospitals and
emergency care centers down here were swamped,
and not just because of the plane crash." There
was an eruption of background noise from her end
of the line—raised voices, the sounds of rushed
activity—but she ignored the distraction.

"We got a couple dozen people who were convinced they'd been irradiated and almost as many
who'd demolished their cars trying to get out of
the D.C. area. One guy T-boned an oil tanker with
his Winnebago, set fire to a half mile of interstate.
Then of course there were the usual number of
real and imagined heart attacks and 'spells' we get
whenever there's a local disaster."

"Sounds like you've been busy," Lucas remarked. He made a mental note to assign some-

body to put together a piece on local ERs. "I guess things have calmed down by now."

The nurse's laugh was dry, a little mocking. "Not so you'd notice, but I think the worst is past. Most of the new cases we're seeing now are your garden variety eccentrics. A lady brought her Pekingese in a little while ago. He had a couple of bald spots and she was afraid it was radiation sickness. Dr. Ellis— he's the resident who treated your friend— assured her it was just mange, gave her a prescription and sent her on her way."

"He prescribed medication for the dog?"

"No, for her. Tranquilizers. He told her to take the dog to a vet."

Lucas was smiling for the first time in two days when he hung up.

Time passed. How much, Sam didn't want to know, so she stopped consulting her watch. The matron didn't return, nor did she receive any other visitors, either real or imaginary. The possibility occurred to her that maybe she'd died and been consigned straight to hell, which in her case meant spending eternity in a freezing jail cell with nothing to eat or drink and no one to talk to. Eventually the unrelieved boredom anesthetized her and she slept, but it was a fitful, exhausting sleep. Her dreams were chaotic, alternately nostalgic and terrifying; happy events from her childhood got jumbled together with horrible images of destruction and death. When she woke, it was to an auditory hallucination: she could have sworn she heard far-off voices singing "God Bless America."

She was lying on the cot, wrapped in the scratchy blanket and immersed in a blue funk, when the matron finally put in another appearance. This time she was accompanied by two men. The one in a navy and gray uniform might have been her twin brother. It was the other one who roused Sam from her melancholy. He was the most gorgeous man she'd ever laid eyes on. She sat up and swung her legs off the cot, then winced when the soles of her feet made contact with the floor.

"You people have a thing or two to learn about prison administration," she groused, clutching the blanket over her chest.

The tall, dark and handsome stranger (who wore a suit and was clearly the person in charge) gestured for the male guard (who was a head shorter and at least eighty pounds heavier) to unlock the cell door. Neither man acknowledged Sam's complaint. The Gray Lady, however, had no reservations about making her umbrage known. Stationing herself against the opposite wall, she folded her arms under her ample bosom and glared at Sam. Sam stayed on the cot and pretended not to notice; instinct told her to concentrate on the men. Evidently the dreamboat didn't consider her much of a threat. He stepped inside the cell as soon as the door was open. His proximity gave Sam's spirits a much needed boost.

"You have some explaining to do, miss."

Joe made his face a stoical mask, determined not to reveal by his expression or the inflection of his voice that he felt as if he were teetering on the lip of a hundred foot precipice and the ground had started to crumble under his feet.

The beautiful redhead glaring at him from the narrow cot was the latest in a seemingly endless succession of shocks. Her unexplained appearance, when it was eventually discovered and reported, had sent a geyser of alarm through several law enforcement agencies, and resulted in Joe's being dispatched to find out what the hell was going on.

It couldn't be true, had been his first, stunned reaction when he heard about the mystery woman. Obviously someone had made a mistake— the jail matron, more than likely. She'd probably gone to the wrong cellblock, or otherwise got her instructions mixed up. People didn't just materialize and dematerialize at random inside locked jail cells.

But standing there in the dank, drafty cubicle, he couldn't deny the proof his own eyes provided. There was no sign of the prisoner who was supposed to be occupying the cell. And while the mystery woman's presence— or, more to the point, her specific location— might turn out to be a mistake, there was no question about her existence. She was conspicuously, vibrantly real. Although she might have sprung from one of his more lascivious fantasies.

She was the most stunning woman he'd ever seen, a miraculous restorative for his bleary, blood-shot eyes: a luxuriant, tousled mane of dark red hair that blazed like fire, defying the gloom of her surroundings; honey-gold skin that belonged on a tropical beach rather than in drab, winter-locked Washington; a full, ripe mouth that evoked disturbing images of sensual pleasures; and of course those startling eyes— the color of emeralds, at the moment they were glittering with overt animosity.

The bolt of sexual awareness that slammed through him unnerved Joe as much as anything that had happened in the past day and a half. But it also angered him, which, thankfully, allowed him to maintain his austere facade.

"You have some explaining to do, miss."

His voice matched his dark, cool looks: all business. In fact everything about him, from his perfect posture to his calm, assured tone, telegraphed unflappable self-confidence. Not surprising, Sam thought; he had to be some kind of cop.

His wardrobe, on the other hand, was something of a surprise. He'd adopted the retro look that had recently come back into style: wide tie and even wider lapels; double-breasted chalk stripes; baggy, pleated and cuffed trousers; high, starched collar. The overall effect was sort of a cross between George Raft and Harry Truman, but his dark, slightly wavy hair and the cleft in his chin were pure Gary Grant. Sam couldn't help thinking that if her 69-year-old grandmother were present, she'd be hyperventilating and fanning her breast.

"FBI?" she said, as casually as if she were asking him to pass the salt.

She was pleased to note that not only did the question take him by surprise, it annoyed him. The pair of creases that appeared between his dark, canted brows made him even more attractive.

"C'mon, fess up," she coaxed. "It's written all over you. Nice stare, by the way— intimidating, but not overtly hostile." She didn't add that no man with eyes that blue and lashes that long and thick should be allowed to circulate among the female population without a bag over his head. No doubt his ego was already the size of Rhode Island.

He ignored the compliment, sliding a graceful, long-fingered hand inside his coat to withdraw a thin notebook and a gold fountain pen. "You don't seem to realize how serious your situation is," he said, as he unscrewed the pen's cap.

Sam was impressed. The pen complemented his wardrobe nicely, adding just the right touch of '40s elegance.

"The Bureau must have relaxed the dress code, though," she observed. She was beginning to relax, even to enjoy the fantasy a little. Well, why not? She was stuck inside it, for however long it lasted. And as hallucinations went, the one standing in front of her with his long legs braced apart and a lock of ebony hair threatening to tumble onto his patrician forehead was certainly tolerable. Much better, for instance, than a wart-covered, fire-breathing demon.

"Terrific suit. Bet you got it in New York, right?"

He lifted his ice blue gaze from the notebook. The look he gave her made Sam's scalp tingle unpleasantly for a moment, before she reminded herself that he only existed in her own mind. She was forced to amend her first impression. "Intimidating" was an understatement; that stare would probably stop an attacking Rottweiler dead in its tracks. She shifted position, tucking her feet under her, telling herself the goosebumps that had suddenly sprouted all over her body were a result of the arctic temperature in the cell. The imaginary cell, in the imaginary prison. But damn, the goosebumps felt real.

"Your name," the dreamboat said flatly.

"Samantha Cook. And you are?"

"Special Agent Joseph Mercer, Federal Bureau of Investigation."

She managed not to smirk, but her satisfaction

must have shown. The corners of his delicious looking mouth turned down in irritation.

"I'd like you to explain how you gained entry to this cell, Miss Cook. It is *Miss* Cook?"

"Actually, I prefer Ms."

The twin frown lines made another appearance. "What?"

"Miz," she said distinctly. "Capital M, small S, period. You know— the courtesy title that replaced Missus and Miss back in the '70s." A hint of sarcasm had crept into her voice. Damn, she couldn't believe her own subconscious would present her with the perfect man and then make him a chauvinist.

Special Agent Mercer's perplexed frown deepened and darkened. "If you intend to represent yourself as mentally unstable, you should know that I can have a qualified psychiatrist here to examine you within the hour."

Sam grimaced. "Please, spare me. I had my annual psych evaluation in August. Anyway, why would I want to plead insanity? Unless of course you're planning to charge me with something, and if that's the case, shouldn't you be informing me of my rights?"

The man was looking more and more provoked. Genuinely exasperated. For the second time since he'd entered the cell, Sam felt a twinge of anxiety. A quick, surreptitious glance at the guard and the matron intensified the uneasy feeling beginning to swirl in the pit of her stomach: they maintained a respectful silence, but their hostility and suspicion were unmistakable. Deciding it was past time she exercised some kind of control, she drew a deep breath and made an effort to organize her thoughts. Should she clue them in, tell them this was all just a very bizarre dream? No, probably not.

"Look, let's start over. My name is Samantha Cook. I'm a 28-year-old, single, Caucasian, female American citizen. I'm a self-employed consultant and I live in Rockville, Maryland. Several hours ago— I can't be sure exactly how long it's been— I woke up here, on this cot. This is all I was wearing."

She stood up and held the blanket open for half a second, long enough to let Mercer see but not ogle. His chiseled features and glacial eyes displayed no reaction whatsoever; not so much as a twitch or a flicker.

"I have no idea how I got here," she said, as she rewrapped herself. She realized that her knees were shaking and sat down again before they could start knocking together. "That's all I can tell you, because that's all I know."

Her composure was a sham, and she was sure he knew it. Her insides were suddenly quivering and cringing, huddling together as a big black wave of premonition rose up out of nowhere and crashed over her.

Joe had almost decided that she was indeed deranged— *back in the '70s . . . my annual psych evaluation . . . self-employed consultant*— the woman was talking gibberish, apparently crazy as a loon. Which still didn't explain how she'd got here, damn it. He'd probably be at the jail the rest of the night, questioning personnel and reviewing stacks of paperwork, before he could file his report and go home.

And then she suddenly stood up and held open

the coarse blanket, and for a moment he forgot to breathe.

He belatedly registered what she'd said a couple of beats after she finished speaking, and experienced a fresh surge of anger. Joe welcomed the emotion, using it to smother his instinctive response to the sight of her lush, nearly nude body. Was that her strategy— to pretend amnesia? He focused his concentration, ordering himself to pay attention to what she said, rather than how she looked. If she was acting, she'd trip herself up, sooner or later.

The impossibly handsome FBI agent sent that laser stare straight through her eyes and into her mind. At least that's how it felt, as if her psyche was being probed with an icicle. After what seemed like a year but couldn't have been more than a minute, he blinked. Sam only realized she'd been holding her breath when it whooshed out of her lungs in relief.

"That's your story?" he said. The blatant disbelief in his voice caused her pulse to pick up speed.

She lifted her shoulders in an apologetic shrug. "It's the only one I have."

"And I suppose you're unaware that the United States is at war."

War?

If the ceiling had caved in, Samantha wouldn't have been more stunned. In an instant, the feeling of premonition was replaced by something much darker and more ominous. She drew the blanket more tightly around her shoulders. It didn't help. The chill that enveloped her seemed to emanate from her bones.

Oh, God. This was no nightmare. The bombing had been real. Everything, all of it, had been real.

"Who?" she whispered. "Iran? Syria?"

Special Agent Mercer looked at her as if he thought it might be a good idea to call in that psychiatrist, after all.

"Japan," he said tersely. "Yesterday the Japanese launched unprovoked attacks on American military bases in Hawaii and the Philippines."

Four

"Japan!"

Her voice was an incredulous croak.

"We were attacked by *Japan?*"

Special Agent Mercer confirmed the astonishing news with a somber, "That's correct."

"But . . . *why?*" Sam demanded. "It doesn't make any sense— we're their best customers, for crissake! They'd be committing economic suicide."

She came off the cot, too distraught to sit still. "Okay, I realize some of the protectionists in this country would love an excuse to declare war on Japan again. *Voilà,* no more trade deficit."

"Again?" Mercer said sharply, but Sam was too worked up to notice.

"But it would be insane for *them* to attack *us!* They have no resources to sustain a war, no way to produce metal, no oil or natural gas— " She took a couple of agitated steps toward the toilet, stopped and spun back to face him. She had to grab the blanket to keep it from falling. "Hold on. Are you sure it was the Japanese— not the North Koreans, or maybe the Chinese?"

"The Chinese?" Now *he* sounded incredulous.

Sam glanced at the guard and the matron. They wore identical expressions of astonished disbelief.

"Hey, it's possible. They have a fledgling free-market economy and a rapidly expanding industrial base. They'd probably profit more than any other country from a conflict between the United States and Japan. And a lot of Americans still can't tell one Oriental face from another."

"It couldn't have been the Chinese," Mercer said flatly.

"Well, probably not," Sam acknowledged with a frown. "They'd never be able to take us by surprise. Our intelligence satellites would pick up any suspicious military movements right away. Must've been the North Koreans, then."

"I assure you, Miss Cook, it was the Japanese who attacked our bases," he reiterated. "First in an early morning raid on Hawaii and later at Luzon and Manila in the Philippines." He jotted down a couple of quick notes, then lifted his head and skewered her with that frosty blue gaze.

"Now let's get back to my original questions."

Sam clutched the blanket and stared at him blankly while her brain struggled to shift gears. Hawaii? And the Philippines?

Hawaii, as in *Pearl Harbor?*

"How did you get into this cell without being observed?" Mercer prompted when she just stood there like a statue.

"What?" Sam blinked, then shook her head, as if that would clear things up. "I told you—"

"You 'woke up' here." He couldn't have injected more sarcasm into his voice if he'd tried.

"That's right," she confirmed, telling herself there was no use getting indignant. Even she realized how lame the story sounded.

"And you have no memory of how you got here."

She studied him in silence for several seconds.

"To be honest, I'm not a hundred percent convinced I *am* here. Or that you are, either, for that matter."

Maybe this *was* a really bizarre dream. The possibility that Japan had carried out sneak attacks on U.S. bases, using exactly the same strategy they'd employed 54 years ago, was just too fantastic to believe.

"Trust me, Miss Cook, we're both here," he said. "Much as I'd prefer to be elsewhere. And I can further assure you that you're going to remain here until you come up with some satisfactory answers."

Samantha didn't respond. She'd spent too much time with law enforcement types to be intimidated by his curt, you'd-better-play-ball-or-else threats. But then, as she stood there shivering with cold and an undefined anxiety that verged on dread, a random thought zinged across her mind like a bolt of lightning. A realization that put this incredible situation in a whole new light.

Fifty-four years ago . . . *to the day*.

She saw Mercer's funky wardrobe as if for the first time . . . and the spartan cell, and the matron's dowdy, calf-length dress and clunky shoes . . .

"What's today's date?" she asked, her voice barely above a whisper.

Mercer's expression said his patience was fast running out. "December 8th."

"Of what year?"

Agent Dreamboat's luscious mouth compressed in annoyance, which he vented by exhaling sharply through his narrow patrician nose. "The year is 1941. The city is Washington, in the District of Columbia, United States of America. The

time is— " with a quick glance at his watch "—
sixteen minutes past two in the morning. And
now, if you don't mind, I'd like answers to some
of *my* questions."

Samantha only dimly registered his testiness.
Her knees almost folded. She stumbled back to
the cot and dropped onto the lumpy mattress.

*Please God, let it be a dream . . . or an hallucina-
tion, or a transient psychotic delusion.* At the moment,
the possibility of mental illness seemed preferable
to the only other explanation she could think of.

It wasn't possible to travel backwards in time.
Was it?

Joe Mercer entered the house by the kitchen
door and crept with cautious stealth across the
freshly waxed linoleum. The shades at both windows had been pulled all the way down, so there
wasn't even a slim shaft of pale winter moonlight
to guide him as he edged past the stove and the
huge old five-legged table that took up most of
the space in the center of the room.

He navigated by memory and instinct, electing
to risk a bruised hip or stubbed toe rather than
turn on a light. Esther would be getting up soon
to start breakfast for the boarders, and he wanted
to be upstairs in his room before she came out of
hers. The past twenty hours had been the longest,
most grueling day of his life. If Esther caught him
before he made it upstairs he knew he wouldn't
get to bed at all, and he desperately needed a couple hours sleep before he had to go back to work.

The sunflower-patterned hall runner muffled
his steps, but the floorboards beneath it creaked
an enthusiastic welcome home. Wincing, he gin-

gerly sidestepped to the narrow strip of polished wood bordering the runner. Halfway down the hall, Esther's door remained closed. Joe listened, heard no telltale squeak of bedsprings. He heaved a sigh of relief and continued toward the front of the house, slipping out of his topcoat as he went.

He hung the garment on an empty hook of the coat tree at the foot of the stairs, then took a minute to remove his shoes before starting up. Each of the worn steps felt taller than the one before and they seemed to go on forever. After a quick trip to the bathroom at the end of the hall, Joe tiptoed to his room, the largest one, at the front of the house overlooking the street. He locked the door behind him, aware that a locked door wouldn't stop Esther if she was determined to interrogate him, but hoping the boarders would keep her so busy for the next few hours that she wouldn't have time for a trip upstairs.

Someone had entered his room and lowered the dark green shades at both windows. Evidently Esther was afraid the Japanese would pick the nation's capital as their next target. Joe considered raising the shades, at least enough to admit a sliver of moonlight, then decided to leave them down. The sun would be up in an hour or so, long before he'd be ready to get out of bed. He undressed in the dark, carefully hanging his trousers and suit coat in the closet out of habit, dropping his shirt and socks onto the floor.

His body was numb with fatigue. His mind should have been, too, but it kept compulsively reviewing the events of the past 24 hours, as if repeated examination might change something, alter some minor detail he'd missed or misunderstood. Of course he knew it was a waste of time and effort. The United States was really at war and Colonel Ethan Herrick was really dead, and no amount of review and analysis would change either of those facts.

And now, as if he didn't already have enough to deal with, this redheaded siren had suddenly appeared out of the blue . . .

Despite his exhaustion, he switched on the desk lamp and retrieved his notebook from the inside pocket of his suit coat. *Miz* Samantha Cook— assuming that was in fact her name— was either mentally deranged or deliberately trying to make everyone think she was. She couldn't possibly expect anyone to believe her extraordinary story.

Joe opened the notebook and flipped through it until he reached the page with her name printed neatly at the top. His eyebrows came together in an unconscious frown as he scanned the notes he'd hastily jotted down in the cold, dank cell. She *must* be pretending insanity. Why else would she suggest that the Chinese had attacked Pearl Harbor? The *Chinese*, for God's sake! Anyone who'd seen a newspaper or listened to the radio in the past four years knew that China was under Japanese occupation. Her claims that the country had a "free-market economy" and an "expanding industrial base" were equally absurd. It was common knowledge that most of China still existed virtually in the Stone Age— uneducated peasant farmers with no electricity or running water.

Then there'd been her repeated references to the "North Koreans." *North* Koreans? And the remark about "intelligence satellites . . ."

Joe closed the notebook with an irritable grunt and tossed it onto his desk. Why was he wasting time trying to make sense of the woman's outlandish rantings, when he should be getting some much needed sleep? He switched off the lamp and climbed into bed, then tossed and turned for several minutes, trying to get settled. Trying to get Samantha Cook out of his mind.

The trouble was that, no matter how things looked, he instinctively knew she *wasn't* a raving lunatic. Far from it— she possessed a keen, quick intellect. And if she wasn't crazy, that left only one obvious explanation for her sudden appearance, today of all days. He'd avoided facing the possibility ever since he left the jail, but in the dark silence of his room there were no convenient distractions to prevent the thought from slipping into his mind.

He didn't want it to be so. He fervently hoped it wasn't so, and only partly because of the complications it would add to his already impossibly complicated life.

"Please, God," he muttered as he sank into an exhausted sleep, "don't let her be a foreign agent."

Shortly after Special Agent Mercer left, the matron had brought her a shapeless, faded blue dress, a brown cardigan sweater, shoes and a pair of anklets. The dress and socks were cotton, the sweater wool and several sizes too large. The shoes fit, thank goodness. If they hadn't, her feet would be bloody stumps by now from all the pacing she'd done.

Her supper tray sat, practically untouched, on the narrow bunk: room-temperature ham, navy beans and cornbread. She'd had to provide her own beverage: a tin cupful of tap water from the basin next to the toilet. The Gray Lady had delivered the tray a couple of hours ago, along with a muttered explanation that the cooks wouldn't be in till 5 A.M. and last night's leftovers were all she could find in the kitchen. Samantha suspected the woman would have preferred to let her go hungry, but Mercer had ordered the meal brought to her when she told him she hadn't had anything to eat since the previous morning.

"Joseph Mercer." Sam murmured his name aloud and discovered that she liked not only the sound but also the feel of it as her mouth formed the syllables. But then there wasn't much not to like about Special Agent Mercer.

She reminded herself, since she seemed to need reminding, that the man's movie star looks were irrelevant. The thing to keep in mind was that she needed to establish a rapport with him, or at the very least that she not make an enemy of him. He was her principal contact in this place.

In this time.

Her logical, analytical mind still resisted the possibility that it wasn't *her* time, even though that was the only explanation she'd been able to come up with so far. And Lord knew she'd strained her gray matter trying to think of some other explanation— *any* other explanation.

She reached the wall, pivoted, and retraced her steps back to the bars. Her thumb constantly rubbed the band of the emerald ring on her right hand. It was an unconscious nervous gesture of long standing, as ingrained as the habit of pacing when she had a problem to work out.

Time travel wasn't possible. It just *wasn't*, period, end of discussion. If it were, everybody would know about it. Wolf Blitzer would have zipped back for a firsthand report of the Revolutionary

War, then forward to broadcast taped interviews
with George Washington and General Cornwallis.
Cindy Crawford would be getting Coco Chanel's
opinions of the new spring fashions on MTV.
Donohue no doubt would have bagged an exclusive
interview with Gaius Julius Caesar.

To Samantha's knowledge, none of those things
had happened. Ergo, it was safe to assume that
time travel was still possible only in the fertile
imaginations of science fiction writers . . . and
that she hadn't really traveled back 54 years to the
original Pearl Harbor Day.

Right, a skeptical voice whispered inside her
head. *So where the hell* are *you, then? And— this is
the question you should be asking yourself—* why *are you
here, wherever "here" is?*

Why? That was the real stumper, wasn't it? Or
maybe: "Why me?"

All right, forget what you *think* you know to be
fact. Assume for the moment that everything
you've seen and heard since you woke up on that
miserable cot has been real— exactly what it appeared to be and not some fabrication of a dis-
eased mind or hyperactive imagination.

Was there a *reason* she'd been catapulted into
this extraordinary situation? Her, specifically, and
not someone else? Was it conceivable that there
was some twisted logic at work here?

Sam abruptly stopped pacing and sat on the
bunk, next to the tray of cold food. "All right,
think!" she muttered. Had something unusual happened recently that might provide a clue about
what was happening to her, and why?

She drew a complete blank. There was nothing.
Absolutely zilch. Until yesterday morning her life
had been cruising along on its comfortably routine

course. She couldn't remember a single bump, dip, or sudden unexpected curve. It had been weeks— no, more like months— since she'd done anything impetuous.

An exasperated frown creasing her forehead, she picked up the bent fork, speared a chunk of ham, and nibbled at it absently. Okay, maybe the trigger hadn't been an event, but a person. Had she come in contact with any potential witches, sorcerers, or extraterrestrials lately?

She tossed the fork back on the tray and shoved both hands through her hair in frustration. Jesus, she was losing it. Maybe she should ask Mercer to summon that psychiatrist he'd threatened her with. Come to think of it, though, she probably wouldn't have to ask him. She suspected the gorgeous FBI agent was already half convinced she was psychotic. Worse, she was beginning to think he might be right.

The agonized shriek of rusty hinges alerted her that she was about to have a visitor and she sat up straight, folding her hands in her lap and arranging her face into what she hoped was a calm, perfectly sane expression.

A different matron, younger but every bit as forbidding as the original Gray Lady, appeared in the corridor. Special Agent Mercer followed about three feet behind her. He was wearing a different suit with a fresh shirt and tie, all in the same outdated style as the clothes he'd had on last night. He waited silently while the matron unlocked the cell door. Samantha picked up the tray and stood to hand it to the woman. The matron accepted it, then stepped to one side. Sam inferred that she was supposed to leave the cell. She glanced at Mercer in question.

"Come with me, please," he said. Despite the "please," it wasn't a request.

Sam took the opportunity to check out the neighboring cells as she followed him down the corridor. All of them were empty, which explained why nobody had responded yesterday, when she'd yelled till she was hoarse.

Mercer led her past a large, sturdy-looking metal door, down another hall, and into a small room that she knew at once was used for interrogation. Not waiting for instructions, she took a seat on one of five straight-backed chairs arranged around a wooden table.

"Is there a reason I have an entire cellblock all to myself?" she asked as Mercer sat down across from her.

He didn't reply right away, taking out his notebook and pen, searching for the page he wanted, studying his notes . . . deliberately drawing out the silence to rattle her. Sam endured his mind game without fidgeting or speaking. She wasn't surprised that he'd arranged an official interrogation, and she expected they'd soon be joined by at least one other person.

While she waited— for the stenographer or whomever to arrive and for Mercer to decide whether he would get around to answering her question— she studied him openly. He must have gone home to change clothes and shave, but if he'd managed to get any sleep, it hadn't been enough. His eyes were bloodshot, with bruised-looking semicircles beneath them that made the incredible blue of his irises even more startling. At length he became aware of her overt inspection, and apparently realized he wasn't going to win this war of nerves.

"The woman who was incarcerated in that cell the night before last was isolated for security reasons."

The terse response only raised more questions. "What woman?" Sam wanted to ask. She didn't, though, because she sensed that he wouldn't tell her. Not until he was good and ready. He was much more severe and focused than he'd been before; in fact, his expression was almost grim. She'd seen the look before, usually on men who'd just come from a meeting with their superiors.

"Hard day?" she said with a tentative smile.

He surprised her by muttering a dry, "You have no idea."

Sam's smile relaxed and widened, but before she could say anything Mercer's gaze shifted to a point beyond her left shoulder and she heard the door behind her open. Seconds later a young woman carrying a stack of steno pads and a handful of pencils took a seat at the end of the table and two middle-aged men claimed the vacant chairs to Sam's left and Mercer's right.

The woman opened one of her pads and waited for the interrogation to begin. She wore the somber, detached expression of a police stenographer, and she avoided making eye contact with any of the other people at the table. A center part divided her glossy brown hair into symmetrical, carefully arranged waves that hugged the sides of her face before sweeping back to an old maid's bun at her nape. It was an odd hairstyle for such a young woman, but no more peculiar than the combination of severely tailored gray suit and frilly white blouse. Maybe she was the religious type, Sam thought. That would explain the absence of makeup or jewelry.

The woman's appearance would have been merely curious, but a quick examination of the men who'd entered the room with her made Sam distinctly uneasy. They were both dressed in the same old-fashioned style as Mercer, and apparently they both patronized the same barber. A flock of butterflies fluttered to life in her stomach when she took in their combed and pomaded hair. One young, attractive FBI agent decked out like a G-man in a '40s movie she could have rationalized as a manifestation of individual style. But three men dressed in the same outdated fashion was a lot harder to explain away.

She realized she was staring at the man next to Mercer and quickly ducked her head, instinctively wanting to hide her anxiety. Her grandfather had a suit just like that. He'd hauled it out of mothballs last Halloween, when he and Gram were trying to put together costumes for the country club party.

"If we're ready to begin . . ." said the man she'd been staring at, drawing her attention back to the small, stuffy room.

He introduced himself as Special Agent William Ragsdale, and the man on her left as Chief of Detectives George Collier of the Washington Police Department. No one bothered to introduce the stenographer.

"For the record," Mercer began when they'd got the basics—name, age, et cetera—out of the way, "tell us how you came to be in the cell where you were discovered by Mrs. Patton yesterday afternoon?"

"That's the matron's name?" Sam said in amused surprise. "Mrs. Patton?" She almost asked if the woman was related to General George Patton, then thought better of it. She could be, though; there was definitely a resemblance.

"Please limit your responses to answering the questions put to you," Mercer said with quiet insistence.

Sam's amusement evaporated. "As I've already told you, I don't *know* how I came to be there. One minute I was in a hotel room outside Alexandria, and the next—"

"That would be Alexandria, Virginia?" Agent Ragsdale interrupted.

"Yes. Alexandria, Virginia." Christ, what did he think she meant— Alexandria, Egypt? She hesitated a second or two, then decided, what the hell? Assuming these people really existed, they already thought she was either crazy or lying.

"Some terrorists had just detonated a nuclear weapon across the river, in D.C. At least, that's what I originally assumed had happened, because of the way the window imploded and the shock wave that knocked me flat. But in the past 24 hours I've been forced to reconsider that assumption. Now I think the whole thing may have been just a really weird—"

Ragsdale broke in again, his tone sharp. "Excuse me! What kind of weapon did you say?"

Sam glanced from him to Mercer, then to the policeman, Collier. They all looked baffled. Not astounded, or suspicious, just confused and uncomprehending.

"A nuclear weapon," she repeated. The butterflies in her stomach suddenly felt more like condors. "You know— a nuke. An atom bomb. Well, strictly speaking, they aren't atom bombs anymore, but . . ."

She trailed off, her pulse thundering at her temples. Mercer's expression had shifted from confusion right into stunned disbelief at the word "bomb."

"Are you saying that someone set off a bomb in Washington, D.C.?" he demanded. "Yesterday morning?"

For a moment that authoritative voice and piercing stare caused Sam to doubt her memory, as well as her sanity.

"Well . . ." She closed her eyes, inhaled deeply, trying to provide her brain cells with some much-needed oxygen. "Yes. That is, I thought . . ."

But then suddenly something inside her snapped. *Stop it!* an angry voice commanded. *Just stop it, right now! You know that's what happened. You know!* And she did know. She wasn't crazy, damn it! It hadn't been a nightmare, or an hallucination. She'd *heard* the window shatter behind her, *felt* the blast . . .

"Yes."

She opened her eyes and looked straight into Mercer's, defying his overt disbelief. "Yes, that's what I said." Her voice gained strength as she continued. "A *nuclear* bomb. It was detonated at approximately eight o'clock in the morning, give or take a few minutes either way. *Yesterday* morning." She paused a beat for emphasis, then dropped the rest of it right into their worsted wool-covered laps. She took pains to clearly enunciate each syllable.

"December 7, 1995."

Five

Of course they didn't believe her. She hadn't really expected them to. Nevertheless, their incredulous, almost stupefied expressions threatened her already shaky composure. Even the stenographer momentarily forgot why she was there. The young woman gaped as if Samantha had jumped up on the table and started yodeling at the top of her lungs.

"Believe me," Sam muttered, "I know exactly what you're thinking. It sounds every bit as crazy to me as it does to you, but I swear I'm telling the truth."

Joseph Mercer was the first to recover. His eyes narrowed shrewdly, concentrating the intensity of that laser gaze so that Sam half expected her flesh to start smoldering.

"Crazy," he murmured. "Yes, I think most people would agree that only someone who's completely insane would invent such an extraordinary story."

"I didn't *invent*— " Sam began.

"Or someone who wants to appear insane."

The quiet observation had an immediate effect on the other two men: their expressions suddenly became as sharp and assessing as Mercer's. Sam felt her face flush with resentment, which she knew all three of them would assume was guilt.

"That's— " She caught the word "crazy," sucked it back, and started over. "Why in heaven's name would I want you to think I was insane?"

The chief of detectives provided a completely unexpected answer. "If you were an agent for the Japanese . . ."

"Or for the Germans," Ragsdale added grimly.

They watched her closely for a reaction, but for several endless seconds Sam was too stunned to do more than stare back at them. "You can't be serious," she said when she found her voice. She was aware that it held more than a hint of derision, but for the moment tact was beyond her. "Do I look Japanese to you?" she demanded of Chief Collier. Then, turning to Ragsdale without giving him a chance to reply, "Or German?"

"You wouldn't have to be either," Mercer said.

"In fact," Collier pointed out, "it would be an advantage for a foreign agent to look like you do— you could pass for an average American citizen."

Sam felt her self-control start to disintegrate. "I *am* an average American citizen, you imbecile! As middle-class, white bread, disgustingly average as they come." She exhaled sharply and raked her hands through her hair, striving to calm herself.

"Think about it for a minute— does it make sense to any of you that either Germany or Japan would send a valuable agent to infiltrate a Washington jail? In her *underwear,* for crying out loud? What vital information could I possibly be after? The only things I've learned so far are that the food is lousy and the matrons check on the prisoners roughly every twelve hours. Christ on a crutch, if I *were* a spy, I could have died of starvation or hypothermia before I managed to get my hands on any national secrets!"

Collier pressed his lips together in disapproval. "I'll ask you to refrain from taking the Lord's name in vain."

Biting back a reply that probably would have sent him into apoplexy, Sam looked across the table, straight into Joseph Mercer's cool, enigmatic gaze.

"Truth time, Agent Mercer. Do you believe I'm a foreign intelligence agent?"

His slight hesitation was encouraging, but his response fell short of the deliverance she'd hoped for. "It's one possible explanation for your sudden appearance."

"And certainly a more plausible explanation than the one I'm offering," she added bitterly, saying aloud what he had to be thinking.

"That you came here from more than fifty years in the future?" Ragsdale jeered. "Yes, I'd have to say the foreign agent theory beats that one hands down."

Sam waited, hoping against hope, but Mercer didn't offer a dissenting opinion. Evidently she had sole responsibility for her own defense.

"All right," she said, forcing herself to concentrate. "Let's explore your theory. If I'm a secret agent working for Germany or Japan, *why* am I here? What information am I supposed to obtain and how am I supposed to obtain it—considering that, except for this little get-together, I'm being confined to a jail cell 24 hours a day?"

Ragsdale didn't have to think about his response. "Perhaps it wasn't information you were after."

Sam shook her head in confusion.

"Perhaps it was a person."

"A person?" She glanced at Mercer, took in his clenched jaw and the taut, white-rimmed line of his mouth. She remembered his succinct reply when she'd asked why there were no other prisoners near her: "The woman who was incarcerated in that cell the night before last was isolated for security reasons."

"A woman," she murmured. "There was another woman in that cell before I showed up."

"Valerie Herrick." It was Collier who provided the name.

"Let me guess," Sam said with a sick, sinking feeling. "She's disappeared."

"Vanished without a trace," Ragsdale confirmed. "Sometime between 12:45 yesterday, when Mrs. Patton collected her lunch tray, and early evening, when she discovered that you were occupying the cell. No doubt you would have been discovered earlier, if the news of the Japanese attacks hadn't caused considerable disorder throughout the city." He paused, leaned forward and clasped his hands on the table.

"A couple of questions occur to me, Miss Cook. One, how did Valerie Herrick manage to escape a locked cell and slip past a dozen police officers without being seen? And two, where the hell is she now?"

Samantha stared at him helplessly. She wished more than she'd ever wished for anything that she could convince herself none of this was happening, that it was nothing more than the world's longest, most bizarre nightmare. But she couldn't. That self-delusion had finally collapsed under the weight of time and physical evidence.

"It's just a guess." Her voice was husky, strained

with the effort of forcing the words out. "But I think she's in a hotel outside Alexandria, Virginia . . . in 1995."

The conjecture provoked a disgusted grunt from Collier and an impatient glare from Ragsdale. Sam's gaze slid to Joseph Mercer's tense, haggard face. His gorgeous eyes reflected a surprising mixture of cynical distrust and anxiety. A shiver of premonition trickled down her spine, leaving a trail of gooseflesh in its wake.

There was something else going on here, something unspoken and unacknowledged; a separate issue that had little or nothing to do with her. Mercer's distrust, she could understand; but the anxiety mystified and unnerved her. She sensed that it was somehow related to this Valerie Herrick's disappearance.

Holding his gaze, she added in a voice that quavered despite her conscious effort to keep it steady, "I also think there's a good chance she's dead."

Levander was worried about the girl. She'd been here almost 24 hours and she still hadn't opened her eyes or so much as wiggled her little finger. Lord knew there hadn't been much of her to begin with. She needed to wake up, eat some solid food. Otherwise she'd waste away till there was nothing left.

He checked in on her as often as he could during his shift, his concern increasing with each visit. According to the paperwork the hospital sent with her, she should have come around by now. She didn't have any skull or brain injuries or broken bones, and the results of all the tests they'd done were within normal limits. Levander took hope from the fact that her pulse was still strong and she was breathing all right. She'd wake up before long, he told himself. And when she did, he would make sure she got something to eat right away, even if he had to fix her a meal himself.

Sam bowed her head and pressed the pads of her fingers against her eyelids. The interrogation was turning into an endurance test. How long did they intend to keep her in this stuffy room, reciting the same answers to the same numbing questions? Apparently they thought if they kept at her long enough, the answers would change. Well, they could think again! She was sticking to the truth, even if it meant spending the rest of her life on this hard wooden chair. Besides, starting to improvise or ad lib at this point would only make them more suspicious than they already were.

"How many times do I have to say it?" she muttered. "I have no idea how Valerie Herrick got out of that cell."

She didn't bother repeating her theory that the woman might have somehow traded places with her. All three men had made it clear that *that* possibility was too fantastic to even consider. If she was right, though, Valerie Herrick was well out of their reach. Maybe farther out of their reach than they could begin to imagine: she might be a charred, unrecognizable lump on the floor of a hotel room in Alexandria, Virginia.

Provided the hotel was still there in 1995.

And that Alexandria, Virginia was still there.

"And you have no idea where she is now?" Ragsdale's voice hammered at her like a blunt instrument.

Sam sat up straight, shoved her hair out of her face and glared at him. Enough was enough.

"That's right," she said curtly. "Furthermore, I really don't give a rat's ass."

Chief Collier stiffened in offense. She gave him a scathing look. "You know, Chief, if strong language bothers you so much, maybe you should consider going into another line of work."

A dark flush spread over his face. "I'm not accustomed to hearing that sort of thing from a woman."

"Really. Well maybe if you hauled your fat political rump out of your comfy office and onto the streets you're supposed to be protecting once in a while—"

"All right!" Mercer cut in. His voice was sharp with surprise, but there was also a thread of what might have been amusement, or maybe reluctant admiration. Sam ignored the interruption.

"— or bothered to take a tour of your own jail—"

"Miss Cook!"

This time there was no mistaking Mercer's message. He made her name an injunction, which he backed up by half rising from his chair. Sam clamped her mouth shut as it suddenly occurred to her that these guys had never heard of the Supreme Court's Miranda ruling. Who was to say what kind of treatment they thought a suspected spy deserved?

"Sorry," she murmured, though she couldn't bring herself to say it directly to Collier. In her considered opinion, political appointees had no place in law enforcement.

Mercer subsided, both figuratively and literally. "Let's get back to the matter of Valerie Herrick's disappearance."

"By all means," Sam agreed. "Let's."

Ragsdale snapped to attention. "Are you ready to tell us where she is?"

From the corner of her eye, Sam saw the stenographer hastily flip to a fresh page in her notebook. "We've already covered that territory," she said. "A couple dozen times, by my count. I've told you I don't know where she is. If I have a sudden revelation— a vision or something— I promise you'll be the first to know."

She paused, giving them some time to adjust to the change in her attitude. During the startled silence that followed, she arched her back and rolled her shoulders, loosening muscles that were stiff from inactivity and emotional tension. Time to shake things up a little, start asking a few questions of her own. Clearly nobody in the room was going to volunteer any information, and there were things she wanted and needed to know. When she was ready, she directed the first question to Ragsdale.

"Why was she here?"

He scowled at her in wary surprise, his intrepid G-man facade wavering. Evidently he wasn't accustomed to having the tables turned in the middle of an interrogation.

"What? Who?"

"Valerie Herrick," Sam said with exaggerated patience. "Why was she arrested? What crime or crimes had she been charged with?"

Ragsdale's scowl turned suspicious, as if he distrusted either the question or her motive for asking it. "She hasn't been formally charged," he admitted, reluctantly, Sam thought. "But she's the principal suspect in her father's murder."

"The only suspect," Chief Collier corrected.

"She was found standing over his body with the murder weapon in her hand."

Sam tried not to show any reaction. *Murder!* Jesus, no wonder they were so bent out of shape about the woman's disappearance.

"Found by whom?"

Ragsdale had turned his scowl on the chief, who was busy pretending not to notice. Mercer took it upon himself to answer.

"Her father's houseboy."

"His *Japanese* houseboy," Collier interjected.

Another chill of premonition slithered down Sam's spine. "And who was Valerie Herrick's father?" Someone important, she'd bet.

The FBI agents consulted one another with a silent look before Mercer responded.

"Ethan Herrick was a colonel serving with Army Intelligence."

The matter-of-fact statement hit Sam like a cannonball. She swallowed the sour taste pooling at the back of her mouth and gave thanks that the leftover ham and beans had been so unappetizing.

"I assume you've questioned the houseboy?" Considering what had happened at Pearl Harbor yesterday morning, she was afraid they might have done a lot more than question him.

Ragsdale and Mercer exchanged another glance, while Collier shifted restlessly on his chair.

"Unfortunately, we haven't had the opportunity," Ragsdale said grimly. "It was the houseboy who called the Washington police to report the murder. The detective who went to investigate— "

"Excuse me," Sam interrupted. "This was two nights ago, right— December 6th?"

"Yes. As I was saying, the detective took the

houseboy's statement, told him the prosecutor would be in touch, then sent him home."

"And the next morning the Japanese bombed Pearl Harbor," Sam murmured, anticipating the rest. "As soon as you heard the news, the FBI started rounding up every Japanese and Nisei in sight. But when you went to collect the houseboy, he'd flown the coop."

"There was no reason to suspect the Jap had anything to do with Colonel Herrick's murder," Collier said in his detective's defense. "After all, he was the one who called us. He heard the shot, ran to the colonel's study, and found the girl kneeling next to the body . . . with the Colonel's gun in her hand!"

Ragsdale gave the chief a look that would have cowed a man whose job security depended on his performance rather than his political connections. "So he claimed."

"The girl didn't deny it!" Collier retorted. "Not the part about him finding her holding the gun, anyway."

"But she did deny killing her father?" Sam asked. The queasiness diminished as professional curiosity kicked in, providing a focus for her nervous tension.

"The prisons are full of convicted murderers who swear they're innocent," the chief growled out of the side of his mouth.

Sam didn't dispute the claim. "Was Valerie Herrick standing, or kneeling?" she asked instead.

Collier frowned as he fished out a monogrammed linen handkerchief to blot his perspiring forehead. "What?"

"First you said she was found standing over her

father's body. Then you said the houseboy found her kneeling next to the body."

He stuffed the handkerchief back in his pocket. "Standing, kneeling, what difference does it make? The point is, she was holding the gun."

Sam drew a deep breath and prayed for forbearance. "If she was kneeling, she might have picked it up. From the floor," she added when Collier just looked at her, an expression of stubborn belligerence on his broad, homely face.

"According to the report, the houseboy claimed she was kneeling on the carpet," Mercer murmured. "Beside her father's body."

His tone was carefully neutral, but Sam thought she detected a hint of *something*— excitement? anticipation?— in his deep, sexy voice. Once again she had the uneasy feeling that there was more going on here than met the eye.

"Was she tested?" she asked, her gaze locked on Mercer's face. Such a cold, beautiful, maddeningly inscrutable face, it might have been carved from marble. He gave a puzzled shake of his head.

"You didn't run an Atomic Absorption Analysis, or SEC?"

"A what?" Ragsdale said sharply. "What the devil is a *seck?*"

"Ess-ee-see," Sam repeated. "It's a test that uses scanning electron microscopy. The SEC and AAA can determine— " She broke off midsentence. Of course they hadn't used or even heard of either procedure, because neither would be available for years. Decades, actually.

"Determine what?" Ragsdale barked.

Sam heaved a sigh and reluctantly finished the explanation. "Whether someone was in close proximity to a firearm that has recently been discharged. But now that I think of it, those tests didn't exist— *don't* exist— in 1941."

All three men made oh-brother-here-we-go-again faces, while the stenographer hunched over her notebook and scribbled furiously. Trying to record the unfamiliar terms as squiggles she would later have to translate back into English was probably giving her fits. Samantha ignored the negative vibes bombarding her and continued her train of thought.

"Besides, even if you had access to a nuclear reactor or an electron microscope and knew how to perform those tests, the results wouldn't be much help if Valerie Herrick had handled the murder weapon." She was thinking aloud, rather than attempting to enlighten her audience, but at this point she stopped and sent an inquiring look across the table.

"You have verified that the gun she was holding was the murder weapon?"

"That information— " Ragsdale began officiously, but Mercer overrode him.

"It was," he confirmed. "Colonel Herrick's government issue sidearm, a Colt .45."

Sam unconsciously leaned toward him, resting both forearms on the table. She sensed a slight softening in his resistance, and she wasn't about to waste time or tempt fate by wondering about the reason.

"How many shells had been fired?"

"One. It was recovered from the wall paneling, about four feet from the body."

Which meant the bullet had passed *through* the colonel's body. And one thing Sam knew hadn't changed in 54 years: a .45 slug fired at close range created a hell of an exit wound. "There must have been a lot of blood."

"The room was a mess," Collier said, forgetting for the moment to be surly.

"Did you do a blood splatter test?" she asked, then grimaced and muttered, "No. Damn, they didn't do that in '41, either."

"Blood splatter test?" the chief repeated.

A quick glance told Sam he was hooked, his hostility replaced by an active if wary interest. Two down, one to go, she thought as she swiveled toward Collier. Maybe in the process of satisfying his curiosity, she could chip away at his resistance to the idea that she'd traveled back in time.

"The pattern of blood splatter from a gunshot wound— where the blood falls, how large an area it covers, and so forth— can provide a lot of information," she explained. "For instance, where the assailant was standing in relation to the victim, the angle and velocity of the bullet at point of entry, whether the victim was moving or stationary— "

"That's absurd!" Ragsdale blurted. "There's no such test!"

"Not yet," Sam said. "But there will be."

"Fifty years in the future," he scoffed.

"That's right." It took a real effort not to snap back at him. She should have known the senior agent would be the toughest convert. Surprisingly, Chief Collier presented himself as a potential ally.

"It makes sense," he said thoughtfully. "That you could figure out some of those things from how the blood splatters, I mean. Just because we haven't developed the test yet— "

"*Yet!*" Ragsdale exclaimed. "For God's sake, man, don't tell me you're starting to *believe* her."

The chief stiffened, his neck and face turning

a deep maroon. Sam had no idea whether his reaction was a response to Ragsdale's contemptuous
tone, the fact that he'd taken the Lord's name in
vain, or both, but Collier looked like he might have
a stroke right there at the table. And of course if
he did, she would be blamed for that, too. She
decided to intervene before the two men came to
blows.

"What would it take to convince you I'm telling
the truth?"

"I can't imagine," Ragsdale began, but Mercer
interrupted before he could finish.

"We'll leave that to you, Miss Cook."

Sam gave him a wry, grudging smile. "Right, I
almost forgot. I'm the one under suspicion here."

She sat back and folded her arms under her
breasts, thinking. What could she say to them,
what information could she offer that would shake
their smug self-confidence? She could tell them
about other advances in forensic science, but there
was no way to back up anything she said with
proof. And nothing less than tangible, verifiable
proof was going to satisfy these guys.

Then it suddenly came to her: World War II.
Both her father and grandfather were WWII fa-
natics. They could spend hours happily rehashing
battles and campaigns, second-guessing strategy
and tactics—and had, during countless evenings
and weekend afternoons for as long as Sam could
remember. Since she didn't have any brothers and
her mother and grandmother were bored stiff by
all things military, she was usually drafted to serve
as their audience . . . and, they hoped, the reposi-
tory of their combined knowledge.

A few years ago Dad, Gramps and several of
their cronies had discovered the board game Axis

& Allies. Fortunately by then Sam was living too far away to be available for their frequent, interminable games, though she was often recruited to take the role of Russia during visits home. Nobody else ever wanted to be Russia, for good reason. Josef Stalin's Union of Soviet Socialist Republics almost always got creamed. Except when Sam played.

Gramps had been an infantryman in the European theater of operations and after the war taught high school U.S. history for forty years. He considered himself an authority on WWII, and delighted in lecturing anyone who would listen about the enormous and costly blunders that had cost Hitler the war.

Gramps loved to take the role of Germany in the Axis & Allies games, to demonstrate how "that demented Austrian paperhanger" might have conquered all of Europe and a large chunk of Asia, if only he'd followed sound military strategy. It irritated him no end when Sam, as Russia, managed to kick the stuffing out of der Führer's war machine. It annoyed him even more when she took the role of Japan and turned against Germany, wreaking havoc with his carefully laid plans at a crucial point in the game.

Anticipation curved her lips in another smile as she prepared to blast her interrogators' stubborn disbelief out from under them.

"How about if I tell you that the attack on Pearl Harbor took place at approximately 7:58 Honolulu time?" she said with calm assurance. "And that Secretary of the Navy Knox had just finished a meeting with Admiral Stark here in Washington when he received the dispatch? I believe that was about 1:30 in the afternoon."

Ragsdale stiffened, then whipped around to demand of the stenographer, "Are you getting all this down?"

"Yes, sir," the woman said nervously. They were the first words she'd spoken since she entered the room.

Mercer was taking his own notes. Chief Collier watched and listened mutely, his interest fully engaged.

"Let's see, what else?" Sam murmured, dredging her memory for details. "The Japanese used several different aircraft— primarily Kawasaki light bombers and Mitsubishi GM4's, I think. If I remember correctly, our military intelligence people referred to the Kawasakis as 'Lily' and the GM4's as 'Betty.' Or was it 'Nell'?" She shook her head impatiently, wishing Gramps were there to consult. "Never mind, I'm sure you can find out. Whatever we called them, they managed to sink, capsize or heavily damage eight battleships, three light cruisers, three destroyers and four auxiliary vessels. Plus a large number of our own aircraft that were caught on the ground. The good news is that most of our planes were— or will be, I guess I should say— salvaged and repaired."

Pleased that she'd remembered so much— it had been years since she'd sat in on one of Gramps and Dad's marathon bull sessions— Sam paused and glanced around, checking the reactions of the people at the table. Mercer and the stenographer were bent over their notebooks, scribbling like mad. Ragsdale had become a grim, stony-faced statue. Whatever he was thinking, he wasn't giving anything away. Collier was staring at her as if she'd suddenly sprouted horns and a tail.

"I don't know how much of that information

you'll be able to confirm right away. I imagine things are still pretty chaotic at Pearl. But there's one detail you should be able to verify through the Department of the Army. There was a Japanese sailor, the pilot or captain or whatever, of one of their two-man midget subs."

Mercer's head snapped up as Ragsdale echoed, "Subs?" in a sharp, alarmed tone.

Sam nodded. "There were a bunch of them that were supposed to penetrate Pearl Harbor and torpedo ships the planes missed, but as far as I know only one was actually sighted inside the harbor. I think the rest had trouble getting past the reef. Anyway, this one pilot was named Sakamaki. Ensign Something Sakamaki. The navigational equipment on his sub went kaput, then the engine died, and he and his crewman had to bail out. The crewman drowned and Sakamaki lost consciousness, but somehow he stayed alive and washed up on the beach. When he came to, an American soldier was standing over him. Ensign Sakamaki of the Japanese Imperial Navy became the United States' first prisoner of war."

She looked straight into Ragsdale's eyes. "His capture should be a matter of record by now. After you've verified that fact, maybe you'll be willing to reconsider whether it might be possible for a person to travel back in time. Because there's no way I could know the things I just told you unless I possess information that will only be available in the future or I was actually *at* Pearl Harbor the morning of December 7th." She paused a beat for effect.

"And we all know I couldn't have been at Pearl Harbor, because I was here, locked up in a Washington jail cell."

Six

Around eleven Friday night Lucas ducked into Vernon Marshall's office for a desperately needed catnap. Unfortunately, Vern's sofa was considerably shorter than his own six-foot, two-inch frame and barely deep enough to accommodate his shoulders. It was also upholstered in slippery black vinyl. Every time he shifted, trying to get comfortable, he started to slide onto the floor. He gave up after a frustrating fifteen minutes that left him cranky and even more exhausted, and returned to the news room.

The station was still on the air, but only because CNN and the networks had been broadcasting both the tape of Andy Budwig's remote feed and the one in which Rashad stated the terrorists' demands every half hour— a situation that had much of the federal bureaucracy up in arms. By noon, Vernon had received phone calls from the State Department, the National Security Agency, several members of Congress and the FCC. All the callers questioned his judgment in making the tapes available to every major broadcaster in the country. A few voiced doubts about either his sanity or his patriotism. One irate senator threatened to bring charges against the station management. Vern told him to take his best shot and hung up on him.

Two FBI agents and a grim young body builder from the CIA showed up just before noon on the 8th to confiscate the terrorists' tape. Vern produced two cassettes, one for each agency. When the older FBI guy reiterated that he'd come for the original, Vernon nodded at the box the man had just accepted, and dead-panned, "That's it." The agent took him at his word and left with a second generation copy.

Lucas suspected the same scenario had been played out at least once in every newsroom that had aired the tape. Washington was an intensely image-conscious town, and the image most government agencies toiled night and day to project was invincibility. At approximately eight o'clock yesterday morning, four anonymous men had annihilated that image, perhaps for all time.

Which, of course, was the real reason the blood pressure of virtually every authority figure in town had reached stroke level. All this rhetoric about national security was so much smoke. The attempts to muzzle everyone in the information-dissemination business were simply the bureaucrats' idea of damage control: Don't let the public know how bad it really is, and for God's sake don't do anything that will encourage registered voters to start questioning *how* or *why* it happened.

Lucas made his way to Cassie McGregor's cluttered desk and perched on a corner while he waited for her to finish a telephone conversation. The two of them had taken on the task of contacting everyone anybody at the station knew who had a link to the intelligence community. Their goal was to convince some brave soul to identify at least one of the terrorists from the tape. So far they'd struck out with every contact they'd made. Not that they'd made that many. Large sections of the telephone system were still out of service, and a lot of the people they did reach hung up the second they heard the words "television" and "news" strung together.

"Any luck?" Lucas asked when Cassie finished her call.

She shook her head no, then amended the response with a tentative, "Well, maybe. A guy my cousin's dating *might* be willing to study the tape for us, but only if we can give him an ironclad guarantee that he'll go to his grave without being identified. Janice says he's *real* nervous about the idea, but she's gonna work on him."

"What is he, CIA?"

"Uh-uh. Army Intelligence. Served three tours in the Middle East before transferring to the Pentagon."

"Sounds promising. When will we have a definite 'yes' or 'no'?"

"Hopefully by tomorrow morning."

"Tell your cousin I'll spring for a bottle of bubbly, if she thinks it'd help," Lucas offered. He stood and arched his back, wincing as the movement produced a symphony of cracks and pops. "If anybody needs me I'll be in my office, trying to get through to the nursing home."

"Good luck," Cassie said as he walked away.

Lucas closed the office door and sat at his desk, then took a minute to psych himself before he reached for the phone. Anxious as he was for news about Sam, he was almost afraid to dial the number he'd memorized the night before and tried calling a dozen times since.

Counseling himself to be patient and keep trying hadn't noticeably reduced his frustration, and not even the endless demands of his job the past couple of days had provided sufficient distraction to let him escape this heavy, smothering sense of dread.

Something was terribly wrong. He knew it in a dark, primitive corner of his mind that had no connection to reason or logic.

Oh, he'd felt better, relieved and encouraged, after he spoke to the ER nurse last night, but only for an hour or so— until the mental agony of not knowing what had happened to Samantha was replaced by this relentless foreboding. Of course he realized it was irrational, probably a reaction to the horror stories he'd heard in the past 24 hours. Not that the realization helped. He was still afraid of what he'd find out when he finally managed to get through to the nursing home.

But he had to *know*. He had to be *sure*, both that she really had been admitted and that she was all right. He closed his eyes and inhaled a deep, fortifying breath, then released it in an impatient rush and reached for the phone.

Levander went straight to Jane Doe's room after clocking out at the end of his shift. During a break in the employees' lounge an hour or so earlier, one of the other aides had mentioned that the last time she'd charted the woman's pulse and respiration, her eyes were twitching beneath the lids. Levander knew this was an indication of REM sleep and hoped it meant Jane was ready to come back from whatever dark place her mind had carried her to.

Sure enough, as he stood beside the bed her right leg shifted under the covers. While he was cautioning himself not to get his hopes up, that it might be just a muscle spasm, the slender fingers of her left hand flexed against the blanket. Levander smiled broadly and pulled a chair next to the bed to sit for a while. He was still there 45 minutes later, when her eyes fluttered open.

He could see that she was confused, a little disoriented as she took in the room— dark now except for the puddle of light produced by a 40-watt bulb in a small lamp on the bedside table. When she slowly rolled her head toward him, Levander's smile returned. He'd been right about her eyes: they were blue. They were also filled with alarm.

"How are you feeling?" he asked, and was gratified to see her apprehension ebb. Levander knew his voice was his best asset. Deep as an ocean, it could roar like crashing breakers or soothe with the steady, reassuring rhythm of an incoming tide. At the moment he was exerting careful control to make it gentle and benevolent.

"I . . ." She closed her eyes, her soft mouth turning down in a faint grimace. Levander suspected she was taking inventory of her aches and pains, or maybe reliving the moment when the airplane crashed into the hotel. He waited patiently.

"My head hurts," she murmured. Her voice was lovely— refined, with the complete absence of an accent that a very expensive education produces.

She lifted a hand and hesitantly touched the bandages that swathed her head. The fear returned, clouding and darkening her eyes.

"There was an accident," Levander said before she could ask. "A plane crashed into the hotel where you were staying. You got a few superficial burns, but that's all. You probably won't even have any scars."

Her fingers lingered for a moment, gingerly inspecting the gauze dressing, then she laid her soft, perfectly-formed hand back on the blanket.

"I don't remember."

"Well, that happens sometimes," Levander assured her. "When you've had a pretty bad shock, usually you lose at least some of what happened right before and right after. I wouldn't worry about it. It's just your mind's way of protecting you."

She lowered her eyelids in lieu of a nod, indicating that she knew this was so. "But . . . I don't even remember being in a hotel."

Levander instinctively hid his surprise, not wanting to do or say anything that might upset her. "Maybe you'd just checked in." He didn't think that was likely, since the plane had crashed early in the morning. She'd probably checked in the day before, in which case the trauma had erased more of her memory than was usually the case.

"Where?" she said, and at his uncomprehending look, "The hotel. Where is it?"

"Just outside of Alexandria."

She frowned. "Are you sure?"

"Yes, ma'am. You couldn't miss hearing about it yesterday. Even before they brought you here, the plane crash and the bomb were all anybody talked about all day."

He immediately regretted mentioning the bomb; she might have had family or friends in Washington. He breathed a sigh of relief when she didn't react to his slip. Maybe she hadn't caught that part.

"Your folks are prob'ly worried sick by now. In all the confusion, nobody got your name, so we didn't know who to contact. If you'll tell me who

I should call, to let them know you're all right . . ."

He trailed off and waited, but she didn't supply any names or phone numbers. In fact, she didn't say anything at all. She lay utterly still, staring at the ceiling. The silence lengthened until Levander began to feel a little uneasy.

"Ma'am?" he coaxed gently. "There must be somebody you'd like me to contact for you. Just tell me who, and I'll— "

"I don't know."

"Your parents, maybe," he prompted. "Or a boyfriend?" She hadn't been wearing any rings when they brought her in, so he assumed she wasn't married. "A pretty girl like you must have a boyfriend."

"I don't know," she repeated. Her voice was little more than a whisper. Turning her head slightly, she looked directly at him. "I don't remember."

"You don't remember if you have a boyfriend?" He spoke slowly, carefully, wanting to be sure he understood.

"Or parents," she murmured. A quaver had invaded her voice. She drew a sharp, shallow breath. "Or my own name. I don't remember *anything* . . . not even who I am."

It took five tries, but Lucas finally got through to the nursing home. The woman who answered had just come back from a week's vacation and didn't know anything about an admission the night before. She put him on hold while she went to look for somebody to answer his questions. Lucas waited anxiously, afraid that he'd lose the connection and it would take another 24 hours to re-establish it.

Finally someone else came on the line. Not an admitting clerk, but a nurse's aide. A middle-aged black man, judging by his voice. Lucas didn't give him a chance to do more than identify himself.

"Mr. Grisham, please, just listen. The phone system's still unstable as hell and we could lose this connection any second. My name is Lucas Davenport. I'm trying to locate a woman I've been told was transferred there last night from an Alexandria hospital. Her name is Samantha Cook. You might have her registered as Jane Doe. She's 28, but looks younger. She was at the hotel, the one—"

"The one the plane crashed into."

"Yes!" If Lucas hadn't been sitting down, he'd have collapsed in relief. "Thank God. She is there, then?"

"Yes, sir, she's here." Levander Grisham sounded almost as relieved as Lucas. "In fact, I was in her room when Miz Williams came looking for somebody to talk to you. It's late, you know? All the office staff went home hours ago."

"Is she all right?" Lucas demanded. "The hospital said she didn't have any serious injuries, but—"

Levander hastened to reassure him. "Yes, sir, that's right. She's got a few minor burns, but that's all. Prob'ly won't even scar."

"Thank God," Lucas said again. "Can you put me through to her room? I'd like to talk to her."

The other man hesitated. Lucas assumed he was worried about policy; maybe patients weren't supposed to receive calls after a certain hour.

"I promise I'll only keep her on the phone a couple of minutes. I just want to hear her voice, and let her know that I'm all right."

"Yes, sir, I understand, but I'm not sure it would

be a good idea for you to talk to her right now. She's pretty upset. In fact, I called the doctor a little while ago and he had the nursing supervisor give her a sedative. She's calmed down some, but—"

"Wait," Lucas blurted. "Back up a minute. Why did she need a sedative, if she wasn't hurt? Is she experiencing some kind of post-traumatic reaction?"

"I expect that's it, exactly," Levander said. "You see, Mr. Davenport, the reason she got so upset was because she doesn't remember what happened yesterday. Not any of it—the plane crash, being taken to the hospital . . . It's like her memory's been wiped clean."

Lucas rubbed the spot in the middle of his forehead where a headache was trying to take hold. "She doesn't remember?"

"That's right. She's suffering from traumatic amnesia. She doesn't remember *anything.*"

It finally sank in—what the man had been tactfully leading up to. Lucas sat up straight. "She doesn't remember me, is that what you're saying?"

"I'm afraid it's worse than that, Mr. Davenport. She doesn't even remember her own name, or where she lives, or if she has family we should contact."

"Her parents," Lucas murmured. "They live in Maryland. I'll call them. What did the doctor say? This is a temporary condition, right? Her memory *will* come back."

"He thinks so," Levander answered. "But there's no telling how long it'll take. He's gonna have her examined by a psychiatrist tomorrow, then maybe we'll have a better idea what to expect. For now, there's not much anybody can do."

"But if I could talk to her—that might help, mightn't it?"

"I'm sorry, Mr. Davenport, but I suspect it might make things worse. Now, if you were *here* . . . if you could sit down next to her and she could *see* you, hold your hand. . . . But from what I've heard, the army's not letting people just get in their cars and go where they want."

"You've heard right," Lucas said. "They've set up dozens of road blocks. Even if I managed to get past them, chances are I'd be stopped by one of the Special Forces teams. Word is they're conducting random patrols, taking everybody they catch trying to leave town into custody. God knows what happens to the people they round up. Our nation's capital is fast turning into a police state."

"It's getting pretty bad down here, too," Levander said. "Today the administrator of this place gave us cards we have to carry 24 hours a day, saying where we live, where we work, and what hours we're supposed to be here. People are scared to make any detours, even for gas or groceries. Not that there's much to buy since the looting started."

"It's spread all the way out there?" Lucas said in surprise.

"Oh, yeah. I had to go a half mile out of my way to get to work this afternoon. There was a riot at one of those one-stop gas and convenience stores and somebody torched the place. When I got there, the fire'd spread several blocks in every direction."

Lucas's professional instincts temporarily overpowered his personal concerns. Grabbing an assignment schedule, he scrawled a terse note about the fire in the margin. While part of his mind continued to wrestle with the problem of how to get to Samantha, another part started indexing contacts in suburban Virginia, reviewing the names of everyone he knew who might be able to get out in the streets and put together a report.

"Mr. Davenport? Are you still there?"

Levander Grisham's deep, resonant voice pulled Lucas back to the present. "Yes!" he blurted. "Sorry, I was distracted for a minute." He told himself the twinge of guilt he felt was foolish. Samantha of all people would *expect* him to keep doing his job. Especially now.

An ominous hissing sound appeared on the line.

"Sounds like we're about to lose our connection," Levander remarked.

"Damn," Lucas muttered. A loud crackle, like bacon thrown on a too-hot griddle, joined the hissing. "Okay, it doesn't look like I'll be able to get out there anytime soon, but I want to keep in touch. Are you usually there at this time of night?"

By now the interference was so bad that he missed the first part of Levander's response, but caught most of the last part.

"— clock out at 10:30 . . . scheduled to work this weekend, both evenings . . ."

"I can barely hear you," Lucas yelled into the mouthpiece. "I'll call again at 10:30 tomorrow night. Here's my number at work, in case— " He floundered, his mind unable or unwilling to complete the thought, then finished in a frantic rush, "In case you need to contact me before then."

He barked out the phone number at the station, hoping Levander Grisham could hear him and had something to write it down with.

After he hung up, Lucas remained at his desk for several minutes, staring at the phone without really seeing it. Sam was alive, and safe. At least he knew that much. And, miraculously, she hadn't suffered any serious injuries. He'd read enough about traumatic amnesia to feel confident that her memory would return, eventually. Maybe not all of it— she might never remember the plane crash or what had happened immediately before— but in time the important things would come back.

He closed his eyes and released a long, pent-up sigh of relief. Now if he could just get a call through to her parents. . . . They must be half crazy with worry by now. They'd probably been trying to reach her since yesterday morning. He opened the center drawer of his desk and took out a small black address book.

Samantha was stretched out on the bunk, propped on an elbow while she examined the September issue of *Good Housekeeping* one of the matrons had brought her, when Joe Mercer appeared at the cell door.

One look at his face told her he wasn't paying a social call. The man really needed to catch some Z's, she thought as she sat up and swung her feet to the floor. The half moons under his eyes had deepened to the color of plums. And while the dark beard stubble added a certain rugged appeal, she suspected J. Edgar Hoover would throw a fit if he found one of his special agents in need of a shave. Though, now that she thought about it, most FBI personnel had probably been running on caffeine and patriotism for the past 24 hours.

"What's up?" she said, as Mercer entered the cell.

He dismissed the guard who'd accompanied him

with a brusque gesture. The man retreated down the corridor, leaving them alone.

"We've been in touch with Army Intelligence," Mercer said as he reached into his jacket for the familiar notebook and pen.

"About Ensign Sakamaki?" Sam guessed. She scooted to the far end of the bunk and patted the mattress in invitation.

"Yes." He hesitated, then gingerly took a seat on the opposite end of the bunk. He perched on the edge, as if at any second he might change his mind and jump back up.

"And?"

She unconsciously leaned forward, needing to hear him say it, to verify that she hadn't gone completely bonkers, that the past couple of days had really happened and weren't just the fabrication of a deranged mind.

"Your account of Ensign Kazuo Sakamaki's capture was accurate." Mercer was flipping through his notebook, not meeting her eyes. "The other crewman's name was Inagaki, by the way. Apparently he drowned."

Sam resisted the urge to say "I told you so." He hadn't come just to tell her the Army had corroborated her story about the Japanese submarine pilot.

"All your other facts also appear to be correct," he added, still scanning pages in the notebook. "Including the code names our intelligence services use for Japanese aircraft."

Uh-oh, Sam thought.

"You're not going to start that nonsense about my being a Japanese agent again, are you?"

He finally looked at her. For an instant Sam thought she saw a glint of amusement in his gorgeous, but dulled with exhaustion, bluer-than-blue eyes.

"I haven't made up my mind about that."

She studied his lean, intelligent face, trying not to let herself be distracted by his drop-dead looks. "But for the time being you're giving me the benefit of the doubt?"

"For the time being," Mercer acknowledged. "I thought of a few more questions after we finished the official interrogation."

"Somehow I thought you might," Sam said dryly. She tucked her legs under her and leaned back against the wall, settling in for the next round. "Okay, Special Agent Mercer. Fire when ready."

His right eyebrow rose a barely perceptible centimeter, but otherwise he maintained a stoic mask as he consulted his notes.

"The first time I came to this cell, you made some puzzling remarks."

Sam was surprised— not that she'd said something he found puzzling, but that he would start with their first meeting.

"Oh? What did I say?" Her own memories of that meeting were mostly about how bowled over she'd been by his looks. Of course, at the time she'd thought he was an hallucination.

"You said it wouldn't make any sense for the Japanese to attack us, that they'd be committing economic suicide because we're their best customers. Then something about protectionists welcoming an excuse to make war on Japan *again*, apparently because of a 'trade deficit.' "

He lifted his head to give her an expectant, questioning look. Sam stared back at him mutely. Yes, now that he mentioned it, she did remember saying those things. Of course they would be puzzling, to put it mildly, to an FBI agent who heard them in 1941 . . . and of course he would want some kind of explanation.

"Oh, boy," she muttered. "I see a problem developing here."

That expressive pitch-dark eyebrow formed a quizzical arch. "A problem?"

"Yeah." She pursed her lips and blew out a stream of air. "A fairly big one. The problem is, exactly how much should I tell you?"

"If you're asking for my advice . . ."

"I'm not. Naturally you want me to tell you everything. That's your job, to elicit whatever information I possess— *all* the information I possess. The problem is, all the information I possess, I brought with me . . . from the future. What if you, or whoever you pass that information on to, uses something I tell you to alter the course of history?"

Both his gaze and his voice sharpened with suspicion. "You have knowledge that could alter the course of history?"

"Maybe." She shifted restlessly. "How do I know? I mean, who's to say? If I told you which side won the war, that probably wouldn't change anything. But if I told you about specific battles that haven't even been fought yet, or things that will happen after the war— about the trade deficit, for example— "

"You know the outcome of battles that haven't been fought?" Mercer interrupted. To say he sounded skeptical would have been an understatement of mammoth proportions.

"Of course. Well, not every single battle, but

most of the major ones in Europe and the Pacific, a few in North Africa."

"North Africa." Now he was looking at her as if she'd started jabbering about Mars, or Jupiter.

"Yes, North Africa." Sam resisted the temptation to reel off names like Tobruk and El Alamein. His blatant disbelief was irritating as hell, but blurting out something she might later regret, just to impress or convince him, would be reckless and stupid.

"Just put your fancy gold pen away," she said. He held it poised over the notebook, ready to jot down anything she said that sounded significant. "I'm not going to tell you anything about battles or troop deployments or give you any other military information till I've had some time to think about the possible consequences."

Mercer stiffened in offense—a reflex Sam had seen often, usually when she'd defied some authority figure or other—and fixed her with a hard stare. "I suggest you also consider the consequences for withholding information that could affect the outcome of this war."

She shook her head. "Save your threats, Agent Mercer. I already *know* the outcome of the war."

"Which you admitted a minute ago probably wouldn't change if you told me what you know."

"Probably not, but how can I be sure?" She paused, tilted her head inquisitively. "You sound like you're starting to believe my story."

He didn't reply, but he didn't have to. They both knew she had him cornered.

"Come on, Mercer, drop the inscrutable federal agent pose. You're at least considering the possibility that I might be from the future . . . aren't you?"

The gold pen tapped a staccato tattoo on the open notebook. Mercer looked frustrated, extremely ill at ease, as if only rigid self-control kept him from squirming. He looked, to be honest, as if he'd rather be anywhere else on the face of the planet. Sam empathized, but she wasn't about to tell him so. Not when she'd finally started to get through to him.

"Time travel is only possible in fiction— pulp novels and movies," he said at length.

"That's what I thought a couple of days ago. Yet here I am, in the flesh." She impulsively reached out to lightly touch the back of his hand. "And you've admitted that I know things nobody from 1941 could possibly know."

His expression suddenly changed from uncertainty to extreme discomfort. Samantha sensed it was because of the unwelcome physical contact, but she left her fingers where they were. If she ever hoped to make an ally of him, she had to get past his professional detachment and make him start thinking of her as a *person*, instead of as a suspect or a collection of notes in his little black book.

The wary, troubled look in his eyes as he slowly withdrew his hand told her she'd made a good start.

Seven

Early the next morning Sam's jailers— or, more likely, Special Agent Ragsdale— sent a psychiatrist and a physician to examine her. Both men asked plenty of questions; neither man answered any of hers. Mrs. Patton stood in the corridor and glared at her suspiciously during both exams.

Apparently whoever was scheduling Sam's appointments intended to keep her busy today. The doctors had been gone no more than two or three minutes when one of the male guards arrived to escort her to the interrogation room. An emaciated, officious-looking man sat at the table, behind a large, unwieldy contraption that Sam guessed at once was a polygraph machine. She spent the better part of the next hour on a hard chair with leads strapped too tightly around her arm, chest and skull, answering still more questions. When the skinny little man finally unstrapped her, she didn't bother to ask about the test results. If he was as close-mouthed as the doctors, it would be a waste of time. Besides, she knew she'd passed with flying colors, for all the good it did her.

Back in her cell, she sank down on the cot and picked up the two-day-old newspaper that had been delivered along with her breakfast. The date at the top of each page was Sunday, December 7,

1941, but since it was a morning edition, there was nothing about the Japanese attacks in the Pacific.

Figuring she probably wouldn't have time to read the entire paper before somebody else showed up with a list of questions, Sam scanned the front page stories. These included a report that Britain, Canada and New Zealand had gone to war with Finland, Hungary and Rumania, following the rejection by the latter countries of Britain's ultimatum that they end their conflict with Russia. There was also another, longer story about Russia: coverage of the ongoing German invasion. Sam skipped over that one. She'd heard enough about Hitler's Operation Barbarossa from Dad and Gramps to fill a couple of history texts. She knew exactly what was happening on the Russian front, probably better than the correspondents covering the story.

On June 22nd, the Führer had sent the greatest mechanized invasion force in history to launch his assault on the Soviet Union. For the past five months the Germans had been ruthlessly destroying every farm and village that stood in their path as they stormed across the Russian heartland. But she also knew that the first week of December would be the beginning of the end for the Wehrmacht. The brutal Russian winter was about to do what no army on earth had managed so far: bring the German army to a dead stop.

She skimmed the rest of the newspaper, looking for coverage of Colonel Ethan Herrick's murder. There was nothing, not even in the obituary section. The paper must have gone to press before the investigating detectives filed their reports.

The sale ads were fascinating, especially the ones for clothes and furniture, but the prices had to be misprints. Good dresses couldn't really be selling for three dollars! Eventually she made her way to the comics. A strip called "Navy Bob Steele" caught her eye because the story line was about the sighting of a "strange submarine." The Navy destroyer crew who spotted the sub were unable to determine its nationality, but the captain immediately forwarded a report to the chief of Naval Operations in Washington. A couple of panels later, an order was issued for "the Pacific fleet to be ready to get underway in half an hour."

Sam shook her head with an ironic smile. If only something like that had actually happened, the U.S. Navy might not have been caught with their collective pants down when the Japanese attacked Pearl. She had moved on to a comic called "Draftie" when the scrape of a key in the lock alerted her that she had another visitor.

At some point in the past couple of days, someone had finally got around to oiling the hinges of the door at the end of the corridor. While Sam didn't miss the agonized shriek every time the door was opened, it was disconcerting to have people suddenly appear outside the cell, without any warning. So far nobody had caught her on the toilet, but she figured it was only a matter of time.

Her lack of privacy and potential embarrassment weren't subjects she cared to discuss with the handsome FBI agent facing her through the bars, though. She waited till Joseph Mercer had entered the cell and the guard had withdrawn, then asked bluntly, "What's the verdict?"

"The M.D. says you're physically fit," he replied as he took a seat on the end of the bunk. "The psychiatrist agrees, but adds that you're obviously delusional."

No surprises there, Sam thought wryly. "And the polygraph test?"

"Agent Harris's report appears to support the psychiatrist's diagnosis."

His attitude— remote, slightly aloof— annoyed Sam, even though she knew it had been programmed into him and didn't necessarily reflect his personality. "Admit it, Mercer, the polygraph test verified that I've been telling the truth all along."

He cleared his throat before he answered, giving her the impression that he wasn't altogether comfortable with what he was about to say. "Agent Harris's interpretation of the test results is that you *believed* you were answering his questions truthfully."

"I get it," Sam muttered. "I'm 'delusional,' out of touch with reality. Very convenient theory, Mercer. Of course it doesn't explain how I know the things I know."

"No, it doesn't."

He spoke so softly that for a second paranoia reared its head and Sam wondered if the cell was bugged. But then she realized that wireless transmitters hadn't existed in 1941, and there were no exposed wires in the cell. If there had been, she'd have found them by now.

"Unless you believe I'm some kind of demented clairvoyant," she said, inviting him to tell her what he really thought. *Was* that what he thought?

Mercer gave an impatient shake of his head. "You're obviously an intelligent, well-educated woman. And despite the psychiatrist's report, I don't believe you have any trouble discerning what's real and what isn't."

"I'd say that makes you a minority of one. So

where does that leave us— is the official line going to be that ridiculous claim that I must be a foreign agent?"

Mercer lifted his left shoulder in a noncommittal shrug. "So far there's no hard evidence to support that theory."

Samantha rolled her eyes toward the fly-specked lightbulb on the ceiling. Of course there wasn't any evidence, for God's sake. There couldn't be, because she wasn't a spy! Not that that possibility would occur to the FBI. She'd spent the past several years working with and for cops— both the federal and local varieties— so she should be accustomed to the bureaucratic mind set, the bullheaded resistance to any explanation that didn't conform to a limited number of comfortably familiar possibilities.

The trouble was that, until now, *she'd* never been the suspect.

"Tell me about this Valerie Herrick," she asked, purely on impulse. She could see that the request surprised Mercer.

"What would you like to know?"

"Well, for starters, why would she murder her father, assuming she did? Had they argued? Was he an abusive parent? Did he make a habit of slapping her around, or humiliating her in public?"

"God, no!" He was clearly appalled by the suggestion. "Colonel Herrick was a rather cold man, but he would never have lifted a finger against Valerie! If anything, he was too protective of her. Almost obsessively so, in fact."

Samantha was surprised by his fervent defense of the late Colonel Herrick, but even more surprised that he seemed to know a lot about the colonel's relationship with his missing daughter.

"So, as far as you know, Valerie had no motive for murdering her father?"

Evidently Mercer realized that he'd overreacted a moment ago. This time he took a few seconds to consider his answer.

"According to witnesses, they'd quarreled earlier in the evening, during dinner."

"At home?"

"No, at a restaurant here in Washington."

"What did they argue about?"

"A man Valerie had been seeing. The colonel disapproved of him, apparently didn't think he was good enough for her."

Something in Mercer's voice, a sort of weary cynicism, made Sam suspect he shared the colonel's opinion. Did he know the man they'd argued about? Evidently he knew the Herricks, or had at least acquired a lot of information about them. Her curiosity sharpened and found a focus.

"What's she like?"

"Valerie?" A small fold appeared between Mercer's dark brows as he considered. "I suppose 'reserved' would be the word that best describes her, both by temperament and as a result of her upbringing. Very conscious of her status, though she couldn't be called a snob. She teaches a Sunday School class, works for all the appropriate charities— Bundles For Britain, that sort of thing. She has a small but close circle of friends. Most of them are women she went to school with, the daughters of Army officers or government officials . . . friends or acquaintances of her father's."

"Sounds like a real daddy's girl," Sam remarked.

He responded with a wryly arched brow. "Very perceptive. Valerie Herrick doesn't utter a word or make a move, in public at any rate, without first considering how it might reflect on her father. Even the men she goes out with are carbon copies of the colonel."

"Except for one," Sam said. And then, in response to his sharp, probing look, "The man she and her father argued about at dinner."

"Oh. Yes, of course."

His knee-jerk reaction disappointed her. Apparently he still harbored some wee suspicion that she knew more than she was telling. Sam tried to shrug off her reaction, telling herself he was only doing his job and it shouldn't matter that he still didn't completely believe her; at least he was talking to her, sharing information.

It did matter, though. She *wanted* him to believe her, to *trust* her. And not just because she was in desperate need of an ally.

"Do you know who this guy is?" she asked, determined to keep herself and the conversation on track. This wasn't the time to examine her feelings about Agent Joseph Mercer. Not that she *had* any feelings to examine.

He gave a negative shake of his head, sending a lock of dark, glossy hair onto his brow. He pushed it back with an absent gesture. "The Washington police have questioned several of her friends. None of them was aware she'd been seeing anyone new."

Sam surreptitiously inhaled a deep breath and uncurled her fingers. For just an instant, the temptation to reach out and brush that lock of hair off his forehead had been so strong that she'd balled her hands into fists to resist it.

"That makes sense," she murmured. "If he was somebody she knew her father wouldn't approve of, Valerie would probably want to keep the relationship a secret."

"Yes, I imagine she would." Mercer reached into his pocket for his notebook and pen. "Chief Collier's men are continuing to question her friends and acquaintances. I'm sure they'll eventually turn up something. In the meantime, I'd like to get back to the conversation we had last night."

The sight of his gold pen hovering above a blank page drove her unsettling physical reaction to him right out of Sam's mind.

"In case you've forgotten," she reminded him, "I told you last night, I don't think I should furnish you with information that—"

"Could allow me or my superiors to alter the course of history. Yes, I remember. But you also said you needed some time to think about the consequences of revealing certain facts." He paused, gave her an expectant look. "You've had several hours."

Sam felt her face flush with indignation. "During which I've been probed, prodded, analyzed and cross-examined by a succession of strange men, all of whom have apparently decided I'm either a raving lunatic or a fiendishly clever criminal. Or maybe both."

Mercer sighed and capped the fountain pen, a gesture Sam knew good and well was meant to relax her and get her to lower her guard.

"Be reasonable, Miss Cook," he said, his sexy voice pitched low and fairly humming with reassurance.

"I'm always reasonable, Agent Mercer."

"You admitted last night that you don't *know* whether you possess knowledge that could affect the course of history."

Sam sat up straighter, her posture telegraphing stubborn resistance. "But if there's even a slight possibility— "

"And how are we supposed to determine that, if you won't talk?" he demanded in exasperation.

"Well, there's our problem in a nutshell, Agent Mercer. I don't believe the FBI *should* be trusted to make that determination."

He recoiled as if she'd accused his grandmother of performing an obscene act in public. Sam reminded herself that this was 1941, a time when most Americans still held the Bureau in high regard. Especially, she was sure, its agents, who hadn't yet started slinging charges of racism, sexism, and homophobia.

"This is getting us nowhere," she said with a sigh. "Look, this will probably strike you as a radical concept, but why don't we try cooperating instead of butting heads."

His eyes narrowed with suspicion, his sinfully luxuriant lashes muting their intensity. "Exactly what do you have in mind?"

"Well . . . you could tell me what you want to know, point by point, and I'll decide whether it's information I feel comfortable sharing."

Mercer's expression made it clear he wasn't bowled over by the proposition. No doubt because it left too much control in her hands. Figuring he was about to reject the idea anyway, so she had nothing to lose, Sam impulsively upped the ante.

"And in return for whatever I tell you, I expect you to do what you can to get me released. I haven't broken any laws. You admitted there's no evidence against me, which means there's no justification for keeping me in jail. *Quid pro quo*, Agent Mercer. I'll do my best to help you out, but I expect something in return."

He didn't reply for a full minute, but Sam could see him thinking, mulling over what she'd said, along with the pros and cons of cooperating with her. Except he probably thought of it as acceding to her demands. Finally he uncapped his pen and gave a brusque nod.

"You have a deal, Miss Cook."

Fifteen minutes later he looked like he was seriously considering stabbing her with the pen.

"You're the most obstinate woman I've ever met! What possible harm could come from telling me who the next President will be? We're talking about *history*, for heaven's sake!"

"*My* history," Samantha shot back. "You and Mr. Hoover haven't lived it yet. And to be perfectly frank, I don't want to be responsible for giving that obsessive megalomaniac even more power than he already has."

She knew she'd struck a nerve when she saw the muscle along his jaw jump. She told herself she should have anticipated something like this. Of course the Director of the FBI would like to know who he'd be reporting to in the future, so he could start compiling secret dossiers full of useful information. Sam couldn't know whether Mercer had been instructed to pursue this line of questioning, or if he'd taken the initiative in hopes of advancing his own career. At any rate, she couldn't work up much concern about his motives. Trying to decide what it would be safe to tell him and what she should keep to herself was turning out to be a lot harder than she'd expected.

"We're wasting time," she said impatiently. "If you're concerned about who'll be running the country five or ten years from now, I suggest you make sure to vote in the next several elections."

"I always vote," Mercer retorted.

"Bully for you. What's the next question on your list?"

His glare simmered with such frustration and resentment that she expected to hear his molars grinding together as he flipped to a new page in the notebook.

"Nice watch," he remarked out of the blue.

The remark threw Sam for a moment, as he'd no doubt intended. "Thanks."

"It looks expensive."

"It is. It was a gift . . . a birthday present."

"From a man?"

She studied him warily, but since he was bent over the notebook she couldn't read his expression. Where was he headed with this?

"Yes, as a matter of fact." The chill in her voice added an explicit: *Not that it's any of your business.*

"And the ring? Was that a gift, too?"

Sam's thumb instinctively tucked into her palm, touching the gold band as if it were a talisman. "In a way. My birth mother left it with the adoption agency to pass along to my parents. They gave it to me on my 21st birthday, as she requested."

Halfway through the explanation, Mercer lifted his head. His handsome features registered mild surprise, curiosity, and what Sam thought was a trace of sympathy.

"What?" She made it a challenge.

His expression immediately smoothed into an impassive mask. "I suppose I'm surprised that a woman who possessed such an obviously valuable piece of jewelry couldn't find some way to keep her child."

Sam shrugged. "Maybe she realized she wasn't up to the job of being a parent, or just wasn't ready for the responsibility." She spread her fingers and studied the large emerald. "I've always thought it must be a family heirloom. That would explain why she wanted me to have it."

Mercer murmured a noncommittal "Mmm" before returning to his notes. He didn't mention the ring again, or make any more remarks about gifts from men. Sam wondered if he thought she was what people in 1941 would consider a loose woman. The possibility that he might be forming judgments about her character didn't sit well. She told herself she didn't care what he thought of her; she only needed his help, not his good opinion.

The trouble was, she didn't quite believe her own disclaimer.

His next few questions were about the Japanese attacks in the Pacific and the effect they would have on America's ability to wage war. Sam figured that by now the Navy had taken stock of its losses and had a fair idea how they would affect the country's ability to wage war, so she recited all the pertinent facts she could dredge from memory, pausing now and then to let him copy the information into his notebook.

Mostly what she recited were names— the names of damaged ships that would soon be made seaworthy, and of men who would earn a place in the history books during the coming weeks and months. She conscientiously skirted any mention of specific naval battles, which rather limited what she could say. She was running out of material when Mrs. Patton arrived with her lunch tray. For the first time since Sam woke up in the cell, she was glad to see the woman.

"This should be sufficient for now," Mercer said. Tucking the notebook and pen away, he stood to leave. "I'll probably be back this afternoon."

Sam gave him a wry smile. "If I'm not in my office, I'm sure Mrs. Patton will know where I can be reached."

She thought he was suppressing a smile of his own as he headed down the corridor.

She *couldn't* be telling the truth.

She *must* be hiding something.

Her story sounded like one of H.G. Wells's fantastic fairy tales, for Christ's sake.

Joe's rational, analytical mind kept broadcasting disbelief and suspicion as he summarized his interviews with Samantha Cook for Bill Ragsdale and a dour deputy director named Harold Boggs. Unfortunately, his instincts were sending out even stronger, contradictory signals.

He tried to ignore his blasted instincts. Listening to them could only get him into serious, career-jeopardizing trouble. He couldn't think of a single reason why he should believe Samantha Cook's incredible story, much less trust her.

Of course, if he really *wanted* a reason, there was her clear, direct, no-bull gaze . . .

She had a way of looking at him— especially when he was struggling to keep his mind on his job, instead of remembering the lush figure he'd glimpsed that first day, when she held the blanket open for half a second. She always met his stare head-on, even when he was being his most severe, letting him know she wasn't at all intimidated by him, personally, or by the authority he represented.

It might be a trite romantic cliché, but her arresting green eyes were truly windows to her mind and soul, allowing him access to every thought, emotion and mood. From the beginning Joe had recognized the fierce intelligence behind those eyes— an intelligence that blazed out at him even during displays of impatience, anxiety, resentment. . . . Equally disconcerting, the strength of her will matched the power of her mind. Despite her precarious situation, he'd never seen the slightest sign of submission or defeat. And he'd been watching, alert for either.

Apparently no one had ever told her that females were supposed to be the weaker sex. Joe had known plenty of strong women— including every female member of his own family— but *Miz* Samantha Cook was a unique experience. When he was with her, he could almost forget she was a woman.

Except, of course, when his concentration wavered and his thoughts drifted to the curves that had been visible under her thin, silky slip. Then his imagination took over and he forgot all about her sharp, incisive mind and the more masculine aspects of her personality. In fact, if he hadn't come prepared with a list of questions the last time he visited her cell, he probably would have forgotten why he was there.

These unfortunate lapses were becoming more frequent, and there didn't seem to be a damn thing he could do about them. He was aware that the very strength and tenacity that provoked and exasperated him were also contributing to his attraction, but the knowledge didn't help. In fact, the more he tried to analyze his disturbing reactions to the woman, the stronger and more out of control they became. Any way he looked at it, Samantha Cook was trouble. And now, to make matters worse, in what had obviously been a moment of temporary insanity, he'd agreed to try to convince the powers that be to release her.

It had seemed like a good idea, at the time. He'd thought— well, hoped, to be honest— that in return for his promise she would furnish invaluable information, about either Valerie Herrick's disappearance or the war America had just entered.

Which was, of course, a tacit admission that he was at least considering the possibility that Samantha Cook really had traveled back in time. From 1995.

Was it a possibility, fantastic as it seemed? He'd racked his brain the past couple of days, but hadn't come up with any other explanation for how she knew the things she knew— things no one, not even a foreign agent, could possibly know.

In 1995 he would be 84 years old. Assuming he was still alive.

"It sounds like you're convinced that whatever she knows, she'll keep to herself."

Bill Ragsdale's terse remark yanked Joe's attention back to the meeting in progress. He took a couple of seconds to consider his reply.

"I'm not entirely convinced that she *does* know anything. At least, anything that would bear on the war effort."

Ragsdale expressed his pessimism with a derisive snort. "I think we should give her another polygraph test."

"There's no point," Boggs said flatly. "She sailed through the first one."

"That could've been a fluke," Ragsdale argued. "The equipment might have malfunctioned, or— "

Boggs cut him off. "Forget it, Bill. We're not wasting time and money on another test. The director has already issued instructions, in case interrogating the woman didn't produce results."

A knot materialized in Joe's stomach. "What instructions?"

Deputy Director Harold Boggs was a stocky, balding man with a bulbous nose, no lips to speak of, and a piercing stare that had a way of making people squirm. He turned that cold, penetrating gaze on Joe.

"We're cutting her loose."

"Releasing her!" Ragsdale said incredulously. "You can't be serious!"

His vehement response gave Joe time to mask his own relief. The decision had already been made! He was off the hook. Still, he reminded himself, Director Hoover never did anything without a reason.

"I assume we'll be keeping her under surveillance," he murmured.

Boggs nodded. " 'Round the clock. You'll be the agent in charge."

Joe stared at the deputy director, too stunned to utter a sound. The relief he'd felt a moment earlier was replaced by stomach-churning anxiety. He didn't want the job of keeping tabs on Samantha Cook! In fact nothing would make him happier than to be told he never had to go near the woman again. She was an unwanted and potentially dangerous complication he'd prefer to be rid of. Permanently. His chief priority was— or had been, until Miss Cook showed up— to find out where

Valerie Herrick had disappeared to. And, even more important, why.

"She'll be released into your custody," Boggs explained. His reptilian mouth stretched into a cold-blooded smile. "You live at your sister's boardinghouse, correct?"

"Yes," Joe muttered. His anxiety climbed rapidly toward alarm. "You intend for Samantha Cook to stay there?"

"She insists she's from the future," Boggs said. It was clear he had dismissed the claim as absurd. "Assuming she sticks to that story, it means she shouldn't know a single soul except the people she's met in jail. She has no family, no visible means of support. I'd think she'll be grateful for the offer of a place to sleep and three squares a day. Your sister can put her to work around the place—cleaning, cooking, whatever she can come up with as payment for Miss Cook's room and board."

"And Mercer and his sister will be able to watch her virtually 24 hours a day," Bill Ragsdale put in. Joe could tell he was warming to the idea. "Sooner or later she's bound to make contact with whoever arranged for her to switch places with Valerie Herrick. As soon as she does—"

"We lower the boom," Boggs finished.

Ragsdale nodded. An eager gleam appeared in his eyes. "It's a good plan. A damn good plan."

Joe disagreed. It was a terrible plan, and he knew Esther wouldn't be any more thrilled with it than he was. But since the director himself had devised it, he kept his opinions to himself.

"We'll assign a few other agents to help with surveillance," Boggs said as he stood and pulled on his top coat. "They'll follow her whenever she leaves the house. We'll rely on you and your sister to keep an eye on her the rest of the time. Of course you'll also monitor her mail and phone calls."

"Of course," Joe muttered. He didn't bother to point out that so long as Samantha Cook stuck to her story, as Boggs put it, she wouldn't be receiving any mail or phone calls. She was far too intelligent to make such a stupid slip. He suspected she was a lot sharper than the two men he followed out of Ragsdale's small, cramped office.

He trailed along as far as his own airless cubbyhole, then excused himself. He had to phone Esther before Boggs or one of his toadies got in touch with her. Joe was confident that by now Harold Boggs knew more about his sister than any of her boarders, possibly more than most of her friends. As soon as he received his instructions, Boggs would have conducted his own, detailed investigation of Miss Esther Mercer. But evidently the one thing he hadn't discovered— yet— was that Esther was constitutionally incapable of taking orders. As Joe was about to duck into his office, Boggs stopped, turning to remark, "I trust there won't be any problem with your sister." His tone and the glint in his eye warned that there'd better not be.

Joe forced a smile. The burning sensation below his breastbone told him he'd better stock up on bicarbonate of soda on the way home.

"I'm sure Esther will be happy to cooperate, once she understands how important it is for us to keep Miss Cook under surveillance."

Sure, a small inner voice scoffed as Boggs gave a curt nod and continued down the hall. *And Adolph Hitler will receive the next Nobel Peace Prize.*

Usually the door to Joe's office stayed open.

Now he closed it behind him, raking a weary hand through his hair as he stepped around the desk. The past few days had been grueling. He'd had little sleep and grabbed his meals on the run, when he remembered to eat. For more than 72 hours now, Samantha Cook had claimed virtually all his time. When he wasn't trying to pry information out of her, he'd been occupied defending his frustrating lack of success to a parade of implacable bureaucrats, or attempting to find out who she was and how she'd managed to take Valerie Herrick's place in a Washington, D.C. jail cell.

And, all the while, struggling to wrestle his unwanted attraction to her under control.

To be fair, though, Samantha Cook wasn't the source of his problems, merely a maddening complication. The nightmare had begun several hours before her inexplicable appearance, with a telephone call early Sunday morning. It was that call from Bill Ragsdale, informing him of Colonel Herrick's murder and sending him out into the cold December dawn, that had triggered the helpless, terrifying feeling that his life was spinning out of control.

The feeling had enclosed him like a dark, suffocating shroud for the past three days. Samantha Cook's appearance— or, to be accurate, Valerie's disappearance— had just made it worse, intensified the sensation of being caught in an dizzying spiral toward ruin and destruction. And as if things weren't bad enough, now Boggs threw this new development at him. Joe stared at the black telephone on his desk as if it were a venomous snake. He didn't know who he dreaded talking to more— his sister or Samantha Cook.

Eight

An involuntary cry escaped Samantha as she thrashed her way to consciousness. The back of her right hand smacked against the wall. Sharp, breath-stealing pain instantly cleared her head and brought her fully awake.

She sat up and leaned against the wall, hugging her knees to her chest. She was shaking uncontrollably. Her skin felt cold and clammy; not surprising, considering that a film of perspiration covered her body.

The scenes in the dream she'd fled had been so vivid, so terrifyingly *real*. Was that what the Washington she had left looked like now? Was that ruined wasteland the world she would return to, assuming a way to return existed? And what of her friends and neighbors, the people she'd worked with, come to like and respect? Her eyes filled with tears as she thought of funny-sweet old Mr. Costas, who owned the corner market and always teased her about her hair— the mark of a passionate woman, he'd vow solemnly, then slip her a lascivious wink.

What had happened to them?

Were any of them still alive? Were they suffering the slow, agonizing death of radiation poisoning?

Lucas.

Sam closed her eyes and dropped her head to her knees. Had he stayed in Silver Spring, like he'd promised, or gone chasing after the story of the century and ended up in the burn unit of some hospital?

"Stop it!" she muttered fiercely. "Just stop it!"

Lucas was fine. He'd been on the phone with her when the bomb went off, seven or eight miles from ground zero. And she knew, thanks to the remote feed she'd been watching, that the terrorists had detonated the bomb under 12th Street, at the central juncture of the Metrorail system. Hopefully that meant most of the radiation had been contained below ground.

Lucas was all right, she assured herself again, and felt her knotted muscles slowly relax. He was safe and sound in Silver Spring, probably burning up the telephone lines— assuming there were any telephone lines left— and working himself and the rest of the news staff into a state of numbed exhaustion. The one thing he *wouldn't* have done was try to get into D.C.; nor would he have allowed anyone else to go. He might be a rabid newshound, but he was neither stupid nor suicidal.

She sat up and shoved her hair out of her face. Christ, she had to get out of this place, before the forced inactivity drove her completely batty. She desperately needed to be *doing* something. *Anything.* Sitting in this cold, dank cell virtually 24 hours a day, she felt like a rat in a cage.

If Mercer could just convince them to release her, she could start to work on solving the mystery of how she'd got here. And why. Specifically, why she'd traded places with Valerie Herrick. Sam was convinced that was what had happened. If she was right, there had to be a *reason* the two of them had

switched places and times. There *had* to be! She
simply couldn't accept all this as a freakish accident of nature or physics . . . or metaphysics.
Given the opportunity, she was sure she'd be able
to unravel the mystery, solve the puzzle . . .

But she couldn't do it from this damn frigid
cage. She needed the freedom to come and go at
will, so she could interview people who'd known
Ethan and Valerie Herrick, start collecting evidence . . . hopefully even examine the crime
scene. Not that the FBI or the D.C. cops were
likely to give her *that* much freedom, but if she
could just get out, she would do her damnedest
to find a way around them. And she was very good
at circumventing bureaucrats.

She was bent over the tiny, stained basin, splash-
ing cold water into her bleary eyes, when she heard
the metallic clink of a key being inserted in the
lock. She grabbed the threadbare towel, hastily
blotting her face as she turned toward the door.

Joseph Mercer entered the cell, cool and composed, looking, as he did on every visit, as if he
owned the place. Except this time there was a subtle difference: the guard remained in the corridor
and the door stayed open. Sam's heart gave an
excited little jump, part hopeful anticipation that
he was bringing good news and part involuntary
reaction to the sight of him.

It really wasn't fair, she thought resentfully. Despite the stress he'd obviously been under, the exhaustion that dimmed his eyes and the taut,
strained set of his mouth, the man got better looking every time she saw him. She glanced from Mercer to the guard, still standing just beyond the
door, then back again.

"You did it," she murmured. "You did, didn't

you? Please, Mercer, tell me you convinced them to let me go. I'll be your slave for life."

"You're being released."

The corners of her mouth started to lift in satisfaction and relief, but then he added in the same solemn tone, "Into my custody."

Sam's smile died before it was born. What was he saying? She was supposed to go with *him*? Go where— to his home? Where he lived . . . where he *slept*? The image that flashed across her mind made her blush furiously.

"Oh, no," she blurted in dismay. "That's— " Realizing how ungrateful she sounded, she belatedly clamped her mouth shut, but the resentment that flared in Mercer's eyes told her the damage had already been done. Sam inhaled a deep breath and asked as calmly as she could, "What does that mean, exactly?"

"Exactly what you think it means," he said coldly. "I'll be held accountable for your actions once you're released from the custody of the Washington Police Department. Believe me, Miss Cook, I'm no happier with the situation than you are. If the arrangement isn't acceptable . . ." He trailed off with a shrug that said he'd just as soon leave her to rot in jail.

"No!" Sam exclaimed, afraid he might do just that if she gave him the slightest excuse. "No, it's acceptable." She forced a smile that felt stiff. "So . . . can I leave now?"

The entreaty in her voice must have gotten to him. Or maybe it was the desperation. His stern expression softened a little and he nodded, then gestured for her to precede him into the corridor.

As she left the cell for the last time, the thought crossed Sam's mind that she might soon start to think of it as a peaceful, longed for sanctuary. She'd bet hard cash, if she had any to bet, that Agent Joseph Mercer approached all his responsibilities with single-minded determination. She'd also bet that, as of today, keeping tabs on her had become his number one responsibility. How the devil was she going to investigate Valerie Herrick's disappearance and Colonel Herrick's murder, with a gorgeous FBI agent dogging her every move?

How long, Joe wondered as he slipped into the kitchen to down a dose of bicarb, did it take to develop an ulcer? He strained to hear the conversation taking place in the hall as he rinsed the glass and placed it upside-down on the drainboard beside the sink. All he could make out were unintelligible mumbles and Esther's throaty chuckle. He suspected that, like his sister, Samantha Cook could make herself heard across a crowded train station when she wanted to, but at the moment both women were speaking in the hushed tones most people reserve for churches or libraries. To make sure he couldn't eavesdrop?

He'd been as forceful with Esther when he phoned her from his office as he'd dared to be, trying to impress upon her the gravity of the situation and that his career could hinge on how well he did or didn't carry out this new assignment. He hadn't mentioned that she was expected to assist him or told her specifically what the assignment entailed, only that it required the presence of a woman who would be staying with them for a while.

Esther hadn't said much, but her disapproving silence spoke volumes. She didn't like the arrangement. Not a bit. Neither did Joe, but they were both stuck with it for God knew how long. If he was very lucky, both his headstrong sister and her equally obdurate new boarder would behave themselves and stay out of trouble long enough for him to find Valerie Herrick. Though considering how his luck had been running lately, that was about as realistic as hoping Stalin's Red Army would drive the Germans out of Russia.

He straightened his tie, smoothed a hand over his hair, and turned toward the door to the hall. When he stepped onto the sunflower-patterned runner he met Esther. She was headed for the kitchen.

"I was just coming to tell you," she said briskly. "I'm putting Sam in the blue room, next door to you."

"Sam?" Joe repeated. At the same time, his mind seized on that matter-of-fact *next door to you* and formed an instantaneous protest, which he managed to refrain from blurting out. He reminded himself that he was supposed to keep the woman under surveillance. That *was* why Boggs had sent her home with him.

"She says that's what she'd prefer to be called," Esther informed him. "And it suits her, don't you think?"

It was obviously a rhetorical question, since she turned her back on him and started toward the front of the house before the last word left her mouth. Joe followed silently. *Sam.* Yes, he thought with ironic amusement, the nickname suited her very well.

"She was dying for a bath, so I sent her on up," Esther remarked over her shoulder. "She needs some clothes, too. I'll see what I can find in the attic— thank goodness Grandma Zlata was tall, too, I think her dresses will be long enough— and then she's going to help get dinner on the table. Stew tonight, half an hour."

Her no-nonsense tone added a tacit, *Don't be late* as she started up the stairs. Joe stood in the small entry and watched her ascent, an affectionate smile tugging at his mouth. His sister didn't so much walk as march. She attacked the stairs as if she were leading an assault on a mountain fortress, slender back ramrod straight, head high, her sturdy shoes clopping like hooves against the wood. When she was four steps from the second floor landing, Alvie Blumberg appeared and started down. Esther paused, moving aside to make room for her boarder to pass.

"Going out, Alvie?" she asked as the slight man drew level with her.

"Evenin' Esther. Just making a quick trip to the market for pipe tobacco. I'll be back in time for supper." He tipped his head back and sniffed the air appreciatively. "Beef stew, right?"

"With buttermilk biscuits and apple pie for dessert," Esther confirmed. "Half an hour."

Alvie's smile transformed his narrow, pointed face into a weblike mask of creases. "Mmm-mmm. I'd better get a move on. We all know how Chet loves your stew, Esther. If I'm a minute late, there might not be any left."

Esther turned and continued on up the stairs, but not before Joe took note of her indulgent amusement. Alvie and Chet Pierce worked for competing small newspapers. During the past few weeks it had become increasingly obvious that their friendly rivalry had extended to vying for their landlady's attentions. Joe doubted that either man was seriously interested in winning his sister's affections, but their good-natured competition didn't worry him. Esther was more than a match for the two of them together.

The thought of Alvie and Chet sitting down to dinner with Samantha Cook produced another concern, though. Both men possessed the limitless curiosity and tenacity all reporters must have— a potential problem Joe hadn't even considered till now. On the way home he'd briefed Samantha on the story he and Bill Ragsdale had devised to explain her arrival at his sister's boardinghouse, sans clothes, luggage or employment prospects. Only now, when it might be too late to do anything about it, did he realize how inadequate their little piece of fiction was.

Alvie and Chet would pick the story apart before the biscuits had been passed around the table, he thought with a sinking feeling as he started up the stairs. Maybe if he and *Miz* Cook put their heads together, they could flesh it out a little, come up with the sort of details that would satisfy those two old newshounds. He waited in his room until he heard Esther leave the one next door, then hurried along the hall and tapped lightly.

"It's me," he murmured. "We need to talk."

When Samantha opened the door he quickly ducked inside, in case one of the other boarders should pick that moment to start down to dinner. He didn't really look at her until she closed the door behind him and he turned around.

For a second he forgot why he'd come.

She was wearing a wine-colored chenille bathrobe that Joe recognized at once: it had been a gift from Esther on his last birthday. He'd worn it only a couple of times. The last time he'd seen the garment it was hanging from a hook on the back of his closet door. He knew in an instant he'd never again be able to touch it without remembering how the soft fabric caressed Samantha Cook's curves.

"What do we need to talk about?"

Joe inhaled a slow, deep breath. He'd have sworn her voice had been different at the jail, not nearly so low and husky. She went back to blotting her still-damp hair with a thick white towel while she waited for him to answer the question. The way she was standing, arms slightly raised, elbows out, pulled the front of the robe apart and exposed the inner curve of one firm, perfect breast.

He averted his eyes and turned toward the dresser. A tortoiseshell brush and comb set rested alongside a jar of cold cream. Joe frowned in surprise. Evidently his sister had already formed an attachment to her unexpected guest. Esther only loaned her personal things to trusted friends.

"The story we came up with," he said brusquely. "A couple of Esther's boarders are newspaper reporters. I'm concerned that— "

"Well, that's just great."

Her acerbic tone made him pivot toward her. She'd stopped drying her hair and draped the towel around her neck. She faced him squarely, shoulders back, hands on her hips. The ends of her hair curled against the towel, catching the light from the ceiling fixture and throwing it back in glints of red and gold. Her stance would have been provocative, even seductive, if not for the resentment that glittered in her eyes. He should have known she and Esther would hit it off right away, Joe thought wryly.

"I suppose we'll all be having dinner together,"

she said. He nodded. "Wonderful. Next to the
FBI, reporters are the world's worst snoops. Trust
me on this, I know whereof I speak. They spend
ninety percent of their time sticking their noses
into other people's business."

Joe suppressed an involuntary smile. "If these
two are representative, I'd have to agree."

"So what the hell am I supposed to do when
they start cross-examining me?" she demanded.
"That pathetic story you and your pal Ragsdale
cooked up won't satisfy them for more than five
minutes."

"I estimate ten, fifteen if we're lucky," he murmured. "But I'm hoping you won't have their un-
divided attention. For the past few weeks they've
both been devoting most of their free time to
courting my sister."

She brightened a little at that. "Oh. Well then,
maybe they'll be so busy trying to score points with
Esther they won't pay any attention to me at all."

Joe slipped his hands into his trousers pockets
and cocked his head to one side. She must be pulling his leg. Alvie and Chet may have convinced
themselves and each other that they were infatu-
ated with his spinster sister, but there wasn't a
chance either man would ignore the presence at
the dinner table of a tall, curvaceous redhead with
eyes like emeralds.

"Unfortunately, neither man is blind," he said
dryly. "Or feebleminded."

Color bloomed in her cheeks. Before Joe could
decide whether the flush was a sign of embarrassment or pique, the bedroom door opened and Esther hurried inside. She was carrying a stack of
clothes draped over one arm. She frowned when
she saw him.

"What are you doing in here, Joe? I thought you two weren't supposed to know each other."

He was used to having Esther lecture him as if he were 10 years old and she'd caught him raiding the cookie jar, but this time for some reason her big-sister tone got under his skin.

"No one saw me come in," he said tersely.

"Well, you'd better leave while you can," she said, as she laid the clothes she'd brought on the bed. "Any minute now they're all going to be heading for the dining room."

Joe didn't move. "Miss Cook and I need to make some modifications to her cover story. It will only take a few minutes."

"You don't *have* a few minutes, Joseph!" Esther said in exasperation. "Unless you want to be stuck in here until everybody else has sat down to supper."

The challenge in the vibrant blue eyes so like his own said she knew he certainly didn't want that. Her boarders were a motley crew, but the one trait they all shared was a lively curiosity about other people's lives. If he wasn't there to steer the conversation in other directions, they'd probably make Samantha Cook the main course. Still, he hesitated. If either Alvie or Chet detected the slightest inconsistency in her story, or started to press her for details . . .

"Sam and I will straighten out whatever needs straightening," Esther said. "Trust me, Joe. I won't try to interfere with your work, I promise. But if anyone should see you leaving this room, the three of us together may not be able to carry off whatever scheme those idiots you work for have dreamed up."

Joe removed his hands from his pockets and

nodded curtly. Esther was right, of course. Wasn't she always? He glanced at Samantha Cook, checking her reaction to his sister's last, tactless remark. She hadn't said a word since Esther entered the room, but she'd been watching and listening closely.

She gave him a wry smile. "Don't worry. I'm pretty good at improvisation."

Improvisation! Joe thought with a sense of impending doom as he descended the stairs. God help him. He wondered if the Navy would accept former FBI agents. Before long the prospect of facing Emperor Hirohito's forces in the Pacific might seem like a picnic in the park compared to dealing with Harold Boggs and Bill Ragsdale. And if worst came to worst and either man uncovered the secrets he was hiding, enlisting might be the only way he could both serve his country during this war and avoid prison.

"Well, that wasn't so bad, was it?"

Esther's chipper remark provoked an incredulous glare from her brother and a dry, husky laugh from Samantha.

"I'm glad the two of you found the ordeal so amusing," Joe said as he accepted a bowl from Samantha's soapy hand and started drying it. He didn't usually help out in the kitchen, but tonight he'd known that if he didn't offer, one or more of the others would, just for the chance to question the intriguing new boarder.

Esther nudged him aside with her hip and shoulder to get at the silverware drawer. "You're going to rub the glaze right off that bowl, Joseph."

He shot her another dark look and turned away

to place the bowl in an overhead cabinet. By the time he got back to the sink, Samantha had stacked three more bowls on the drainboard. Her head was bent, her attention ostensibly on the pan of soapy water in front of her, but he thought she was fighting to suppress a smile.

"Of course you both realize that your little performance succeeding in making everyone think of Miss Cook as some sort of fascinating mystery woman," he said testily.

"Sam," both women corrected at the same time, then looked at each other and grinned.

"A regular femme fatale," Esther drawled as she finished putting away a handful of flatware.

Joe felt his jaw muscles clench in exasperation. "I suspect that no one in this house will give you a minute's peace now, *Sam*. Why in God's name did you have to invent such a sensational story?"

Sam shrugged. "I had to come up with something. As you pointed out upstairs, Alvie and Chet wouldn't have been satisfied with the skimpy details *you* provided. Fortunately, as I believe I mentioned earlier, I'm good at improvisation.

The understatement made Esther laugh. "Are you ever! You should go to New York, audition for one of those Broadway plays."

Samantha gave the other woman an appreciative smile. "Thanks, Esther, but I couldn't have carried it off without you. You were terrific, so sympathetic and concerned. For a minute there you had *me* believing I'd been kidnapped and robbed at gunpoint."

"When you've finished complimenting each other for being such good liars," Joe said tightly, "I'd like to point out that tomorrow morning your little melodrama will probably be repeated in the newspapers Alvie and Chet write for!"

Both women stared at him as if he'd suddenly started snarling and foaming at the mouth. After a moment Sam ducked her head and went back to washing dishes, while Esther reached out to rescue her good linen dishtowel from his clenched fist.

"Joe, dear," she said patiently. "In case it's slipped your mind, this country went to war yesterday. I doubt Alvie's and Chet's editors will consider a random assault on a woman traveling alone more newsworthy than that."

Of course she was right. Again. Joe stepped away from the sink, unconsciously raking a distracted hand through his hair, giving himself a minute to get his temper under control. And, if he was honest, his resentment. Damn it, he'd introduced these two scarcely an hour ago, yet they were already so chummy you'd think they'd shared a cradle and been best friends ever since.

He tried to tell himself their instant rapport only bothered him because it created a potential danger to his sister, but his conscience wasn't buying that lie. God knew what Samantha Cook had told her. One reason he had been deliberately evasive with Esther was because the less she knew, the less likely she'd be to get herself or him— or both of them— into trouble. But another, equally cogent, reason was because his work was the only area of his life Esther didn't dominate. God knew he loved his sister, would willingly lay down his life to protect her, but she was such a formidable, relentless presence that every so often he longed to spend an entire day without seeing her or hearing her voice.

"You're overlooking something."

Samantha Cook's subdued, husky voice pulled

him back around to face her. He was surprised to find her standing right behind him, drying a heavy iron skillet. Esther had taken over at the sink and was energetically scrubbing the stewpot.

"Oh, really?" Joe murmured. He tried not to notice the way her long, glossy hair fell in soft waves that caressed her face, or how it gleamed when she gave an impertinent little toss of her head.

"Yes, really," she said. "The story I improvised included a kidnapping, and kidnapping is a federal offense. Now, if anyone sees us with our heads together, they'll probably assume I'm filling you in on the pertinent facts."

Joe casually folded his arms across his chest. "For example, providing a description of your fictitious bearded assailant."

His sarcasm didn't faze her. "That, and providing other information as it comes back to me. You should know that it can take quite some time for the victim of a crime to remember every little detail— weeks, even months. If you think about it, I did you a favor. From now on, if you want to talk to me you won't have to wait until no one's around and sneak into my room."

Esther snorted trying to stifle a laugh. Joe pretended he hadn't heard. Miss Samantha Cook was not only strong-willed and sharp as a tack, she also seemed to know quite a lot about law enforcement. That business about crime victims not being able to remember everything right away, for instance. . . . He remembered the claims she'd made about forensics tests no one had ever heard of— Atomic Absorption Analysis, and the other one, what was it? SEC. She'd said that test required some kind of special microscope that hadn't been invented in 1941.

God, was it possible—

He ruthlessly cut off the thought and made his face a mask, not wanting her to see his uncertainty.

"Let me guess— I'm supposed to be overwhelmed by gratitude for your foresight in doing me this 'favor'," he murmured.

"All right, I wasn't *only* thinking of making things easier for you," she admitted with a crooked, slightly mischievous smile. "I was having a little fun at your expense, too. You could really stand to lighten up, you know."

She paused, as if she expected a reply to that. Since Joe wasn't a hundred percent sure what she meant by "lighten up," he said nothing.

"Besides, it's the end result that matters, right? And I kept the skeleton of your original story— I was coming to Washington to look for work, but along the way I lost my luggage and my purse, which held all my money and personal papers, including a letter of recommendation from my former employer. I didn't change any of that, I just tossed in a few details to make it more convincing . . . and a little more interesting."

"Interesting!" Joe exclaimed. "You thought a roomful of strangers would find it *interesting* that you were abducted at gunpoint, dragged through the countryside by your crazed abductor, then left to perish in the wilds of Maryland? My God, you made it sound as if there's nothing but unpopulated wilderness between Baltimore and Washington! I half expected you to claim you'd been attacked by a tiger or barely escaped being trampled to death by a herd of elephants."

She blithely waved away his indignation and set the dry skillet on the table in the center of the room. "I may have gotten a little carried away, but it worked. They all bought it— including Alvie and Chet."

"Especially Alvie and Chet," Esther put in. "They believed every word, Joe. You know they did. Sam could have thrown in the herd of elephants and they probably would have believed that, too." She turned the stewpot upside down on the drainboard and turned to face him with a smile. "I thought *you* were going to choke on your stew when she got to the part where the bearded man made her jump off the train, but everybody else was eating out of her hand."

Joe grimaced. His stomach was reacting to Esther's delicious meal as if he'd swallowed a gallon of sulfuric acid.

"Maybe she should try her hand at writing pulp fiction," he muttered. "She'd probably make a fortune."

Samantha lowered her eyes and started folding the dishtowel into a tidy rectangle. "Actually, it occurred to me during dinner that I'll need to find a way to earn some money."

Joe's eyes narrowed with suspicion. Her matter-of-fact tone didn't match her tense posture, and she kept her gaze averted.

"Esther agreed that you could repay her for your room and meals by helping with the housework and cooking," he reminded her.

"For which I'm grateful, but after a few days the other boarders are going to think it's strange if I'm not at least looking for some kind of work."

She had a point. But then he realized that she'd said "some kind of work," not "a job." A second later he remembered that Alvie and Chet had been needling each other about their abysmal typing skills during dinner.

"Let me guess," he murmured. "You just happen to be an excellent typist."

She finally lifted her head. Determination glinted from her eyes. "As a matter of fact, I type a hundred words per minute, with no mistakes. Of course that's using a computer keyboard or an electronic typewriter. I may not be that fast on an old manual machine. Still, considering the number of typos Alvie and Chet both claim—"

She broke off suddenly, her eyes flying open wide as she realized her blunder. Joe darted a quick glance at his sister, hoping she hadn't noticed. He should have known better, he thought as she leaned back against the sink and planted her hands on her hips.

"A computer keyboard?" Esther echoed Samantha's words in a tone that was simultaneously inquisitive and wary. "An electronic typewriter?" She studied Samantha and then Joe for several interminable seconds, taking in their worried expressions and their uneasy silence.

"All right, what's going on here? Don't say 'nothing' and try to convince me I'm imagining things!" she warned when Joe opened his mouth to do just that. "Ever since you phoned me this afternoon I've known something odd was in the works. The FBI doesn't make a practice of arranging lodging for stranded women, and if Sam's a secretary from Baltimore, I'm Veronica Lake. This is my house. If it's going to be used as the base for whatever the two of you are up to, I have the right to an explanation. Otherwise, you can find someplace else to play your secret government games."

Joe shoved his hands deep in his pockets and scowled at the toes of his shoes. He'd been half expecting a scene that went something like this—

his sister was nobody's fool—but he'd hoped the big confrontation wouldn't come for a day or two, till Samantha Cook had settled in and been accepted by Esther's boarders. He still hadn't decided how much to tell her.

Evidently she had leaped head-first to the conclusion that Samantha had been installed here to perform some kind of undercover work. It was funny, in a way. Esther thought Samantha Cook was an FBI agent, probably that she'd been sent to spy on the neighbors, several of whom were of German descent, or even on one of the boarders in this very house. Should he encourage that mistaken belief? It would certainly make things a lot easier. Unfortunately, Samantha spoke up before he could decide.

"I'm not playing any government games," she declared. She spared a quick glance for Joe before turning her attention to Esther. That look he'd already come to dread was back in her vivid green eyes—a look of challenge, almost defiance.

"Nor am I the stranded, out of work secretary they're trying to pass me off as," she added bluntly. "The truth, which your brother and everybody else I've met in the past four days refuses to accept, is that on the morning of December seventh, an explosion somehow knocked me from Alexandria, Virginia into a Washington jail cell."

She paused a beat, studying Esther's blank-with-confusion expression before delivering the coup de grâce. "That's not the half of it, though. The explosion took place on December seventh, 1995."

Joe closed his eyes and silently prayed for divine guidance as his sister uttered a sharp, startled, *"What!"*

Nine

Lucas and Levander Grisham managed a ten-minute telephone conversation Saturday night. Before they lost their connection, Levander passed on the disappointing news that the consulting psychiatrist hadn't been able to get to the nursing home to examine Miss Cook. He had, however, phoned to say he'd try again on Sunday, when traffic would hopefully be lighter. Lucas hadn't wasted time voicing his opinion, which was that there would be more traffic clogging the streets on Sunday, not less.

The good news was that Sam's physical condition continued to improve. The relief and satisfaction in Levander's voice came through clearly when he reported that she'd eaten every bite of every meal she was served, "even the rice pudding, and the rice pudding in this place tastes like wallpaper paste with raisins." Lucas was thankful that if he couldn't be with Sam, at least she was in the care of someone like Levander Grisham.

More good news came his way early Sunday morning, in the form of a message Cassie relayed from her cousin: Janice's friend in Army Intelligence was willing to study the terrorists' videotape and see if he could identify any of the four men on it, but only in the privacy of Janice's apartment.

"He's afraid the CIA or somebody is watching the station," Cassie explained. She was slumped in a chair on the other side of Lucas's desk. Her speech was slurred and raspy and there were dark semicircles beneath her eyes.

"He's probably right," Lucas muttered. "Find a way to get a copy of the tape to her, then I want you to go home and crash for a few hours. That's an order."

Cassie gave him a tired smile as she pushed herself out of the chair. "Yours to serve and obey, o glorious leader. And I'm way ahead of you on the tape. Yolanda and Janice are both going to order pizza for dinner tonight."

Lucas smiled and sketched a salute before waving her out the door. Yolanda Johnson, the station's receptionist, had a brother-in-law who owned three pizza parlors in Silver Spring and two in Bethesda. Lucas assumed Yolanda would place her order first, and slip whoever made the delivery a videotape cassette along with the tip.

After Cassie left, he took advantage of a brief pause in the continuous parade of traffic through his office to remove his glasses, lean back and close his eyes for a few minutes. At times, the past three days had seemed like a nightmare—a really, really bad dream he couldn't wake up from. He knew that was a perfectly understandable form of denial at work, his mind's way of rebelling against the constant bombardment of unspeakable images and information; but the longer he went without sleep, the harder it became to convince himself that the nightmare was real.

The figures were too outrageously exorbitant, the reality too obscene. Thousands dead within the first three to four hours, thousands more condemned to the agonies of radiation sickness before they, too, succumbed. And why? Because some crazed, hate-filled bastards had wanted to make a goddamned *statement*, get the world's *attention* to promote their precious cause . . . and had been willing to die to do it.

Well, they sure succeeded, Lucas thought bitterly, and nothing inspires imitation like conspicuous success. Where would the next bunch of deranged terrorists strike— New York? London? Disney World?

He pressed his thumb and index finger against his closed eyes. *Think of something else. Get your mind off the insanity for a while.* He groped for an image that didn't inspire horror or despair and found Sam's surprised, smiling face, the night he'd given her the gold watch. Her 28th birthday.

She'd been wearing a slinky emerald green dress that was almost a perfect match for her extraordinary eyes, and of course the ring, which he'd never seen her without. He'd taken her to dinner at her favorite Italian restaurant. Her hair blazed like flame in the candlelight, a cascade of luxuriant, glossy waves that stopped just short of her shoulders. Sam liked clothes that exposed her shoulders and back, enjoyed showing anyone who cared to notice that she didn't have the freckles that were the bane of most redheads. And most people who saw her noticed. Especially the men.

Remembering that night, and the way her emerald ring flashed green fire as she helped him fasten the watch, Lucas made a mental note to mention the jewelry to Levander Grisham the next time they spoke. He'd ask Levander to make sure both items were locked up somewhere safe until Sam was ready to leave the nursing home. The watch had cost a pretty penny, but it was insured. The ring, however, was irreplaceable. She would be heartbroken if anything happened to it.

A brisk rap on his office door roused him from his reverie as one of the production staff stuck in his head to ask for instructions about editing a taped interview. Lucas put his glasses back on and reluctantly re-entered the nightmarish reality of the present.

She knew her name now because he'd told her, but she still didn't remember where she lived, her phone number— any of the common, ordinary details people take for granted. Her mind had held onto the important things, though. For instance, she could read . . . and not just English.

One of the resident patients, Mrs. Cecile Foret, had come to America from France after World War II, and some of her family who still lived over there sent her a French newspaper every week. But Mrs. Foret's eyesight was failing; she had trouble with the small print. Levander had mentioned Mrs. Foret to Samantha Cook yesterday afternoon, just in passing, trying to do what he could to help keep her mind off her problems. She asked if she could visit the woman, so he got a wheelchair and took her to Mrs. Foret's room. He'd thought it was a good sign that she was interested in other folks and *their* troubles. Not that he was surprised. He'd known an hour after she opened those clear blue eyes that she was that kind of girl. She'd parked the wheelchair next to Mrs. Foret's bed and inside of five minutes she was reading the newspaper to the old woman. Reading it out loud, in French! And she must have done a good job of it, because

Mrs. Foret didn't interrupt or ask her to repeat anything.

When Samantha finished reading and the two of them started chatting in French, Levander tiptoed out. Neither woman noticed. He had Samantha's supper tray taken to her in Mrs. Foret's room, where she'd stayed until the old woman went to sleep a little before nine. When Levander went to take her back to her own room, she was so quiet and serious that he wondered what she and Mrs. Foret had been talking about for the past couple of hours. He hoped the old woman hadn't upset her. Mrs. Foret could be cantankerous at times, but she seemed to enjoy the younger woman's company. He decided if Samantha was still in this brooding frame of mind tomorrow, he'd try to find out why.

He'd been half hoping that Lucas Davenport wouldn't call tonight, or that if he tried he wouldn't be able to get through. But the phone at the front desk rang at 10:31 on the dot, just as he headed for the exit. Levander knew it couldn't be anybody else calling at that hour. And wouldn't you know, there was nobody at the desk. For a second he considered ignoring the phone, but his conscience wouldn't let him. Just as it wouldn't let him hold back information when Lucas asked about Samantha. If she'd been his lady, he knew he'd want to know every little detail, too.

"To tell the truth, she seemed a little down tonight," he said reluctantly, then went on to explain about her long visit with Mrs. Foret. "It was probably just listening to the old woman go on and on about her family. You know how old folks can be when they start reminiscing. That's bound to be upsetting to Samantha, when she can't remember her own family or if she even has one."

The silence at the other end of the line stretched out until Levander began to wonder if they'd lost the connection. But just as he opened his mouth to ask if Lucas was still there, the other man spoke.

"You say Sam read these French newspapers to the old woman?"

"Sure did. Caught Mrs. Foret up on all the news. It was a really nice thing for her to do."

There was another silence, not quite so long as the first one, and then Lucas said slowly and carefully, as if he wanted to make sure Levander understood every word, "Was Sam wearing any jewelry when she was admitted? Specifically a gold watch and a large emerald ring on her right hand?"

Levander didn't have to think before he answered. "Why, no. She didn't have any jewelry at all. If she was wearing a watch and a ring when they found her at the hotel, somebody must've taken them off. The hospital, maybe. Would they do that?"

"I suppose it's possible," Lucas murmured. He sounded doubtful, though.

"What's wrong?" Levander asked in concern. Something was bothering Lucas, he could tell. The first thing that occurred to him was that the jewelry must be valuable, and Lucas was afraid someone had stolen it. He wasn't at all prepared for Lucas's startling disclosure.

"Levander, Sam doesn't speak or read French." Before Levander could take in the revelation, much less decide what it meant, Lucas hit him with something even more startling.

"I hope I'm wrong, but I suspect this woman may not be Samantha Cook."

The worst was past. At least that was what Joe kept telling himself. Considering how direct both his sister and Samantha Cook were— and that was a charitable way of putting it— it had been inevitable that sooner or later Samantha would confide her extraordinary tale to Esther. That much he could have anticipated, and would have, if he'd spared fifteen minutes to think about the two of them living under the same roof. What he never, not in a hundred years, could have anticipated was his sister's reaction.

Damned if Esther didn't believe every incredible word.

Not right away, of course. At first she'd been stunned speechless. Unfortunately that state hadn't lasted long, and Esther had always possessed a lively and fertile imagination. Five minutes after Samantha started talking, Joe saw the curiosity and excitement glittering in his sister's eyes, and knew she was hooked.

He left the women in the kitchen long enough to run upstairs and fetch a new box of bicarbonate of soda. When he returned, they were seated at the big old table in the middle of the room with glasses of milk and a plate of oatmeal cookies.

"Stomach bothering you, Joe?" Esther asked as he filled a water glass at the sink.

"Now why on earth would my stomach be bothering me?" he muttered sarcastically.

Samantha got up and got another glass from the cabinet, then a fresh bottle of milk from the Fridgidaire. "Drink this," she said, taking the full glass to him. "It should help. God knows there's enough butterfat to coat a giraffe's digestive tract. I guess they don't sell Maalox yet?"

Joe gave her a sardonic look as he accepted the glass. "Thank you. Maalox? No, not to my knowledge. I suppose that's something else we'll have to wait for— along with electronic typewriters and nuclear reactors."

"Nuclear what?" Esther asked.

"Never mind," he said sternly.

Samantha capped and replaced the bottle of milk and returned to her seat at the table. "Don't mind him. He thinks I'm a Japanese agent."

Esther expelled a startled, incredulous laugh. "A what? You're joking."

Samantha shook her head and helped herself to a cookie. "Or is it the Germans you think I'm spying for, Joseph? You don't mind if I call you Joseph, do you?"

Actually, he very much liked having her call him Joseph. Or would have, if she hadn't been doing it to goad him. He carried his milk to the table and took a seat.

"I don't believe you're here to gather information for any foreign government," he said, as he reached for a cookie.

"Well, hallelujah," Samantha muttered. "Think there's any chance you could convince your pals Ragsdale and Boggs of that?"

Joe dunked half the cookie in milk and bit off the wet part before it could fall into the glass. He didn't answer till he'd swallowed. "At the moment, I doubt my opinion carries much weight with either of them."

"And you're reluctant to shove it down their throats," Esther commented. "At the moment."

He lifted the glass of milk and gave her a look over the rim. She must have been feeling generous, because she inclined her head in a discreet little nod and didn't say anything else.

"Because of the declaration of war, you mean," Samantha said. "And Colonel Herrick's murder, of course." She took another cookie from the plate and followed Joe's example, giving it a quick dunk and then biting it in two before it could disintegrate.

"You said he was with Army Intelligence. What was he working on, specifically?"

Joe sent her a droll look. "You don't honestly expect me to tell you that?"

"Why not?" she countered. "His work is probably the reason he was murdered."

Joe darted a nervous glance at the closed door to the hall. He fervently hoped all of Esther's boarders were either still listening to the radio in the parlor or had gone up to their rooms.

"I thought the police arrested Valerie for her father's murder," Esther said. She sounded surprised. "Wasn't she found standing over him with the gun in her hand?"

"Kneeling beside him," Sam corrected. "Doesn't mean she killed him. She could've come into the room, seen him lying there on the floor with the gun next to him, and picked it up without thinking . . . acting purely on impulse. That happens a lot more often than you might think."

Esther turned to her brother for confirmation, her forehead puckered in a troubled frown.

"It happens," he agreed reluctantly. "People usually aren't thinking too clearly when they've just discovered a dead body."

"Especially if the dead body is someone they were close to," Sam added.

Esther's distressed gaze darted from one of them to the other. "So Valerie might *not* have killed him?"

"I don't think she did," Samantha said flatly. "Why would she? From what Joe's told me, they got along fine except for the colonel's disapproval of this man she'd been seeing, and that's hardly a motive for murder. I mean, Jesus, if every woman killed her parents just because they objected to her boyfriends, we'd all be orphans before we got out of high school."

Neither the speculative glint in Esther's eyes nor her next remarks did a thing to relieve Joe's tension.

"So you think someone else murdered Colonel Herrick. Do you have any ideas about who it could have been?"

"I might, if your brother would share some pertinent information," Samantha replied. She swiveled to confront Joe with that observant, penetrating gaze. Her hair swung with the movement, brushing the tops of her shoulders, a red-gold bell framing her oval face.

"There's no reason to keep the nature of Colonel Herrick's work secret, and you know it," she said. "Especially now that America's entered the war. By now it must have occurred to everybody that he may have been killed because of intelligence information he'd recently acquired."

Joe hesitated a moment before conceding, "That possibility is being investigated."

"Well, then— "

He cut her off with a brusque, "No. Stop right there. The FBI and the Army have assigned agents to study Colonel Herrick's intelligence work and interview the people he'd recently had contact with, including a classified list of informants. I am *not* one of the agents assigned to that investigation. So you see, Miss Cook, I couldn't give you any 'pertinent information' about that kind of thing, even if I were willing to jeopardize my career to satisfy your curiosity.

Samantha's sour expression said she wasn't happy with the situation, but she accepted it . . . for now. Joe reached for another cookie to cover his relief. His sister decided to jump in with her two cents' worth while his mouth was full.

"I bet if you could get your hands on some of that information, though, you could do more with it than those FBI and Army clowns," Esther observed. "Considering you know things they don't— I mean, things they *can't* know yet."

"How right you are," Samantha drawled. "If I could just get into the autopsy room, or at least sneak a peak at the medical examiner's report . . ."

Joe choked on the last bite of cookie. Esther got up and stepped behind his chair to deliver a couple of hard whacks between his shoulder blades, while Samantha sighed and pushed his glass of milk toward him.

"Don't have a stroke, for pity's sake. I'm not planning to break into the morgue."

"Good!" he said when he'd caught his breath.

"But only because I know you and Esther would be held responsible if I got caught."

"Well, for heaven's sake, don't let that stop you," Esther said.

Joe had been about to take a sip of milk, but he changed his mind and set the glass down, so hard that milk sloshed onto the flower-patterned oilcloth Esther kept on the table to protect the wood.

"Esther, for God's sake!"

"You want to find out who killed Colonel Herrick, don't you?" she fired back. "And why?"

"There are at least a dozen people working on that investigation, probably closer to two dozen."

"And you want to find out what happened to Valerie. Sam thinks she and Val switched places . . . and times."

He glared at Samantha. She responded with an apologetic shrug that wasn't the least convincing. "I know that's what she says," he began, struggling to keep his temper under control.

"But you don't believe her." Incredibly, Esther made it sound like an accusation.

Even more incredible, the remark triggered a sharp twinge of doubt that shook Joe and fed his anger. "And you do? You actually believe she traveled back in time from 1995? Don't you realize how insane that sounds!"

"Of course I do. It sounds like something out of one of those cheap pulp magazines Chet sometimes reads. But fifteen years ago people would have said the idea that a man could fly nonstop from Long Island to Paris was crazy, too."

"Until Lucky Lindy did it," Sam put in.

Joe gave her another dark look. "Flying across the Atlantic is hardly comparable to traveling 54 years back in time."

Esther continued as if neither of them had spoken. "And who would have believed we'd be listening to Lamont Cranston and Margot Lane or Fibber McGee and Molly on the radio, or that I could pick up the telephone and call someone in California?"

Joe could see that she'd built up a good head of steam and there'd be no stopping her until she wound down.

"Who's Lamont Cranston?" Samantha asked.

He murmured a resigned, "The Shadow. A character in a radio serial."

"Oh, right— Alec Baldwin!"

Joe was beginning to feel like a character in a radio drama himself. Alec Baldwin?

"Or England!" Esther exclaimed. "I could even phone someone in England. If I knew anyone in England, that is, which unfortunately I don't. But the point is, all those things would have sounded like crazy, impossible dreams to our grandparents, Joe, or even to our parents. Nevertheless they're real— *now* they're all real! We can't even *imagine* what kind of wonderful, miraculous things might be possible in the future!"

"Miraculous?" he echoed.

"That's what I said, Joseph." Obviously unfazed by his cynicism, Esther turned to Samantha with an abrupt and, Joe could tell, completely unexpected demand. "Tell us, Sam. Tell us about some of the things people will take for granted in 1995."

Joe felt the tension that had been building all day suddenly collapse like a balloon that had been pricked with a pin. His mouth tilted in an ironic smile as he leaned back in his chair and seconded the request.

"Yes, Sam. By all means, tell us about some of the miraculous things our great-grandchildren will take for granted."

The pompous, manipulative *ass!*

Samantha paced from the foot of the iron bedstead to the window and back again, still too worked up to sleep an hour after she'd come upstairs. Damn him! He'd sat there with that confident sneer on his handsome face and dared her to do what she'd made clear back at the jail she wouldn't do: provide him with information that would allow him— or, more likely, one of his fascist superiors— to change the future.

She was beginning to realize that she just might have been a little too inflexible on that subject, but damned if she'd admit as much to Joseph Mercer. She was too steamed by his smug, supercilious attitude. She'd seen the change that came over him as soon as Esther, in all innocence, made her request. He'd known he had her, that she was trapped. It had shown in the narrowing of his bluer-than-blue eyes and that infuriating smirk.

"Yes, Sam. By all means, tell us," she mimicked as she completed another bed-to-window-and-back circuit.

She was barefoot, because she didn't want her pacing to announce to anyone else that she was still up. Especially the person in the room next door. So when, in her anger, she spun around too fast and rammed the toes of her right foot into the dresser, there was no padding, nothing to protect her foot from the impact. An involuntary yelp escaped her as she stumbled back against the bed.

She was sitting on the edge of the mattress, her right foot resting on the opposite knee while she massaged her toes and cursed under her breath, when the door opened and Special Agent Joseph Mercer stepped into the room.

Sam registered several things all at the same time as he silently closed the door behind him: he must have heard the collision between her foot and the dresser or her yelp of pain, or maybe both; he was more than a little put out that she was making such a racket in the middle of the night; and he slept in his underwear.

The last was a guess, based on the available evidence— his trousers were zipped but not buttoned and he was wearing an undershirt instead of a pajama top. Not the kind of undershirt Sam was accustomed to seeing on males and females of all ages, sizes and shapes, but one of the old-fashioned tank top variety. The kind people in the '90s called a muscle shirt. Obviously for good reason.

Sam tore her gaze from his impressive biceps and trapezius muscles and gingerly set her throbbing foot on the floor. A second later she remembered to tug the hem of the nightgown Esther had lent her over her knees.

"Are you all right?" he asked softly.

She ducked her head in an embarrassed nod but didn't meet his eyes. She was suddenly and acutely aware that, apart from a pair of cotton underpants, the thin flannel gown was all she had on. His robe lay across the foot of the bed. For a second she was tempted to grab it, but decided that would be a foolish, adolescent gesture. Though God knew she *felt* like a foolish adolescent— flushed and flustered and generally discombobulated, which had the effect of resuscitating her anger.

"I stubbed my toe on the dresser," she explained. It came out sounding surly, as if he were to blame for her clumsiness.

"Mmm, I heard you kicking the furniture."

The dry comment brought Sam's head up. Was he mocking, or teasing? Before she could decide, he sat down next to her— on top of the robe— and bent to lift her foot back to her knee. In the process, his shoulder pressed down on her left thigh for a long three or four seconds. Sam held her breath till he straightened.

"If you make a habit of venting your anger that way, you should at least wear shoes," he said, as he examined her foot. "Or heavy boots."

"I'll keep that in mind," Sam muttered. *"Ow!* Damn it to hell, that hurts!"

He stopped wiggling her big toe but left his right hand resting lightly on the arch of her foot. "It isn't broken. Do all women in 1995 swear like teamsters, or are you the exception rather than the rule?"

"I could've told you it isn't— " she began irritably, then broke off and stared at him in astonishment. "Does that mean— Mercer . . ."

The snap had left her voice; now she sounded tentative, almost wistful. Sam didn't like that, not at all, but at the moment it was a minor aggravation.

"Do you finally believe me?"

He didn't answer, just stared long and hard into her eyes. As the silence stretched out, a disturbing jumble of emotions began to swirl in Samantha. Desperate hope that he'd say yes. Fear that he was only setting her up so he could slap her down with more hard-nosed cynicism. Dread that she was about to be subjected to another cross-examination.

Gradually she became aware that a similar internal chaos was reflected in the mesmerizing blue gaze that searched hers so intently. The knowledge sent a jolt of surprise through her. He was wrestling with his own doubt and uncertainty, even as he tried to probe her mind for the truth! He wasn't sure, *couldn't* be sure, what to believe.

The mental and physical contact was suddenly too intense, almost threatening. Instinctively seeking to withdraw, Sam eased her foot from under his hand and placed it on the floor. But instead of withdrawing the hand, he let it settle on her knee. She felt the warm imprint of each finger through the flannel gown.

"Joe." His name emerged as a husky, breathless whisper. She experienced another small seism of surprise, and something else— something both exciting and alarming, triggered by the flare of emotion in his eyes. Without thinking, she laid her hand on his, and instantly knew that had been a mistake. She snatched it back, curled her fingers into a fist, enclosed the fist in her other hand. Her eyes shied away from his.

"I swear to you . . ."

She trailed off in consternation. Her voice sounded even more provocative than it had a moment ago, a smoky, seductive contralto. She swallowed, cleared her throat. This was no time to be sidelined by rampaging hormones. She stared at her hands and made up her mind to ignore the warm, hard body next to her . . . the muscular shoulder nudging her arm . . . the lean hip that pressed against hers where the mattress sagged under their combined weight . . .

"Improbable as I know it seems, everything I've told you has been the truth."

Much better, she thought with a swell of relief; she sounded like herself again, confident and self-assured. She lifted her gaze to assess his reaction, and was struck dumb by what she saw in those hypnotic blue eyes. Her mouth went dry.

Her stomach muscles contracted in automatic reflex.

His long, curling lashes descended— to mask his
thoughts? A second later he lifted his hand from
her knee to brush a wisp of hair off her cheek.
Sam heard her breath catch, felt his fingers trem-
ble at the sound.

"You're an incredibly beautiful woman."

He spoke so softly that if she hadn't been sitting
right beside him, she probably wouldn't have been
able to make out the words. She concentrated on
pulling air into her lungs and then pushing it out,
because if she didn't think about it she was afraid
she'd forget to breathe. His fingers drifted across
her cheek, paused to gently caress her temple, then
slipped into her hair.

"Beautiful," he murmured. "Every part of you.
Your bewitching green eyes . . . your golden
skin . . . your glorious hair . . ."

His hand closed into a fist and he tugged gently,
forcing Samantha's head back so that her face was
raised to him.

"Your mouth."

His lips hovered over hers for a heartbeat that
felt like infinity before he lowered his head and
kissed her. Not hard, but not tentatively either.
Testing. Gently exploring. Sam knew she could
have pulled away, pushed at his chest, merely
turned her head, and he'd have released her. She
did none of those things. She was aware that she
should, that it was foolish and reckless and probably downright stupid to let this happen, but she
couldn't summon the will to move. So much easier
to just feel. And, God, the things she was feeling . . .

"Such a sensuous, inviting mouth," he breathed

against her lips. "It tempts a man to believe it could never lie or deceive."

A warning went off in Sam's head, but she scarcely had time to register it before his mouth locked on hers with a fierce, almost angry passion that obliterated conscious thought. When he released her just as abruptly seconds later, her heart was hammering against her ribs and she was gasping for breath. She stared at him mutely as he rose from the bed and scowled down at her.

"I apologize," he said curtly. "That was . . . a mistake."

Sam closed her eyes and bent her head while she struggled to regain her composure. A *mistake?* She couldn't decide whether she was more inclined to laugh or stand up and slap his handsome face. She tried to remember the last time a man had apologized for kissing her, and when she couldn't, she realized it was because no man ever had.

But this is 1941, Sammy, she reminded herself wryly. *FBI agents don't go around seducing single young women nowadays.* Especially, she was sure, single young women who were officially suspected of being either spies or mentally deranged.

"Apology accepted," she murmured, lifting her head to give him an inquiring look. "So, Agent Mercer, do you believe my story or not?"

He blinked, obviously unprepared for the question. He recovered quickly, though, which pleased Sam.

"I haven't decided," he admitted.

She liked that, too. She nodded, then gave him a smile to show there were no hard feelings.

"Be sure to let me know when you do."

He was looking at her as if she were a strange

insect he'd discovered crawling out of the bathroom drain. "I will," he said solemnly after a moment. And then he turned on his heel and left.

Ten

Lucas kept telling himself that what he was thinking wasn't possible. The woman at the nursing home *had* to be Samantha. The hotel register had identified the female guest staying in that room as Samantha Cook. Besides, he'd been talking to her on the phone seconds before the bomb was detonated. There hadn't been time for Sam to leave the room and someone else to take her place.

But Sam didn't speak or read French.

And the only time she took off that emerald ring was just before she got into the shower. She put it back on as soon as she got out.

He was on his way to the station after spending the first night in his own bed since the terrorists' attack. Thank God he lived only 10 minutes away; any farther than that and he probably wouldn't have made it home. All the major streets inside the beltway were littered with abandoned vehicles, many of them stripped and gutted by the roving gangs of young punks who'd transformed themselves into capitalist entrepreneurs in the last few days. Word was you could pick up a brand new stereo system, including CD player, for a couple hundred bucks.

As Lucas pulled into the station parking lot he impulsively reached for the cellular phone and punched in the nursing home number. Levander wouldn't be there at this time of day, but maybe he could connect with someone else who'd be able to answer a few critical questions.

Fifteen minutes later he entered the station lobby, frowning and distracted, and almost collided with Cassie McGregor as she hurried out of the news room.

"I saw you sitting out in the lot," she said breathlessly. "I was just coming out to tell you— Jan's friend identified two of the men on the tape."

Lucas grasped her arm and hustled her toward his office. "He's positive?"

"Oh, yeah. He's handled their files— the files Army Intelligence has on those two, that is. The one named Rashad was one of the key strategists for Hezbollah, Hizballah, however you pronounce it."

"I think how you pronounce it depends on whether you're a Middle Eastern Islamic fundamentalist or a Western infidel," Lucas said as he ushered her into the office and closed the door behind them. He'd already shunted his conversation with one of the nursing home aides to the back of his mind. For the present, that dilemma would have to be put on hold.

"Did our source provide any details— Rashad's full name, aliases, known political contacts . . . any other terrorist attacks he may have taken part in?"

Cassie nodded eagerly. "He wrote it all down for Jan, then had her record his notes on tape so the government couldn't ID him with a graphology or voiceprint analysis. Then he burned and flushed the notes. This guy is *really* cautious."

Lucas dropped into his chair and swiveled to

power up his desktop computer. "Good. His caution will probably keep him out of federal prison. Okay, here's how we'll handle this. Somebody left the tape at reception while Yolanda was away from her desk. She came back, found it, turned it over to you. You listened to it and immediately passed it to me." He brought up the news schedule, then glanced at her. "Make sure you get rid of your cousin's fingerprints."

Cassie nodded. "Right." She remained standing, poised to get moving as soon as he gave the word.

"Is her voice distinctive in any way— does she have a lisp or a regional accent, anything like that?"

She thought for a moment. "No. Jan sounds like a well brought up young lady from Virginia."

"Okay, good." He turned back to the computer and created a new file for news copy as he continued improvising strategy. "I took the tape to Vernon and he approved it for broadcast. Let's see, if we say we got it early this morning—"

"Lucas," Cassie interjected. "You haven't asked about the second terrorist Jan's friend ID'ed."

The barely contained excitement in her voice brought his head around. She was biting her lower lip, restlessly shifting her weight from one foot to the other.

"Nicolai from Kazakhstan?" he guessed.

"Bingo. His full name is Nicolai something Kalashnikov, like the guy who invented the rifle. Army Intelligence had a file on him because of his family connections— father's Russian, but his mother's Muslim parents emigrated to Kazakhstan from Yugoslavia, and they still have lots of relatives there, or did, before war broke out in Bosnia— combined with the fact that he was a nuclear technician in the Soviet Army." She paused, her eyes glittering with excitement.

"You remember how Kazakhstan rang a bell, but we couldn't remember why?"

Lucas nodded brusquely, impatient for her to get on with it.

"Well, it was because of a story one of the wire services broke a couple years ago, not long after the breakup of the Soviet Union. Seems several nuclear warheads that had been deployed in Kazakhstan turned up missing. So far as I've been able to find out, they were never accounted for."

"Jesus," Lucas murmured. "Of course. I remember now. There was some speculation that Soviet physicists had smuggled the warheads out, might even be planning to sell them if the government didn't come up with the back pay they were owed."

"Yeah, but a lot of people suspected that if the physicists didn't get to them first, Soviet Army personnel had appropriated them to use as bargaining chips. A lot of the army brass didn't like the breakup one bit. A few of 'em made some pretty scary threats."

"So Nicolai may have been the one who provided the bomb," Lucas said. "And he was almost certainly the only one of the four qualified to arm and detonate it. But it was probably the Palestinians who got it into the country."

He abruptly stood up and waved Cassie behind his desk. "Get over here and start putting the story together."

She reared back as if he'd taken a swing at her. "Me? You want *me* to write the copy?"

"You've got all the background and the facts. We can't afford to screw this up, Cassie. We have to be damn sure we've crossed all the T's and dotted the I's. This story's so hot we may only get one chance to broadcast it. Where's the tape your cousin made?"

"In my desk. Top left-hand drawer. You're gonna leave me here to do this on my own?"

Lucas paused on his way out of the office to give her some reassurance. "Just get down what you've got so far. We can flesh it out later. Vernon and I will have to listen to the tape, see how many questions it leaves unanswered, then I'll start trying to reach everybody I know who can help us fill in the blanks. You can do it, Cassie. Think of it as on-the-job training."

"Great," he heard her mutter as he left. "But will it prepare me for stamping out license plates?"

Distraction furrowed Lucas's brow as he hurried to Cassie's desk in the news room. It looked as if he would be tied up here for the rest of the day, at least. There was no way he'd get free long enough to find a way around the roadblocks and patrols and drive to the Eldercare home between Alexandria and Virginia Hills.

Which meant that for the time being he wouldn't be able to confirm that the woman the hotel had identified as Samantha Cook was in fact a petite, blue-eyed blonde who couldn't remember her name or how she'd come to be in Sam's room.

Joe hadn't slept well, and he knew it showed when he went downstairs the next morning. If he needed confirmation, the worried look his sister gave him as she poured him a cup of coffee provided it.

"Thank you," he murmured, then, before she

could ask whether he wanted bacon or sausage with his eggs, "Coffee is all I have time for."

He avoided making eye contact with either Esther or Samantha Cook, who had apparently risen early to help serve breakfast. Joe slid a surreptitious glance at her while she was busy stacking empty plates and noted with a touch of resentment that she looked fresh as a daisy.

"You have to eat something, Joe," Esther chided.

Samantha turned to him and added an annoyingly cheerful, "How 'bout a couple of pancakes?"

He gave a terse shake of his head and took a cautious sip of coffee. Experience had taught him not to gulp. Esther's coffee was strong enough to strip paint and always scalding hot. This morning he welcomed both the bitter taste and the tongue-blistering heat. He needed a physical jolt to get him going.

One good thing about coming down late—both Chet and Alvie had finished breakfast and left for work. Joe hadn't been here much since Sunday afternoon, when the radio networks broadcast news of the Japanese attacks, but whenever he'd managed to get home for a change of clothes or a few hours' sleep, both reporters had pestered him for information.

At the moment, the only other people in the long, narrow dining room besides Esther and Samantha were Owen Nordstrom and Martha Hampton. A small, dapper man in his late fifties, Owen was the accountant for a furniture store. Martha was a middle-aged spinster who worked as a secretary-typist for a large law firm near Capitol Hill. They'd both nodded in greeting and given him subdued "Good mornings" when he entered the dining room, but characteristically neither attempted to start a conversation. Joe thought of Owen and Martha as "the mice." Gertrude Willis, the most garrulous of Esther's boarders, must have already left to catch the bus to work. Gert sold ladies' dresses in a large, fashionable department store.

As Joe took his third sip of coffee Owen and Martha rose together, as if on cue, and silently left the dining room to collect their coats and hats. Esther had their dishes and silverware added to those Samantha had stacked almost before they were out the door. She paused next to Joe's chair on her way to the kitchen. Her expression told him she had quite a bit to say to him, and that he probably wouldn't like any of it.

"Don't," he said. He spoke quietly, but firmly.

For a moment he thought she would disregard the injunction, but then she pressed her lips together, gave an exasperated shake of her head, and marched off. The heels of her shoes made angry clacking sounds on the strip of bare wood at the edge of the carpet.

"She's worried about you."

Joe glanced around and saw that Samantha was sitting in the chair Gertrude Willis usually occupied. Someone, probably Chet, had been reading the *Post*. She pulled the newspaper across the table and studied the banner headline which was, of course, about America's entry into the war. There'd been nothing else on the front page all week.

"She thinks you're in trouble," she said in the same matter-of-fact tone. She was looking at a photograph of a somber President Roosevelt, sitting behind his desk in the Oval Office.

Joe curled both hands around his coffee cup. "She told you this?"

"No." Her head came up, those perceptive green eyes searching his face. "She didn't have to. It's obvious."

He averted his gaze and lifted the cup for another sip. "You're imagining things."

"No I'm not. And my guess is, neither is Esther. She's worried all right, and she isn't the kind of woman who worries for no good reason."

Joe was starting to regret not having taken those pancakes, or at least a piece of toast— something to soak up the coffee that was affecting his stomach like molten lava.

He'd lain awake for hours, rebuking himself for kissing her. For letting her get to him . . . for letting *himself* forget things he couldn't afford to forget. For example, how astute she was. And now here she sat, wide-eyed and bushy-tailed, apparently unfazed by the kiss that had kept him awake half the night, scrutinizing him as if she were the FBI agent and he were the suspected criminal. He couldn't help being just a little amused.

She suddenly reached out and laid her hand over his. Joe's amusement vanished.

"Is it because of me?" she asked softly. "Am I the reason Esther's worried?"

Oh, yes, she was too perceptive by far. Joe withdrew his hand. "No," he said dryly. "Your arrival was merely a catalyst. My sister has been convinced for some time that I'm headed for ruination."

Knowing he'd already said too much, he abruptly pushed back his chair and stood.

"I have to get to work. I presume you know better than to try to leave Washington."

She shrugged. "Where would I go? And what

with? I don't have a dime to my name. Even the clothes I'm wearing are borrowed."

Joe didn't think for an instant that a lack of money would stop her if she decided to get on the next train out of town, but he decided to interpret the reply as a tacit assurance that, for the moment at least, she wasn't making any such plans.

"I assume there are agents watching the house who'll follow me if I leave," she said. She didn't sound especially indignant or resentful, just resigned.

"That's a safe assumption," he murmured. And then he left, before he could tell her anything else he shouldn't.

"Is there a pawn shop anywhere near here?"

The question made Esther gape in surprise, but then her mouth curved in a mischievous smile as she dried her hands on a dishtowel.

"I have no idea, but I bet Chet and Alvie would know!"

A minute later she was on the phone in the hall, asking the operator for the number of the newspaper where Alvie Blumberg worked. Sam stood a couple of feet away and listened to Esther's half of the conversation. Apparently Alvie was a bit taken aback by the query. Esther sent Sam a grin and a wink as she explained to him.

"No, Alvie, I promise I'm not planning to hock the family silver. It's Samantha Cook who wants to know." Lowering her voice to a sympathetic murmur, she added, "You know, that terrible man took all her money. Every cent. She's literally penniless. I told her she can stay here as long as she wants and help me with the cooking and housework in exchange for room and board. But that's only a temporary solution. Sooner or later she'll need to buy some clothes so she can go out and look for a job. I think she's planning to pawn her watch."

There was a short silence while Esther listened to something Alvie said. She mimed wiping sweat from her brow, a gesture Sam took as a sign that Alvie still wasn't questioning the yarn she'd spun at dinner the night before.

"Oh, yes, it's a very nice watch. Gold, I think. You're so knowledgeable about this kind of thing, Alvie, I was sure you'd know of a good, honest pawnbroker— that is what they're called, isn't it?"

A little later Esther hung up and turned to Sam with a satisfied smile. "He's coming home during his lunch hour to take us to a pawn shop. Most of them are in bad neighborhoods, he says, not the kinds of places ladies like us should go alone."

Samantha pursed her lips and studied the watch on her left wrist. Alvie was sure to get a good look when the pawnbroker appraised it.

"What's wrong?" Esther asked.

Sam extended her arm. "Can you tell by looking at it that it's the only watch of its kind in 1941?"

"Oh, my, I hadn't even thought of that. What'll we do if Alvie starts asking a lot of questions?"

Samantha made a wry face. "Lie, I guess. It's the only thing I have to pawn."

"What about that ring?" Esther asked, indicating the emerald stone on her right hand.

Sam shook her head. "I'd starve to death in the gutter before I'd part with it. It belonged to my mother."

"Well, if I were you I'd take it off. A stone that big is sure to draw attention."

Sam hesitated, but only for a moment; she knew

Esther was right. She removed the ring with reluctance and put it in the pocket of her borrowed flowered housedress. Her hand felt strange, unnaturally light. But then they went upstairs to start stripping the beds so they could wash five sets of sheets— Esther informed her on the way up that her's and Joe's had been done separately, on Monday— and she was too busy after that to think about how naked her hand felt without the ring.

She was falling-down exhausted long before Esther called a break to fix something for Alvie's lunch. Good grief, did women work like this every day fifty years ago? It was a wonder any of them had lived past thirty. Just cranking the sheets through the wringer contraption on the washing machine had given her a harder workout than four straight aerobics classes. Not to mention the exertion of lugging wicker baskets piled high with wet sheets down to the basement, where she and Esther draped them over heavy cotton cords strung near the furnace.

On the third and last trip down the narrow, dimly lit steps, Sam told herself she should be thankful Esther had decided it was too cold to hang the bedclothes outside; she *could* have a case of frostbite to go along with her aching muscles.

Esther explained as she sliced leftover chicken for sandwiches that normally neither Joe nor any of the boarders came home for lunch. But since Alvie was using his lunch time to escort them to the pawnshop, she thought the least she could do was have something ready for him to eat. Sam drained the water from a pan containing a dozen hardboiled eggs and murmured agreement, and didn't say what she was thinking— that Esther's explanation sounded just a teensy bit overdone.

Alvie arrived at a few minutes past noon and hustled them out to a taxi that was waiting at the curb. Ten minutes later they were deposited in front of a two-story brick building with hand-painted signs on the windows that proclaimed "Honest Prices" and "Fair Treatment" and "Cash for Your Trash."

"This guy's all right," Alvie assured Sam as they approached the entrance. "Any offer he makes will be fair, but if it isn't as much as you think you need, there's another place we can try over on Ninth Street."

Once they were inside and Alvie had introduced the women to the proprietor— a burly man named Sylvester something or other— Esther drew him away by pointing out a Royal typewriter she'd spotted on top of a solid-looking wood and glass display case. The two of them stood in front of the machine, their heads together in murmured conversation, while Sam and Sylvester haggled over his first offer for her watch. She knew by the gleam in his eye that he realized he'd be able to make a handsome profit on the watch, so she pressed hard and came away with $125. Nowhere near what it was worth, even at 1941 prices, but probably as good a price as she'd get anywhere else. Besides, she didn't want to troop to every pawnshop in Washington; the fewer people who saw the watch and would be able to connect it to her, the better.

She was stuffing a wad of Silver Certificates into the pocket of her borrowed coat— Lord, what would these bills be worth in 1995?— when Alvie came over to ask what Sylvester would take for the typewriter. Esther caught her eye and slipped her a wink while the men dickered over the price. Sam responded with a barely perceptible nod. Apparently she'd just landed a part-time typist job.

Alvie arranged to stop by the pawnshop and collect the typewriter on the way home from work, insisting it was too heavy for the women to take with them on the bus. Sam started to argue—either of them could probably bench press the reporter ten times without breaking a sweat—but clamped her mouth shut when she felt Esther's elbow in her ribs. Esther thanked Alvie profusely for his time and trouble, Sam also expressed her appreciation, then Esther thrust a brown bag containing two chicken sandwiches and an egg at him, grabbed Sam's arm, and they hurried to the corner to catch the bus that had just pulled to the curb. Esther and Alvie waved goodbye to each other through the grimy window as the bus pulled away.

"How much did you get?" Esther asked, still waving.

"One twenty-five. Esther, you can tell me to mind my own business if you want, but are you . . . um . . . ?"

The bus turned a corner and Esther turned away from the window. "Sweet on Alvie? Of course not. But he's a nice man, and I'd hate to hurt his feelings." She lowered her voice to an excited whisper. "He gave you $125?"

Sam nodded. "It cost about three times that, but I figured one twenty-five was the best I could hope for. He'll probably sell it to a jeweler and make close to a hundred percent profit."

"You're joking! A watch costs almost four hundred dollars in 1995?"

"Not all watches," Sam said with a smile. "You can get one for about fifteen dollars at Walmart. This one was a birthday present."

"Oh." Esther's excitement flagged a little. "It's too bad you had to sell it. Walmart— is that a jewelry store?"

Sam laughed softly. "Well, yes and no. I guess you could say Walmart is the late twentieth century equivalent of an old-fashioned general store— everything you could possibly need and a lot of stuff you'll never need under one roof. They sell everything from watches to sanitary napkins to Nintendos."

"Nintendos?" Esther repeated curiously.

"Oh, boy," Sam muttered. How to describe a Nintendo to someone in 1941? "It's a video game. You hook it up to your TV set— " She broke off when Esther shook her head in puzzlement. "Never mind. I probably shouldn't be telling you about Walmart or Nintendo anyway."

"Because it might somehow change history?" Esther scoffed. "I know that's why you won't tell Joe anything about the future, and I think you're probably right since he works for the government. But you can't honestly think *I* could do anything that would affect history one way or another."

"But how can I be sure? Think about it, Esther. Just by using what I've already told you, you could start a chain of discount stores that would get the jump on Walmart, or an electronics company that would beat Nintendo to the video game market. Not that either of those things would be a global catastrophe," she conceded dryly.

"Exactly! Nothing I do could possibly cause a global catastrophe, for heaven's sake. And I'm dying to know about the future, Sam. You would be, too, you know you would."

Yes, Sam thought. If she were in Esther's place and had the opportunity to pick the brain of someone from her own future, she'd probably chain the unfortunate soul to the wall and use thumbscrews or hot coals to extract every piece of information she could get.

"I'll think about it," she conceded. "About what it would be all right to tell you, I mean. But to be honest, my first priority is to figure out what the hell I'm doing here— how, or at least *why* I woke up in that jail cell— and whether there's any way to get back where I belong. There's a *reason* I'm here, I know there is! I don't know what the reason is— yet— but every instinct tells me it has something to do with Valerie Herrick. There's some connection between us, some kind of . . . link."

She shook her head in frustration. "She was put in that cell after her arrest. So far as anyone knows, she was still there right up until the instant I took her place."

"Or until the two of you switched places," Esther remarked.

"You don't think that's a completely insane idea?"

Esther lifted her shoulders in a small, "who knows?" shrug. "No more so than the idea that people can jump 54 years across time. In fact, if you think about it, it makes a crazy kind of sense. She has to have gone *somewhere.*"

"Precisely! I may never be able to prove the two of us switched places, or how. But so help me, Esther, I'm going to figure out *why* or die trying. And the first step has to be finding out everything I can about her."

Esther caught her lower lip between her teeth, a pensive frown replacing her expression of avid interest. Sam leaned toward her eagerly.

"What? You know something, don't you? Something about Valerie Herrick."

Esther's uncertainty showed in the blue eyes so like her brother's, and yet so different. While Joe's eyes usually brought to mind images of glacier-fed mountain lakes, Esther's were clear, temperate pools.

"Yes," she said eventually. "I know something." Casting an uneasy glance at the few other passengers on the bus, she lowered her voice to a stage whisper. "I'll tell you when we get home."

Eleven

"She was having an affair with my brother."

Sam stared at Esther as if she didn't think she'd heard right. She wished that were the case, but unfortunately her ears seemed to be working fine. Of all the things she might have guessed Esther would tell her about Valerie Herrick, that bombshell wouldn't even have made the list.

"With *Joe?*" she said, feeling slow and stupid. "Are you saying that she and Joe— "

"For about two months," Esther confirmed with a nod.

They were sitting at the big square table in the kitchen, warming themselves with cups of hot cocoa topped with dollops of real whipped cream. Sam couldn't remember the last time she'd had real whipped cream. She usually bought the low-cal version of the artificial stuff.

"I think one of her friends must have introduced them. I can't be sure though, because he refuses to talk about Valerie."

"Then how do you know— "

"I saw them. At a hotel downtown."

Esther got up to collect the half dozen oatmeal cookies they hadn't finished the night before. Must be her comfort food, Sam thought. She helped herself to a plump, chewy cookie. It was hers, too.

Whipped cream and homemade oatmeal cookies. For a moment she felt like a little girl again, visiting her Gramma and stuffing herself with her favorite goodies till she thought she'd pop. But then Esther resumed her narrative and the image disappeared.

"I'd been shopping for a new winter coat and a couple of everyday dresses with an old friend," Esther went on between bites of cookie and sips of cocoa. "We hadn't seen each other for more than a month— Bernice had been out in Illinois, visiting her parents— and we decided to treat ourselves by stopping in at one of those fancy tea rooms for lunch before we headed home.

"We'd just been shown to a table. The tea room was right off the lobby, and I was sitting so I had a clear view of about half of the lobby and one of the elevators. Bernice had her back to the door, thank goodness. I saw them get off the elevator together— Joe and Valerie Herrick. I didn't know who she was at the time, understand. I was just surprised to see Joe there at the hotel, in the middle of the day. But then I realized it was probably his lunch hour. Except he hadn't been in the dining room, he'd got off the elevator, which meant he must have been upstairs. So then I thought maybe he was running an errand, or interviewing someone at the hotel— you know, for the Bureau."

"Maybe he was," Sam murmured hopefully.

Esther raised her eyebrows and gave her an eloquent look over her cup of cocoa. "No, they were together, all right. Or I should say they'd *been* together, if you catch my meaning. That was clear enough. She walked partway to the hotel entrance with him, then put her arm around his neck and stretched up to kiss him goodbye. Right there in the lobby! Took Joe by surprise, I could tell. I could also tell he didn't like that little public display at all. He has this way of scrunching his eyebrows down and smashing his lips together when he's annoyed, you know?"

Sam nodded. Oh yes, she knew.

"But that goodbye kiss didn't surprise him half as much as when he sort of gently pushed her away and turned around to leave. When he turned, he just happened to swing toward the tea room."

"He saw you?"

"He not only saw me, he knew *I'd* seen *him*. His expression was black as thunder, and he left in a hurry, like he was afraid I was going to jump up and run over to ask him a bunch of questions. As if I would, with Bernice there. Bernice is a terrible gossip."

But at some point Esther *had* asked Joe about the woman she'd seen him with. Sam had no doubt whatsoever about that, or that Esther would tell her all about it in her own sweet time. She absently dunked a cookie into her cocoa, stunned by the information Esther had dumped on her like the proverbial ton of bricks. Special Agent Joseph Mercer and Valerie Herrick had been having an affair!

Of course, now that she knew, a lot of things made sense. Especially the feeling she'd had, several times since she woke up in that jail cell, that there was more to Valerie's disappearance than met the eye. She'd sensed mysterious undercurrents, that information was deliberately being concealed. She'd assumed it was Ragsdale who was doing the concealing. Now she understood it had been Joe, all along.

And no wonder— *he* was the man Colonel Herrick disapproved of. The man Valerie and her father had argued about the night the colonel was murdered.

Joe replaced the telephone handset on its base, folded his hands on the desktop and glared at the instrument. He'd just been informed that Alvie Blumberg had rushed home at a few minutes past noon and escorted his sister and Samantha Cook to a pawn shop, where Miss Cook pawned a gold watch for $125.

The watch was at that moment being taken apart and examined by various scientists and technicians in a government-funded laboratory. The initial report wasn't encouraging— no one at the lab had ever seen a timepiece like it before. They were inclined to think the watch must be Swiss, or maybe German.

Grimacing, Joe unclasped his hands and brought a fist down on the desk with a restrained thud. *Damn* it! He should have known it wouldn't take long for her to acquire some ready cash. Of course he'd noticed her jewelry, both the watch and the ring. After what she'd told him about the ring, he hadn't even considered that she might sell or pawn it, but he should have identified the watch as a liquid asset.

He wished he'd taken a closer look at it. If a pawnbroker had given her more than a hundred dollars for it, it was worth twice that. At least. And the people who were examining it thought it might be German. He could imagine what Bill Ragsdale and Harold Boggs would make of that.

He closed his eyes and pinched the bridge of his nose. Every instinct he possessed rejected the theory that Samantha Cook was a German agent.

The idea was even more preposterous than her story about being from the future.

A small, annoying voice reminded him that she *had* known about Ensign Kazuo Sakamaki, *and* that the losses she'd catalogued from the attack on Pearl Harbor had now been verified. She'd been dead right about the numbers and classes of the ships that were damaged or destroyed. No German or Japanese agent could possibly have known those things; even the U.S. Navy had taken almost three full days to confirm her figures.

But if she wasn't a foreign agent and she hadn't traveled fifty years back in time, then who the devil *was* she and how had she managed to materialize in a jail cell in the nation's capital on the day war was declared?

Joe released a gusty sigh and raked both hands through his hair in distraction. He'd been asking himself those questions for the past four days, and so far he hadn't come up with a single plausible answer to either of them.

In the beginning, he'd assumed that since Samantha's arrival coincided with Valerie's disappearance, the two events must be related. But in the short time he'd known Valerie, she had prattled endlessly about her friends— their names, who their parents were, what schools they'd attended, who they were seeing and even which shops they patronized— but she'd never mentioned anyone named Samantha Cook. He'd heard all about Melissa and Constance and Veronica and Joanne, and not one but two Marilyns, but no Samantha. And certainly no one called Sam.

Besides, back at the jail Samantha had asked him to tell her everything he knew about Val. He was certain she hadn't been putting on an act, playing

Little Miss Innocent just to find out what they
knew about Val's disappearance. For one thing,
those eyes of hers would have betrayed the lie even
before it passed her lips. For another, she was too
shrewd to take such an unnecessary risk.

So he had to conclude that she didn't know
Valerie. And if she didn't know Val, she probably
hadn't known Colonel Herrick either.

Which brought him full circle back to the original questions: Who was she and why was she here?

It was after eleven before Lucas got away from
the newsroom. Much too late, reason dictated, to
start the circuitous and probably dangerous trip to
the Elderare home. He topped off his tank at one
of the few gas stations still open— a Platolene one-
stop where two burly men with shotguns guarded
the pumps and a third sat inside next to the clerk
manning the cash register— and set out anyway.

Viewers were still feeding the station information about roadblocks and patrols, so Lucas had a
good idea what areas to avoid. Even so, he drove
most of the way without benefit of headlights, and
pulled his sapphire blue Capri to the curb a couple
of times when he detected activity ahead. He
wished he'd thought to take a CB unit from the
station. All he had in the car was his cellular
phone, which might come in handy if some punk
took it into his head to carjack the sporty little
convertible— assuming of course that he'd have
time to use the phone before he was dragged out
of the car and clubbed senseless— but was useless
when it came to letting him know what might be
around the next corner.

By the time he found the nursing home— in a

semirural area where large houses sat at the end of long, private, tree-lined drives— every muscle in his body was knotted with tension. He parked the Capri, then got out and spent a couple of minutes stretching out the kinks while he studied the building's darkened windows and tried to figure out what to do next. He hadn't been aware of the cold while he was in the car, but he was certainly aware of it now. He shivered, his breath forming small clouds that looked solid enough to catch in his hand.

He suddenly felt incredibly foolish. He must have been out of his mind to drive down here at this time of night. He hadn't even thought to phone ahead. Levander Grisham was the only employee he'd had any contact with, and Levander's shift had ended a couple of hours ago. What if whoever was on duty wouldn't let him in? He supposed he could sleep in the car, if it came to that. Of course he'd wake up in the morning looking and feeling like a frozen pretzel. Assuming, he thought as he glanced uneasily at the trees and expensive, frost-coated landscaping surrounding the building, that he woke up.

He pushed a button on the side of his watch and checked the illuminated time: 12:38. It had taken almost an hour and a half to get here from Silver Spring. He didn't even want to think about making the return trip, either in daylight or dark.

His breath was a plume of vapor that preceded him as he stepped over the curb and started up the cement walk to the nursing home. The only light visible through the wide plate glass door was a flickering fluorescent fixture on the far side of the lobby, at the entrance to a long, dark hall. He was trying to psych himself for the likelihood that he was going to spend the rest of the night scrunched behind the Capri's steering wheel, when a white-clad figure suddenly appeared from the dim recesses beyond the light and headed toward the front right corner of the reception area. Probably an orderly or nurse's aide. A man, judging by his height and bulk.

Lucas broke into a run, at the same time waving wildly and yelling, *"Hey!"* to attract the guy's attention. For a second he thought he'd been neither seen nor heard, but then the man stopped and turned toward him.

"Hallelujah," Lucas muttered as he sprinted the last few feet to the door. He jiggled the metal hand grip and gestured for the man to let him in.

The man was standing to his right and about ten feet away, in the gloom where the light from the hall merged with the darkness. Dressed entirely in white, he looked like some kind of supernatural apparition. Lucas barely made out the brusque negative movement of a large, square head that topped an equally impressive physique. Jesus, the guy was a giant! Casper the Friendly Ghost on steroids. Except, with his face shrouded in darkness, he didn't look all that friendly.

"Please, unlock the door," Lucas said as loudly as he dared. God knew what kind of predators might be prowling the night, hoping to come across an idiot so stupid as to have wandered outside the city alone and unarmed. "It's important. I have to see one of your patients."

"Can't do it, man," a sepulchral voice responded. "You'll have to come back in the morning."

Lucas stiffened in reaction. That voice! He impulsively pressed his hands against the door and leaned close. "Levander? Levander Grisham!" His breath fogged the glass, blurring the image on the other side. "It's me— Lucas Davenport!"

He saw the indistinct white form twitch in surprise, and then Levander was on the other side of the glass, digging a set of keys out of his pocket, opening the door. He grabbed Lucas by the arm and dragged him bodily across the threshold, then quickly relocked the door.

"Are you crazy? Damn, you must be, to drive all the way down here after dark."

"I've been telling myself the same thing," Lucas muttered. "But I had to see her, Levander. I had to be *sure.*"

Levander stood there for a minute that felt like an hour, studying him in silence. Anxiety began to nibble at Lucas. Had something happened? Had someone come to claim her, taken her away? Had she checked herself out?

"Well?" he said curtly when the silence and the darkness became intolerable. "She's still here, isn't she?"

Levander nodded. "She's still here. Still awake, last time I checked. Where's she gonna go? You should be thanking your lucky stars *I'm* still here, and that you made it here in one piece. It's got so bad the last couple days that some of the staff is afraid to work nights. We just rearranged the shifts this afternoon."

Lucas made a mental note to follow up on that, but later. After he'd seen the woman everyone had assumed was Samantha Cook.

"Take me to her," he asked.

Levander nodded again and turned toward the hall. "Her room's down here."

It was a small, private room, the last one before

the corridor ended at a fire exit. Levander opened the door without making a sound, a skill he'd probably mastered so he wouldn't disturb the patients or residents or whatever they were called in case they were napping.

Lucas hesitated before he stepped inside. He was relieved she didn't have a roommate; this was going to be hard enough, without a deaf octogenarian yelling questions at him from the sidelines. He became aware that his palms were damp and rubbed his hands down the legs of his trousers.

The room was dark except for the pale circle of light provided by a small table lamp next to the bed. At first all Lucas could make out was an amorphous lump, but then he realized that she was lying on her side, facing away from him, the covers tucked snugly around her shoulders.

The light was so dim that he couldn't distinguish the color of her hair, but even without that identifying detail he knew right away that the person on the bed couldn't be Samantha. No one who'd ever seen Sam would describe her as petite; this woman took up roughly the same amount of space as the average 12-year-old.

He closed his eyes against a wave of despair that almost drove him to his knees. He'd thought he was prepared. He'd been wrong. Until that moment, a small, stubborn part of him had clung to the hope that the woman Levander Grisham described on the phone was some other amnesiac from the hotel—that when he got here, he'd find Sam, waiting for him to tuck her into his little blue car and take her home.

Dear God, where *was* she?

He opened his eyes just as the woman sighed and rolled onto her back. For half a second Lucas considered backing away from the door and gesturing for Levander to close it. She turned her head and saw him before he could act on the craven impulse.

"Hello," she said.

That was all. Just "Hello," in a genteel, ladylike tone he hadn't heard used in years. Not "Who the hell are you?" or "What are you doing here?" She didn't seem upset or even particularly surprised to find a strange man standing at the door, obviously watching her. Lucas found himself inside the room without having willed his feet to move.

"I apologize for disturbing you," he murmured. "I just wanted to . . ."

He trailed off, feeling foolish. How could he possibly explain his rash late-night trek through dangerous streets to stand in a doorway and stare at a perfect stranger? The woman sat up and hugged her knees to her chest. The change in position brought her face into the light. Lucas felt his heart stumble in surprise. She was incredibly lovely.

"See me?" she finished for him. "You're the man Levander told me about, aren't you— the one who's trying to find his friend?"

Lucas nodded, afraid to try to speak around the sudden thickness in his throat. She smiled and patted the mattress.

"Come and sit down. I have a feeling we both need someone to talk to."

Joe didn't get home until Sam and Esther were putting the finishing touches on dinner. As Sam carried a platter of sliced roast beef into the dining room, she wondered if he'd timed it that way deliberately.

Of course he couldn't know that Esther had spilled the beans about him and Valerie Herrick, but he might be avoiding her for some other reason. It had been obvious at breakfast that just being in the same room with her made him uncomfortable. He hadn't wanted to look at her or talk to her, clutching his coffee cup as if it were a crucifix and she were one of the living dead.

She set the platter on the table, straightened, and planted her hands on her hips while she considered what Mercer's problem might be. She knew he resented being saddled with the responsibility of keeping an eye on her, and he'd been thoroughly pissed that he'd had to bring her home with him. But even so, he'd been carrying on manfully, doing his duty like the upright, true-blue G-man he was. Until this morning.

In the kitchen last night he'd been more relaxed than she'd ever seen him. Not loose as a goose, life-of-the-party relaxed— she doubted Joseph Mercer would ever be a rip-roaring extrovert— but he had seemed comfortable, at ease. Once or twice he'd even displayed a droll humor she found extremely appealing. In fact for a minute or so, when she and Esther were ganging up on him, she'd actually sympathized with him. But then this morning he'd unaccountably reverted to being the stolid, all-business FBI agent. Why?

Sam suddenly stiffened with a smack-your-forehead flash of insight. The kiss! *That* was the burr under his blanket, the reason for his backslide into stiff-necked stoicism. Of course, that must be it. She knew a moment's impatient pique— for heaven's sake, it was only a kiss— followed by a warm flush of something close to, but not quite, embarrassment. Right, and the Cathedral of Notre Dame was *only* a church.

Her mouth curved in a secretive smile. It *had* been quite a kiss. All things considered— his position, and hers— she could understand how it might have rattled him.

"Are you thinking of eloping with the roast?" Esther asked as she placed a bowl of mashed potatoes next to the platter.

Sam felt heat flood her face. To make matters worse, she realized that Martha Hampton and Gertrude Willis had come into the dining room. Before she could think of anything to say, Esther winked and added, "Frankly, I think you can do better. There's a really handsome Virginia ham in the ice box down in the basement."

Sam laughed self-consciously. "Thanks for the tip. Once rationing starts, that ham will probably be worth a year's supply of sugar."

"Rationing?" Martha said in surprise. "What's this about rationing?"

Martha wasn't the only one who reacted to the thoughtless remark; Esther gave Sam a sharp, questioning look.

"It's bound to happen," she said with a shrug. "Especially for anything we import from other countries— sugar, coffee, rubber . . . things like that."

She escaped to the kitchen to collect the deviled eggs and biscuits before anyone could ask how and why she'd come by that opinion. Fortunately, Joe and the other three boarders filed into the dining room as she and Esther put the last dishes on the table, and for the next several minutes everybody was occupied taking their seats and making polite chitchat while they filled their plates. Sam slid into the chair on Joe's left and concentrated on keeping her mouth full, which she hoped would keep her from making any more stupid slips.

Of course the conversation quickly focused on war news. The topic on everyone's lips tonight was the sinking by Japanese war planes of two British ships— the new 35,000-ton battleship *Prince of Wales* and the battle cruiser *Repulse*.

"That has to be a hard blow to the Brits," Chet Pierce said as he ladled gravy over his mashed potatoes. "But at least we got one of the Japs' ships. That should help even the score. Some of our Army bombers sank one of their battleships off the northern coast of Luzon."

Sam felt Joe's eyes on her as Alvie demanded, "Where'd you get that information, Chet?" She kept her own gaze on the plate of food in front of her and didn't react. Was he wondering if she'd pass that bit of news on to her German or Japanese employers, for pity's sake?

"From the War Department, of course," Chet replied with a grin. "What'sa matter, Blumberg, did you miss that story?"

"Guess I must have," Alvie muttered. "I thought I caught every press notice that came out of the War Department today, but I sure didn't see anything about our bombers sinking a Jap battleship."

"It was called the *Haruna,* if you're interested."

"Yeah, yeah, all right. Pass the gravy, would you."

Sam felt a twinge of guilt. Had Alvie missed the story because he was escorting her and Esther to the pawn shop when he should have been at his desk?

"Did anyone hear the report on the radio about

those fires they found out west?" Martha asked. "I only caught the end of it."

Gert nodded and quickly swallowed a mouthful of roast beef. "It was out in Washington state. The police found several fires in the form of arrows pointing toward Seattle. Of course everybody thinks they were set as markers for Japanese planes, so they'd be able to find the city in spite of the blackout."

"Holy cow, I hadn't heard about that!" Chet exclaimed. "Did they catch whoever started the fires?"

Gert shook her head. "No, but the police put them out right away and nobody reported seeing any suspicious planes—planes that weren't supposed to be in the area, that is."

"Thank goodness," Martha murmured. "I certainly wouldn't want to live out there now. One of the secretaries I work with says people in California have reported seeing submarines offshore."

"I seriously doubt those reports are true," Owen remarked. "People expect to see submarines, so they see submarines."

"Mass hysteria," Sam agreed.

The observation earned her a keen glance and a hopeful "You think so?" from Esther.

"Absolutely," she said firmly. "The Japanese will never attack the mainland."

"Well, now, they just might," Chet said. "If I lived out on the west coast, I sure wouldn't be taking it for granted that they *won't.*"

Sam opened her mouth to either argue or reassure him, she wasn't sure which, but Alvie spoke before she could.

"What about it, Joe? The Japs got as far as Hawaii. Does the government think they'll try to come the rest of the way?''

Joe dabbed at his mouth with one of Esther's snowy napkins before he answered. Everyone at the table, including Sam, stopped eating and looked at him expectantly. She sensed that both the question and the attention made him uncomfortable.

"Not to my knowledge," he said. "But you should remember, I don't work for military intelligence. And the War Department isn't about to tell anyone else what they know or don't know about the enemy's plans, or what our own plans might be."

"Plans!" Chet said with a contemptuous snort. "I sure hope whoever was in charge of *planning* for the Navy doesn't have any pull at the War Department. Honest to Pete, I'd like ten minutes alone with that blockhead, whoever he was. To let us get caught with our pants down like that!"

"But the Japanese attack was a complete surprise, Chet," Martha said. "Coming at dawn on a Sunday morning like it did, while their ambassador was still carrying on peace talks with our State Department. How could anyone have expected that sort of treachery?"

"Military leaders are expected to anticipate such things, Martha," Owen pointed out. He smiled to show it wasn't a reproach. "Chet is right, we got caught with our pants down."

"Boy, did we ever," Sam said with a grimace. "Did you know that 1941 was the first time in more than twenty years the Navy didn't schedule large-scale maneuvers in the Pacific? If they had, the entire Pacific fleet wouldn't have been one gigantic floating target in Pearl Harbor."

"If that's true, they're a bigger bunch of block-heads than I thought," Chet grumbled.

"Oh, it's true," she assured him. A second later she felt a sharp pain in her right foot as Joe's shoe pressed down on the arch. "Uh, at least, according to one of the policemen who interviewed me after I was robbed. He has a cousin in the Navy. The policeman, that is. That's what his cousin told him."

The pressure on her arch increased. She abruptly stopped babbling and stuck a forkful of green beans in her mouth, but at the same time she shoved her knee against Joe's, hard enough to dislodge his foot and make him drop the biscuit he'd started to butter. Fortunately it landed on his plate, on top of the roast beef.

She fumed in silence for the rest of the meal. When the boarders adjourned to the parlor to listen to the radio, Joe stayed in the dining room, once again pitching in to clear the table and carry dishes to the kitchen.

"We can manage the rest, thank you," Sam said coolly as she took a bibbed apron from a hook next to the stove.

He removed his tie, then his suit coat, draping both over a chair before he also collected an apron. "It's no trouble."

Esther looked from one of them to the other and shook her head with an ironic smile. "If I'd known having a German agent in the house was what it took to get you to help in the kitchen, I'd have written Mr. Hitler years ago and offered to board a few of them for him."

Joe's expression made it clear he didn't find the remark in the least amusing. "I told you both last night, I don't believe Samantha is a foreign agent.

Unfortunately, I'm afraid some of the people I work with are convinced that she is."

Sam had been scraping food scraps into an empty lard can, but that remark made her stop and look at him in concern.

"And your little excursion today didn't exactly put their suspicions to rest," he added grimly.

"How do you know about— Oh, shit. Of course. They followed us to the pawnshop." A horrible thought occurred to her. "Do they have the watch?"

Joe merely nodded, which for some reason disturbed her more than if he'd ranted and raved.

"*Who* followed us?" Esther asked.

"The Federal Bureau of Inquisition, of course," Sam muttered. "Mr. Hoover's corps of professional snoops. *Damn* it!"

"Excuse me for pointing out that your indignant outrage is uncalled for," Joe said dryly. "Since just this morning I told you you'd be followed if you left the house."

"Well, I forgot! It's not like I don't have other things on my mind. I was flat broke, and the watch was the only thing I had that I could convert to hard cash. I couldn't very well take out a classified ad— for sale: one-of-a-kind gold lady's watch that won't be available again for fifty years."

"It sounds like you might as well have," Esther observed.

"Yes," Joe said with a sigh. "The men who are studying it have never seen a watch like it, but they're certain it wasn't made in this country. They believe it's either German or Swiss."

"The innards are probably Swiss," Sam murmured. "Are Boggs and Ragsdale going to use the watch as an excuse to lock me up again? Because if that's the plan— "

"What?" Joe interrupted. "You'll run, catch the first available transportation out of Washington?" He stepped to the sink and turned on the hot water faucet with a vicious twist. Neither woman pointed out his error when he dumped in about half a pound of soap flakes, but Esther did hurry to open the cold water tap so he wouldn't scald himself.

He unbuttoned his cuffs and rolled up his sleeves, his movements quick and precise. "That would only convince them you're guilty . . . of something."

Sam picked up a plate and started scraping again. Of course that was exactly what she'd been about to say she would do. "Would they come after me?"

"You can bet on it," he said, then glanced over his shoulder to add a snide, "Now that you have some hard cash to bet."

She lifted her chin stubbornly. "I won't let those shortsighted, tight-assed bureaucrats put me back in jail."

"I doubt they'd ask your permission."

"I haven't committed any crimes, damn it!"

Joe turned off both faucets and pivoted to face her, blistering her with a look. "The United States is at *war*, damn it! Individual rights have to take a backseat to national security."

"Now where have I heard that before?" Sam muttered. "So are you saying they do plan to arrest me?"

He released a gusty breath and came to the table to pick up a stack of dirty dishes. "No, that isn't what I'm saying. So far as I know, the plan is still to watch you, and wait."

"Wait," Sam repeated in a flat, hard tone. "For me to contact my control, I suppose?"

Joe had started back to the sink with the dishes. He stopped and frowned in confusion. "Your what?"

"My control. You know— someone who passes orders to intelligence agents."

His right eyebrow rose a skeptical inch. "I see. That's what you call such people in— "

"Nineteen ninety-five," Sam said tightly. She wanted to hit him. Hard. He was still resisting the truth out of plain, ornery pigheadedness, but she knew he was more than halfway to accepting it. She *knew* it! Why did he always have to act like such a cynical hard-ass?

But she knew the answer to that, didn't she? Valerie Herrick.

"Yes, that's what we call such people. It describes their function. What are they called in 1941, Agent Mercer?"

"I have no idea."

He continued on to the sink and carefully lowered the stack of dishes into the steaming water. If he burned his hands, he gave no sign. Esther darted a worried glance at Sam as she left the kitchen, dishrag in hand, to clean the dining room table.

"Have you heard that the Bureau has begun to detain enemy aliens for interrogation?" Joe asked quietly as soon as his sister was out of earshot.

The question, and his timing, surprised Sam. "Yes. According to the radio, they've already rounded up over twelve hundred Japanese and eight hundred Germans."

"And more than a hundred Italians," he murmured. He sounded . . . disturbed.

Sam pressed the lid of the lard can in place and carried the rest of the dishes to the sink. "It's only the beginning. There'll be a lot more, mostly Japanese and Japanese-Americans. And they won't just be interrogated."

He gave her a wary, questioning look. "What do you mean?"

"Their property will be confiscated— homes, businesses, virtually everything but the clothes on their backs— and they'll be put into internment camps for the duration of the war. In effect, they'll become prisoners of war in their own country."

He stared at her silently for a full minute. When he finally spoke, it was to utter a stunned, unconvincing, "No. I don't believe that."

"Yes, you do," Sam said. "You believe it, and you realize there's only one way I could know about it. For God's sake, Joe, it's in *history* books."

She went to the drawer where Esther kept the dish towels, using that as a reason to turn her back before her frustration precipitated a real explosion. When she got back to the sink, he had all the flatware and three dishes washed, rinsed, and placed on the drainboard. Sam collected a handful of forks, then almost dropped them when Joe said quietly, "I think it would be a good idea for you to give me a few more history lessons." He glanced at her, took in her blank amazement. "Whatever you feel you can tell me."

Twelve

Lucas propped his elbows on the desk and rested his head in his hands. It was just past six in the morning. He'd spent the past couple of hours on the phone, in an office Levander had unlocked for him, questioning various staff members at the hotel in Alexandria, the Red Cross, the emergency rooms of three hospitals and a handful of funeral homes.

All the fatalities from the hotel had now been identified and their remains turned over to their families. Samantha Cook hadn't been among them; nor had there been a female Caucasian who might have been mistaken for Samantha Cook. Two hospitals had patients from the fire in their intensive care burn units, but both patients were men.

Lucas was completely whipped, numb with fatigue. He'd taken in all the facts, but his exhausted mind short-circuited when he tried to process them— to sort and combine and dismiss, then organize the relevant pieces of information in some kind of logical order until the obvious conclusion was revealed. There *was* no obvious conclusion. There was no logical order. The facts didn't add up.

He sat up, scrubbed his hands over his face and

reached for his glasses. The plaid-upholstered sofa against the wall beckoned, but he resisted the temptation to stretch out and catch an hour or two of sleep. Maybe later, if he didn't head back to Silver Spring right away.

Pale morning sunlight squeezed between the slats of the miniblinds at the eastern window. It was a nice office, and Levander had said he could use it as long as he liked. The former occupant—an assistant administrator who'd been shot by a carjacker the day before when he refused to hand over the keys to his BMW—wouldn't be coming back to work anytime soon. When Levander said last night that things had gotten bad in the last couple of days, he hadn't been exaggerating. Evidently the D.C. suburbs had descended into near total anarchy.

Lucas's thoughts turned to the fragile-looking young woman with the clear, vulnerable blue eyes in room 156. She had no idea how she'd come to be in the hotel four days ago and no memory of having been brought here. But though she was understandably frightened and confused, she possessed a quiet strength and serenity that had impressed him. He couldn't help comparing her to Sam. Amnesia or no amnesia, if Samantha Cook had awakened in a strange place, she would immediately start trying to find out how she'd got there. This girl, on the other hand, seemed content to wait for the answers to present themselves, and confident that everything would become clear, in time.

Lucas wished he could share that confidence. No, to be honest, what he wished was that she would show a little more impatience. Then he wouldn't feel so guilty for his own. He wanted to question her relentlessly, poke and prod until he *forced* her to start remembering. Of course he knew that would be both pointless and insensitive as hell, which was why he felt guilty.

Adding to his impatience and frustration was the gut feeling that Jane Doe held the key to finding out what had happened to Sam. Everyone else who'd been at the hotel had now been accounted for. There had to be some sort of connection, some link, between these two women. There *had* to be!

The door opened and Levander slipped into the office. Lucas was struck once again by how gracefully the big man moved.

"Any luck?" Levander asked.

Lucas shook his head. "All the corpses have been identified, and nobody's been asking around about a missing petite blue-eyed blonde."

"Too bad. I think she was sort of counting on you to turn up something."

"So was I," Lucas muttered. "Are you on your way home?"

"Not till seven. That is unless somebody else on the day shift calls in to say they can't make it, then I'll stay over. So far we've heard from three people. One had her van stolen last night and the other two are just plain scared to come out of their houses."

Lucas glanced at his watch. Still too early to phone the station and get somebody started on a piece about the breakdown of law and order in the suburbs. "What does your family think of your staying here day and night?"

"There's just the wife and me," Levander said with a shrug. "Ginnie's an aide, too, works the evening shift at one of the hospitals. Usually I pick her up after I leave here, but I called her at work last night and told her to stay there. I didn't want her to be at home by herself. She was glad to stay. They're having staff shortages, too."

Lucas nodded. "No kids?"

"Yeah, a son and a daughter. They're both grown, though. Tyrone works for a computer software company in Chicago, and Elise and her husband live outside Detroit. He's an auto worker. The kids see more of each other than they do of us, but they both manage to get home a couple of times a year."

He hesitated, then remarked, "You may not have noticed, but our Jane Doe was pretty taken with you."

The observation startled Lucas. "It's probably just that she hopes I'll be able to find out who she is and where she belongs. You know— turn out to be her white knight."

"Maybe so," Levander murmured, but he didn't sound convinced. "You know, it doesn't seem right to keep calling her Jane Doe."

Lucas agreed. He always associated the name with a tag fastened to the big toe of an unidentified corpse. Now that he'd seen the girl, spoken to her, he wanted her to have an identity to go with her personality.

"Yeah, but what else can we call her? We don't have any idea what her name is."

"Grace," Levander said without hesitation.

Lucas's mouth slowly stretched into a smile. It was a strange feeling. "Grace," he repeated. "It fits, doesn't it? All right. If the lady has no objections, Grace it is."

Levander gave one of his calm, unflappable

nods. "You hungry? They'll be serving breakfast in a little bit."

Lucas started to say no, then realized he was starved. "As a matter of fact, I am." He stood and stretched. "So you think our Grace has already formed an attachment to me, huh?"

"Seemed that way to me," Levander said as he opened the door.

Lucas preceded him into the hall. "She's been through a lot, and she may have even worse to deal with when her memory comes back."

"That's a fact."

"I wouldn't want to do anything to . . . well, you know . . ."

"Add to her troubles."

"Right."

"Then don't."

The stern remark sounded very much like a warning. Lucas glanced at the huge man in surprise.

"I'm not saying you shouldn't talk to her, spend time with her," Levander said. "Lord knows the girl needs all the friends she can get. But I know what you're thinking— when she starts to remember, she might know something that'll help you figure out what's happened to your Samantha. It wouldn't be right to lead her on just so you can use her."

"Levander, I swear to you, the thought hadn't crossed my mind."

"Good," Levander said mildly. " 'Cause if I thought that was happening, I'd be obliged to do something about it. Here's the dining room. Grace will prob'ly be along in a minute or two. Enjoy your breakfast."

Lucas stood at the dining room entrance and

stared after him as he walked away down the corridor. There went a good man, he thought with another small smile. Too bad there weren't more like him.

And then Grace came around a corner, saw him, and beamed at him in greeting. Lucas forgot both Levander and the admonition he'd just delivered. She really was a lovely girl. He went to meet her, wondering what she'd think of the name Grace, hoping she would approve.

"Don't pretend you don't know, that you haven't seen the newspaper stories," Sam said curtly. "American papers have carried reports of the Nazis' anti-Semitic policies for more than a year, for God's sake! The State Department sure as hell knows. They've lodged official protests, though that's virtually all the spineless wimps have done."

She, Joe and Esther were once again seated at the square table in the middle of the kitchen. When Esther returned from tidying the dining room and realized that in her absence her brother had undergone an abrupt attitude adjustment, she immediately started a fresh pot of coffee. Sam reflected that it was a good thing she had, because this promised to turn into a long, wearing night. Once Joe finally accepted that she'd been telling the truth all along, he was full of questions, all of which he wanted answered without delay. As for Esther, she'd made it clear that it would take a crate of dynamite to get her out of the kitchen.

"Of course we've seen the stories," Esther said quietly. "Everybody has. But we thought . . . I don't know, I guess we assumed they were . . . exaggerated."

"Exaggerated," Sam repeated, her voice laced with bitterness.

"Yes, exaggerated," Joe said. "A lot of newspaper publishers have been pressuring Congress to move this country toward joining the war in Europe."

"And at least as many of them belong to the America First Committee," Sam retorted. "Did you think the stories their papers ran were exaggerated, too?"

"Those papers don't print much about that kind of thing," Esther murmured. She looked troubled, anxious. "That the Germans have been rounding up Jewish people and putting them in prison camps, I mean."

Sam closed her eyes and exhaled a heavy sigh. These were good people, not racists or bigots. Did they truly not realize what was happening in occupied Europe, or was it simply that it was more convenient, less troubling to the conscience, to avoid facing the truth?

"They aren't prison camps, Esther," she said, striving to keep her tone nonjudgmental. "Not the way Americans think of prison camps. Some of them are already death camps, and before long there'll be others— places built and maintained for the express purpose of exterminating every Jew in Europe."

She looked them straight in the eye; first Esther, then Joe. They both looked stunned, incredulous.

"It's true. Hitler calls it the final solution. In February of this year he predicted there'd be no Jews left in Europe after the war. In Poland, all the Jews who didn't manage to escape are being confined to ghettos until the gas chambers and the ovens are ready. Right now, at this minute, the Nazis are testing Zyklon B on Russian prisoners of war and Polish Jews at Auschwitz."

"Gas chambers?" Esther whispered in horror. "Ovens?"

"What is this Zyklon B?" Joe demanded.

Sam was heartened by the fact that, while he still appeared shocked, he was paying close attention to every word. "It's a crystallized form of hydrogen cyanide."

She told them about Auschwitz-Birkenau and the other camps, and that sometime during December the Vatican would report that the Germans had already executed more than 40,000 Polish Jews, moved 60,000 to concentration camps, and were using over a million people as forced labor. When she mentioned the Vatican, Joe took his pen and notebook from his coat and started copying down the figures.

"I'm not sure that's such a good idea," Sam said.

"I don't intend to show this to anyone," he replied without looking up.

"Just want to be able to verify what I've said, huh?"

"Yes." He stopped writing and looked at her. "Don't take it personally."

"I don't. If our positions were reversed, I'd want independent confirmation, too."

He nodded, then got up to refill his coffee cup. Esther was dabbing at her eyes with a corner of her apron, obviously badly shaken. She suddenly looked across the table at Sam, her eyes dark with concern.

"What about Yugoslavia? Can you tell us what's going on there?"

"Yugoslavia?" Sam repeated blankly. It took her a moment to remember that it *was* still Yugoslavia.

Esther nodded anxiously. "We have relatives in Belgrade, most of our father's family. At least, we think they're still . . . We haven't heard from them in months."

Joe brought the coffee pot to the table and refilled both women's cups.

"Our family name was originally Mirkovic," he said in explanation. "It's Serbian. Our father's oldest brother was one of the air force officers who took part in the coup last March."

Sam remembered Gramps telling her about the coup. A General Simovic, vice-marshal of the Yugoslavian Air Force, had led a group of military officers in overthrowing the government rather than see their country aligned with Germany. It had been a brave and noble gesture, but had only succeeded in enraging Hitler. By the end of the day he'd signed a directive that sent wave upon wave of German bombers to destroy Belgrade and the country's military installations. Of course Herr Hitler couldn't have anticipated that his impulsive act of vengeance would ultimately cost him the war.

But that casual "Our family name was originally Mirkovic. It's Serbian," took Sam aback. During WWII the Serbs had paid dearly for their defiance, but they'd continued to resist the Nazis with ferocious determination and incredible courage. Who in 1941 could possibly foresee that today's victims and freedom fighters would become tomorrow's most ruthless oppressors?

"I'm sorry," Sam murmured. "I can't tell you much about the situation in Yugoslavia. Only that the Serbs won't give up."

"That goes without saying," Joe murmured. He resumed his seat and flipped to a fresh page in his notebook. "Let's concentrate on the immediate future."

Sam gave him an ironic smile. "The war, you mean."

"Yes."

"Quid pro quo, Agent Mercer, remember?"

She watched his frown of confusion become a scowl when he remembered the deal she'd offered him back at the jail.

"I've already told you, I don't have access to information from the investigation into Colonel Herrick's murder."

"Come on, Joe," Sam said impatiently. "You're FBI. We both know you can *get* access any time you want."

He folded his hands on top of the open notebook. "Possibly. But not without substantial risk. You're suggesting that I should jeopardize my career just to satisfy your curiosity?"

"No, of course not! That isn't why I'm asking." She was offended that he assumed her motive was so frivolous. Did he really have such a low opinion of her? "It isn't just curiosity."

She laid her arms on the table, unconsciously leaning forward. "Ever since I woke up in that jail cell, I've been trying to figure out the answer to one question: *Why?* Why has this happened, why am I here— why *me,* and not someone else?"

"You believe you and Valerie Herrick switched places," he murmured.

"I'm convinced of it," she said firmly.

"So am I," Esther said. When her brother turned a quizzical, faintly amused look on her, she sat up straighter and lifted her chin. "For heaven's sake, Joe, if you'd think about it for five seconds you'd see it's the only possible explanation. Val was in a locked cell, inside a jail full of police officers. How could she have gotten out without being seen?

"And even if she could have managed that," she went on without giving him a chance to answer, "where would she have gone? You know good and well her friends wouldn't hide her from the police, not when she's suspected of murdering her father. That would make them accessories or something, wouldn't it?"

"Yes, it would," Sam confirmed. Go, Esther! Maybe the two of them together could convince Joe to give her the help she needed.

"You're both overlooking one minor detail," he said dryly. "Even if this wild conjecture is true, there's no way to prove it."

"No," Sam admitted. "But— "

"So what's the point? What do you hope to accomplish by convincing me— or anyone, for that matter— that you and Val somehow traded places and she ended up more than fifty years in the future? If that is what happened, she isn't going to be found and taken into custody. And if the two of you would think about *that* for five seconds, you'd realize your fantastic theory puts Samantha in an even more precarious position."

"I do realize that," Sam said tersely. "As long as she's missing, the police will be trying to find not only Valerie, but whoever helped her 'escape.' And of course I'm the obvious suspect. Hell, I'm the *only* suspect. Don't you see, that's why I have to find out who killed her father!"

"You," Joe said flatly. Neither his voice nor his expression could be called encouraging.

"Yes, me! *That's* why I'm here! It's the answer

to the question that's been driving me batty for the past four days."

"You mean, 'Why me?' " Esther said. Her eyes glittered with excitement. "Of course! It makes perfect sense. That's what you *do*— help the police solve crimes!"

"Right." Sam looked at Joe as she said it. "That's what I do. Do you get it now?"

He didn't answer for so long that she thought he was putting together an argument, or maybe several arguments. Sam tried to anticipate him, come up with a rebuttal. Unfortunately, she'd never had any talent for reading people's minds.

But then he said, very softly and with utter seriousness, "I think I'm beginning to."

Lucas made a couple of phone calls— one to the station and one to Cassie McGregor at home— then spent the rest of the morning with Grace. She'd had no objection to the name, in fact she told him she preferred it to either Jane or Samantha.

He learned that she was indeed fluent in French and also spoke a smattering of Spanish and German. That last was important, because she *remembered* it, while they were sitting on a comfortable sofa in the large, sunny lounge.

"Isn't that odd?" she said, her head cocked to one side. "I remember that I know a little German and a little Spanish, but not where I learned either language, or when."

"It was probably in school," Lucas said with pretended nonchalance. "That's where most people learn a foreign language." It was hard to hide his elation. He had to forcibly restrain himself from pressing her, trying to stimulate more memories.

"Yes, I imagine you're right," she murmured. "Still, I wish I could remember what schools, and where they were."

"Be patient. It'll come."

One of the resident patients came into the lounge, picked up the remote control from a table, and turned on the large television in the far corner. Grace jumped when Bernard Shaw's mellifluous voice suddenly erupted from the stereo speakers.

"What's that?" She was looking around the room, her eyes wide and startled.

Lucas impulsively reached out and clasped her hand. "Take it easy, it's only CNN." He gestured toward the television. Lowering his voice, he added, "The old geezer's got the volume maxed out. I'd ask him to turn it down, but he's probably deaf as a post."

She leaned forward, staring at the television screen on the other side of the lounge. Her hand squeezed his so hard that Lucas winced and rearranged their fingers. Bernie Shaw's voice continued to boom from the speakers as a panning shot of a D.C. street littered with abandoned vehicles, some of which were burning, replaced the newsroom set. Lucas realized that she was seeing the destruction and chaos for the first time. It must be horrifying for her. He almost slipped a comforting arm around her shoulders, but then he remembered Levander's warning.

"CNN?" she asked. She sounded confused, and just a little anxious.

"Cable News Network," he said in surprise. "You don't know CNN?"

She shook her head no. Weird, Lucas thought. Maybe she'd been living in a convent. *Everybody* knew about CNN, for crissake. Even Saddam Hussein had been a regular viewer via satellite during Desert Storm.

Just then the old man pointed the remote at the set and switched to one of the home shopping channels. Grace gasped in either amazement or alarm, Lucas couldn't tell which. The next thing he knew she was on her feet, hurrying toward the television set. He got up and followed.

She crouched down to one side of the set, apparently mesmerized by the porcelain dolls that were being hawked. "What is this?" she asked in wonder.

"Legalized theft," the old man replied from his overstuffed chair. "I know folks who've ordered stuff from those crooks. Half the time it's damaged or doesn't work when they get it. The other half the time it's not the same thing they showed on the tube."

He switched to another channel in disgust. Indiana Jones and Marion Ravenwood were trying to find a way out of the pit they were trapped in without stepping on any of the snakes that covered the floor. Grace gave another startled jerk and almost lost her balance.

"There you go!" the old man said in satisfaction. "This is one terrific movie. I love to see those damn Nazis get their butts kicked." Grace swiveled to stare at him. "Pardon my French," he said with a sheepish grin.

"You can have movies shown right in your home?"

"Sure, long as you've got cable. Most of the stuff on the networks nowadays is trash— stupid soap opera junk. This is a good one, though. It's got everything, even God," he added with a dry chuckle. "Too bad we came in in the middle. Tell you what, pull one of those chairs over here and I'll fill you in on what we've missed."

"God?" Grace said as she got to her feet. She dragged a maple captain's chair across the carpet and positioned it next to the one the old man was using.

"Well, I can't swear it's really Himself," he said with a wink. "But the special effects are so good I couldn't swear it isn't, either."

Lucas stood frozen in place several feet behind them. What the hell . . . ? She'd never heard of CNN, didn't know about home shopping channels or that you could watch movies on television? Had the amnesia wiped all that from her mind along with her name? No, he didn't think that could be the case. She hadn't forgotten about newspapers, or radios— when he first went into her room the night before, the clock radio next to her bed was tuned to a classical station.

His scalp tingled; a finger of misgiving tickled the base of his spine. She was reacting as if she'd never *seen* a television set before.

"You're taking a lot for granted," Joe said. There was a slight edge to his voice. "I may not be able to get a look at any of that information."

"But— " Sam began, and was rudely ignored.

"And even if it's possible to examine the reports, there's no chance I'll be able to remove anything from the offices that have been assigned to the investigating team."

"But you have an excellent memory," Esther pointed out. "Even if you can't bring the reports home, you'll be able to memorize most of what's in them."

He gave her a repressive look that had no visible effect. It was almost eleven, late for the two women to be up since they'd have to rise at daybreak to start breakfast.

"I don't expect you to try to sneak any of the reports out," Sam said quickly. "I know how risky that would be. I wouldn't even be asking you to help if I could think of any other way to find out what the investigation's turned up."

Joe heaved a resigned sigh and conceded, "I'll see what I can do. No promises, though."

"I don't expect any," she assured him. "Whatever you can find out will be more than I know now."

He nodded brusquely, then picked up his cup and realized it was empty. "Time to call it a night, I think."

"I'll second that," Esther said.

She pushed back her chair and had just stood up when the door to the hall opened and Alvie Blumberg staggered in. He was carrying the typewriter he'd bought at the pawn shop. A stack of loose papers teetered precariously on top of the machine. He lugged the typewriter to the table and set it down with a thump, then had to grab the papers to keep them from spilling to the floor.

"I didn't want to barge in while you were cleaning up after dinner," he said with a grin. "Esther might've put me to work. Another wonderful meal, Esther."

"Thank you, Alvie," she murmured. "It's a pleasure to cook for people who enjoy good food."

Alvie beamed at her. "Well, it goes without saying that anybody would love your cooking." He cleared his throat softly and turned to Samantha. "I hope you won't be offended, Miss Cook, but Esther and I came up with a plan for you to earn a little pocket money."

Sam didn't dare look at Esther or Joe. "Yes, Esther mentioned it this afternoon," she said, hoping to forestall a long-winded explanation. Surely he didn't want her to type up the copy for one of his stories tonight? "Of course I'm not offended. It was very thoughtful of both of you."

"Not at all," Alvie said, sending another broad smile in Esther's direction. "It'll be a mutually beneficial arrangement. You need a job, and I need a good, reliable typist— somebody who can translate my chicken scratchings into copy my editor can read, so he won't have a heart attack or make me go back to school to take a typewriting class."

He separated the papers into two stacks and handed her the larger one. "These are my notes for a couple of stories I plan to file tomorrow morning." The second stack of paper he deposited next to the typewriter. "And this should be enough typing paper to last you a few days."

Sam riffled through his notes and reflected that the term "chicken scratchings" perfectly described his handwriting.

"I thought ten cents per page would be a fair payment. I'll provide the typing paper, and I'll bring home a new ribbon for the typewriter tomorrow. I noticed that this one's pretty worn."

Sam was still marveling over that "ten cents per page," when he said he'd collect the copy from her after breakfast in the morning and excused himself to go up to bed. By the time she roused herself to protest that if she stayed up to decipher his notes and type the copy she wouldn't get to bed at all, Alvie was gone.

"I'll start another pot of coffee before I head up to bed," Joe offered as he turned for the sink. "Looks like you're going to need it."

Sam frowned at his broad back, wishing she could see his face. She suspected he was grinning from ear to ear.

Thirteen

It was after three when Sam finished typing the last page of Alvie's copy. She stood and arched her back, then rolled her shoulders, wincing at the ominous cracking sounds that emanated from her spine. She couldn't remember ever feeling so exhausted. Of course, she didn't usually expend the physical effort she had today.

"Get used to it, kid," she muttered as she turned off the kitchen light and headed for the stairs. Unless she could find a way back to her own time, she might spend the best years of her life as an unappreciated beast of burden.

Maybe she could get the feminist movement off to an early start, or find some ambitious inventor and feed him suggestions for a few labor-saving devices. A microwave oven and an electric clothes dryer would be right up there at the top of the list. And a dishwasher. God, yes, a dishwasher would be priority number one.

Esther, or maybe Alvie, had left the light on the second-floor landing turned on. Sam switched it off when she reached the landing, started toward her room . . . and a few feet later wished she'd left the light on. The hall was as dark as a mine shaft. She held her left arm out from her side, running her hand along the wall so she'd know when she reached her room, and tried to decide whether she could stay awake long enough to take a bath. She'd used the toilet downstairs, and washed her hands and face twice in the last couple of hours to keep herself awake and alert. Or had it been three times?

To hell with it. A bath could wait till tomorrow.

Her fingers encountered the solid oak door of Martha Hampton's room, which was the first one past the landing. Only another nine or ten feet to go. Her room would be next, the last door before Joe's at the front of the house.

When she finally reached it, she eased the door shut behind her and immediately started fumbling with the tiny buttons on the bodice of her borrowed dress, not bothering to turn on the light. God, she was whipped. And damn it, she still had to wrestle with these clunky old-lady shoes. She shrugged out of the dress and flopped down on the bed, bending over to untie the laces and tug off the shoes, then the white cotton anklets. She noticed that she needed to shave her legs. Maybe Esther had a razor she could borrow till she could get out and buy one. Did they make electric razors in 1941? Did women even shave their legs in 1941? Funny, she hadn't noticed.

Reaching behind her to pull back the covers with one hand, she smothered an enormous yawn with the other as she slipped between cool cotton sheets.

Oh, *heaven* . . .

A lean, muscular arm slid across her stomach and a deep, sexy baritone murmured in her ear, "I believe one of us is in the wrong bed."

Sam almost strangled on a gasp. Her heart leapt into her throat. She instinctively tried to sit up, but Joe's arm held her firmly in place.

"What— ? How— ?"

"Turned off the light, didn't you?"

Her right hand had flown to her chest in spontaneous reflex. She could feel her heart galloping like a thoroughbred in the final stretch of the Kentucky Derby. She tried to breathe normally in the hope that would slow her pulse, as well. If she died of a stroke or a massive coronary, she'd never find Colonel Herrick's murderer.

"Yes. I turned it off. Jesus, you scared me out of ten years growth!"

"Sorry, but you gave me quite a start, too."

His tone was dry, just a tiny bit amused. The realization of where she was, and with whom, suddenly slammed into Sam and her entire body started to burn with embarrassment. At least, she told herself it was embarrassment.

"Oh, God, I'm sorry," she mumbled. "I must've gone right past my room and didn't even realize it." She started using her bottom and shoulders to work her way toward the edge of the bed. "I'm just so exhausted, you know? It's a wonder I didn't fall asleep on the stairs."

She managed to scoot a couple of inches before his hand curved around her waist and he hauled her back against him.

"What are you— ?" she blurted, and that was all she got out before his mouth found hers in the dark.

Stupid question anyway, she thought in the first second or two, while she was still able to think. She'd known the instant she felt his arm tense against her ribs what he was going to do, and it hadn't entered her mind to say the word "No" or roll off the bed or push his hand away.

His mouth was hot, eager, hungry. Sam felt a

ribbon of desire unfurl in her lower abdomen. She was desperately trying to dredge up some willpower when Joe smoothly slid one hand beneath her and splayed his fingers across her back, just below her shoulderblades. His other hand shifted to her right hip, his touch firm and assured. The next thing she knew, he'd turned her onto her side and pressed her against him from collarbone to knees. His mouth never lost contact with hers.

Sam heard a feeble moaning sound and was appalled to realize it had come from her own throat. "Joe," she gasped against his lips. "No. Stop. We can't—"

He responded to the feeble, halfhearted protest by pressing her closer still, pushing his pelvis against hers, making it devastatingly clear that "can't" didn't apply.

"I've wanted to do this since the first time I stepped into that freezing cell." His voice was a hoarse, ragged mutter. "You were wrapped up in a blanket, remember?"

"Yes." Sam barely got the word out. God, yes, she remembered. The first time she'd seen him, she'd thought she was hallucinating. Partly because he was the most magnificent man she'd ever laid eyes on. And now here they were . . . in bed . . . together.

Maybe this was the hallucination.

"You said 'My name is Samantha Cook. I'm a 28-year-old, single, Caucasian, female American citizen.' Then you said you'd woken up in the cell several hours before, and this—" His left hand drifted up her side, carrying her silk slip with it. "—was all you were wearing. And you held the blanket open. Just for a second."

His hand reached her breast. Froze. Caressed

her through the crumpled silk. Sam momentarily forgot how to breathe.

"You weren't wearing a bra then, either."

His voice deteriorated to a splintered whisper as he reclaimed her mouth and suddenly rolled, covering her body with his. Whatever discretion or good sense Sam still possessed was buried under an avalanche of physical sensation. She was surrounded, trapped, by both his weight and her own instantaneous sexual response.

The cool sheet and soft mattress beneath her made her even more aware of the lean, hard strength in his body. And of his heat. Her skin felt scorched everywhere they touched. The scrape of his beard stubble against her jaw was a sharp, sensual contrast to the smooth, wet stroke of his tongue. The fragile material of her slip magnified the gentle abrasion of his thumb as it rubbed back and forth across her nipple. And even if she'd been able to ignore all that, there was the brand of his erection against her stomach.

She was drowning in desire. She'd never known such urgency, such desperate *need*. Yet somehow the tiny part of her mind that was still functioning managed to transmit a faint, fuzzy warning that this wasn't right. *Why*, was unclear, but the admonition was enough to check her hands when they would have reached for him.

As if he'd somehow picked up the message, too, Joe lifted his head to mutter, "I resent this attraction as much as you do, you know. I don't *want* to want you, Samantha Cook. To be brutally honest, I wish I'd never set eyes on you."

Stung, she impetuously retorted, "The feeling is mutual," and instantly knew it for the lie it was. She might wish she was back in her own time— and did, a dozen times a day—but she would never, not in a million years, wish that she'd never met Special Agent Joseph Mercer.

The realization shook her. What did it mean? Surely getting back where she belonged would mean leaving him behind. She *did* want to get back where she belonged . . . didn't she?

"But I do want you," Joe said as if she hadn't spoken. "And I'm tired of pretending I don't. Which only leaves the obvious question."

Sam became aware that he was lying very still, the rise and fall of his chest the only movement she could detect. He gazed down at her in silence, waiting. She couldn't see the incredible blue of his eyes, only a faint glimmer in the darkness, but she felt their searing intensity as if they were in fact the lasers she'd compared them to.

"I want you," she whispered. "You know I do."

Her voice wavered on the last word and she tensed in anticipation of the sensual onslaught she expected the admission to provoke. When he still didn't move—didn't kiss her, or caress her, or even breathe a satisfied sigh—she experienced an unsettling combination of confusion and disappointment.

"Show me."

Her heart stumbled in surprise. *Show* him?

"Show me," he repeated in the sexiest, most seductive voice she'd ever heard.

Sam knew a dare when she heard one. Her hands lifted, found his upper arms. His biceps flexed at her touch, an involuntary reflex that made her smile in the dark. She slowly ran her fingers up over his shoulders, around to his nape, clasping the back of his head as she raised herself to kiss him.

She teased him with her tongue, tracing the seam of his closed mouth, withdrawing the instant his lips parted, returning to offer him the briefest taste before she shifted her attention to his jaw, and then his ear. Joe let her weight pull him down, apparently willing, for the moment, to allow her to set the pace. Sam sensed that this passive acceptance was uncharacteristic. She knew without having to think about it that in bed Joseph Mercer was the archetypal dominant male, the initiator and the tutor. He would make love *to* a woman, rather than *with* her.

But not tonight; not with her. For some reason she didn't pretend to understand, he was abdicating control, inviting her to take the lead. Sam didn't waste time speculating about his motives.

Her hands abandoned his thick, silky hair for his undershirt, impatiently tugging it up and over his head. He gave her only minimal assistance, twisting and shrugging his torso to free the front of the shirt. Nor did he try to reclaim her mouth, though she knew he wanted to. She could feel his self-restraint— and what it was costing him— in the knotted muscles beneath her hands, hear it in his increasingly disturbed breathing. His rigid control was both an aphrodisiac and a provocation. How much could he take? How long could he keep up this submissive act?

She tossed the undershirt aside and reached for his boxer shorts. He gave her a little more help with those, but still he only responded to her cues, leaving the initiation to her.

All right, Joseph, you asked to be shown . . .

She let her hands roam where they wanted, and they wanted to explore every sleek, taut, burning inch of him. She pushed at his shoulder in impa-

tience, urging him onto his back. He rolled silently.
Sam went with him. Her mouth joined her hands'
exploration, tasting, nipping, caressing . . .

He finally began to move. Nothing voluntary,
just restless jerks and twitches that let her know
his control was badly frayed. She smiled and laid
a string of kisses across the hard slab of his stomach, pausing to dip her tongue into his navel. At
the same time, she trailed her right hand up his
thigh, her touch so light that the pads of her fingers barely registered the coarse texture of his
body hair.

His low, tormented groan affected her like a
match set to dry kindling. Suddenly who was in
control no longer mattered. Her trembling hands
deserted his body to grope for the bottom of her
slip. Just as she found it and rose to her knees,
Joe's fingers curled inside the waist of her panties.
Sam wrestled the slip over her head while he
dragged the panties down. There was an awkward
second or two while she wobbled from one knee
to the other to get them off, and then she was
straddling him and he was gripping her hips, guid-
ing her over him and onto him.

When she took him inside her, for a moment
Sam felt as if her entire body was about to dis-
solve— her muscles were melting, bones disintegrating. But then his hands firmed their hold and
he started to move, and she caught fire. She was
oblivious to the protesting creak of the bedsprings,
the soft, needful murmurs that slipped past her
own lips, the chill of the air. Nothing existed but
Joe, and the extraordinary, electrifying feelings he
was giving her.

His hands slid up her back to pull her down.
His mouth closed on the peak of her breast and

she moaned with pleasure. The sound drew an answering groan from Joe as his tongue stroked her nipple. He began to suckle, gently at first, then harder, the tugs perfectly matching the rhythm of his thrusts. Sam's fingers closed like talons on his shoulders. She bit her lip to keep from crying out.

And then suddenly she was on her back and he was devouring her mouth, swallowing the wild sounds she couldn't hold back as he swept her with him to a shattering climax and sweet, dark oblivion.

Sam drifted, weightless, through a fine, enveloping mist that gradually resolved into a pair of arms that cradled her against a warm chest . . . lips that brushed her temple in a feathery caress. She sighed and nestled closer, pressing her face into Joe's neck.

"Are you all right?" he murmured against her hair.

He sounded concerned, so she made an effort to shrug off her delicious languor and speak. "God, yes. The question is, am I still alive?"

His chest jiggled with silent laughter. "I sincerely hope so. I'd hate to think a corpse could affect me the way you do."

Sam ran her hand down over his stomach to administer a light, teasing caress. "Mmm, I see what you mean."

Joe covered her hand with his. "Not yet, you don't, but if you keep that up . . ."

Unsure if it was a warning or an invitation, and too spent to accept if it were the latter, she withdrew her hand and stretched up to kiss him. She only meant it to be a soft affirmation of the intimacy that still cocooned them. The instant resurgence of desire—both hers and his—took her by surprise. His arms swept around her and he kissed her as if he were starved for the taste of her. When he finally released her mouth, they were both trembling.

"Damn," Joe muttered. "I knew you were trouble the second I set eyes on you."

The resentment in his voice was like a slap in the face. Sam eased away from him and sat up. He didn't try to hold her.

"I wonder, would your reaction have been the same if Valerie Herrick had been in the cell with me?" she said, as she rummaged among the bed-clothes for her slip and panties.

There was a long, pregnant silence before he murmured, "What do you mean?"

Sam gave up trying to find the underwear and left the bed to retrieve her dress. Anger started to simmer inside her.

"Nothing." She found the dress, scooped it off the floor and yanked it over her head. "I don't mean a damned thing." One of the tiny buttons popped off and disappeared into the darkness. *"Shit!"*

The box springs screeched as if a grizzly bear had fallen through the ceiling and landed on the bed. "What?" Joe said sharply.

"Nothing," she snapped again. "I lost a button."

Damn him! Damn *her!* What in God's name had she been thinking, to make love with him after what Esther had told her? Dumb question. Obviously, she *hadn't* been thinking. She dropped to her knees on the rug to search for her shoes and socks, and a second later nearly jumped out of her skin when Joe's hand clamped on her upper arm. Before she could collect herself, he gave her an impatient jerk. Sam lost her balance and fell against him, her partially covered breasts colliding with his bare chest. His arms came around her, steadying them both.

"Let go of me!" She planted both hands on his shoulders and shoved. The only thing the gesture accomplished was to remind her that he was still naked. As if she could have forgotten.

Joe ignored the demand. In fact, if anything, he held her tighter. "Not until you tell me what the hell's going on. A minute ago you couldn't get close enough. Now all of a sudden you're acting like I've got the plague."

The reminder of her brazenness made Sam stiffen in anger and embarrassment. Of course Joe felt the instinctive reaction.

"Damn it, what's wrong?

"I know!" she said between clenched teeth. "That's what's wrong."

"You know *what*, for God's sake?"

"About you and Valerie Herrick!"

She flung it at him like an accusation. Which, of course, it was. He expelled a stunned breath, as if she'd punched him in the stomach, and abruptly released her.

"Esther told you."

It wasn't a question, so Sam didn't bother to reply. She took advantage of her freedom to resume searching for her shoes and socks. She was thoroughly disgusted with herself for blurting it out like that, even more upset about the *reason* she'd given in to the rash impulse. The resentment she'd heard in his voice, so soon after what had been the most extraordinary sexual experience of her life, had triggered a ferocious jealousy that completely demolished her self-control. Not that she'd ever possessed much self-control where Joe Mercer was concerned.

The irony didn't escape her. She was insanely jealous of a woman she'd never set eyes on and probably never would. A woman who had almost certainly died in a nuclear bomb blast 54 years in the future.

None of which meant a blessed thing. The very thought of Joe and Valerie Herrick together made her sick with anxiety. Even worse was the horrible suspicion that Val had meant more to him than she ever would.

God help her, she'd gone and fallen in love with the man.

"Stupid, *stupid!*" she muttered as she dragged the second shoe from under the bed and scrambled to her feet.

She'd located only one of the anklets, but she didn't dare stay in the room another second, for fear she would utterly humiliate herself. She had her right hand on the doorknob, and the shoes and lone sock clutched to her chest, when Joe caught her by the left shoulder and spun her around. She dropped the shoes and sock.

"Of course it was stupid. Damned moronic, in fact."

Sam was so startled—by both the way he'd grabbed her and the barely contained anger in his voice—that it took a moment for what he'd said to sink in.

"What?"

He grasped her other shoulder and gave her an exasperated shake. "I said you're right, it was stupid of me to get involved with Val. Does hearing me admit it make you happy?"

Sam felt her mouth fall open. "No. I mean, that

wasn't—" She broke off, took a deep breath, and tried to get her brain and her mouth in sync. "I was referring to my own stupidity, not yours."

His fingers dug into her shoulders. "I see."

Judging by his flat, hard tone, Sam didn't think so, but she sure as hell wasn't going to enlighten him. She stiffened her spine and asked bluntly, "When you said you knew I was trouble the first time you saw me, did you mean because you thought I had something to do with her disappearance?"

"Of course I thought that, but—"

"Were you afraid somebody in the government had found out about the two of you and arranged her escape, as a trap or something?"

"A *trap?*" he barked. "What the devil are you talking about?"

Sam bristled at his tone. "I'm talking about the fact that apparently *you* were the man Valerie and her father argued about the night he was killed. If anybody besides Esther knew about the two of you—"

"No one else did, until Esther decided to take you into her confidence."

"Are you sure?"

"Positive." He seemed to realize that he was still gripping her shoulders, and removed his hands. But slowly, almost reluctantly. Sam tried not to feel disappointed.

"Then how did Colonel Herrick find out?"

"Val told him. That night. At least, she was planning to, and considering that the waiter who served them told the police they were arguing about a man—"

"Yes," Sam murmured. "Considering. But, if

you didn't think I was there to entrap you, then what did you mean— "

"When I said I knew you were trouble?"

His voice had deepened, taken on a slight rasp. A shiver of awareness rippled over Sam's skin. She was trying to decide whether she should answer him, retract her original question, or just beat a fast retreat, when he moved— so quickly and smoothly that she couldn't have evaded him if she'd tried.

He pressed her back against the door, one hand sliding inside her bodice to close over her breast, the other burying itself in her hair as his open mouth fastened on hers. Sam thought about putting up a token resistance— for about half a second, till she realized he was giving her her answer. Relief and joy magnified the desire that swept through her like a flash fire. She reached out blindly, locking her arms around his neck.

"Does Esther come to wake you," he asked between voracious kisses, "or is there an alarm clock in your room?"

She sighed the answer into his mouth. "A clock."

His hands shifted to her bottom and he lifted her against him. Her feet left the floor, her pelvis nestling perfectly into the wider structure of his. Sam stopped breathing for the few seconds it took him to carry her back to the bed.

This time they had neither the need nor the patience for foreplay. He entered her before she finished wriggling out of her dress. She launched herself off the mattress to meet every deep, driving thrust. They fused their mouths to muffle the sounds neither could contain, feeding one another's frenzy. When they finally separated to lie side by side, spent and gasping, slick with sweat, Joe's back and buttocks bore scratches in a dozen places and Sam's lips were bruised and swollen. And even then they couldn't stop touching, their wondering caresses accompanied by soft, apologetic kisses and inarticulate murmurs.

"On second thought," Joe said as he rubbed a gentle finger across her lower lip, " 'trouble' was an immense understatement."

Sam reached up to capture his hand. "Having regrets?"

"God, no." The fervency in his voice erased her fears even before he lowered his head to give her a kiss so sweet and tender it brought tears to her eyes.

"Though I suspect we both will be," he murmured against her lips, "if you don't get up and leave in the next five minutes."

She knew he was right; she barely had time for a bath before she went downstairs to help Esther start breakfast. And postponing a bath was no longer an option. She pushed herself up and out of bed with a groan and began to hunt down her clothes.

"Something tells me it's gonna be a long day."

"Maybe longer than you think," Joe said. A new, solemn note in his voice made her look at him in question. Enough pale gray light had forced its way around the window shades for her to make out his worried expression.

"Your watch," he reminded her. "They think it's German, remember? Boggs will probably want to question you about it."

Fourteen

"They'll have to find me, first," Sam declared as she and Esther finished washing the breakfast dishes.

She'd just told Esther about Joe's prediction. Of course she'd neglected to mention what had immediately preceded the remark and the context in which it was made, but she suspected Esther already had a pretty good idea what her brother and her new boarder had been up to during the night.

Sam knew she looked like death warmed over. A cold bath and two cups of Esther's industrial strength coffee had allowed her to get through breakfast without falling on her face, but now the caffeine fix was starting to wear off. She longed to go up to her room and crash for a few hours, but she didn't dare, in case Joe was right and Boggs sent someone to collect her. The next best thing would be to get out and get some exercise.

A worried frown settled on Esther's face as she upended an iron skillet on the drainboard. "But there are FBI agents watching the house. If you leave they'll follow you, just like they did yesterday."

Sam nodded. "That's what I'm counting on. I thought I'd go shopping today, use some of the money I got for my watch to buy a few dresses, some cosmetics, maybe a couple pairs of shoes or some lingerie. . . . Thing is, I'm a very fussy shopper. I wouldn't be surprised if I hit a dozen stores before noon."

A conspiratorial smile replaced Esther's frown. "The agents assigned to follow you will be bored stiff after the first two or three stops."

"Of course. They're men. And believe me, Esther, a bored watchdog is remarkably easy to lose. So what do you say, are you up for a shop-till-you-drop binge?"

Esther laid the dishcloth over the edge of the sink. "Just let me get my purse and coat."

The plan had worked beautifully, except for one thing. This wasn't the Washington Sam knew. The streets had the same names, but the bus schedules and routes were different, cabs were few and far between, and apparently a lot of the buildings had been either torn down and replaced at some point between the '40s and the '90s, or repeatedly refurbished and remodeled until they were unrecognizable.

After she ditched the FBI tails— who were probably still waiting for her to emerge from the ladies' room of a department store packed with Christmas shoppers— she took two cabs and a bus before she finally located the upscale neighborhood where the Herricks had lived. She'd been surprised to find Ethan Herrick listed in the telephone book before she and Esther left home. Evidently not even high-ranking Army Intelligence officers considered it necessary to have an unlisted number in 1941.

But she was beginning to think that discovering the Herricks' address so easily had used up her allotment of luck. First, Esther had stubbornly insisted on staying with her after she lost the FBI watchdogs. Sam had quickly realized that arguing would be a waste of time. Esther Mercer shared her brother's bulldog tenacity. So she did the only thing she could think of, which was to lose Esther along with the FBI agents. By now Esther was probably good and steamed. Sam had not only given her the slip, she'd left Esther to carry home all their purchases.

It belatedly occurred to her, as she froze her buns off trudging up and down vaguely familiar yet strangely foreign-looking streets, that maybe she should have brought Esther along after all. Very few of the houses displayed their street numbers; worse, a lot of them looked deserted, as if maybe the owner had recently been murdered and his only relative had mysteriously disappeared. For that matter, the streets themselves weren't well-marked, either, and they twisted through the neighborhood like a mass of snakes, frequently looping back to intersect with themselves so that a couple of times Sam found herself retracing her own steps.

Damn it, what street was she on now? Was it a tree, or a flower? Jasmine Way? Magnolia Avenue? Elm Drive? She felt like she'd hiked ten miles already, and she was no closer to finding Ethan and Valerie Herrick's house than when she and Esther had left home— how many hours ago? Double damn it, why hadn't she taken time to buy a new watch in one of the stores they'd trekked through?

"Ready to admit you could use some help?"

Instantly recognizing the self-satisfied voice, Sam spun around to find Esther standing in the street a few feet behind her.

"How did you get here?" she said in surprise.

Then, glancing around anxiously, "Were you followed?"

"I took the Alabama Avenue bus, of course. And nobody followed me."

"Are you sure?"

"I'm sure. Oh, there was a heavyset man in a government car parked across the street when I got home. He waited around about half an hour, then drove away when you didn't show up. They probably sent him off to join the others scouring the city for you. You're lost, aren't you? I knew you would be."

"Well, you were right," Sam muttered. "Okay, I'd appreciate some help finding the house, but then you should get back on another bus and go home."

"And miss out on the excitement?" Esther said indignantly. "Not on your life."

"Esther, for heaven's sake! This isn't some glamorous adventure, like in the movies. Assuming we can find the address in this damned maze, I plan to break into a private residence that's also a crime scene. I may end up tampering with evidence. I'll be breaking at least half a dozen laws. If you come with me, and we get caught—"

"We won't," Esther interrupted. "We'll be careful. I think you're on the wrong street. This is Hyacinth Drive. We want Hibiscus Lane. Come on, I believe it's a couple of streets north of here."

She marched past Sam, obviously expecting her to follow. Sam heaved a resigned sigh and hurried to catch up. "If you get into trouble tagging along with me, Joe will murder us both."

"Me, maybe," Esther said wryly. "But you? I think not. Which reminds me—I changed Joe's bed linens and tidied his room while I was waiting for the fat man in the government car to go away. I found a couple of articles that looked like they might belong to you, so I put them in your room."

Sam bit her lip and didn't say a word. *A couple of articles.* Specifically, a white cotton sock and her slip. Thank God she'd found the dress and panties Esther had lent her before she left Joe's room.

Esther had been right about the street, and she located the house with no trouble. It was a two-story brick Tudor, set well back from Hibiscus Lane behind several big old trees and surrounded by a forest of evergreen shrubbery. The landscaping provided a substantial privacy screen. It would also provide cover for anyone who wanted to sneak up to the house without being seen.

"It doesn't look as if there's anyone around," Esther remarked.

"No," Sam agreed. "The police probably collected their evidence and closed the place up."

"Then why don't we just walk up to the front door and ring the bell?"

Sam considered the suggestion. "Good idea. If somebody answers the door, we'll say we're trying to find our cousin Agnes's house."

"On Hyacinth Drive," Esther added with a wicked grin.

They exchanged an encouraging look and started up the long, narrow drive of crushed stone, walking side by side and with matching purposeful strides. When they reached the small brick stoop, they discovered a sheet of paper tacked to the door that said unauthorized entry was prohibited by the order of the Washington, D.C. Police Department and the Department of the Army. Two officials had scrawled their names at the bottom of the document. Sam took a deep breath and pushed the button for the doorbell before intimidation could set in.

A faint, shrill *brinnggg* sounded inside the house, but no one came to open the door.

"Ring again," Esther whispered. "Just to be safe." Sam pressed the little black button a second time. Another *brinnggg*, but still no sign of life. "Okay," she muttered. "Here goes nothing."

She grasped the doorknob and tried to turn it. It rattled a little but otherwise refused to budge.

"Darn, it's locked," Esther said.

"Of course it's locked. Did you think the cops would stick that sign on the door and then leave the house unlocked? We'll have to break in."

Sam glanced at Esther to assess her reaction. Apparently the prospect of committing both forcible entry and trespass didn't faze her. She backed away from the stoop to study the windows at the front of the house, then bent over and started inspecting the grass and flowerbeds next to the stoop.

"What are you looking for?" Sam asked.

"A brick, or a big rock."

"Jesus, Esther, we can't go pitching bricks through the windows! Especially not on the side of the house that faces the street."

"You're right," Esther said with a nod. "Let's go around to the back."

Fortunately they found a set of French doors at the rear of the house. Sam knew that French doors— at least the old-fashioned, low-tech kind— were a snap to break open. Esther produced the silver dollar she requested, then watched in fascination as she used the coin and carefully applied leverage to pop the latch.

"That's amazing! Where did you learn to do that?"

"Actually, a cop taught me," Sam said, laughing at her expression. "Burglars love these doors. A five-year-old with a screwdriver can get past 'em. But since neither of us thought to bring a screwdriver, I'm glad you had that silver dollar. They're scarce as hen's teeth in 1995."

"What, silver dollars?" Esther said in surprise.

Sam nodded as she brushed the sheer curtains aside and stepped across the doorsill. "I'm not even sure the government still mints them." She stopped and wrinkled her nose. "Phew. Something tells me this is where the colonel met his untimely end."

Esther crowded against her back. "Really?"

"Either that or somebody butchered a steer in here."

"Blood?" Esther's voice sharpened with excitement. She stood on tiptoe, craning her neck to look over Sam's shoulder. "Where?"

"Pretty much everywhere," Sam murmured as she gingerly moved into the room and took a look around.

It was true. She didn't remember ever seeing so much blood from a single gunshot wound. It had showered the sofa sitting at a right angle to the French doors and an end table and Victorian lamp at the far end of the sofa, splattered on the dark-paneled wall beyond the table, pooled on the wool rug in front of the sofa.

"Must've severed an artery," she observed as she skirted the still-tacky stains on the rug to go switch on the table lamp. "Or else it was a direct hit to the heart. Turn on the desk lamp, but don't touch anything else."

Esther tiptoed past the French doors and along the wall to the big old roll-top desk in the corner.

When she switched on the banker's lamp, the quantity of blood Ethan Herrick had lost became even more obvious.

"My God," Esther whispered.

Sam gave her a sharp look. "If you think you're going to faint, go back outside and take a few deep breaths."

Esther shook her head firmly. "I'm not going to faint."

"Don't throw up, either."

"I won't. What are we looking for, exactly?"

"Evidence," Sam muttered. She stood in front of the sofa and rotated slowly to study the room. "Things the police detectives may have missed, either accidentally or deliberately."

"Deliberately!"

"Yeah. One thing I can tell you right now is that Ethan Herrick's daughter didn't kill him, and neither did his houseboy."

"How can you possibly know that? We've been here less than five minutes."

"Look around," Sam said. "How many ways are there to get into this room?"

Esther looked. It took her less than five seconds to come up with the answer. "Two. The French doors, and that door in the far wall."

"Right. And where do you think the interior door leads?"

"To a hall, probably. Or maybe to a parlor, or the dining room."

"Some other area of the *house*. But the killer came in the same way we did. See how the blood fell after the colonel was shot? It sprayed over the sofa, the end table and the lamp." Sam gestured without touching anything. "And those big splotches on the wall are from the exit wound. The bullet probably ripped out a fist-sized hole when it left the body."

"This is what you do for a living?" Esther said with a grimace. "Pointing out things like that to the police?"

"And to private investigators, and prosecuting attorneys, and defense attorneys," Sam confirmed absently. "It looks like he was moving toward the interior door when he was shot, maybe going for help."

"Or just trying to get away from whoever was pointing the gun at him," Esther muttered.

"His own gun," Sam observed. "According to Joe, Colonel Herrick was shot with his Army side-arm." She turned to the roll-top desk. "And I bet that's where he kept it."

She walked around the sofa and went to the desk. "Let's hope it isn't locked. Do you have a pencil or pen?"

"Why?" Esther said as she opened her purse to look. "Surely the police took the gun. Yes, I have a pencil."

Sam accepted the pencil and slipped it inside the handle of the desk's wide center drawer, then tugged hard. Too hard. If she'd been standing a few inches back, the drawer would have come all the way out and dumped its contents on the rug. Instead, it banged into her hip.

"Ow! Damn."

Esther hurried to catch the drawer before Sam could remind her not to touch it, but at least she grabbed hold at the bottom, so that the pads of her fingers were on the rough underside. Sam used the pencil to poke around, but the drawer contained only a few receipts, a checkbook, some pencils and a handful of banker's clips.

"There's something taped to the bottom," Esther said. "It feels like an envelope."

Sam got down on her hands and knees and crawled under Esther's arm to look. "Yep, it's an envelope. Hold the drawer while I pull it loose."

"Oh . . . are you sure you should?"

"Let's not get started on 'should' or 'shouldn't.' This qualifies as tampering with evidence. Could mean a count of obstructing justice, too, depending on what I do with the envelope after I have a look at it. Okay, got it. You can close the drawer."

Sam sat on the floor to examine the long, cream-colored vellum envelope, while Esther perched on the edge of Ethan Herrick's desk chair, leaning forward, her expression a mixture of curiosity and apprehension. There was an embossed "H" on the envelope's flap.

Sam remarked, "Looks like some of his personal stationery."

"Good. Maybe whatever's inside doesn't have anything to do with his murder."

"Maybe not, but it was important enough for him to hide from anybody who decided to snoop around in his desk."

"Aren't you going to open it?"

"Not yet," Sam said. She stood up, tucked the loose ends of tape around the envelope, and slipped it into her coat pocket. "I'll wait till we get home. Let's check the rest of the desk."

"You're going to take it with you?" Esther said in alarm.

"Well, I'm sure not going to leave it here." Unfortunately, all the other drawers and the roll-top cover were locked tight. "Think about it, Esther. There were at least a half dozen police officers in this house the night Ethan Herrick was killed, and probably about that many the next day. Maybe they didn't find the envelope because it wasn't here. Somebody may have hidden it *after* Herrick was murdered. On the other hand, if it was here all along, either the Washington cops are incredibly incompetent or for some reason they didn't conduct a thorough search of the murder scene."

"You keep implying that the police deliberately bungled the investigation. Do you have some reason to think that?"

"Nothing concrete," Sam admitted. "Just a bunch of little things. Look at this room—they should have rolled up the rug and taken it, but they didn't. In fact, except for some knife marks on the paneling where somebody dug out the bullet, it doesn't look like they collected any evidence at all. Not even blood samples."

"But why would they need to? It's obviously Colonel Herrick's blood all over the place, you said so yourself. And he was the only corpse in the room, after all."

Sam cocked her head to one side. "Yes, but was he the only person who *lost blood* in this room? What if he fought with whoever killed him, managed to inflict an injury or two before he died?"

"Well, he must not have," Esther said reasonably. "Except for the blood, the room is perfectly in order. It certainly doesn't look as if there was any kind of struggle." Her forehead suddenly puckered in a frown. "But come to think of it, that's odd, isn't it? You'd think— "

"You'd think that since Ethan Herrick was a career military officer, he'd at least have put up a fight," Sam finished.

"Unless it was his daughter holding the gun. If it *was* Valerie, he might have thought she didn't really intend to shoot him, or maybe that she did intend to but wouldn't be able to actually pull the trigger."

"In which case he probably would've tried to take the gun away from her," Sam pointed out. "But I don't think it was Valerie. The two of them had gone out for dinner, during which they had an argument." She saw no point in mentioning what— or more to the point, who— they'd argued about.

"Evidently they came home together. Valerie was probably in her room, crying or sulking or something, or maybe in the kitchen fixing herself a cup of cocoa. Why would she leave the house and walk around to the backyard, just to come back inside this way?"

Esther glanced at the open French doors. "How can you be sure the murderer did come in this way?"

"I can't be," Sam acknowledged. "Not a hundred percent. But there's no blood on the rug between the sofa and the French doors, and none on the curtains. Ethan Herrick was shot while he was moving toward the interior door, *away* from the French doors." She walked to the end of the sofa, studied the blood splatter patterns, took a step backward.

"The murderer was standing right about here." She extended her arm, aiming an imaginary gun, took another step back and to the left. "No, about here."

She was just inside the French doors, about two feet to the left of center and roughly six feet from the rear corner of the sofa. She sighted down her index finger and verified that the bloodstains on the sofa began at the spot where a line drawn from the end of her finger to the door across the room would intersect the front of the seat cushions.

"Amazing," Esther murmured.

"It's just a necessary job skill, like typing or taking shorthand," Sam dismissed. "Okay, the colonel's sidearm was a Colt .45, so the spent casing would have ejected to the right." On impulse, she knelt and began eyeballing the edge of the rug and the narrow strip of bare wood near the French doors.

"What are you looking for now?" Esther asked "You said the police dug the bullet out of the wall."

"They did, but the shell casing would've been ejected from the gun when it was fired. If they didn't take this place apart till they found it, they were even sloppier than I— Bingo!"

She stood up, triumphantly holding the empty casing out for Esther to see.

"It looks like somebody stomped on it."

"Yeah." Sam shook her head in disgust. "Some klutz in a police uniform, most likely. Can you imagine putting your foot down on this and not checking to see what it was?"

"No, but I *can* imagine five hungry boarders and one irritable FBI agent who'll be wondering why their dinner isn't on the table if we don't start for home."

"So can I," Sam muttered, dropping the bent shell casing into her pocket along with the envelope.

The prospect of facing Esther's hungry boarders didn't bother her, but the FBI agent was another matter. She suspected that Joe was going to be more than merely "irritable" when he got home— assuming he wasn't there already, working himself into a foul mood while he waited for the two of them. Boggs and Ragsdale had probably held him responsible for her disappearance, never mind that he wasn't one of the agents assigned to follow her.

Sam was jiggling the handle on the outside of the French doors, making sure the latch was securely seated, when she felt Esther tugging on the sleeve of her coat.

"What?"

"There's a man watching us," Esther said in a frightened whisper. "He's hiding behind the big maple tree. I think he's Japanese."

Sam bit her lip, thinking furiously. "How far away?"

"Ten or fifteen yards, at least. Should we run for the street, or just pretend we don't know he's there?"

"Neither. And relax, he's probably more afraid of you than you are of him. Give me that pencil I used to open the desk drawer, and something to write a message on."

Esther looked at her as if she was convinced Sam had taken leave of her senses, but she fished the pencil and an old grocery list from her purse and handed them over.

"What's your phone number?" Sam asked as she held the paper against the doorframe and printed a quick note.

"What! You're not going to give some strange Japanese man my phone number!"

"He's probably Colonel Herrick's missing houseboy," Sam hissed impatiently. "I need to talk to him, but if I head toward that tree, I guarantee he'll take off. C'mon, Esther, I really don't want to chase him through a bunch of hedges and lily ponds. Besides, I left my running shoes in 1995."

Esther's lips pinched into a thin line, but she reluctantly recited the number. Sam added it at the bottom of the note, then turned toward the maple tree and waved the paper, displaying it for whoever had been hiding and watching.

"Okay," she said, as she stooped to lay the note on the ground in front of the French doors. "Let's go. Don't hurry, just stroll back around to the street."

Esther fell in beside her, but kept glancing back until Sam grabbed her arm and gave her a yank.

"Stop that! You'll scare him."

"Good!" Esther snapped. "Maybe he'll stay behind the tree till we're a safe distance away."

She was still grumbling about Sam's having given her phone number to a potential Japanese agent when they got off the bus several blocks from her house. She abruptly stopped fussing, though, when they turned the corner and saw the big black Oldsmobile sedan parked in front of the house.

Fifteen

Lucas was utterly confounded. He was also starting to be seriously worried. Apparently not only had Grace never experienced television or Indiana Jones, she hadn't even been aware of their existence.

It didn't seem possible to him that a woman could make it to her early twenties without having spent *some* time in front of the tube. Even if her family hadn't owned a set, or she'd grown up in some remote orphanage run by aesthetic types who considered television poison to the mind and soul, she had to have at least been exposed to it.

Yet after watching her interact with the old man and the TV set in the lounge, he was convinced that she *hadn't* been. Ever.

Where was she from, anyway?

The first time the question crossed his mind, it was one of those random, extemporaneous thoughts that don't hang around long enough to demand acknowledgment or examination. But then it returned, lingered, taunting him until he could neither ignore nor dismiss it.

Where *was* she from?

She spoke American English, but her vocabulary and speech patterns weren't quite right. She sounded like . . . like someone older, Lucas realized when he took the time to be analytical. Like his mother, come to think of it.

From that point on he was hooked, a puzzle junkie in possession of a few loose pieces but no idea what the completed picture was supposed to be. Discovering the answer to *Where was she from?* quickly became an obsession. Somehow he knew that if he could put the puzzle pieces together in the right order, the answer to that question would also tell him what had happened to Samantha.

He managed to pry Grace away from the television when the soaps started and the old man dozed off, and took her to the solarium. At some point during the morning it had started to snow. So far the lawn and shrubbery bore only a light, powdery dusting, but if it kept up the roads would soon be slick and hazardous. Not that Lucas planned to drive anywhere.

Cassie and Vernon Marshall had the terrorist story well underway. They'd started snipping and splicing tape from the station's archives to put together a video that would run while one of the news anchors provided the voice-over. The pièce de résistance would be a series of tight, digitally sharpened head shots of the four terrorists as the anchor identified Nicolai and Rashad and reported the information "an anonymous source" had supplied about them.

Lucas suspected all hell would break loose when the story was broadcast. Vernon thought so, too. In fact, he'd advised Lucas to stay away from the station and preferably out of Silver Spring for the next couple of days. Lucas hadn't argued.

He settled Grace on a loveseat in the solarium, facing the wide sweep of lawn at the rear of the building and a grove of trees beyond, and went to get them each a cup of coffee from the lounge. When he came back she was nestled into a corner of the loveseat, her legs tucked up beside her, watching the snow fall.

"How long do I have to stay here?" she asked, surprising him. "Does someone have to claim me, or can I leave whenever I want?"

Lucas sank down on the other end of the loveseat and sipped at his coffee. He knew it was an unforgivably selfish reaction, but all he could think was that if she left the nursing home— disappeared— he'd lose whatever chance he might still have to find Sam.

"I guess you could leave, if you had somewhere to go," he said carefully. "But until your memory starts to come back, it would probably be best— "

"Couldn't I stay with you?"

He gave a startled jerk. Coffee sloshed onto his thigh. "What?"

Grace swapped her coffee for a handful of tissues from a box at her elbow and leaned over to blot at the stain. But then, as if she suddenly realized what she was doing, she dropped the tissues, blushed and ducked her head.

"I meant temporarily. Just until I can remember where I belong."

"Oh, Jesus," Lucas muttered. He picked up the damp tissues and took a couple of swipes at the leg of his trousers. Levander Grisham's warnings and his own code of ethics waged a furious battle with his self-serving interests.

"Listen, I'd be happy to sign you out of here, but I don't have anyplace safe to take you. For the time being I can't even go back to my own apartment. I'd probably be arrested before I could get my key in the lock."

"Why?" she asked, her self-consciousness forgotten. "Are you some kind of criminal?"

Lucas sighed and lobbed the soggy tissues into a wastebasket on the other side of the solarium. "There are plenty of people who'd argue the point, but no, I'm not a criminal. I'm the news director of a television station in Silver Spring. During the past few days I've authorized the broadcast of a couple of stories the government would have preferred to keep under wraps. As a result, a bunch of folks at the FBI and NSA would like to 'interview' me. I imagine there are some military types who'd like a shot at me, too."

"Military types." Grace repeated the words slowly, thoughtfully. "Do you mean . . . Army Intelligence?"

"Especially Army Intelligence," Lucas confirmed. "They probably have somebody watching my place right now." He belatedly noticed her pensive expression. "What is it?"

"I'm not sure." She gave an impatient little shake of her head. "As soon as you said 'military,' I felt . . . I don't know . . . *something*. And then the words 'Army Intelligence' just leaped into my mind. I have a feeling that term holds some special meaning, but if it does I have no idea what the meaning is."

"Maybe you know somebody in Army Intelligence," Lucas said. God, he hoped not. His life was a big enough mess already. "Your father, or a brother?"

She tilted her head to one side, considering. "I don't have any brothers. Or sisters." She sat up straight, an excited laugh bubbling out of her. "I'm an only child. I *remember* that! How wonderful! Or maybe not—I suppose I could be an orphan, too, but somehow I don't think I am."

"Considering the way my luck's been running, it's probably your father who's with Army Intelligence," Lucas said with a wry grin. But then another thought occurred, and the grin faded. "Or maybe a boyfriend."

Grace also sobered as she returned his gaze. Her burns were healing rapidly; the only signs of the ordeal she'd been through were a few shiny pink spots on her forehead and arms. Strangely enough, her missing eyelashes emphasized her clear blue eyes, made them more startlingly lovely. Lucas knew he shouldn't ask, but he couldn't help himself.

"Is there a boyfriend, Grace?"

"I think there was," she said, so softly that he had to lean forward to hear. "But . . . something happened. I don't remember what, or why . . . but somehow I know he's no longer a part of my life."

Lucas felt his heart thudding against his ribs. "And how do you feel about that? Does knowing make you sad, or depressed?" He held his breath until she shook her head no.

"I remember—there was an argument, a rather nasty one." She tilted her head again, as if she were trying to hear a faint, faraway voice, then released a resigned sigh. "I can't remember what it was about. But no, I don't feel sad. Maybe that means I didn't really care for him."

Lucas found himself hoping that was exactly what it meant. God, what was happening to him? He'd come here to meet her, talk to her, out of a desperate hope that she could provide some clue about what had happened to Sam. When had his focus started to shift? When had a pair of gentle, trusting blue eyes replaced the image of astute green ones that fired sparks of anger and passion?

There were two men in the Oldsmobile. Sam was immensely relieved that they didn't get out when she and Esther passed the car on the way into the house. Her relief was short-lived, though. Joe was waiting in the foyer. Evidently he'd been home for a while. He'd removed his suit coat and tie and draped them over the newel post, and Sam caught a whiff of Scotch as she brushed past him.

"Don't start," she said, as she shed her coat. "We're both beat, and we have to get dinner on the table."

Joe collected his suit coat and followed them down the hall to the kitchen. "Had a busy day, did you?"

"You could say that," Esther muttered as she tied an apron around her waist. "Are those men outside going to arrest anybody? Because if they are, I hope they'll wait until I've fed my boarders."

Sam went to the pantry for a bag of potatoes. When she returned, Joe had thrown his coat over the back of a chair and was setting a small dishpan and a pot for the potatoes on the table. He rolled up his sleeves and went to collect two paring knives.

"If they intended to arrest either of you, they'd be in the house by now," he replied as he dropped the knives on the table and took the chair next to Sam's.

She grabbed a knife and a potato and started peeling, glad for something to keep her hands busy, so she wouldn't give in to the almost over-whelming urge to reach out and touch his arm. Hard to believe that less than twenty-four hours ago he'd been smashing her foot under the table to silence her when she started telling Owen and Chet about the Navy's fateful decision not to hold maneuvers in the Pacific this year. What a difference a day makes, she thought in amazement. Yesterday they'd been polite— well, most of the time, anyway— adversaries. Today they were lovers, and just being in the same room with him was making her hot and bothered.

She dropped the peeled potato into the cooking pot and took another from the bag. "If they aren't going to arrest anybody, why are they here?"

"To make sure you don't embarrass the Bureau again, I imagine."

Joe glanced at her as he said it. The instant their eyes met, the droll amusement in his vanished, replaced by the same excruciating sexual awareness that had Sam almost squirming in her chair. He shot a quick, surreptitious look at his sister. Fortunately she was turned away, vigorously pounding a slab of meat with a wooden mallet. Sam concentrated on the potato she was peeling— or, more accurately, on not slicing off a finger.

"Did Ragsdale and Boggs give you trouble because I ditched the watchdogs?"

Joe released a pent-up breath and reached for a potato and the other paring knife. "No. The agents who were supposed to keep you under surveillance have been reassigned, though. The men in the car outside have taken their place. I should warn you, they'll be a lot harder to lose."

She frowned in disappointment. "Damn. I

wanted to take another look at the Herricks' house."

"So that's where you went," he murmured. He didn't sound terribly surprised. He peeled his potato in about fifteen seconds and dropped it into the pot, then reached for his coat and withdrew a folded paper from the inside pocket.

"This is all I managed to copy this morning, before the investigative team arrived. It's mostly the names of people they've interviewed or plan to interview— Valerie's friends, Colonel Herrick's subordinates, a few neighbors. There wasn't time to summarize the interview reports, but I read the ones that looked most promising."

Sam smiled with pleasure and repeated what Esther had said the night before. "And you have an excellent memory."

His gaze focused on her smiling mouth. "Which is sometimes more a curse than a blessing."

Her right hand jerked and a chunk of potato flew onto the table. Joe picked it up and put it in the dishpan along with the peelings. She noticed that his hand wasn't altogether steady, either.

"There's one other thing," he said a little too casually. "It seems Colonel Herrick wasn't killed with his own sidearm, after all. A sergeant in Army ordnance notified his superior, who in turn reported to the D.C. police, that the Colonel turned in his Colt almost two weeks ago. It needed the safety mechanism repaired and a new firing pin. They'd just used the last spare firing pin and had to order a shipment from the company. The shipment still hasn't arrived. The gun has been sitting in a box at Fort McNair since the sergeant picked it up at the Colonel's office."

Sam glanced up and encountered Esther's astonished gaze.

"That covers my news," Joe said, fishing another potato out of the bag. "What about the two of you— did you find anything interesting today, or was your visit to the Herrick house a complete waste of time?"

Sam could tell from his tone that he assumed it had been a waste of time. She glanced at Esther again. About to place several breaded veal cutlets into a sizzling iron skillet, she made a face at her brother's back and mouthed, "Smart ass."

"As a matter of fact, we did stumble across a couple of interesting items," Sam replied. She laid the paring knife on the table and stood up. "I'll get them."

When she returned to the kitchen Joe leveled a stern frown at her. "You removed evidence from a crime scene?"

"Would I do that? These things *can't* be evidence, because the police didn't bother to collect them."

She placed the shell casing on the table in front of him and sat down again.

"You did say the bullet they recovered from the wall was a .45, didn't you?"

"According to the ballistics report," Joe murmured. He was studying the end of the casing. "This is the spent casing from a .45 shell."

"Give the man a cigar. It would appear there are *two* Colt .45 semiautomatic pistols. That shell casing is from the one Valerie was holding when the houseboy rushed in and found her kneeling beside her father's body."

"Where did you find it?"

"Exactly where I expected to find it, once I'd

placed the shooter's position. The question is, why didn't the cops find it first?"

Joe shook his head. "Surely you know how chaotic the scene of a murder can be in the first hour or so after the police are called. The first people in the house were probably uniformed officers."

"Who didn't know squat about preserving evidence," Sam said in disgust. "By the time the medical examiner arrived, there were probably a half dozen people milling around, leaving their fingerprints all over the place, destroying trace evidence. . . . I want a look at the body."

He reared back as if she'd waved a rattlesnake under his nose. "You must be joking."

"I'm not. I need to see the wound. And the clothes Ethan Herrick was wearing."

Joe shook his head adamantly and started peeling another potato. "You know that's impossible."

"Have they already buried him?"

"No."

"Then it isn't impossible."

"I said *no*, damn it! Absolutely not!" He threw the potato into the pot. "What's in the envelope?"

Sam realized she was still holding it. "I don't know." She picked up the paring knife and used it as a letter opener. "It was taped to the bottom of a desk drawer in Ethan Herrick's study."

"What! Jesus Christ!"

"Joe!" Esther said in a fierce whisper. "I think I just heard Owen and Martha come in."

He gave Sam a tight-lipped glare and got up to check. When he returned a minute later, he nodded grimly and started cutting up the peeled potatoes. The way he wielded the paring knife made Sam suspect he longed for something animate to use it on.

"Well?" he said curtly. "You risked going back to jail to take the damned envelope, aren't you going to see what's inside it?"

His palpable anger made Sam decide to abandon the idea of examining Ethan Herrick's body. She slipped a single, folded sheet of heavy cream vellum out of the envelope. The paper contained several lines of precise, closely spaced writing. Printing, actually.

"What is it, a letter?" Joe asked.

"No. It's a short note, written like a report. It isn't addressed to anyone, and there's no signature." She shook her head in bewilderment. "This doesn't make sense. It looks like a sheet of Ethan Herrick's personal stationery." She held up the note and the envelope, side by side.

"See, they both have the same embossed capital H. The note says that someone called Falconer—sounds like a code name— repeated to Colonel Herrick on the night of December fourth that the plans for Operation Sea Lion are almost complete, and that Hitler will take advantage of England's preoccupation with the submarine attacks in the Atlantic and the Russian front to launch an invasion before spring. The last sentence says that Falconer was most insistent that this information should be forwarded to Colonel Herrick's superiors immediately. The word immediately is underlined."

Esther had abandoned her cutlets, drawn to the table by the mysterious note. "Dear God! Hitler's going to invade England?"

"No," Sam said, looking first at Esther, then Joe. "He isn't. That's why this doesn't make any sense. Hitler knew— *knows*— that Germany would have to establish air supremacy over the English Channel before he could stage an invasion. But the Luftwaffe will never take control of the skies from the RAF." She gave the paper an angry shake.

"This is a classic example of the disinformation campaign that damned Nazi used to keep the Allies off balance."

"Which means this Falconer must be a German agent," Joe surmised.

"Who's been feeding false intelligence information to Colonel Herrick and God knows who else," Sam added.

Esther reached between them to pick up the pot of potatoes. "But who wrote the note?"

Sam glanced up at her, and knew from Esther's expression that the same thought had occurred to both of them.

"Do you think— ?" Esther began.

"No question— the houseboy. Had to be. That's why he was watching the house, to see if anybody would find it."

"Hold it," Joe interjected. "You *saw* the colonel's houseboy?"

"Well, I'm pretty sure it was him," Sam said. She explained what had happened as they were leaving the house.

"And you gave him our phone number?"

"How else was I supposed to let him know I wanted to talk to him?" she said reasonably. "I couldn't give him the address, not with the FBI watching the house twenty-four hours a day."

"Oh, dear, I just remembered," Esther murmured. Sam and Joe both turned to her with worried, questioning looks. "What are we going to have for desert?"

Sam stood up. "I'll throw the leftover biscuits from breakfast in with that stale bread you were saving for stuffing, and whip up a pan of bread pudding. We have plenty of eggs, don't we?"

Esther nodded and carried the potatoes to the sink. "Mountains. The egg man came on Tuesday, and he always looks so raggedy I end up buying twice as many as I need. I suspect he has a closet full of nice suits and only wears those old rags to take advantage of soft-hearted women like me. Use plenty of cinnamon. Alvie and Chet both love cinnamon."

Sam and Joe exchanged fondly amused smiles. When she turned from the table to start assembling utensils and ingredients, he caught her hand.

"Can you really make bread pudding, or should I lay in a fresh supply of bicarb?"

His tone and expression were dead serious, but even if the twinkle in his eye hadn't given him away Sam wouldn't have been able to take offense. Not with his palm pressing warmly against hers.

"My bread pudding will make you think you've died and gone to heaven," she promised, and had the pleasure of seeing the twinkle become a spark of desire.

He lifted her hand and kissed the knuckles. "God help me," he murmured against her skin. "She cooks, too."

The conversation around the dinner table was mostly about Germany's declaration of war against England and the United States. Chet reported that in Hitler's address to the Reichstag, the Fuhrer had called President Roosevelt both insane and a gangster, and that Mussolini had informed 150,000 Romans gathered in the Piazza Venezia that Italy was also at war with the U.S.

Not to be outdone, Alvie announced that tomorrow's edition of the newspaper he worked for would carry the English translation of the Axis pact between Germany, Italy and Japan. This pact, Alvie claimed, not only committed the three countries to a joint war against the United States and Britain, but also prohibited any of them from making a separate peace.

"Looks like we're in it for the long haul," Owen Nordstrom remarked. The others nodded and murmured agreement, but the mood was one of determined resolve rather than apprehension or dread.

"By the way, Samantha," Alvie said halfway through the meal. "I meant to tell you, that copy you typed was a big hit with my boss. He trimmed a couple of sentences and handed everything right over to the typesetter."

Sam gave him a tepid smile. "I'm glad it worked out for you, Alvie." Before everyone sat down to dinner, he'd slipped her two dollars, for the twenty pages she'd typed. She hoped that wasn't going to represent a typical day's notes. Typing on the old Royal was like breaking rocks with a sledgehammer, compared to the computer keyboards she was accustomed to.

The conversation turned to a discussion of the America First Committee's announcement that the organization had been officially dissolved.

"I guess even Lucky Lindy couldn't keep insisting we should stay out of the war after the Japs attacked us," Gertrude Willis remarked.

"Wouldn't it be something if he was drafted," Chet said with a grin. "Now that the Selective Service Act is official, they'll be conscripting experienced fliers."

"He's too old," Alvie scoffed. "He'll have to register like the rest of us, but they won't draft anybody over forty."

"You're probably right, but wouldn't it be ironic if he and those other mucky-mucks disbanded their group, then the government up and drafted him? After he argued so loud and long for keeping America out of the war, I mean."

Esther had been unusually quiet during the meal. When she finally ended her silence, it was to insert a matter-of-fact question that almost caused Sam to choke on a mouthful of Wiener schnitzel.

"Has anyone heard anything new about that army colonel who was murdered last weekend?"

Sam felt Joe, who was sitting at her right, stiffen in surprise. Or maybe it was horror.

"All I know is they arrested his daughter," Gert said as she helped herself to more potatoes. "What kind of world is it, when children murder their own parents?"

"According to my sources, there's some doubt she did it," Chet remarked.

"And what sources would those be, Chet?" Alvie asked. "The beat cops you buy an occasional beer for at Sweeney's?"

Chet's face turned an unattractive shade of red. "As a matter of fact, Alvie, I got the tip from one of my contacts at the War Department."

"That would be a major scoop," Alvie admitted. "If it's true. I assume you couldn't get it confirmed, since I haven't seen the story in that rag you write for."

Chet looked uncomfortable. As if, Sam thought, he was regretting that he'd mentioned the tip in the first place. He slid a concerned glance at Esther before he answered.

"My source spoke off the record, and since she was repeating something she'd overheard, it was secondhand information. Of course I tried to follow up, but everybody I contacted gave me the cold shoulder. Which makes me think there's probably something to it."

Sam resisted the impulse to look at Joe, but the tension radiating from him made her suspect this was news to him.

"So your source is a 'she,' huh, Chet?" Alvie said.

"A lot of my sources are women," Chet replied defensively. "So are yours, I expect. Working women— secretaries, file clerks, switchboard operators— are often in a position to hear and see all kinds of things that can lead you to an important story. And they're usually more observant, too. They notice things men overlook."

"Amen," Sam murmured. Joe bumped his knee against hers to let her know he'd heard, but didn't withdraw his leg once he'd made the point.

"Did your source say why they think the daughter may not be the murderer, Chet?" Martha asked. "One of the lawyers I work for said she was found kneeling beside her father with the gun in her hand. That sounds pretty incriminating, to me."

Chet shook his head and grimaced. "Unfortunately, all she knows is just what I said— that some of the big shots have doubts it was the daughter. Personally, though, I think they may suspect a foreign agent. The colonel was assigned to Army Intelligence, you know."

"He was?" Owen said in surprise. "I don't remember reading that in the newspapers.

"You wouldn't," Alvie said. "Because it wasn't published. Now that we're in the war, the government's handed down some pretty strict rules about what we can print and the radio news departments can broadcast—and what we can't, which is anything that might be a threat to national security. So far everybody's playing ball, but I don't know how long that'll last since it means we're only reporting half the story if it has anything to do with defense or the military. It's true, though. Colonel Herrick was with Army Intelligence."

"I wouldn't be surprised if he was receiving information from several of our agents in Europe," Chet said.

Alvie nodded, then sent a wry smile across the table at Joe. "I guess even if you knew something about the murder, you couldn't say so. Right, Joe?"

"That's right," Joe said tersely, then relented enough to add, "But if it's any consolation, the two of you seem to know more about that investigation than I do."

The disclaimer seemed to satisfy both Alvie and Chet, and the conversation moved on to other topics. By now Joe's habit of helping his sister and Samantha clean up after dinner had become established. No one remarked about the fact that he remained in the dining room when everyone else headed for the parlor, though Martha and Gert did exchange a knowing look as they left. Joe noticed; he also noticed that Esther noticed.

"What was that look about?" he asked her as they carried serving dishes into the kitchen.

"It's just a guess, but I think it was about the whisker burns on Sam's face this morning," Esther replied.

Sam was at the table, scraping plates. She pretended she hadn't heard the exchange, telling herself there were much more important things to worry about than whether Esther's boarders knew about her and Joe.

"I've been thinking about what Chet said, and how it might relate to Falconer," she said, as Joe set a stack of plates on the table.

He nodded. "You mean was Falconer a German agent feeding Colonel Herrick false information, or is he in fact one of ours?"

"One of ours?" Esther repeated in surprise.

"If somebody in the War Department suspected Ethan Herrick was working for the Germans, they may have been using Falconer to test him," Sam explained.

"Or trap him," Joe added. He shook his head with a frown. "I can't believe Colonel Herrick was a German agent, though."

"Maybe he wasn't. Maybe our original assumption was right and Falconer is the agent."

"And Colonel Herrick found out and was about to expose him," Joe murmured thoughtfully. "In which case Falconer is probably our murderer. The problem is, we have no idea who Falconer is or where to start looking for him."

"Maybe we do," Sam said. "That list of names you brought home— people the special investigative team is interviewing. They all had some connection to Ethan Herrick, didn't they?"

"Or to Valerie." He nodded and a rare smile lightened his brooding expression. "It's a good starting point, at least."

Esther came to the table and handed each of them an apron. "The two of you can stay up all night pouring over that list if you want to, but first we've got a stack of dirty dishes to wash."

Sixteen

Grace's memory was returning, but it was an agonizingly slow process. So far she hadn't regained any whole, uninterrupted chunks, only fragments that often revealed themselves as insubstantial impressions or insights before crystallizing into actual memories of people and events.

She and Lucas spent one more night at the Eldercare home before he thought of moving them to Samantha's apartment. He was annoyed that it hadn't occurred to him sooner. Sam lived in Rockville, a safe distance from the station and his own place. And even if one or more of the petty bureaucrats who wanted to talk to him knew about Sam, by now they would have sent someone to check her apartment and discovered that nobody had been there for days.

He suspected Grace would be much more comfortable and relaxed away from the nursing home, and Sam's place also boasted another attraction, in addition to safety, privacy and comfort— her top-of-the-line computer setup. Maybe he could use the computer to search the dozen or so databases she had access to, for information about both Sam's whereabouts and Grace's identity.

Assuming, of course, that he could smuggle Grace past Levander Grisham, get them both to

Rockville in one piece, and then figure out Sam's access codes and passwords.

The first task was accomplished easily enough when Levander finally went home to catch some sleep. The drive to Rockville provided a couple of hairy moments, but Lucas drove the Capri up on the sidewalk to evade one group of threatening young punks and aimed the little car straight at a second group, who evidently weren't as tough as they looked because they scattered like stray cats fleeing a garden hose.

The encounters frightened Grace badly, which troubled him, but he didn't dare stop the car to comfort her. Besides, what would he say? He couldn't tell her not to be afraid; any sane person would be scared out of her wits. If either gang had managed to waylay them, the creeps probably would've taken the car, raped her, and shot them both.

She huddled in the passenger's seat and didn't speak for the rest of the trip. The possibility occurred to Lucas that the two close calls, combined with the ruined urban landscape they were passing through, might send her into some kind of traumatic shock. God knew what she'd already endured, but whatever it was had been bad enough to short-circuit her memory. Damn, it had been reckless and stupid of him to take her out of the nursing home. At least there she'd been safe, insulated from the grim reality waiting outside. What if she couldn't deal with that reality? What if her mind shut down completely?

By the time they reached Sam's apartment complex, he felt tied in knots. He'd been gripping the steering wheel so hard that it took several seconds to straighten his cramped fingers.

"Well, we made it." He turned toward her as he spoke, half afraid she'd be curled into a fetal ball. Relief washed through him when he saw that she was studying the buildings' pseudo-Georgian architecture.

"This is where your friend lives?"

"This is it. Come on, let's get inside. I don't know about you, but I could use a stiff drink."

Before they left the nursing home Lucas had phoned Rob David, Sam's next door neighbor, to make sure the spare key to Sam's apartment would be available. He stopped at Rob's just long enough to collect the key and explain that they'd be staying next door for a few days. The slight elevation of Rob's plucked and penciled eyebrows was his only comment.

"Does he give her key to anyone who asks for it?" Grace asked as soon as they entered the apartment.

Lucas set the deadbolt and turned from the door with a wry smile. "No way. He knows me."

She gave him a long, considering look that made him wonder if he should have phrased that differently, but then she murmured, "I see. You and Samantha are more than just friends, aren't you?"

Lucas found himself hesitating, and wondering why. God knew she had a right to ask, and she deserved an honest answer. The trouble was, he wasn't sure how to describe his relationship with Sam.

"We've been seeing each other exclusively for a couple of months. Neither of us has made a serious commitment, yet, but I thought— that is, I *think* we're headed in that direction."

The slip unnerved him. He told himself he'd

only used the past tense because of his uncertainty about where she was, whether she was still alive.

"She's a very independent lady," he added, not entirely sure whether he was explaining to Grace or to himself. "She won't be pushed, or rushed."

Grace nodded firmly and said, "Good for her." The remark surprised Lucas a little. He hadn't taken her for a feminist.

"Well, make yourself at home. I'm going to check the fridge and the freezer. Sam's a terrific cook, but she's usually too busy to spend much time in the kitchen. I'll probably have to make a run to the supermarket." He paused, smiled. "And maybe we can find a store that hasn't been emptied by looters and get you some clothes. For now, though, I think the only thing of Sam's you wouldn't get lost in or trip over would be a pair of sweats."

"Sweats?" Grace repeated curiously.

"Yeah, you know— sweatshirts and pants. Not exactly high fashion, but they're comfortable and one size almost does fit all. I'll see if I can find a set."

He headed for the kitchen, leaving her to explore the apartment. When he returned to the living room some time later, carrying a navy blue sweatshirt and a pair of gray sweatpants, a shopping list tucked in his shirt pocket, she was standing at the large window that overlooked a central courtyard.

Lucas noticed that she'd turned on the television, but either there was no one left to man the equipment at the station the set was tuned to or they'd lost the network feed. The screen displayed the all-purpose "We are temporarily experiencing technical difficulties. Please stand by" text message over a stock graphic.

Ordinarily he would have turned away as soon as he registered the message, but the graphic caught and held his attention. It was a lovely watercolor landscape depicting a romantic picnic for two, laid under a Japanese cherry tree in full bloom. A golden loaf of bread protruded from an old-fashioned wicker basket, and on the picnic cloth were arranged a bouquet of lilies, an opened bottle of white wine and two stemmed glasses. Bright spring sunlight filtered through the cherry blossoms, striking pink and yellow sparks off the crystal and highlighting the silken texture of the lilies' petals.

As Lucas stood admiring the scene, he experienced a sudden overwhelming sense of loss. Would the irradiated cherry trees be replaced someday? Would grass grow beneath them? Would such an idyllic setting ever again exist in Washington?

His gaze was drawn to Grace. She stood quietly at the window, her expression pensive, a little melancholy. If he was feeling depressed and anxious, what must she be going through? She'd lost all memory of the world she belonged to and then, before she had a chance to adjust, she'd been tossed into a post-apocalyptic nightmare that must be terrifying. Anyone else would be a basket case by now, but her poise never seemed to desert her. While Lucas admired her calm self-possession, it was a little intimidating. There were times— like now— when he wanted to offer her comfort and reassurance, but her quiet strength was a barrier he couldn't quite overcome. And then of course there was his own self-imposed constraint, the result of Levander's friendly warning.

"This is all I could find," he murmured, dropping Sam's sweats onto the oyster-colored sofa.

"Everything else is in the dirty clothes. If you want to come out with me, you should probably change. What you have on doesn't look very warm."

She was wearing the plum-colored dress she'd had on when they found her in Sam's room at the hotel. The nursing home staff had cleaned and pressed the dress and polished her black high-heeled pumps. Lucas was no authority on women's fashions, but he thought the dress was a little out-dated. Still, it suited her.

"Lucas," she said without turning from the window. She spoke so softly that he started across the room to be sure he could hear her.

"Yes, Grace."

"I'm scared."

The quaver in her voice pierced him. He was beside her, wrapping her in his arms, before he had time to consider whether he should. She turned into his chest and put her arms around his waist, hugging him tight.

"This is all . . . wrong. Terribly strange and wrong."

Lucas stroked her back, sincerely wanting to ease her distress and at the same time guiltily aware of his instinctive physical response to the feel of her, the smell of her . . . the *rightness* of holding her in his arms.

"What's all wrong, Grace?"

"Everything— the people, the automobiles, even the language you use. I feel like . . . I don't know how to describe it. It's as if I went to sleep and when I woke up I was someplace else . . . someplace I don't belong."

He held her closer, an involuntary reaction to the fear that suddenly gripped him.

"No," he muttered into her hair. He had no

idea where the words came from. He didn't think about them; they just spilled out. "No, Grace. I don't know what's happened, how you came to be in that hotel room or why, but one thing I'm absolutely sure about. You do belong here."

It was true, he realized with a painful combination of guilt and exultation. He'd known it the moment she sat up in bed, back at the nursing home, and he'd looked into those clear, guileless blue eyes for the first time.

"You do belong here," he repeated. He spoke softly, but his voice was rock solid with conviction. "Right here."

In case she didn't understand his meaning, he lowered his head and kissed her. Gently, tenderly, not wanting to frighten her or exploit her vulnerability. He needn't have worried. After a second's confused surprise, her lips parted beneath his and she kissed him back. And suddenly his guilt and uncertainty were gone, eradicated by a rising tide of joy and desire.

He swept her up in his arms, cradling her against his chest, and carried her into the master bedroom. He didn't let himself think about the fact that it was Sam's bedroom until much later.

Sam and Joe had pared the list to nine suspects: two junior officers Ethan Herrick had recently caused to be demoted and reassigned for dereliction of duty; a member of the America First Committee who had publicly accused Army Intelligence of feeding the President and members of Congress false information in order to achieve the commitment of American forces to the war in Europe; four leaders of the German-

American Volks Bund, a large organization of Hitler's supporters who wore Nazi uniforms and displayed the Nazi flag at their gatherings; and, of course, Valerie Herrick and the Japanese houseboy, one Kyoshi Takamura.

They'd argued about whether to eliminate the Volks Bund group and the isolationist. Sam thought all of them were far too conspicuous to be effective spies. Joe claimed that was exactly why they might have been recruited— Hitler would assume the FBI would use the same reasoning and fail to seriously consider that they might be agents of a foreign government. To that she replied that if Adolph Hitler knew anything at all about J. Edgar Hoover, he'd never assume any such thing. Joe bristled at the implied criticism of the Director, dug in his heels, and all five names stayed on the list.

"Well at least we can scratch Valerie and Mr. Takamura," Sam said as she drew a line through each of those names.

"We can't discount him," Joe insisted. "For all we know he could be a Japanese agent who was placed in Colonel Herrick's house to collect information."

Sam cast a nervous glance at the door to the hall. Esther had gone to the parlor, promising before she left to make sure all the boarders stayed there for the next hour or so, but Sam kept expecting Alvie to burst into the kitchen with another stack of notes to be typed. She listened for several seconds; then, telling herself she was being paranoid, she reluctantly erased the pencil line she'd just drawn through Kyoshi Takamura's name. Fortunately Joe had written the names in ink.

"All right, we'll leave him on the list . . . for now. But my gut tells me he's innocent, on both counts. If he was a Japanese agent, they'd have grabbed him and gotten him out of the country right away. And if he was the murderer, he sure as hell wouldn't still be hanging around the scene of the crime, much less planting clues."

"You don't know for sure it was Mr. Takamura behind the tree," Joe pointed out.

"Who else could it have been, for pity's sake? In case you hadn't noticed, the Washington area isn't a real friendly place for people with Oriental features right now. Everybody of Asian descent is going out of their way to *not* attract attention. Besides, you said yourself that the note was probably taped to the bottom of the drawer *after* the police cleared out early Sunday morning."

"Probably," he agreed. "But only one person knows for sure."

"Mr. Takamura."

"Assuming he's the one who put it there."

Sam scowled at him. "You really enjoy arguing with me, don't you?"

His rich, throaty laugh was incredibly sexy. "As a matter of fact, I do. You argue so well—like a man."

"If that's supposed to be a compliment—"

"But there are other things I enjoy doing with you much more," he added in a suggestive murmur.

Sam tried and failed to hold onto her indignation. "Well, I should hope so."

Joe pulled the pencil from her hand, then gathered up the list of names, refolded it and slipped it into the envelope with the note about Falconer. His beautiful eyes had turned a smoky blue-gray.

"As a matter of fact, I was just thinking that we should put all this aside for tonight, go upstairs, and—"

A couple of brisk raps were the only warning Alvie Blumberg gave them before he barged through the door. He was clutching a fistful of papers, which he slapped down on the table in front of Sam.

"I was enjoying myself so much talking with Esther I almost forgot to bring you these notes, Samantha," he declared, beaming at them both. "It was awfully nice of the two of you to finish the dishes so she could relax for a bit before bed. I want you to know, I do appreciate it."

"Glad to be of service, Alvie," Joe replied. "Maybe you can return the favor sometime."

Evidently the faint sarcasm in his voice went right past Alvie. The reporter looked puzzled for a moment, then grinned and gave him a conspiratorial wink. Sam stifled a snort of laughter.

"Any time, Joe. Any time at all." Alvie stretched and yawned. "Think I'd better call it a night. I'll have to be on my toes tomorrow. Got a couple of big stories in the hopper, including one that'll blow the lid off this town. It's a follow-up to one of the 'unconfirmed rumor' pieces you typed up for me last night, Samantha."

"Oh?" Sam said. She'd been so zonked the previous night that she couldn't remember more than a dozen of the 5,000 or so words she'd pounded out on the old Royal. "Which one?"

He leaned forward slightly and lowered his voice. "The rumor about Hitler's plans to invade England."

Sam's heart banged against her ribs. She didn't dare look at Joe. "You've confirmed that it's true?"

"Not yet, but I plan to camp out at the War Department tomorrow until I get either an official confirmation or an official denial. If it's a denial, we'll run that, and make it sound like they're covering up, which they will be. Ol' Blowhard Chet isn't the only one with contacts over there," he said with a complacent smile.

"According to *my* source, word from Navy Intelligence is that the invasion is definitely a go. They'll probably try to pull it off while everybody's busy helping Uncle Joe Stalin save Russia. My contact says we're already making plans to put the Atlantic fleet on standby. Looks like we would've been in the war before spring even if the Japs hadn't pulled off those sneak attacks."

"But doesn't the Navy need to keep the Atlantic fleet available to transfer to the Pacific, to fight the Japanese?" Joe asked.

Alvie shrugged. "You'd think so, with so many of the ships that were at Pearl out of commission."

"No, they wouldn't transfer the Atlantic fleet," Sam said. "Those ships are needed to combat the U-boat wolf packs, and to defend the east coast. Besides, all the aircraft carriers in the Pacific were away from Pearl when the Japanese attacked, so they're still in service."

Alvie was clearly impressed. "I hadn't thought of that—about the wolf packs and the carriers, I mean. You're very well-informed, Samantha. Sharp, too. You'd make a good reporter."

She shook her head with a dubious smile. "I don't know about that, Alvie."

"I'm serious. Listen, if you spot any mistakes in my notes, or if I leave out something important—like that business about the U-boats, for instance—

would you mind fixing the copy when you type it up?"

"Do a little line editing, you mean? Would that be ethical?"

He laughed. "You're asking a reporter about ethics? I'd be willing to pay more for edited copy. Say, fifteen cents per page."

"Make it twenty, and you've got a deal."

He agreed, but not without some grumbling. When he'd left, Joe got up to collect the typewriter from a buffet in the corner and carried it to the table.

"What are you up to?" he asked as he set the machine in front of her.

Sam gave him an innocent look. "What makes you think I'm up to something?"

He put his hands on his hips and stared her down.

"Oh, all right. I was thinking I might slip something into one of Alvie's stories that would draw Falconer into the open."

Joe pursed his lips, considering. "You mean feed him some disinformation?"

"Exactly. He's been a busy boy, spreading this garbage about an invasion of England all over the place. It's time somebody turned the tables, used his own game plan against him. What do you think?"

Before he could answer, Esther opened the door and stuck her head around it. "Sorry," she said with a grimace. "I went to the bathroom, and when I got back to the parlor he'd escaped."

"It's okay," Sam assured her. "Alvie just provided us with a way to trap Falconer."

"We hope," Joe amended. "If it works."

Of course Esther insisted on being brought up

to speed. By the time they finished filling her in, it was almost ten. She made a big to-do about the lateness of the hour, said goodnight and headed off to bed, leaving Sam and Joe alone.

"I never would've guessed she could be so diplomatic," Sam remarked as she walked into his arms.

"Don't kid yourself," he drawled. "She's probably got her ear pressed against the door."

"That's not nice."

She nipped at his chin. He grasped her bottom and snuggled her pelvis into his. She tugged the tail of his shirt out of his trousers and reached under it, running her hands up and down his back.

"I'd appreciate the gesture more if it wasn't wasted," he murmured against her cheek. "How long will it take for you to type those damned notes?"

"Not as long as last night—there aren't as many pages." She reached for his mouth, but he evaded her. "Joe." She made his name both a plea and a demand, curling her fingers into his taut, warm skin.

He sucked in his breath, but continued to deny her. "How long?"

"I'll set a new words-per-minute record. I'll pound that ugly hunk of metal to pieces, melt the keys right off the sucker. Kiss me, damn it."

"An hour?"

"An hour," she agreed. "But only if I don't die of frustration in the next ten seconds."

He finally brought his mouth down on hers, but she got much, much more than the simple kiss she'd asked for. He was rapacious, plundering and devouring. At the same time, his hands wreaked havoc everywhere they could reach.

"Too long," he growled into her mouth, and rocked his hips against her.

"Oh, God," Sam moaned. "Stop. I'm going to pass out."

He released her but didn't step back, so that all the places that burned and ached were still pressed together. Sam reached out blindly, grabbing the edge of the table to brace herself upright.

"We can't have that," Joe said softly. "Not for another hour, at least." He lifted a hand and brushed his knuckles across her cheek. "I'll shave before I go to bed."

He gave her a parting kiss, hot and yearning but all too brief, then left. Sam inhaled a deep, steadying breath, sat down, and rolled a sheet of paper into the typewriter. She was less exhausted and more motivated than she'd been the night before, and from now on she intended to pay close attention to every word of Alvie's notes.

That would be a lot easier, though, if she wasn't weak and trembling from Joe's kisses and impatient to be in his bed when she sat down to turn the notes into typed copy. One thing was glaringly apparent— if they hoped to carry off this scheme and uncover Falconer's identity, they were going to have to work out some kind of schedule. Let's see, something like: dinner at 5:30; KP from 6:30 to 7:30; consultation and typing from 7:30 to 9:00; and the rest of the night for making love. Yeah, she thought with a grin as she began pounding the keys, that was a schedule she could live with. Maybe she should post it on the refrigerator door.

Seventeen

Lucas spent almost an entire day looking for a list of Sam's passwords and access codes. He knew the list had to exist; she was too compulsive about organization not to have kept a record of everything, *somewhere*. He finally found it in an encrypted file on a backup diskette. It took him another two hours to figure out the password that unlocked the encrypted file— AXIS&ALLIES. If she hadn't told him about her father's and grandfather's obsession with the game, he never would have figured it out.

He ran the search he dreaded most first, checking law enforcement databases for unidentified female corpses that had turned up in the D.C. area during the past week. There were six, four of which were the wrong race or age. The remaining two corpses had been discovered miles from the hotel, and one of them was badly decomposed. He heaved a massive sigh of relief as he logged off.

Grace sat beside him in the small bedroom Sam had converted to an office, fascinated by the technology that gave him access to information stored in mainframes hundreds of miles away.

"This is all brand new," she said, her voice hushed and wondering.

"Not really. National databases have been

around for years, though until the phone companies started using fiber optics and the Internet opened its gateways to casual users, the average person couldn't access them from home."

She shook her head. "No, Lucas. I mean it's all brand new to *me.*"

He swiveled Sam's ergonomically designed chair to face her. "What are you saying, that you've never seen a personal computer before?" He wasn't really surprised— she hadn't known about television, after all— but he didn't want her to worry. "Maybe it's just one of the things you've forgotten."

"No," she said firmly. "I didn't want to tell you, because I was afraid you might insist on taking me back to that nursing home, or to a hospital or something. I've been having strange . . . flashes, for lack of a better word. They're like dreams, except they only last a few seconds. But they aren't dreams, Lucas, or hallucinations. The people and things I see are real, I know they are. They're just not *here*. They must be memories, or at least parts of memories."

"How long has this been going on?" he said anxiously. "And what do you mean, they're not 'here'? Not in Washington? Not in the United States?"

"The first time was yesterday afternoon, after we made love." A faint blush stained her cheeks when she said it, but she didn't stumble over the words. Lucas smiled into her eyes.

"But the spooky part is— and this is why I was afraid you might overreact— it *is* Washington I see. Just not *this* Washington. Last night I saw the Capitol Building, and this morning the Lincoln Memorial. Both places looked exactly the same as they do now. That is, the same as the pictures I've seen of them on television. But the *people* I saw were different."

Lucas felt the hairs on his arms stand at attention. "Whoa. This is beginning to sound like something out of *The Twilight Zone*."

"I don't know what you're talking about." Her voice held a hint of impatience, or maybe it was irritation. It was the first negative emotion she'd displayed, and it threw Lucas for a moment. "But I have the feeling you're not taking me seriously. Do you think I'm crazy, is that it?"

He hurried to reassure her. "No. I swear, I don't think you're crazy, and I am taking you seriously. Okay, let's get specific. You say the people you see in these flashes are different. How, exactly? Describe them. Be as precise as you can."

"Well, now that I think of it, I suppose the people themselves aren't really different, but their clothes certainly are. A lot more . . . conservative. Most of the people I've seen since we left the nursing home have looked like either tropical birds or hobos. But these people are wearing much more simple clothes, in plain colors— browns or blues or grays. Oh, and all the men and most of the women are wearing hats."

Lucas grabbed a notebook and pen. "What kind of hats?"

This was getting weirder by the minute. It had been years since he saw a woman wearing a hat. Caps, sure. Everywhere you looked there were women wearing caps emblazoned with everything from the names of professional baseball teams to political slogans designed to shock or offend. But no hats.

"Nothing special," Grace said with a shrug. "Just hats. Mostly brown felt fedoras on the men— "

"Like Indiana Jones's hat?"

"Yes, like that. The women have more different styles, but their hats are all small and feminine. Some have little veils that can be pulled down over your eyes." She stopped, her lips curving in a soft, reminiscent smile. "One woman at the Lincoln Memorial was wearing a dark blue cloche just like Joanne Winston's mother bought on her last trip to New York. It had little pleats around the bottom, and— "

She abruptly broke off and they stared at each other in stunned comprehension. It was Lucas who finally spoke, sending each word into the charged silence as carefully as if it were a live grenade.

"Who is Joanne Winston?"

Every trace of color had drained from Grace's already pale complexion, so that her blue, lashless eyes blazed like sapphires set in an alabaster bust.

"A friend." Her voice was less than a whisper. "An old friend from school. Oh, God, Lucas, I remember her . . . and her mother, and the hat her mother brought back from New York . . ."

He saw that she was trembling and leaned over to take her hands. They felt like ice.

"It's all right," he murmured. "Just take it one step at a time. What else do you remember?"

She nodded and gripped his hands. "Our house— it's a lovely old house, with lots of trees. My bedroom. Oh, Lucas, I can *see* it— my bed, and my writing desk in front of the window! And my father's study . . ." She stopped and closed her eyes. Her forehead wrinkled in a frown of concentration.

"Don't try to force it. Just let it come."

"You were right, my father is assigned to Army Intelligence. He's very worried about the situation in Europe. He thinks the United States will eventually have to become involved."

Lucas nodded encouragement. He assumed she was referring to the war that had begun in Bosnia and now threatened to spread across several borders. But the next words out of her mouth blew that assumption to smithereens and left him dumbfounded.

"Daddy says that madman Hitler means to take over the entire continent, and America is the only country that can stop him."

"Hitler?" Lucas repeated hoarsely.

Absorbed in the memories that were suddenly flooding back, Grace acknowledged the name with a distracted nod. Then she suddenly stiffened and stood up, letting go of his hands. She took several agitated paces, stopped and spun back to face him.

"The argument I remembered earlier— it wasn't with the man I'd been seeing, it was with my father, *about* the man I'd been seeing." She shook her head, obviously distressed. "It was a terrible fight, but I have only myself to blame. I should have waited till we got home to tell Daddy about Joseph. I knew he'd disapprove, but I was sure I could reason with him, that he wouldn't make a scene in public."

Lucas squashed the urge to follow up on that reference to Hitler. He sensed that the memory stream she was experiencing was important— both the actual memories and their sequence— and also that he shouldn't interrupt or try to direct the process.

"Why did your father disapprove of this man?"

"Partly because of his job, I think," Grace murmured. Her frown returned briefly. She paced off a few more steps, pivoted, returned to her starting point. "Yes, that's right— Joseph works for the FBI, and Daddy doesn't trust Mr. Hoover."

Mr. Hoover! The name brought Lucas out of his chair. Dear God, she was talking about Adolph Hitler *and* J. Edgar Hoover— and referring to both of them in the present tense!

"But Daddy also disapproved because Joseph's parents and grandparents were Yugoslavian immigrants," she continued, oblivious to the effect her revelations were having. "I hate to say it about my own father, but he's a terrible snob. I wouldn't have told him about Joseph at all, but Joseph insisted."

She crossed her arms under her breasts and started pacing again. She looked more intent now, more deeply submerged in the memories pouring back into her mind.

"He said he was tired of sneaking around like a criminal, that if we couldn't be seen together in public, we'd better call it quits. I knew it was a mistake, but I promised to tell Daddy that night. We went out to dinner, to one of my favorite restaurants. I wore my new purple dress. When I told Daddy about Joseph, he turned cold and angry and ordered me to break it off at once. Of course I argued, but he wouldn't listen. We both said some hateful things."

She stopped pacing, closed her eyes and released a trembling sigh. Reliving the argument with her father was obviously taking an emotional toll. Lucas impulsively moved closer, but he stopped short of making physical contact. He was torn between the desire to pull her into his arms and comfort her and a compulsive, jealous need to know more about this Joseph she'd been involved with.

"In the end, I promised not to see him again," she said before he could resolve his own inner conflict and decide what to do. "It was easier than continuing to fight Daddy, and anyway, I could see that he wouldn't change his mind. When we got home I went up to my room, to write Joseph a letter." She paused again, hugging her arms as if she'd had a sudden chill.

"And then—" Her voice changed, became thin and tight, as if she were forcing the words past a constriction in her throat. Lucas took another step closer. "And then I heard this strange sound . . . like a car backfiring out on the street, only not exactly like that, and much closer."

A chill trickled down Lucas's spine. He reached out and clasped her arms, just above the elbows. She stood as stiff and still as a statue, not responding to his touch. Her eyes were clouded, unfocused; she was looking straight at him, but he knew she didn't see him. He gave her a little shake.

"Grace." He was careful to speak quietly, his tone low and urgent. She didn't react to either the shake or the sound of his voice.

"I looked up from the letter, out through the window over my desk, just as someone ran out of Daddy's study and around the side of the house. That's strange. Who would be visiting at this hour? And that loud noise. . . . Maybe Kyoshi was trying to use the pressure cooker and it blew up again. I'd better go down and make sure everything's all right."

When she unconsciously slipped into the present tense, the chill spread over Lucas's entire body. He shook her again, harder. "Grace, no. Stop."

Her head flopped back, then forward, whipping her hair into her face, but her eyes still had that glazed, unfocused look.

"Daddy's study. That's where the sound came from."

"Grace! Snap out of it!"

"Daddy? Is everything—" The rest was choked off by a terrible, tortured sob as her eyes widened in horror. "Daddy? Oh, God, nooooo! *Daddy!"*

Lucas caught her as she fainted.

The stories that appeared under Alvie Blumberg's byline over the next few days attracted a lot of attention, including, eventually, that of the War Department. Alvie announced at dinner one evening that a Major Connors, from Army Intelligence, had visited him at work to ask where he was getting his information about the Russian front.

"I've been wondering the same thing," Chet Pierce remarked. "You've been reporting news from Russia almost before the correspondents over there can pass it on. What's the deal, Alvie? Is your new source a gypsy fortune teller, or maybe a Russian general?"

"Neither, Chet," Alvie said with a smug smile. "Just someone with a very good understanding of military strategy and a knowledge of how brutal the Russian winters are— something Herr Hitler should have taken into consideration before he sent his tanks across their border."

"I especially like the predictions you've been making," Martha said. "It's interesting to read what you say will happen, then check the papers over the next day or two to see if you were right."

"Apparently a lot of people are doing that," Alvie replied. "Our circulation manager says sales are increasing every day."

"But do you really think the tide has turned in Russia?" Owen asked.

Alvie darted a surreptitious glance at Sam under cover of taking a sip of water. Conscious of Joe's size-ten shoe nudging her right foot, she pretended not to notice. While Alvie hesitated, Chet jumped into the breach.

"I wouldn't bet on it, Owen. Two of my government contacts tell me the Jerries are too solidly entrenched for the Russians to have any hope of routing them on their own. Uncle Joe's Red Army may manage to drive 'em back in a few places, for a while, but they'll regroup and come on stronger than before."

"Well, we have Chet's prediction," Gert observed. "What do you think, Alvie?"

He grinned at her across the table. "I think you'll have to buy a copy of tomorrow's paper to find out what I think, Gert."

The cocky response drew a chuckle from Owen, Martha, and Gert and perfunctory smiles from Sam, Joe and Esther. Chet, however, reacted with a derisive harrumph. He clearly wasn't happy with Alvie's new popularity.

"I warned you not to give him too much, too soon," Joe said later, as he and Sam stood at the table scraping plates. "The little rooster's drunk on power."

"There's no need to be insulting, Joseph," Esther admonished. To Sam, she added a solemn, "But I admit I'm starting to worry, too. If the War Department sent someone to question Alvie— "

"They've probably already started an investigation," Joe said grimly. "Next thing you know, Deputy Director Boggs will be calling all four of us in for a cozy little talk."

"You're overreacting," Sam said. "This is the U.S. government we're talking about, remember. The right hand never knows what the left hand is doing. Even if the War Department is keeping an eye on Alvie, there's no reason to assume they'd inform the FBI. In fact, they probably wouldn't."

"Joe?" Esther asked. "Is that true?"

"Answer your sister, Joe," Sam said when he didn't immediately reply.

He gave her a hard, thin-lipped look. "Yes, it's true, especially if Army Intelligence is involved. Our military leaders don't appear to have a great deal of respect for Director Hoover."

"On the contrary, I imagine they respect him a lot," Sam said. "The same way you'd respect a cobra. They just don't trust him."

"And I don't appreciate your comparing the Director of the Federal Bureau of Investigation to a snake," he bit out.

"Don't be so touchy. I was only making an observation."

Esther stepped between them to collect the stack of dishes. "I've had just about enough of this foolishness. The two of you had better work out whatever it is that's got you snapping and snarling at each other, or I'll lock you in the cellar together until you either kill each other or decide to kiss and make up."

Twin smears of red appeared on Joe's high, slanting cheeks before he turned away to slap the lid on the can of table scraps.

"He just doesn't like admitting that I'm right and he's wrong," Sam muttered.

As soon as the words left her mouth, she wished them back. Joe spun around and sent a frigid glare from those laser eyes straight through her heart.

"And you're always right, aren't you? You always know exactly what to do, and you just go out and do it. You never experience a second's doubt or uncertainty, and of course you've never made a mistake in your life."

"No," she said defensively. "Of course I've made—"

"It must be a wonderful feeling, this unshakable confidence in your own infallibility."

The corrosive sarcasm in his voice made her flinch. Before she could pull herself together and form a response, he was headed for the back door.

"Joe!" Esther called after him. "For heaven's sake!"

"I need some fresh air," he snarled over his shoulder. A second later the door slammed behind him.

Esther turned to Sam, her expression a mixture of astonishment and concern. "Well! That was certainly enlightening."

"He'll freeze out there," Sam said miserably. "He didn't even take time to put on his coat. One of us should go after him."

"Be my guest. But if I were you, I'd take along a whip and a chair."

"You shouldn't joke," Sam said. She managed to sound disapproving, but she was having a hard time keeping her mouth in a straight line. "He's really pissed."

"I noticed. Do you want to wash or dry?"

Sam sighed and collected a dishtowel. "I'll dry." After a few minutes, she said, "Aren't you going to ask what started this mess in the first place?"

"Are you going to make me ask?" Esther countered. "I thought we were friends."

"Of course we're friends, but Joe's your brother. I don't want you to feel caught in the middle, or that I expect you to take my side."

"I'll only take your side if you're in the right." Esther gave her a sidelong look. "Are you in the right?"

"Of course I am! Well, mostly. Oh, hell, I don't know. Probably not. The argument that started everything was my fault, but since then we've had a series of skirmishes that wouldn't have amounted to anything on their own. Unfortunately they've all just sort of piled up on top of each other."

"That can happen," Esther murmured. "So what was the first fight about?"

"I told him it was stupid of him not to tell his superiors about his affair with Valerie after her father's murder."

Esther winced. "I bet that went over like a lead balloon."

"Well, it *was* stupid of him. If they find out now, he's going to look guilty as hell. They'll figure Joe had something to hide— especially if they also find out he was the man Valerie and her father argued about the night he was killed."

"And what did Joe say when you gave him the benefit of these insights?

Sam heaved another aggrieved sigh. "He said he was trying to protect both of them, that he didn't want to say anything until he'd had a chance to talk to her."

"And of course he never got that chance because the two of you switched places."

"Which he was quick to point out, as if it was *my* fault he didn't get to ask Val what she'd said to the cops. The point is, the more time passes, the guiltier he's going to look if anybody ever does find out about them."

"I'm sure Joe realizes that," Esther said. "What were the other skirmishes about?"

"Well, he threw the watch up to me, reminded me it had been foolish to take it to a pawnshop when I knew the FBI was watching every move I made. Although that turned out all right, because— I don't think I told you this— they brought in a German watchmaker who'd recently immigrated to examine it, and he told them it wasn't German or Swiss. In fact, he said he'd never seen anything like it and couldn't figure out how it worked."

"No, you didn't tell me that. It's good news, though, isn't it?"

"It would be, except apparently the watchmaker made such a big deal about the watch— how it must be the only one of its kind and so on— that now they've sent it to some engineers to study."

Esther murmured a noncommittal, "Mmmm," and placed the last plate on the drainboard.

"And of course Joe's given me grief over every single piece of information I've passed on to Alvie, no matter how small or insignificant. The really irritating thing is, he was right, damn it. Less than a week ago I was dead set against revealing anything about the future. Yet once I came up with this scheme to flush Falconer out, I conveniently forgot all my idealistic scruples."

"Don't be too hard on yourself," Esther advised. "I think it's more likely that you just got a little carried away."

"I've created a monster, is what I've done," Sam muttered. "That first time, when I added a couple of sentences to Alvie's story about the siege against Moscow, he almost scratched them out. He was afraid he'd lose his job if I was wrong and the Red Army didn't manage to repel the Germans. I convinced him to leave in the stuff I'd added, and of course the next day the news came over the wire that the Germans were in retreat. Ever since, he's been feeding me every scrap of news about the Russian front he can get his hands on, and expecting me to make bigger, more impressive 'predictions.' "

She finished drying the last dish and carried the stack to the china cabinet. "Unless I can come up with a way to make him back off, by this time next month I'll be able to teach a course in Russian military history," she grumbled. "To Russian army officers."

"You'll think of something," Esther said placidly as she wiped off the oilcloth that covered the table. "And if you don't, Joe will."

"Assuming he ever speaks another word to me."

Esther merely smiled.

"What did you mean when you said 'that was certainly enlightening' after Joe stormed out?"

Esther opened her mouth to answer, but Alvie made his nightly appearance, bearing a handful of fresh notes, before she could say anything.

Esther and everyone else had gone to bed and Sam was halfway through the fourth typed page when Joe re-entered the kitchen through the back door. He looked half frozen. Without saying a word she got up and started making a pan of cocoa. He thawed out next to the radiator until it was ready.

"Thanks," he said when she carried a cup to him.

"You're welcome," she murmured, and then, before she could lose her nerve or manage to do or say something to piss him off again, "I'm sorry I've been such an obnoxious, know-it-all bitch queen."

He curled both hands around the cup and lifted it to his mouth, but she saw his lips twitch.

"I put in extra marshmallows."

"Thanks," he said again. "But you didn't have to bother. I'm not terribly fond of marshmallows."

Sam waited until he'd finished the cocoa, then took the cup from him and set it on the china cabinet. "I know. They weren't for you."

His eyebrows were still quizzically raised when she stretched up and ran her tongue over his upper lip.

"I love melted marshmallows," she said against his mouth. "But not as much as I love you, Joseph Mercer."

She was close enough to feel the shock that punched through him. He went absolutely still. She thought he even stopped breathing. She backed out of his personal space and smiled at him.

"Don't panic, I don't expect you to say it back. Not till you can't help yourself. You'd better go climb into a hot tub."

She took the cup to the sink and washed both it and the pan, then returned to the table to finish typing Alvie's copy. Evidently she'd rattled Joe even more than she thought. So far as she could tell, he hadn't moved a muscle. Maybe it had been a mistake to just lay it on him like that, without any warning. She placed her fingers on the home keys and tried to concentrate on producing legible sentences and paragraphs for Alvie's editor.

"If there's any justice in this world," Joe said in

a wry, resigned tone that sent relief surging through her, "someday, somewhere, when you least expect it, some intrepid soul is going to take you completely by surprise and leave you not knowing up from down."

"Someone already has," Sam said without looking up. She heard him inhale sharply. "In fact, he does it a couple of times a night."

She didn't hear him move, but suddenly he was on the other side of the table, hands planted on the oilcloth, leaning over the typewriter to read the page she was typing. Of course he had to read it upside-down, but that was a skill most FBI agents mastered early in their careers.

"I hope we're not talking about Alvie Blumberg."

She laughed softly. "Well, come to think of it . . ."

"What are you giving him tonight?"

"General Zhukov's armies have cut off Guderian's Second Panzer Army south of Moscow, and Marshal Timoshenko is attacking northwestwards, between Livny and Yelets, to hit their right flank. Timoshenko's forces will mangle the Germans and Guderian will have to retreat. It's the beginning of the end of the German offensive."

"I'll take your word for it," Joe muttered. "Isn't that a lot to give him in one lump?"

"Not really. I took everything except the stuff about Timoshenko's forces mangling the German's right flank from the info Alvie furnished. He could've come up with most of this himself, if he'd just sat down and studied the correspondents' reports."

The right corner of Joe's mouth lifted in a surprised smile. "Do my ears deceive me, or have you actually started to exercise some discretion?"

"Better late than never, right?" she said with a sheepish grin.

"Absolutely."

His smile lingered, became soft and warm . . . was complemented by a flicker of emotion in his eyes. Sam reminded herself that she still had at least four pages of copy to type.

The phone in the hall rang shrilly.

Joe got to it first, as Esther opened the door of her room. She stood there in a long flannel gown, a yellow scarf wrapped around her pincurls, blinking in confusion.

"Who on earth would be calling at this hour?" she complained sleepily.

Sam's shrug turned into a surprised start as Joe held out the phone and said in a tense murmur, "It's for you."

"Hello," she said tentatively. "This is Samantha Cook speaking."

"I'm phoning in response to your advertisement," a slightly accented male voice said.

Sam frowned. "My advertisement?"

Joe stepped in close and she tilted the receiver to let him listen.

"Yes," the man on the phone said. "You desire a companion to accompany you on a trip to the south of England, is this correct?"

Joe clamped his hand over the mouthpiece. "Sea Lion," he whispered fiercely. "It's Takamura, the houseboy."

"Yes!" Sam blurted. "Yes, that's correct. I'm sorry, you took me by surprise. I placed the ad several days ago, and since no one had responded . . ."

"I apologize for the delay," Kyoshi Takamura

said with formal courtesy. "I'm sure you understand that committing oneself to make such a journey, particularly at this time, requires most careful thought. I am now prepared to discuss the matter with you, if you would agree to meet with me."

"When and where?" Sam said without a second's hesitation.

Eighteen

Lucas tiptoed into the bedroom to check on the sleeping girl, then slipped back out and returned to Sam's office to phone Levander. He wasn't at work, so Lucas had to hunt down the home number Levander had given him. He found it in the pocket of a pair of slacks he'd stuffed into the laundry hamper.

"I wanted to let you know Grace is all right," he said quickly, trying to forestall a lecture. "We're at Sam's apartment in Rockville. Her memory's come back, Levander. Most of it, at least. She knows her name. It's Valerie Herrick."

There was a long, strained silence before Levander replied. "Are you making sure she eats?"

Lucas closed his eyes and released a gusty sigh of relief. "She's got an appetite like a horse. Or she did have, until this morning."

"Why? What happened this morning?"

"That's what I'm calling about. I was planning to anyway, to apologize for sneaking out like that and let you know she's all right. But after what happened this morning— God, I feel shell-shocked. I had to talk to somebody I could trust, somebody I know for sure is sane, and you're the only person I could think of who meets both criteria."

"Just *tell* me, man," Levander said impatiently.

"All right, all right. You're probably going to think I've gone off the deep end, but just listen till I finish, okay? She's from 1941, Levander. The last thing she remembers before she woke up in the nursing home was going to sleep in a D.C. jail cell. She was there because she was discovered kneeling on the floor next to her dead father, holding the gun that killed him, the night before the Japanese attacked Pearl Harbor."

There was another long silence, and then Levander said quietly, "You're right. I think you've lost your mind."

"No I haven't, damn it! I thought I had, or *she* had, until I logged onto a couple of historical databases we use at the station and checked her story. It's true, every word! Her father was a colonel in Army Intelligence. His name was Ethan Herrick, and he was murdered in his home the night of December 6th, 1941 . . . *exactly* like she said!" He paused, raked a trembling hand through his hair.

"The police arrested the colonel's daughter, *Valerie Herrick,* for the murder. But— get this, this is going to blow you away— she was never indicted or tried, because she mysteriously disappeared while in police custody. *While in police custody,* Levander. Fantastic as it seems, there's only one possible explanation for her disappearance— one second she was locked up in a jail cell in 1941, and a second later she was in a hotel room outside Alexandria, a bunch of Islamic terrorists were nuking D.C., and it was 1995."

"That's— "

"Crazy. I know. Christ, don't you think I know how crazy it sounds? But this girl can't be more than twenty-three or four. She couldn't possibly know the things she told me about a murder that happened 54 years ago. And that's not the half of it."

He told Levander about her references to Hitler and J. Edgar Hoover, and how she'd reacted the first time she encountered television and Sam's desktop computer.

"She'd never heard of CNN, for God's sake. I'm telling you, somehow she traveled more than half a century through time. Don't ask me how, because I don't have a fucking clue, but that has to be what happened. And if she's here— "

"If she's here, you're thinking maybe your friend Samantha is there— in '41," Levander interrupted. "Now that's *really* crazy."

"Maybe not," Lucas said. "In fact, that may be the key that explains the whole thing. Sam is a forensic scientist. Do you know what that is?"

"Some kind of scientific detective who helps the police solve crimes."

"Right. Well, mostly what she does is study the evidence and provide an independent expert opinion, or testify in court."

"And you're thinking that's why she got sent back to 1941, assuming she did," Levander said thoughtfully. Lucas couldn't tell by his voice whether Levander was seriously considering the possibility, or only humoring him.

"That's what I'm thinking," he confirmed, and prayed Levander Grisham wasn't planning to show up at Sam's door in a few hours carrying a straight-jacket.

"Well, that doesn't sound any crazier than the rest of it," Levander allowed. Lucas felt every muscle in his body go slack. "One question, Lucas. Why did you call me and tell me all this?"

"Damned if I know," Lucas said with a shaky

laugh. "I guess I needed to tell *somebody*—you know, lay it all out, see if it sounded as insane as I thought."

"It does, and then some. Take my advice and don't put this on the six o'clock news."

"Don't worry."

"So . . . what happens next? If you didn't get hold of some funny mushrooms and you're right about all this, I mean? If Samantha solves the murder, will these two women change places again, just hop back where they came from?"

That was the one question Lucas had steadfastly refused to let himself consider. "I don't know," he said. "Maybe. Or maybe they'll both be stuck where they are."

"But what if there's something you can do to affect how things turn out?" Levander persisted.

"Like what?"

"Hell, how should I know! You're the one who came up with this screwy idea. But if people can travel backwards and forwards across 50 years, it seems to me there ought to be a way to get them back where they started."

Levander hesitated a moment, then added in a tone rife with insinuation, "Assuming, of course, that somebody wants to get them back where they started . . . and that where they started is where they want to be."

Which pretty much covered *why* Lucas hadn't let himself think about what would happen if Sam found Ethan Herrick's murderer. He still wasn't ready to deal with the possibilities, so he changed the subject.

"A minute ago you said 'if Samantha solves the murder.' How do you know the police didn't arrest the right person?"

Levander made a scornful sound. "Come on, Lucas. Anybody who's spent five minutes with that girl knows she couldn't kill a fly. Is Samantha good at what she does?"

"Yes. She's very good."

"Then maybe you'll be seeing her again before too long. In the meantime, make sure you take good care of . . . what did you say Grace's real name is?"

"Valerie." Just saying it sent a sweet, sharp pain through his chest. "Her name is Valerie."

The apartment building was on N Street, between 7th and 8th. Sam stood shivering on the brick sidewalk while Joe paid the cab fare. The shivers got worse as the two of them crept down a dark alley beside the building, and they weren't entirely a reaction to the cold. There were rustling, scrabbling noises in the dark. Joe must have heard her teeth clicking together, because he slipped an arm around her waist and whispered,

"It's only rats."

"Only?" she whispered back. "Do you have any idea how many diseases rats carry?"

She'd argued when he insisted on coming with her, afraid his presence might spook Mr. Takamura, but now she was glad he was there. Being an independent, self-sufficient modern woman was well and good, but there were times when an old-fashioned brawny male came in handy. She wondered how far Joe would be able to kick a rat.

He'd phoned for a cab and arranged for them to be picked up two blocks from home, then they'd sneaked out by way of the back door. The agents in the black Olds hadn't been around for the past couple of days. At least they hadn't been continuing their covert surveillance from an ugly black car the size of a barge parked scarcely a dozen yards from the front door. Joe said Deputy Director Boggs was still having her watched, though, which was why Sam's feet were cold and wet and she had a scratch on her right shin. Joe had led her through several backyards and one rose garden to get to the corner where he'd told the dispatcher to send the cab.

"Why didn't you think to bring a flashlight?" she asked, still whispering.

"Why didn't you? This is your rendezvous. I'm just the bodyguard."

"These buildings look abandoned. There are no lights in the windows."

"Blackout shades," he said succinctly. "Besides, all the tenants are probably in bed. Which, if you don't mind my saying so, is where— "

"I do mind you saying so. Besides, you want to hear what Mr. Takamura has to say as much as I do. We should be getting close to the end of the alley."

Mr. Takamura had directed her to come to a door at the rear of the apartment building, just before the alley dead-ended at brick wall. He said he'd wait there for twenty minutes. Almost that much time must have passed since Joe called for the cab.

"Here," Joe said suddenly. Sam didn't know how he could see the door in the darkness, but there it was, exactly where Mr. Takamura had said it would be.

Joe knocked, two sharp raps. The door opened almost immediately and he stepped inside, pulling her after him. They had entered a large storage room that was almost as dark as the alley had been. The only illumination came from a small bulb above a door on the other side of the room. Someone had thrown a cloth over the bulb.

"Who is this man?"

The suspicious question came from behind a stack of wooden crates to the right of the door they'd just entered. Sam couldn't see the speaker, but she recognized his voice from their brief, cryptic phone conversation.

"It's all right, he's a friend. He wouldn't let me come by myself."

"Very wise." A slender Japanese man stepped from behind the crates. He took a moment to size up the two of them, then went to remove the cloth he'd thrown over the light. He folded it into a perfect triangle as he recrossed the storage room, and slipped the triangle into his trousers pocket.

"You and the other woman found my message."

"Yes."

"It was not intended for you. Please return it."

The polite request was so unexpected that Sam felt her jaw drop. *"Return* it?"

"Yes, please."

"I don't have it. I didn't think you'd want it *back,* for God's sake."

Joe reached into his suit coat and produced the envelope Esther had discovered taped to Ethan Herrick's desk drawer. Before handing it over, he withdrew the folded list of names he'd copied.

"Thank you," Mr. Takamura said as he accepted the envelope.

"Who was it intended for?" Joe asked.

"I am not at liberty to say."

"Someone in the War Department, I'd guess. Or

maybe the Coordinator of Information for the Joint Chiefs."

"I am not at liberty to say," Mr. Takamura repeated stoically.

"Time out," Sam interrupted. "Let's see if I can save all three of us a little time and frustration. Exactly what *are* you at liberty to say?"

"What would you like to know?" Mr. Takamura replied.

"Well, for starters, did you see who murdered Ethan Herrick?"

"Unhappily, I did not. But I believe it was the man known to me only as Falconer."

"Did you tell the police about Falconer?"

"No," Joe said before Mr. Takamura could answer. "He couldn't. It's classified information."

"Oh, Jesus," Sam muttered as the light finally dawned. "You *were* spying on Colonel Herrick, but for *us*, not the Japanese."

Mr. Takamura looked startled. "Goodness, no," he said. "There was no reason to *spy* on Colonel Herrick. He was an exemplary officer and a loyal American. Unfortunately, however, the quality of the information he was collecting had been deteriorating for some time. At first it was only small discrepancies, for example, numbers concerning troop strengths that didn't agree with confirmed intelligence reports."

"And when nobody followed up on the discrepancies, the amount and importance of the bad information he was getting increased," Joe murmured.

"Yes. Eventually it became obvious that one of the colonel's informants was a German agent."

"How many informants were feeding him intelligence about the Germans?" Sam asked.

"Too many, I'm afraid, and several of them had insisted on keeping their identities secret, even from him. They still have relatives in Germany, you see. Often it is these relatives who pass on the information. It was the colonel who suggested placing someone in his home, someone who could assist him in identifying which of the informants was providing the false information."

"Which, I presume, is when you entered the picture," Joe remarked.

Mr. Takamura nodded. "I had served as a translator for the colonel on several occasions. He asked if I would be willing to pose as a servant, providing him with an extra set of eyes and ears. A servant is invisible to many people, like the wallpaper or the furniture," he added in an aside to Sam. She nodded, though her personal experience with servants was nil.

"Of course I was honored by the request and agreed at once. We were able to clear all the informants whose identities were known to us of suspicion, and to identify and also eventually absolve four of those who had insisted on using only code names. Unfortunately, the man who called himself Falconer was not one of the four."

"But why didn't you figure out that Falconer was the German agent right away?" Sam asked. "I mean, Colonel Herrick knew what information Falconer was giving him, right?"

"Yes, of course the colonel knew which information had come from each informant, but often lies aren't discovered to be lies for weeks or months. Also, honorable people with the best of intentions can make mistakes, accurate information can be misinterpreted, military strategy can change without warning . . ." He lifted his shoulders in a fatalistic shrug.

"It is not so simple as it might seem. A cunning, well-trained agent can provide false information for years without being discovered. But I believe Falconer may have realized that his time was running out. In the past, he had always insisted on meeting Colonel Herrick in person, alone and at a place and time he selected. But he phoned the colonel several times recently, and came to his home twice."

"Sloppy," Joe commented. "He was getting careless."

Kyoshi Takamura nodded.

"But that doesn't make sense," Sam objected. "Not if he thought Colonel Herrick might be on to him. You'd think he'd become *more* cautious, not less."

Mr. Takamura hesitated a moment before replying. "The colonel suspected that for some reason Falconer had suddenly been feeling a lot of pressure."

"From the Germans?" Joe asked sharply.

"It seemed very likely. Since the end of November, all his messages concerned Operation Sea Lion. It was as if he'd become obsessed with convincing Army Intelligence that the invasion of England was imminent."

"And not only Army Intelligence," Sam remarked. "Remember Alvie's story?" she said to Joe, and then to Mr. Takamura, "Alvie Blumberg is a local reporter, and he claims a source in *Navy* Intelligence told him the invasion was 'definitely a go.'"

Mr. Takamura frowned. "If both the Army and Navy are receiving the same information—"

"But it's bad information," Sam interrupted. "Believe me, Hitler has no intention of launching an invasion of England. He abandoned those plans months ago."

"Don't ask how she knows," Joe said dryly. "Just take it as fact. Operation Sea Lion is a red herring, intended to distract the U.S. and England from the Russian Front."

"Where the Germans are about to get their collective butts kicked," Sam put in. "Falconer is the German agent, I'd bet my last dime on it. You'd better go straight to whoever's in charge and tell him not to buy anything else Falconer tries to sell you. God knows how much damage he's already done."

Mr. Takamura gave a troubled shake of his head. "Even if everything you say is true, where is your evidence, your proof? Do *you* know Falconer's identity?"

"No such luck," Sam muttered. "We don't even have a clue what he looks like."

"I can describe him to you."

She gaped at him in astonishment. "You've seen him? Well, why didn't you say so, for pity's sake?"

"I saw him only once, very briefly, two nights before Colonel Herrick was murdered. He arrived unexpectedly at a few minutes before eleven. I had already gone to my room and changed into my pajamas. The colonel called out that he would answer the door, but by then I had already put on my robe and come into the kitchen. Colonel Herrick saw me as he reached the foyer. He gestured for me to stay where I was.

"He opened the door and exchanged a few words with the man standing there, and then they went to the colonel's study. But as Colonel Herrick turned away, he made a little sign to let me know the visitor was someone important. I knew at once it must be Falconer. He stayed ten or fifteen minutes, then left by the French doors in the study. I wanted to see him, so I ran to the living room and watched through the window as he walked around the house."

"And this was the meeting you referred to in the note?" Joe asked. "The one you taped to the drawer of the colonel's desk."

"Yes, of course. But I was about to describe the man— the man I'm sure was Falconer."

"By all means," Sam said impatiently. "What does he look like?"

"He is of average height, for a Caucasian, a little less than six feet, I think. Neither heavily built nor slender. He moved quickly and it was late at night, but I think his hair is brown. Of course I couldn't see the color of his eyes."

"Great," Sam muttered. "So far we've got average height, weight, and hair, eye color unknown. He could be anybody."

"But wait!" Mr. Takamura said. A note of excitement had entered his voice. "I haven't finished. When he passed the corner of the house, the light from the kitchen window fell on his face." He paused. Sam thought he was getting a kick out of building the suspense.

"And?" she said.

"He has a scar. A very prominent one, like a scar from a knife wound. It extends from the corner of his left eye almost to his mouth."

She grinned at him. "Now that was worth the wait, Mr. Takamura."

"And it's a good way to bring this little get-together to an end," Joe said abruptly. "We'd better leave, just in case we were followed."

"Yes, I agree," Mr. Takamura said. But then he frowned, as if he'd suddenly remembered something, and reached back to pull a folded piece of paper out of his hip pocket.

"I feel badly that Colonel Herrick's daughter was arrested, but I don't know what I can do to help her. I'd be in trouble with his superiors if I went to the police and told them about Falconer, and I doubt they would believe me anyway. I tried to tell them that night that she didn't shoot her father."

"And if you went to the police, they'd probably turn you over to the FBI as a possible Japanese agent," Sam said quietly.

"Yes," he said with a resigned sigh. He held out the paper. "After the policemen left, I went up to Valerie's room to turn off the lights and the radiator. This was on her desk. It's a letter to someone named Joseph."

He glanced down at the letter and missed Joe's involuntary jerk of surprise.

"She must have been writing it when she heard the gunshot. I don't know why I took it, perhaps to keep the police from finding it. It's rather personal. She tells him she can't see him anymore. I don't know who this Joseph is, or how to get the letter to him. What do you think I should do with it?"

Sam looked at Joe, not wanting to force him to decide, but without an idea in her head what she should say. "I— "

"Burn it," he said without a trace of emotion. "I think that would be best."

Mr. Takamura hesitated a moment, then nodded. "Yes, you are probably right."

They were about to leave, when Joe thought of one last question. "Do you know if Colonel Herrick ever provided any of his informants with a gun?"

"Yes, he did, at least three times. In each instance, the informant was afraid he would be found out by German sympathizers. Whether their fears were justified, I don't know, but the colonel took them seriously enough to acquire a gun and a box of bullets for each of them."

"You're thinking he probably gave them Army Colts, aren't you?" Sam asked as they retraced their steps down the alley.

"And that one of those Colts was the gun used to kill him," Joe confirmed.

"We need to find out whether the two junior officers Colonel Herrick had demoted can account for their sidearms. If they can— "

"We'll cross them off the list." They reached the deserted street. "Damn, we'll never find a cab at this hour." He took her arm and started heading for the corner. "C'mon, I think there's an all-night diner a couple of streets over."

"Don't you think we can scrap the list now?" Sam said dryly. "It's obvious that Falconer is the murderer. Somehow he found out Colonel Herrick was on to him, or at least that he was getting suspicious. Falconer was under pressure to keep up the Operation Sea Lion disinformation campaign, and he had to get rid of the colonel before his cover was blown. If he'd known Mr. Takamura was working with Colonel Herrick, he probably would have gone after him, too."

Joe didn't say anything, just kept walking. They

reached the corner and turned left. The street-lamps had been left off as part of the blackout. Moonlight glinted in his dark, glossy hair and washed his classically chiseled features with silver. He was so beautiful it hurt to look at him.

"You agree with me, I know you do," she said huskily. "Why won't you admit it?"

He glanced down at her and grinned. "If I admit it, what would we have to argue about?"

Sam grinned back and hugged his arm. "I'm sure we'll think of something. Now all we have to do is snoop around till we find out who Falconer is."

"No, we don't."

She'd been expecting something like this. "Yes, we do," she said firmly. "So save the speech about how we should leave it to Army Intelligence or the FBI or the War Department to expose him, because the Army won't want to believe he managed to pull the wool over their eyes and the other two don't even know he exists."

"No," Joe said calmly. "I meant we don't have to snoop around until we find out who he is, because his picture was on the society page of this morning's paper."

Sam abruptly stopped walking, dragging him to a halt with her. "Are you sure?"

He nodded, but before he could say anything a black Oldsmobile sedan pulled to the curb and whoever was inside cranked down the passenger's window.

"Get in," a man's voice ordered. "Deputy Director Boggs wants to talk to both of you."

Nineteen

They rode in the back seat, with two grim-looking FBI agents up front. Neither of them spoke, but Joe took Sam's hand and held it in a firm grasp for the duration of the trip. She wasn't sure if he was trying to reassure her or warning her to behave herself.

They were taken to a small conference room at FBI headquarters. An Army sergeant who'd been standing at ease in the hallway snapped to attention and opened the door when they approached, at which point their FBI escorts disappeared. Bill Ragsdale and two other men Sam had never seen before were waiting inside the room. One of the men was an Army officer whose uniform bore the insignia of a major. Bad sign, Sam thought. She assumed the third man was Deputy Director Boggs. There was no stenographer present. That could also be a bad sign. When she and Joe had taken seats across the table, the civilian with a nose like a turnip and no lips spoke.

"Good evening, Miss Cook. I'm Harold Boggs, Deputy Director of the Federal Bureau of Investigation, and this is Major Connors, from Army Intelligence. I believe you've already met Agent Ragsdale."

It had already been a long, trying day, and something about the man set Sam off. Probably the mean look around his eyes, or the way he conspicuously slighted Joe by refusing to acknowledge his presence. Impulsively deciding to give Mr. Boggs a taste of his own medicine, she deliberately turned her gaze away from him without responding and dipped her head in greeting at the other two.

"How's it going, Bill?" she said to Ragsdale. "Found Valerie Herrick yet?"

She heard Joe's long-suffering sigh, but didn't look at him. Ragsdale looked as if he were about to swallow his tongue. Boggs's lipless mouth stretched into a tight, nasty smile. Sam leaned back in her chair and crossed her arms, daring them to try to intimidate her. Surprisingly, it was Major Connors who spoke.

"I suspect you know the answer to that question, Miss Cook. Valerie Herrick is still missing. Since you've put the subject on the table, do you have any idea where she might be?"

"Yes, Major, as a matter of fact, I do. I explained my theory about Valerie Herrick to Agents Ragsdale and Mercer several days ago. I seriously doubt you'd find it any more credible than they did."

The major folded his hands on the table and leaned forward. "Try me."

She gave him a wry smile. "Trust me, Major Connors, you don't want to hear it."

"You couldn't be more wrong, Miss Cook," he said, then amazed her by adding emphatically, "I want to hear everything you have to say. That's why we're here."

Sam eyed him warily. "*You* had us picked up?"

He nodded solemnly. "I've been planning to talk

to you for several days, but I thought I'd wait a while and see what new information you might give Mr. Blumberg."

"You're the intelligence officer who visited Alvie at work," Joe remarked.

"Correct," Major Connors said. "Miss Cook seems to know things about the German offensive in Russia that haven't even made it into our intelligence reports."

"I knew she was a German agent," Ragsdale muttered.

Connors fixed him with a frosty stare. "If we don't have the information yet, I guarantee you no German agent has it, either."

A dark flush spread over Ragsdale's face, but he judiciously swallowed whatever he wanted to say. Connors turned back to Sam.

"For instance, Mr. Blumberg claims you furnished the information that the Russians would concentrate on retaking Klin, on the Moscow-to-Leningrad railway route."

Sam managed a nonchalant shrug, but her mind was racing. She couldn't decide whether she was more angry at Alvie for ratting on her, or at herself for not listening to Joe when he'd warned her about giving Alvie too much information.

"Anybody who took the time to study a map could have predicted they'd want to regain control of the railroad," she pointed out.

"True enough," Connors agreed. "But no map I know of would have told you that the Commander in Chief of the German Army tendered his resignation to Hitler on December 7th."

"Holy cow!" Ragsdale blurted. "The head Nazi general resigned?"

Sam knew when to admit defeat. "His name is

von Brauchitsch," she muttered. "He had a heart attack not long ago. The date he resigned stuck in my mind because it was the same day as the Japanese attacks—" She suddenly stiffened, her eyes narrowing to suspicious slits. "Wait a minute! I don't remember adding that to any of Alvie's stories."

"You didn't," Major Connors admitted.

She gaped at him. "You tricked me!"

"And very skillfully," Joe commented. "I wouldn't want to play poker with you, Major."

"We just found out about von Brauchitsch's resignation yesterday afternoon," Connors explained. "So it was fresh in my mind."

Annoyed that he'd bamboozled her so easily, Sam asked, "Did you also find out that Hitler refused to accept his resignation?"

Her churlishness didn't seem to bother the major in the least. "As a matter of fact, we did receive that information, as well."

Evidently Harold Boggs had tired of being merely a spectator. "Do you still maintain that she isn't a German agent, Major?" he demanded. "The woman knows things only an agent *could* know. And as for you, Mercer—"

"Leave him out of this!" Sam snapped. "If you narrow-minded imbeciles had believed what I told you in the first place—"

"That you're from 1995, you mean?" Ragsdale sneered.

"That's right, you idiot!"

She was so incensed that she didn't feel Joe's hand on her shoulder until he shoved her back against her chair and barked, "Samantha! Shut up, before you give them a reason to arrest you!"

"She's already done that," Boggs said with obvious satisfaction. "I've heard more than enough to charge you with failure to register as an agent of a foreign government, Miss Cook. Ragsdale, place her under arrest."

"With pleasure," Ragsdale said as he got to his feet.

"Hold it right there, Agent Ragsdale," Major Connors ordered. "You're not arresting anybody."

"You're out of line, Major," Boggs snapped. "This is a civil matter."

"No, sir, it isn't. If you'd care to get on the horn to your Director, he'll confirm that I have jurisdiction here."

"On whose authority?" Boggs said furiously. "The FBI does not take orders from the United States Army."

Sam had to hand it to Major Connors. He didn't lose his cool or his military bearing. He remained composed and respectful, and his voice never rose above a conversational level.

"I believe you'll find the order was passed down from the Attorney General's office about the time Agent Mercer and Miss Cook arrived here."

The Attorney General? Sam turned to Joe in amazement. He was frowning slightly, apparently as surprised by this development as she was.

"Now I'll have to ask both you gentlemen to leave the room," Major Connors said, adding insult to injury. "The things I need to discuss with Miss Cook involve information that's been classified for military intelligence personnel only."

My, my, Sam, thought; the major was just full of surprises. She sat back and waited to see what the next one would be.

"Surely you're not suggesting that she's an agent for *our* military," Boggs said. His indignant outrage had been tempered by a trace of uncertainty. He was probably trying to decide whether Connors was bluffing him now, Sam thought. "You just said she passed on information that you hadn't even received yet."

Major Connors gave him a long, hard stare. "Army Intelligence operatives aren't the only people collecting information for the United States, Mr. Boggs."

That effectively put an end to Boggs's protests, but Ragsdale was still miffed that he wasn't going to get to arrest anybody.

"What about Mercer?" he demanded. "He's FBI."

"Agent Mercer has also been working with us since you released Miss Cook into his custody," Connors said tersely. "And that's all I'm prepared to say at this point. Now I'll have to insist that you leave so I can get on with this debriefing. If you have any more questions, take them to your director."

"Very impressive," Sam said to the major when Boggs and Ragsdale had huffed out of the conference room. "I don't think I've ever seen anybody tell so many lies in such a short period of time without tripping himself up."

"I was highly motivated," Connors said dryly. "Arrogant FBI pinheads tend to have that effect on me. No offense intended, Agent Mercer."

"None taken," Joe drawled. "Provided you enlighten us about what that elaborate flimflam was all about."

"I was there tonight when you met with our Japanese friend, observing from behind that stack of packing crates."

"That note Esther and I found was intended for you!" Sam exclaimed.

"It was, indeed. Mr. Takamura had tried to contact me the morning after Colonel Herrick's murder, but unfortunately I was . . . out of town."

He probably meant out of the *country*, Sam thought. Maybe in London, comparing notes with the British?

"I didn't arrive back in Washington until late that afternoon," he went on. "By which time the news about the Japanese attacks had hit. Kyoshi decided he'd better disappear for a while. He went into hiding with some Filipino friends before I could get to him. I only managed to track him down late this afternoon."

"When did he leave the note?" Joe asked.

"Two days after the murder. He watched the house till he figured the police were finished, then let himself in with his key, wrote the note, and fastened it to the bottom of the desk drawer. He knew the desk was the first place we'd look. By then the FBI was rounding up every Japanese in sight and he was afraid to try to contact me directly, but he figured that sooner or later I'd either show up at the house or send somebody to have a look around."

"But when you got there, there wasn't any message for you to find," Sam murmured. "I'm sorry. I should've known somebody would show up to collect it."

Major Connors tilted his head and studied her through narrowed eyes. "What I couldn't figure out was why you'd broken into the house in the first place."

Sam shifted on her chair, uneasy under that relentless stare. "Well, that's a long, complicated story."

"So I gather," he said dryly. "According to Mr. Blumberg, you're a secretary from Baltimore, yet we haven't been able to find any record of your ever having lived or worked there. You were also supposedly abducted at gunpoint and forced to jump off a train— taking your luggage and your handbag with you— but we haven't managed to locate any witnesses to confirm that story, either. You'd think the other passengers would remember something like that, wouldn't you?"

"Thank God you didn't throw in the tiger or the herd of elephants," Joe muttered. Sam felt embarrassed color flood her face.

"Add these things to your inexplicable knowledge about the fighting in Russia, and the facts and figures you gave the FBI about the losses at Pearl Harbor— which Navy Intelligence subsequently confirmed— and we have the makings of a fascinating mystery," the major added. He leaned on his arms, his expression solemn but intensely interested.

"I never could resist a good mystery, Miss Cook. Now, what was this about your being from 1995?"

Lucas was beginning to think his *Twilight Zone* quip had been prophetic, a weird flash of clairvoyance or something.

"The story's changed." Valerie pointed out what he'd already seen for himself as she leaned over to read the text on the monitor screen. "This reference to an 'unidentified mystery woman' who was also questioned by the police wasn't there before, was it?"

Lucas took a deep breath. "No. It wasn't there before."

"Well, then . . . I don't understand. Did someone go into the computer and add that?"

He shook his head. "This is a read-only library file. You can't change it. Well, you could download it to your own computer and *then* change it, but you couldn't upload the altered text, and you can't change what's stored in the mainframe."

"Then how did that part about the unidentified woman get added?"

"Damned if I know," he said honestly.

He had logged on to the database the day before, to let her see the archived 1941 newspaper reports of her father's murder for herself. He'd thought reading about the details— specifically her own arrest and mysterious disappearance— would help nudge her into accepting the fact that she'd somehow been transported more than 50 years into the future. The idea had worked, but it had been a traumatic experience for her, a hell of a thing to deal with on top of her father's death. She'd spent the rest of the day either crying or staring vacantly into space. For a while Lucas thought he'd have to get her to a doctor— maybe a psychiatrist. But then this afternoon she'd asked him to access the database again. She wanted to follow the story through, find out whether the police ever caught her father's murderer.

And that was when they discovered that the text of the original stories had changed overnight.

"This is majorly spooky," he murmured, more to himself than to Valerie.

"You're thinking the same thing I'm thinking, aren't you?" she said.

Lucas shook his head again. "Don't say it. It isn't possible."

"A few days ago you'd have said traveling through time isn't possible, wouldn't you?" she retorted. "But it happened. I'm here, and Samantha is there, in 1941. She must be the woman an 'anonymous source' told this reporter about."

"Jesus," Lucas whispered. He stared at the screen in disbelief.

"I wonder why the police questioned her."

He closed his eyes and massaged the bridge of his nose. "I think I can guess," he said dryly. "When the two of you switched places— and times— she was in that hotel room outside Alexandria, so that's where you landed. And you were— "

"Oh my goodness! I was in *jail!*"

Lucas started to laugh softly.

"I don't see what's so funny," Valerie said. "The poor woman must have woken up or come to or whatever in a jail cell, with no idea how she got there."

His chuckles subsided, but he couldn't help smiling at the irony. "On December 7th, 1941," he murmured. "God, they probably figured she was a spy, or maybe some kind of smart-mouthed psychic. And when she found out the police had an unsolved murder on their hands . . ."

"You don't sound very worried," Valerie said. She sounded disapproving.

Lucas swiveled the desk chair and reached out to squeeze her hand. "I am, a little. But not as much as I was. Sam's in her element. Christ, she's got World War II *and* an unsolved murder! If she had to get zapped to some other time and place, this is exactly what she would've picked."

"Do you think she'll be able to do it— find the person who killed my father?"

"Oh, yeah. I think she'll find the murderer."

"And then what will happen?" Valerie asked with quiet intensity.

Lucas took her other hand and looked into her eyes. "What do you want to happen, Val?"

She closed her eyes and winced, as if she'd had a sudden pain. "I don't— I can't— "

"Just tell me. Be honest."

Her eyes opened, she met his questioning, anxious gaze. "I want to stay here. With you."

He lifted her hands with a shuddering sigh and kissed each palm. "That's what I want, too."

"But if I stay here, she'll have to stay there, won't she? And she probably wants to come back to her own time. Can we both be here, Lucas? Together, at the same time?"

He knew she wanted him to say yes. And heaven knew he wanted to say yes. But he had to be as honest with her as she'd been with him.

"I don't know, Val. I wish to God I did."

Neither Sam nor Major Connors had seen the photo in that morning's paper. The major went to the door and directed the sergeant standing guard outside to go find a copy. The sergeant was back in fifteen minutes. Sam wondered who he'd mugged to get a newspaper so fast at that time of night.

"I don't know, Joe," she said, as the three of them crowded together to study the photo. "It looks like a scar, but maybe it's just a shadow, or a flaw in the film. This picture is pretty grainy."

"It's a scar," Joe said. He'd obviously made up

his mind and wasn't going to change it just because the picture was a little fuzzy.

The major agreed that the line along the man's face looked like a scar to him. "From a knife wound, in fact," he added. "Just like Kyoshi said."

"Well, even if you're right," Sam pointed out, "he isn't identified in the caption under the photo, which means you're going to have to show it to at least a couple of the other people in it and ask them to identify him. And if he *is* Falconer, and he finds out the Army is asking questions about him, he'll be on the next plane to South America."

Major Connors looked at her in surprise. "Exactly what is it you do— or I suppose I should say *did*— in 1995, Miss Cook?"

The forthright question made Sam smile. She was still amazed at how quickly the major had accepted the truth. Of course he'd been dubious at first, but he hadn't let his prejudices get in the way of analyzing the evidence in his possession and acknowledging that it led to only one logical conclusion.

"She caught crooks," Joe answered before she could. There was a touch of pride in his voice that gave Sam a warm glow.

"I helped catch crooks," she corrected, then grinned. "When I wasn't listening to lectures about the second World War or beating the pants off my dad and granddad in a game of Axis and Allies."

"Ah, yes," the major murmured. "Sounds like a fascinating game. Too bad it hasn't been invented yet. Now, as for identifying the man in this photo— you're right, we'll have to be discreet. Especially considering where the picture was taken."

The event had been a fund-raiser for Bundles

For Britain, and the people grouped in the fore-
ground were all well-known socialites and prominent businessmen. The man who might or might
not be Falconer was standing behind and between
two of them. His head, the left half of his torso,
and his left arm were visible.

"You know, it looks like maybe he was trying.to
hide his face— as if he started to turn away at the
last second," Sam observed. "See, the image of the
woman standing next to him is sharper. Golly,
y'think maybe he didn't want his picture taken?"

"She's an attractive woman." Major Connors
tapped an index finger against the paper. "We
might have more luck if we asked about her. I
wonder if she was with him, or just happened to
be standing there when the photographer snapped
the picture."

"I think she's with him," Joe said. "She has her
hand on his arm. That is her hand, isn't it? Sam's
right, this picture is awfully grainy."

"We can take care of that," the major said.
"First thing tomorrow I'll send somebody down to
the newspaper to get the negative."

"I guess there's not much we can do for the
time being, is there?" Sam said hopefully. She was
dead on her feet. Now that Army Intelligence was
on to Falconer, Major Connors could take over.
She was looking forward to a long soak in a hot
tub, and then. . . . Her gaze slid to Joe's elegant,
long-fingered hand, resting on the table next to
the newspaper. Well, she'd see how tired she was
after a bath.

"On the contrary," the major said, dashing her
plans. "I want you to continue planting information about the Russian Front in Mr. Blumberg's
stories. In fact, I think we should up the ante."

"Up the ante?" Sam repeated, not liking the idea already. Damn, more late nights pounding away at that antique typewriter. "How do you mean?"

"Apparently Falconer is feeling the heat to convince us Operation Sea Lion is still on. How do you think he'd react if Mr. Blumberg started dropping hints that we're far from convinced?"

"He'd probably freak out," Sam murmured. "Maybe do something reckless."

"Like go after Alvie," Joe said solemnly.

"I'll provide protection for Mr. Blumberg," Connors promised. "Keep in mind that we have no proof either that Falconer is a German agent or that he murdered Colonel Herrick. Hell, I have only Miss Cook's word for it that Hitler's scrapped his plans for Sea Lion. Don't take this personally, ma'am, but I can't see myself trying to convince a U.S. Attorney to bring charges against him, based on nothing but the testimony of a woman who claims she's from the future."

"No," Sam murmured. "You'd probably be the one who ended up behind bars . . . or in a padded cell."

"Even after we've identified Falconer, we could pick him up for questioning, but we couldn't charge him without some kind of evidence. And as soon as he was released he'd be on the next flight to South America, just like you said."

"What about Samantha?" Joe asked. "Would you also provide protection for her?"

"Why would I need protection?" Sam asked. "We're the only three people besides Alvie who know I've been augmenting his stories. Besides, I have a live-in FBI agent to protect me."

"But maybe not for long, after tonight," Joe said

dryly. "Boggs and Ragsdale are going to have to take their anger out on somebody, and I'm the most likely candidate."

"Leave those two to me," Connors said. "What I told them about Attorney General Biddle ordering Mr. Hoover to back off was true."

"Wonderful," Joe muttered. "That should guarantee I'll be out of a job when this is all over."

"Well, if worst comes to worst," the major said matter-of-factly, "I'd be happy to put in a good word for you with Major General Donovan. The scuttlebutt is he's been tapped to head up some new intelligence agency."

Judging by Joe's expression, Sam didn't think the offer gave him much comfort.

Twenty

Most of the next morning was a blur. The sun was peeking over the horizon by the time Sam finished typing Alvie's copy. She almost fell asleep over her scrambled eggs and toast. Then when Joe and the boarders had left for the day, she had to deal with Esther's endless stream of questions while the two of them washed the breakfast dishes.

She'd already decided to tell Esther everything. It was her house, after all, and she should be forewarned in case Falconer did decide to come after Alvie. There was also the "protection" Major Connors had promised— Sam suspected Esther would notice right away if armed soldiers set up camp in her backyard.

"It sounds like the neighborhood is going to get pretty crowded," Esther remarked as she swept the kitchen floor. "What with the FBI agents already keeping you under surveillance and now who knows how many soldiers from Army Intelligence moving in. I wonder what they'll do if they bump into each other."

"Probably shoot first and ask questions later," Sam mumbled. "Hopefully they'll shoot each other and not us or the neighbors."

Esther put the broom and dustpan away and came to pluck the dish towel out of her hands.

"Go upstairs and take a nap. You can finish telling me about your meeting with Major Connors later."

Sam didn't even make a token protest. "Bless you, Esther," she said with feeling. "I owe you two chocolate cream pies and a huge batch of oatmeal cookies. But there isn't much more to tell about last night's little get-together." She lifted a hand to cover a yawn. "Oh, there was one other thing— the major's going to send somebody to the newspaper, to collect the negative of that picture that was in yesterday morning's edition."

"The one of the man Joe thinks is Falconer?"

"Right. Frankly, it's a long shot. The mark that looks like a scar will probably turn out to be a shadow or a dirty spot on the camera lens, or the guy will turn out to be a U.S. Senator or somebody from the British Embassy. Really, what are the odds that a photo of the very man we're looking for would conveniently show up in the newspaper?"

"Probably not very good," Esther admitted. "But stranger things have happened. For instance, people jumping across 54 years in the blink of an eye."

Sam gave her a tired smile. "All right, it's possible, but I'm not getting my hopes up. If I'm not downstairs by the time you're ready to start dinner, come and wake me."

Esther appeared in her bedroom to shake her awake a couple of hours later, but not because it was time to start dinner.

"Sam. *Sam!* Wake up!"

Samantha dragged the pillow over her head, but Esther yanked it away and shook her shoulder again, hard enough to rouse her from a coma.

"You have to wake up. This is important!"

"All *right!*" Sam sat up and shoved her hair out of her face. "What? Is the house on fire?"

"No, it's nothing like that. Where did you put your ring?"

Still a little groggy, Sam swung her legs off the bed and rubbed at her eyes with the heels of her hands. "What?"

"That big emerald ring, the one you were wearing when you got here— where is it?"

"Middle drawer of the dresser, in the right hand corner, under the panties." She was awake now, but more than a little bewildered. She collected the dress she'd removed before crawling under the covers from the foot of the bed and pulled it over her head. "What's going on?"

Esther tossed a large manila envelope onto the bed and went to rummage among the new underwear Sam had bought during their shopping excursion. She found the ring and brought it to the bed. Her eyes glittered with feverish excitement.

"Major Connors sent a soldier to deliver a copy of that photo that was in the newspaper, for you and Joe to study. It's in the envelope. Take it out and look at it."

Sam finished buttoning the bodice of her dress and picked up the envelope. The photo inside was an 8-x-10 black and white glossy. The first thing she noticed about it was that the resolution was much sharper. The second thing she noticed was that the mark on the unidentified man's face— which was about four times larger than the reproduction in the newspaper— was definitely a scar, and not a shadow or a flaw in the film.

The third thing she noticed was the right hand of the woman standing next to him, resting with casual intimacy on his left sleeve. Or, more accurately, she noticed the large ring on the woman's third finger.

Esther held Sam's ring next to the one in the picture. "It's the same ring, isn't it? Surely there can't be two just like this one."

Sam suddenly felt lightheaded. She sank down on the bed, her mesmerized gaze fixed on the ring in the photo.

"No," she murmured. "It looks the same, but it can't be."

The denial sounded hollow even to her. It was the same ring. She knew it, without knowing how she knew.

"It is," Esther argued. "Look at it, Sam! It's exactly the same! Didn't you say your ring was a family heirloom or something—that it belonged to your mother?"

Samantha felt cold all the way to her bones. "Yes."

"Well then . . . what does this mean? How can the woman in the picture be wearing the ring, when you have it?"

"I don't know," Sam said. Her voice sounded as if she were speaking from inside a long, deep tunnel.

"Do you think— Could she be— "

"I don't know," Sam repeated. Esther didn't have to finish the question. The same thought had occurred to her: Could the woman in the photo— the woman who had evidently attended this charity affair with a man who was more than likely a German spy—be related to her?

The possibility gnawed at her the rest of the afternoon, while she helped Esther dust and polish and mop. Should she try to contact Major Connors, tell him about the ring? No, she decided. For one thing, there was no way to be sure it *was* the same ring; she had only her own gut certainty to offer as confirmation, and she doubted he'd be willing to accept that. The major had already swallowed the premise that she'd traveled here from more than 50 years in the future; Sam was reluctant to strain her own credibility more than she already had. Besides, if she told him about the ring and he believed her, what then? Establishing a connection between herself and the man in the picture might place her under suspicion, as well.

She desperately wanted to know about the woman in the photo, though— who was she, and what was her relationship to the man with the scar?— and Major Connors was probably the only person who could provide that information. Assuming he'd managed to find out who the man was.

In the end, the major contacted her before she could decide whether to try to get in touch with him, or how. The telephone rang in the middle of dinner. Joe got up to answer it, and was away from the table less than five minutes. When he returned, he said only that he'd have to go out for a while later.

"This wouldn't have something to do with the order the Attorney General issued yesterday, would it, Joe?" Alvie asked slyly. "I heard all the U.S. Attorneys have been told not to prosecute anybody for seditious speech without Biddle's consent."

"If I were you, Alvie," Chet remarked, "I'd be more worried about the censorship office Roosevelt just named AP's executive news editor to head up. Considering the things you've been publishing lately, they might be calling Joe in to ask if he thinks one of your sources is a Nazi agent."

"Give it up, fellas," Joe said flatly. "You both know I won't talk about my work."

Sam hadn't had much appetite to begin with, and it deserted her altogether after the mysterious phone call. She hoped Joe would hang around long enough to explain what it had been about. To her surprise, he loitered at the end of the meal and began stacking plates.

"I'll help clear the table before I leave."

He said it loudly enough to be heard by Owen and Martha, who were the last to file out of the dining room. Sam followed him into the kitchen, but he deposited the plates on the table and hurried out again before she could ask about the call. He was back seconds later, though— carrying both his coat and hers.

"Come on, Major Connors has a car waiting for us a couple of blocks up the street."

"Us?" Sam asked uneasily as she pulled on her coat.

"That's what he said."

The major was sitting in the front seat with his driver, who pulled away from the curb as soon as the rear door was shut.

"We have a problem," Connors said without preamble. "My superiors aren't buying your claim that Operation Sea Lion is a no-go. The way they see it, Falconer provided Colonel Herrick with a lot of reliable information over the past year or so, and there's no reason to assume his Sea Lion intelligence isn't just as sound."

Sam was stunned. "I don't believe it!"

"Not only that," he added. "There's some concern about why you would try to convince us that Hitler's scrapped Sea Lion."

"Shortsighted idiots," Joe muttered.

"I'm still trying to identify the man in the newspaper photo," Connors said. "But if I can't convince anybody at the top that he's the one who's been feeding us false information, I don't know how much good it's going to do." He paused, laying an arm along the back of his seat, his attention focused intently on Samantha.

"I've been thinking about what it might take to persuade the top brass you're on the level. Is there anything else you could give me to pass on to them— something so hush-hush that even my superiors would have to go higher to check it out?"

She closed her eyes and tried to think. Anything that hadn't happened yet would be impossible to confirm. It would have to be something from the past . . . before America got into the war . . .

"Yes," she said quietly. "There is something else, but nobody's going to want to hear it. In fact, it might cause a lot of trouble for both of us."

Connors didn't hesitate. "Tell me."

Sam took a deep breath. "Last January the American Ambassador to Japan sent a coded message to the State Department. The message said the ambassador's staff had heard rumors the Japanese were planning a surprise attack on Pearl Harbor. The State Department passed the message to the Department of the Navy, and Naval Intelligence passed it on to Admiral Kimmel."

"The Commander in Chief of the Pacific fleet!" Joe exclaimed.

"None other," she confirmed. "Nobody, including Admiral Kimmel's staff, took the rumors seriously."

"And you say this happened last *January*?" Connors demanded. Sam nodded. "Jesus Christ! Heads will roll for sure."

"And yours may be the first," she pointed out. "You know that old saying about killing the bearer of bad news."

"She's right," Joe said solemnly. "Nobody's going to want to hear this. Especially not now, with the Pacific fleet reduced to so much scrap metal."

Major Connors slammed his fist against the seat. "But damn it to hell, people *should* hear it! It should be rammed down their throats. Almost three thousand men were killed at Pearl Harbor."

"Wait!" Sam muttered. "Hold on a sec. I just thought of something else you could use to convince them— Magic."

"Magic?" Joe repeated. "Samantha, this isn't the time for jokes."

"I'm not joking. Magic is the name the Signal Intelligence Service gave the project to break Japanese codes. The toughest one was called Purple. It was a diplomatic code, and they finally managed to break it last summer. The naval codes were a lot harder to break, partly because the Japanese kept changing them, but the United States has been decrypting Japanese diplomatic messages for months." She leaned forward to make sure she had Major Connors's full attention.

"On December 1st, we intercepted a communiqué to Japan's Ambassador to Germany, in which he was instructed to tell Hitler it was likely that war would soon break out between the United States and Japan. You could tell your superiors about Magic, and Purple, and save the December 1st message as a trump card in case they still aren't convinced. Do you think that might do the trick?"

He smiled with grim satisfaction. "I think it just might, Miss Cook."

* * *

Major Connors had promised to let them know as soon as he identified the man in the photo. In the meantime, he instructed Sam to beef up the information she was adding to Alvie's stories.

"Add some heavy-duty details," he encouraged. "Things that will get Falconer's attention and make him start to sweat. Can you do that?"

"I can do it," Sam said. "The question is, will Alvie and his editor go along?"

"Leave them to me. I'll have a little talk with the two of them first thing tomorrow morning."

"But what about the new censorship office?" Joe said. "This is precisely the sort of thing they've been authorized to suppress."

"Not exactly," Connors replied. "Mr. Price is supposed to prevent people from leaking our plans to the enemy. I don't think he'll squawk much if American newspapers start publishing the Nazis' secrets."

The next day, Alvie's paper carried another story about the Russian Front under his byline. The article reported that General von Brauchitsch had ordered Field Marshal von Bock's army to withdraw and establish a winter line ninety miles from Moscow, but that Hitler, upon learning of the order, had flown into a rage, countermanded it, and sacked von Bock. The story ended with the prediction that Hitler would replace all his generals in Russia before the New Year. Anyone who read between the lines couldn't help but conclude that der Führer was at the very least out of touch with reality, if not stark raving mad.

Alvie went pale when he first read the copy, but that night he was strutting like the rooster Joe had labeled him. He didn't mention the visit he'd received from Major Connors or ask Sam any questions she wouldn't have been free to answer, for which she was grateful. Obviously whatever the major said to him had erased any lingering doubts Alvie had about the information she was providing.

His lead story the following day disclosed that "an anonymous, knowledgeable source" had confided that Admiral Wilhelm Canaris, chief of Germany's Foreign Intelligence and Counter-Espionage Bureau, was convinced the Führer's insane lust for power would lead his country to humiliating defeat. According to this source, Alvie reported, Abwehr personnel under Canaris had warned European leaders that their countries were about to be attacked as early as May of 1940. And, as if these revelations weren't sensational enough, the same anonymous source claimed it was only a matter of time before Germany's most senior military leaders would band together and attempt to remove Adolph Hitler from power.

"Don't you think you went a little overboard?" Joe asked that night, when he and Sam were alone in his room. "Predicting Hitler's own generals will turn against him?"

"Major Connors said he wanted heavy-duty details," she replied as she draped her slip over the back of the desk chair. "And every word of it's true."

He waited till she'd climbed under the covers and nestled against him to ask, "I don't suppose you'd tell me whether they'll succeed."

Sam kissed his chest and ran her hands down his body. "Not a chance."

"That they'll succeed?"

"That I'll tell you."

He caught her to him for a long, deep kiss. "You're a hard woman, Samantha Cook."

Her hand administered an intimate caress that made him moan. "That's definitely a case of the pot calling the kettle black."

"It's no use trying to distract me. If you won't talk, I guess I'll just have to seduce you to get the information I want."

"I'd like to see you try," she murmured with a wicked grin.

Lucas scowled at the monitor as if he could will the text to change.

"I don't understand why you're so upset," Valerie said. "If it's true, why shouldn't the newspaper have printed it?"

"Because nobody in 1941 could have *known* about it," he said in exasperation. "At least nobody in Washington, D.C."

"Obviously one person knew," she pointed out. "The reporter who wrote the story."

Lucas shook his head and started scrolling backwards through the text, checking to see what other surprises he might have overlooked.

"Impossible, unless he was a fortune-teller, or somebody inside the Third Reich was feeding him information." He abruptly stopped scrolling. "Or—no, surely she wouldn't—"

"Who wouldn't?" Val asked. "Are you talking about Samantha? Oh, of course! *She* would know things other people in 1941 couldn't possibly know. Well, there's your explanation. She must have told this reporter that Hitler's generals would try to overthrow him."

"But why?" He was utterly confounded; it didn't make any sense. "She had to have realized that revealing information about the future might *change* the future— *her* future."

"And make it impossible for her to return to her own time, you mean," Val surmised. "Then, if she's the one who gave the reporter this information, she must have thought it was necessary." She paused a beat, then murmured, "She must be quite a woman."

"Yes." Lucas turned from the monitor and lifted a hand to gently caress her cheek. "She is."

Valerie captured his hand and kissed the palm, letting him know she wasn't feeling jealous or insecure. "Where did you meet her?"

"At a Halloween party. I went as Clark Kent. I hate trying to put together a costume, so I always go as Clark Kent. All I have to do is load my hair with styling gel, stick a notebook and pen in my pocket, and leave my glasses on all night. Sam was— "

"Let me guess. Lois Lane."

He laughed and shook his head. "Sherlock Holmes, complete with cape, Meerschaum pipe and deerstalker cap. She asked if I was supposed to be an accountant, and when I said no, I was Superman's alter ego, she said if I couldn't come up with anything better than that I should've stayed home."

Valerie laughed. "Ouch! So it wasn't exactly love at first sight."

"No," Lucas murmured. "That's only happened once." He leaned over to kiss her, marveling that he should be sitting here telling her about Samantha, and that she was laughing and encouraging him.

"It was sort of a rocky start," he said when he straightened. "But it was a boring party and we ended up in the kitchen telling each other our life stories. We discovered we were both adopted and that neither of us had ever had the slightest desire to search for our biological parents. That gave us something in common, a sort of bond, I guess. By the time the party broke up, we'd made a date for dinner the next night."

"I don't think I've ever known anyone who was adopted," Val said. "Did your parents tell you when you were little?"

Lucas nodded. "When I was six or seven. Does that bother you—that I can't trace my ancestry back for fifty generations?"

"Of course not!"

"Because I could find out who my birth parents were, if I wanted. My mother told me when I was sixteen that the records are accessible."

She reached out and gripped both his hands, hard. "Lucas, it doesn't matter to me."

"Well, it might, someday."

"I can't imagine why."

He turned his hands and linked their fingers. "Sometimes it's good to know your biological family history. For example, if you decide to have children."

"Oh," Val said faintly.

"You know, so you'll be aware of any genetic problems that might get passed on. Not that I have any genetic problems," he added with a crooked smile.

She smiled back. "None that I've noticed, anyway."

He stood, pulling her out of her chair and into his arms. A few minutes later he remembered to disconnect from the news database he'd been scanning and switch off Sam's computer.

There'd been no word from Major Connors, and Sam was starting to get antsy. She decided to go for broke with the next story.

"Are you sure you want to do this?" Joe asked when she showed him the copy.

"Yes. No." She heaved a frustrated sigh. "Damn it, nothing's happening. Somebody has to do *something* to shake things loose."

He frowned for a moment, then acceded with a nod. "You're probably right, but I'm not crazy about the idea of you being that somebody."

Sam thought she knew what was bothering him. He was the man—the stalwart FBI agent, for crying out loud—and it was 1941. *He* was supposed to be the one who made the decisions and then set events in motion. At least that was probably how he saw it. Then again, he'd grown up with Esther for a sister, which you'd think would have cured him of any chauvinist tendencies long ago.

She wished she could think of a way to let him know how necessary he'd become to her, without giving him the idea that she would ever permit him to "take care" of her. God forbid. A pedestal was probably a neat place to hang out if you were a marble bust or a fern, but Sam had never been able to comprehend why any woman would allow herself to be *placed* on one. Which, she suspected, was exactly what Joe Mercer would try to do to a woman he was out-of-his-gourd, head-over-heels in love with.

But then he'd never said he loved her—not even when he was making exquisite love to her—so it wasn't a predicament she needed to waste time fretting about. Damn it.

She was tempted, for about the five hundredth time, to tell him about the ring. Not because she expected or wanted him to do anything about it, of course, just because she would have liked to ask what he thought, and maybe what he thought *she* should do. And for the five hundredth time, she repressed the urge. It would only give him one more thing to worry about, in addition to catching a German agent, solving a murder, and whether he was going to have a job next month.

Besides, if she got the chance, Sam planned to make contact with the woman in the photo, find out everything she could about her. Because it *was* the same ring.

Twenty-one

Alvie still hadn't come home from work when everyone else sat down to dinner.

"Gosh, I hope nothing's happened to him," Gert Willis remarked. "I've never known Alvie to miss a meal."

Chet's mouth twisted in a sardonic grimace. "After the story he ran today, I wouldn't be surprised if the censorship office had both him and his editor arrested and the newspaper building boarded up."

"Wasn't that incredible?" Martha exclaimed. "How does he find out about these things?"

"I wish I could say he makes them up, Martha," Chet muttered. "But the truth is, he's latched onto one heck of a source. I'd give my left arm to have a contact like that. So would every other reporter I know."

"So you think what he said in today's paper is true, then?" Owen asked.

"Yeah, I do. It sounds like just the kind of scheme Hitler would come up with. Besides, Alvie doesn't have that good an imagination."

Sam listened and kept her head down, figuratively and literally. She hoped Alvie's lead story was generating this much interest in dining rooms all over Washington.

It had been a follow-up to the "Hitler Plans to Invade England" piece. Except that today Alvie had astonished his readers by repudiating the rumors that his newspaper and several others had been reporting for the past couple of weeks. This afternoon's headline had read "Invasion Plans Determined To Be Nazi Hoax." According to Alvie's (by now famous) anonymous source, military intelligence had concluded that a German invasion would be impossible so long as the RAF controlled the skies over the English Channel . . . a situation that wasn't expected to change for the duration of the war.

The story had been picked up by the radio networks, and would no doubt be passed on by the wire services and appear in other newspapers tomorrow morning. Unless Falconer never read a newspaper or turned on a radio, he was sure to hear about it.

Of course, so were Major Connors's superiors. Sam hadn't heard a peep from the major, and since Joe hadn't said anything, she assumed neither had he.

When Alvie still hadn't shown up by the time dinner was finished and the other four boarders trooped off to listen to the radio in the parlor, Sam started to worry.

"Do you think Army Intelligence might have picked him up for questioning?" she asked Joe as they carried dishes into the kitchen.

"I doubt it," he replied. "Since Connors knows it was you who wrote that story. I'm more concerned about Falconer."

"So am I," Esther said. "And where's this protection the Army was supposed to provide for Alvie? I've been keeping an eye out, but I haven't seen any strangers who look like they might be Army bodyguards."

"Why don't we phone the newspaper offices?" Sam suggested. "Maybe he's just working late."

If he was working late, he didn't answer the phone.

"Shouldn't *somebody* be there to answer?" Esther said anxiously.

Sam shook her head. "If they put out a morning edition, that crew would be working now, but since it's an afternoon paper everybody probably went home hours ago."

The three of them were still standing in the hall, trying to decide what to do next, when the phone rang. Esther snatched up the handset and barked a tense, "Hello." A second later she handed the phone to Joe. "It's Major Connors."

The conversation lasted only a minute or two, during which Joe spoke four terse sentences: "Yes, sir," "No, that won't be a problem," "Yes, of course," and "I'll be ready."

"What's going on?" Sam asked when he hung up.

He was writing a number on a sheet of the note paper Esther kept by the phone. He handed the paper to Sam.

"He's sending a car for me. They've collected some photos of men who might be Falconer. Mr. Takamura's coming in to have a look at them."

"But you've never seen him," Sam pointed out. "In the flesh, I mean. What possible help can you be?"

Joe shrugged. "I assume Connors wants somebody from the Bureau on hand, in case Boggs finds out they're using a possible Japanese agent to identify a suspected German agent, and raises a fuss. That phone number is for the major's office. There's always somebody there to take messages. If you hear from Alvie, let us know."

He headed for the stairs. Sam followed. "Maybe I should come with you. I'd like to talk to Connors about how much more information it would be safe to use in Alvie's stories."

Joe was already halfway up the stairs. He abruptly stopped and jerked around to rap out a sharp "No!" that froze her in the process of reaching for her coat.

"No," he said again, his tone more moderate. "It's better if you stay here, in case Alvie calls. It shouldn't take long for Mr. Takamura to look at the photos. I'll tell Major Connors you want to talk to him, but right now I have to hurry. The car he's sending should be here any minute."

Sam frowned as she watched him take the rest of the stairs to the second floor landing two at a time. Maybe that spontaneous, autocratic "No!" had been his latent chauvinist streak bursting forth, in which case she would straighten him out as soon as he got back from this males-only powwow.

But maybe— and this possibility was even more disagreeable— he and Connors just didn't want her around when they identified Falconer.

Esther returned to the kitchen to finish washing the dinner dishes, but Sam was waiting at the bottom of the stairs when Joe came back down. She handed him his topcoat.

"Is Connors planning something important tonight?" she asked bluntly. "Something besides looking at pictures?"

He slipped the coat on and gave her a quizzical look. "Nothing I'm aware of."

Sam studied him intently. He looked and sounded sincere. Still, she couldn't shake the feeling that he was holding out on her. The mellow sounds of Frank Sinatra crooning "All Or Nothing At All" wafted from the parlor. Sam remembered what she'd thought the first time she'd heard Old Blue Eyes on the radio: He's no Harry Connick, Jr., but he'll do till the real thing comes along. The song ended and an annoying jingle for Pepsi Cola started playing. Joe headed for the front door. She went with him.

"I just thought maybe something new had come up . . . something you don't want me to know about."

He peered through the glass of the door. "The car's here." Already reaching for the doorknob with his right hand, he slid his left arm around her waist for a quick hug and a brief but hard kiss. "Fat chance I'd have of keeping anything from you. This shouldn't take long. Call the major's office if you hear from Alvie, all right?"

Sam nodded silently. She stood at the door, arms folded and forehead crinkled in an irritated frown, until he'd climbed into the car and it pulled away.

"Liar," she muttered under her breath. He was hiding *something*, all right. When he'd pulled her against him in that one-armed hug, she'd felt the unmistakable bulge of the shoulder holster and gun he'd gone to his room to collect.

If she'd had any idea where he was headed, she'd have phoned for a cab and gone after him. She unfolded her arms and scowled at the phone number he'd jotted down, tempted to dial it and give both Joe and Major Connors a piece of her mind. Arrogant, tyrannical men! How dare they shut her out, just when it looked like they were about to nab Falconer! But then she remembered that Joe hadn't said they were meeting at Connors's office, only that someone would be there to take a message.

"*Damn* it!" she said fiercely as she turned from the door to go help Esther with the dishes. It was just as she'd suspected— Joe Mercer was too much a product of his time to ever accept her as an equal. No doubt when she confronted him, he'd spout some macho bullshit about it being his responsibility to protect her, keep her out of harm's way. What garbage!

She was halfway down the hall when the phone rang again. "I've got it," she called to Esther before marching back to pick up the receiver and greet the caller with a rude, "Yes, who is it?"

There was an uncertain silence before Alvie Blumberg replied, "Samantha? Is that you?"

Sam released a gusty sigh and leaned against the wall. "Yes, it's me, Alvie. Sorry, I'm in kind of a bad mood right now. Where are you? We were worried when you didn't show up for dinner. Esther's keeping a plate warm for you, but if you don't get home soon, Chet's liable to— "

"Can you talk?" Alvie blurted.

Sam blinked in surprise. He sounded nervous. And maybe a little scared?

"If you mean is Esther around, no," she said wryly. "She's in the kitchen. Relax, Alvie, she's not gonna scalp you for missing dinner. Want me to call her to the phone?"

"*No!* No, it's you I called to talk to, Samantha."

Sam straightened from the wall, her amusement evaporating. Yes, there was definitely a thread of fear in his voice.

"What's wrong?"

"Well, uh . . . there's somebody here who wants to—"

"Where?" Sam interrupted. "Where are you? At the newspaper?"

Alvie didn't respond. There was some background noise, someone speaking in an angry, threatening tone.

"Alvie?" she said, keeping her voice low so Esther and the boarders wouldn't hear. "Are you there? Are you all right? Say something, damn it!"

"Mr. Blumberg is quite all right," a new voice said coolly. "For the time being."

It was the German accent, rather than the implied threat, that made Sam snap to attention.

"Who is this?" she demanded. "What's going on?"

"An excellent question," the man said. "I'm hoping you can provide the answer, Miss Cook. Mr. Blumberg has informed me that you are the 'anonymous source' who has furnished much of the information contained in his newspaper articles during the past week."

Sam's hand clenched on the receiver. *Falconer!*

"Is this correct?" he asked.

She squeezed her eyes shut and tried to think. If she said no, what would he do to Alvie? *Stall,* her instincts urged.

"And if it is?" By sheer force of will she managed to sound as cool and suspicious as the man on the other end of the line.

"Then it's imperative that we talk."

Sam's knees almost buckled. He wanted to talk to her? "Talk" being a euphemism for what?

"I'm . . ." She swallowed, trying to work up some spit. "I seriously doubt I could tell you anything you don't already know."

He laughed harshly. "On the contrary, Miss Cook. You obviously know a great deal more than I do. Surely you understand the extremely hazardous position your meddling has placed me in."

"And surely you knew the dangers when you accepted your present assignment," Sam shot back. The nerve of some people. He was a *spy* for God's sake!

"I have a family! A wife and a daughter. I was assured that I would be warned if their safety was about to be compromised."

Sam's eyebrows jerked together in surprise. "Excuse me?"

"You *owe* it to me to explain your actions. I'll be waiting at Mr Blumberg's newspaper."

Sam's mouth fell open. She *owed* it to him? By the time she untangled her tongue, he'd hung up. She replaced the receiver in its cradle and stared at the phone for a full minute. And then it suddenly hit her.

He thought *she* was a German agent.

The E-mail message was waiting the next time Lucas logged onto the Internet gateway. He reread it twice, then printed it and read it again. He didn't recognize the sender's ID number, but the message had obviously come from someone who knew him. It looked like part of a genealogy chart, only reversed. His name and date of birth were at the top, followed by a line that read "Josephine Mirkovic, b. July 12, 1944, Munich, Germany," and a third line filled with question marks.

But it was the brief personal note at the end of the message that left him stunned and shaken:

"I've discovered who my birth parents were, Lucas. Isn't it time you did? I'll contact you two weeks from today and we'll make plans for that steak dinner you owe me."

There was no name, but the message could only have come from one person. Which meant Samantha was back.

Here . . . in 1995.

Sam had experienced a fleeting moment of panic— neither Joe nor Major Connors was available and God knew how long it would take to get a message through to them— and then she realized that this was probably the only chance she'd ever get to talk to Falconer, alone and in person.

He'd said he had a wife and daughter. Was his wife the woman standing next to him in the photo? Was that even *him* in the photo? There was only one way to find out. She looked up the number of a taxi company and ordered a cab, then grabbed a pen and scribbled a quick note, which she left next to the phone.

Expecting Esther to appear any minute to ask who the second phone call was from and why she wasn't in the kitchen drying dishes and silverware, she dashed upstairs to collect a few dollars for the cab, snared her coat from the coat tree at the foot of the stairs, and slipped out to wait on the porch until the cab arrived.

She didn't remember the FBI agents who'd been assigned to watch her until the cab was on its way. Were they still hanging around? Damn, she'd hate for Boggs to get the credit for capturing Falconer. Of course, as far as she knew Boggs wasn't even aware that Falconer existed, but she decided not to take any chances. She leaned forward and instructed the driver to drop her off a couple of blocks from the address she'd given him.

She sprinted between buildings and down a couple of alleys and arrived at the newspaper where Alvie worked, out of breath and with a stitch in her side, only to find the main entrance locked. Well of course, it would be, she told herself as she leaned a shoulder against the brick wall. Her breath puffed out in small, chained clouds of vapor that gradually became larger and spaced further apart.

What now? Had Esther found her note yet, and called Major Connors's office? If she had, the 1941 version of the cavalry might come charging up any second now. Of course it was just as likely that a pair of FBI agents would cruise around the corner and spot her before she could find a way into the building. She probably didn't have much time, in either case.

She found three more doors. The first two were locked. The third wasn't, but it admitted her to a huge warehouse-type area that was apparently where the newspapers were brought to be loaded onto delivery trucks. Enough moonlight filtered through the tall, grimy windows for her to see that, at the moment, the cavernous room was empty. No bundled and stacked newspapers, but no Alvie and no German agent, either.

"Great," Sam muttered. If she'd gone to all this trouble and Falconer had taken off before she could get here, she was going to be highly pissed. She impulsively turned around and engaged the deadbolt on the door she'd just come through, then started toward an open staircase that looked like it might lead to offices.

At the top of the stairs was a narrow hallway.

Yellow light spilled through an open door about halfway down. Sam squared her shoulders, took a deep breath, and started toward the door. She didn't try to be quiet; that might get her killed. The clunky heels of her old-lady shoes hammered against the hardwood floor, announcing her approach to anyone who wasn't stone deaf. The pounding of her heart was almost as loud.

"Come in, Miss Cook," the voice from the phone said as she neared the door.

Her step faltered for a second, but then she jacked up her courage and moved into the doorway. The man from the newspaper photo stood in front of a large wooden desk placed at a right angle to the door. The prominent scar on the left side of his face was sharply highlighted in the glare of the desk lamp. Sam was aware that part of her mind registered the fact that Joe had been right—the man in the photo was Falconer. But the larger part of her consciousness was busy trying to cope with an astonished comprehension that threatened to take her legs out from under her. The man's stunned greeting betrayed that he was just as unnerved by the sight of her.

"My God!" he murmured, his voice hushed with something like awe. "Who *are* you?"

Sam was very much afraid she knew. Suddenly everything fell into place. The question that had plagued her since she woke up in that freezing jail cell— why me?— was answered the instant she saw him. The answer was manifested in his gleaming dark auburn hair and astute emerald eyes, in the sharply defined features that were larger, stronger copies of her own.

She was looking at a masculine version of herself.

"That's Samantha Cook. You told her to come."

It was Alvie who spoke, from a chair in the corner. The response jolted them both out of their dazed paralysis. Falconer gestured brusquely for Sam to move into the office. She stepped to the middle of the room and he closed the door behind her.

"Are you all right, Alvie?" she said. It took every ounce of self-control she possessed to present a facade of cool composure. Questions she couldn't ask and might never have answered were shrieking inside her head, demanding recognition. She tried to shut them out.

"Yeah," Alvie muttered. "He roughed me up a little, but I'm okay. He's got a gun."

Sam turned to Falconer. "Let him go. He's only a pawn."

"And as such, expendable," he replied without a second's hesitation. "Answer my question. Who are you?"

The shock she'd experienced when she first saw him was ebbing, but the fear that seeped in to take its place was almost as debilitating. There was a deadly menace in those eyes so like her own, a coldness that would numb her mind if she let it. *Think!* she told herself fiercely. Whatever else he might be, he was a German spy who had already committed one murder to protect his identity. And Alvie had said he had a gun.

She remembered locking the door downstairs—the only door that had been *un*locked—and her stomach roiled.

Think, for God's sake!

She needed an advantage, something she could use against him. Suddenly she remembered what he'd said on the phone— "You owe it to me to explain your actions." Evidently he had assumed, because of the information she'd been inserting into Alvie's stories, that she, too, was a German agent.

"More to the point," she said, making her voice flat and hard, "who are you, to call me out like this? Why have you risked exposing me to the Americans?"

"The *Americans?*" Alvie blurted.

Sam whipped her head toward him and snarled, "Shut up, you little worm, or I'll shoot you myself!"

The threat may have been empty but her anger was real, though only partly directed at Alvie. Where the hell was the protection Major Connors had promised to give him? For that matter, where the hell was Major Connors? Surely Esther had phoned his office by now.

"Well?" she said, turning her attention back to Falconer. "Explain yourself."

Miracle of miracles, the arrogant demand worked. A slight adjustment to his posture, the unconscious twitch of his hand, told her she'd managed to put him on the defensive.

"I had to know who was providing this man with such high level intelligence," he said curtly. "And to what purpose."

"My reasons for giving him the information are none of your concern," Sam said coldly.

"It *is* my concern when what you are doing subverts my mission!" he retorted furiously. "I agreed to bring my wife and child to this nation of mongrels. I've subjected them to living among halfbreeds, and worse. I've dishonored myself and my family by publicly renouncing the Fatherland, and provided the enemy with military intelligence that could result in the deaths of loyal German soldiers . . . all to establish my credibility. And with one stroke, you have managed to destroy everything— *everything!*"

The hatred and bitterness in his voice spewed like venom. Sam had to steel herself not to flinch, or show any sign of weakness or fear. His fanaticism and bigotry had made him as twisted as the sadistic madman whose values and beliefs he obviously shared. The thought that his blood might be flowing through her own veins sickened her.

"It is you who owe me an explanation," he said, eyes narrowing with sudden suspicion. "On what authority did you make this information public?"

Sam swallowed the sour taste pooling at the back of her mouth. She didn't know how much longer she'd be able to stall. "My orders came from the highest level of the Abwehr."

"Canaris!" He hissed the name, his voice filled with loathing. "I might have known. The traitor!"

Bad move, Sam thought. She'd assumed he worked for military counter-intelligence and would be impressed, if not intimidated, by the mere mention of Canaris's bureau. Obviously she'd been mistaken.

"If you weren't sent by Admiral Canaris— " she began.

"I report directly to *Sicherheitsdienst* headquarters," he informed her proudly.

Sam's blood ran cold. The SD! The Nazi party's security service had been run by Heinrich Himmler, the most powerful and dangerous man in Germany after Hitler. The SD, like Himmler's blackshirted *Schutzstaffel* troops— the more well-known and universally feared SS— were the elite of the elite.

"But the SD has no authority to operate outside

the Fatherland," she stammered, automatically quoting from one of Gramps's interminable lectures.

"Patriotism does not recognize national borders," he replied haughtily. And then he suddenly moved, grasping both her arms in a painful grip. "We have wasted enough time! Tell me why Canaris ordered you to sabotage my mission."

Sam stared into the green eyes that might have been mirror images of her own and knew this was it, the end of the line. She'd run out of doubletalk, he'd called her bluff, and now he would kill both her and Alvie. Incredibly, her fear drained away. She wasn't ready to die, and especially not like this, at this man's hand— she suddenly realized that she didn't even know his name— but there was nothing more she could do. She decided she might as well go with a clean conscience.

"Admiral Canaris didn't send me," she said huskily. "You're going to find this hard to believe, but I came here from— "

Before she could finish, the door to the office crashed open. Falconer instantly released her to reach inside his coat for his gun. Sam looked around in time to see Joe shoulder his way past the splintered door, a .38 revolver in his hand.

"No!"

She didn't realize she'd cried out. Acting purely on instinct, she threw herself at Falconer, arms flying up and out to shove him off balance. As she slammed into him, the small office was filled with two deafening explosions.

Twenty-two

It might have been seconds or months later that Sam realized she was lying on the floor and someone was kneeling beside her, calling her name in a frightened voice.

Joe's voice.

"*Samantha!* Oh, God. Please, sweetheart, if you can hear me, open your eyes."

Sweetheart?

She pried her eyes open, then squeezed them shut again as pain shot down her right arm.

"What— ? Damn, that hurts."

"Thank God." His voice shook with relief. And maybe something else? He sat on the floor and gently lifted her head and shoulders onto his lap, folding her injured arm across her stomach. "Don't move. There's a doctor on the way."

"You just moved me," she pointed out. "And I wish you wouldn't do it again until somebody shoots me full of morphine." She became aware that Major Connors and another officer were hauling Falconer off the floor and slapping a set of handcuffs on him. "God, my arm feels like it's broken."

"You were shot," Joe said.

"*I* was?" She lifted her head and stared at her arm in amazement. Since she was still wearing Esther's borrowed coat, she couldn't see much—just a hole in the sleeve and some blood. It wasn't gushing out, at least. She dropped her head back on Joe's lap. "Who shot me?"

He winced. "I'm afraid I did."

"What!"

"Well, it was your own fault. You jumped in front of me at the last second."

"Why in God's name did you do that?" Major Connors growled from the doorway as he handed his prisoner over to two MPs standing in the hall. "You could have been killed!"

The major didn't appear to expect an answer. He moved aside to make way for the doctor, who'd just arrived. Sam felt Joe's hand tenderly stroke her hair as the doctor gingerly picked his way around the shattered door, and lifted her gaze to his face. One look at his expression told her he would never ask why she'd thrown herself between him and Falconer. He knew why.

The doctor knelt at her right side and began peeling the coat off her shoulder and arm. To take her mind off the pain and keep herself from swearing at him, she said, "What took you guys so long? I thought you'd never get here."

"As soon as Mr. Takamura positively identified Falconer, we went to his house to take him into custody," Joe answered. "Needless to say, he wasn't home. We were on the way back to the major's office when the man he'd assigned to keep an eye on Alvic radioed in to report that the suspect was here at the newspaper, and that an unidentified woman had also arrived. When I heard that, I almost had a heart attack."

So Esther hadn't phoned the major's office, Sam thought ruefully. Or if she had, he hadn't received the message. The doctor finally got her arm free. He poked at it and made a clucking sound. Sam gritted her teeth.

"I don't suppose it occurred to you that maybe I'd have liked to be there when you arrested him."

Major Connors dismissed the complaint with a terse, "You're a civilian. We couldn't have taken you along if we'd wanted to."

"Don't blame me," Joe murmured. "It was the Army's call."

The remark and his apologetic smile went a long way toward erasing Sam's disappointment. Unfortunately, she didn't have time to savor the feeling of gratification because the doctor started swabbing her arm with what felt like hydrochloric acid. Joe gave her his hand to squeeze.

"I thought I heard two shots," she said. "Was anybody else hurt?"

"Just the reporter," Connors said dryly. "When he fainted, fell off his chair, and hit his head on the floor. He's got a pretty good lump, but he'll live. He's down the hall, writing the story that'll probably make him a household name. Falconer's shot went into the ceiling." He hesitated, then added grudgingly, "Thanks to you. If you hadn't thrown his aim off, he might've hit Joe or me."

She lifted her brows in question. "So it's 'Joe' now?"

Connors met her inquiring, slightly reproachful look with a straight face and a twinkle in his eye. "Sorry, you're right. Agent Mercer. But why the surprise? You were there when I told Boggs that he's been working with us since the FBI had you released into his custody."

"But I thought you were lying! You knew I did!"

"Miss Cook, the United States Army doesn't

lie," he said with the same deadpan expression. The doctor— who was wearing an Army uniform— snorted rudely as he began to bandage her arm.

"Didn't you think it was a little strange that I bought your . . . er— " The major's gaze darted to the doctor. "— improbable story so quickly?"

"Well . . ." Sam murmured. Now that she thought about it. . . . So Joe had already convinced him she was from the future, even before Connors had them picked up. She felt ashamed of the unfair things she'd been thinking earlier in the evening. Of course, Joe never had to know about that.

"Colonel Herrick had tipped us to Falconer a couple of months ago," Major Connors continued. "But we decided not to move until we could prove he was the German agent who'd been feeding us false information. His name's Ernst Reiner, by the way, in case you're interested. He and his family immigrated to America about a year and a half ago."

Sam nodded mutely. She was indeed interested, for more reasons than he had guessed, evidently.

"We suspected right away that Reiner had murdered Colonel Herrick, because we knew the colonel couldn't have been shot with his own weapon, which was in an ordnance storage room at Fort McNair. Of course, we weren't in any hurry to share that information with the FBI."

"You just said the Army doesn't lie," Sam reminded him.

"Withholding information for reasons of national security isn't lying. Besides, we couldn't tell the FBI about the second gun without also telling them we suspected a German agent of committing the murder."

"A German agent who'd managed to fool Army Intelligence for, what— close to a year?"

Connors frowned at her while the doctor finished securing the bandage and removed a bottle of pills from his bag.

"Take one of these if the throbbing gets too bad," he instructed as he handed the bottle to Sam. "But no more often than every four hours. You'll need to have your arm looked at tomorrow, but it should be fine in a week or so. It's a fairly minor flesh wound."

"Thank you," she murmured. She cautiously sat up, Joe's arm at her back to give assistance. The doctor closed his bag, got to his feet, and left.

Sam returned her attention to Major Connors. "You knew Valerie hadn't killed her father," she accused. "Why didn't you tell the police and the FBI right away?"

"As I believe I explained earlier," he said patiently, "I was out of town when the colonel was murdered."

Joe lifted Sam from the floor and deposited her on the chair Alvie had fallen off of. "He wouldn't have left her in jail," he said in the major's defense as he went to perch on a corner of the desk. "But by the time he got back to Washington and found out what had happened, she was gone."

"And a mystery woman who knew all kinds of things she shouldn't have known had taken her place," Connors pointed out. "I'm sure you can understand our intense curiosity about you, Miss Cook. We knew we'd been getting false information. Suddenly it looked like somebody had been leaking ours, too. The decision was made to put someone in place to watch you, find out how you knew what you knew, and whether you were responsible for Valerie Herrick's disappearance. For all we knew, *she* may have been the leak. Agent Mercer was the obvious choice for the job, since he'd known Valerie and had now been given responsibility for keeping tabs on you."

That "since he'd known Valerie" hit Sam like a bolt of lightning.

"The letter Valerie was writing to Joe that night!" she exclaimed. "Mr. Takamura found it after the police left. Did he— ?"

"I didn't find out about the letter until the afternoon before you met Kyoshi," the major said with a shake of his head. "Though of course we'd known about Agent Mercer and Miss Herrick all along. I saw no point in telling her father," he said before she could ask. "They were both adults, and it's a free country."

"But then why— ?" Sam looked at Joe and shook her head in confusion. "How did they convince you to work with Army Intelligence?"

"They didn't blackmail me, if that's what you're thinking." He glanced at the major to ask a silent question. Connors hesitated briefly, then nodded. "I've been offered a different job, with a new government agency," Joe explained. "It would be a step up, but the offer was conditional on a brand-new, top-level security clearance."

"Something tells me this new job isn't with Army Intelligence," Sam murmured.

"No. But agreeing to place myself under Major Connors's command allowed him to move ahead with the security clearance, and at the same time gave me the chance to learn a little more about what would be required of me."

Sam bit her lip. She thought she could guess what would be required of him. "You wouldn't by chance be going to work for 'Wild Bill' Donovan, at— ?"

Major Connors cleared his throat loudly. She gave him a droll smile. "What, it's so top secret I can't even say the name?"

"The agency doesn't even officially exist yet," he said sternly. "Besides, I don't think it's been given a name."

"Well, when somebody gets around to picking one, it'll be the Office of Strategic Services," she told him.

Connors gave her a perturbed look. "Miss Cook, please don't be offended by this, but being around you for very long could wreck a man's nerves."

The remark provoked a sheepish grin from Sam and a secretive smile from Joe, who murmured, "You can't begin to imagine, Major."

Later, after the major's driver had taken them home, they'd calmed a near-hysterical Esther, and Sam had promised to replace her coat, they retreated to the peace and quiet of Joe's room.

"Do you need one of those pills?" he asked solicitously as he placed a glass of water next to the bed.

"I'll take one in a minute," she said, then gave him a provocative look. "Right now I could use some help undressing."

He performed the task with such gentle, tender care that her eyes were moist when she slipped beneath the covers. He noticed, of course, and immediately reached for his trousers.

"I'm going to call our doctor, have him come over and give you a shot or something."

"No." Sam reached out with her good arm to stop him. "I don't need a shot. What I need is for you to hold me."

He hesitated, but he didn't make her ask twice. He carefully settled her on his chest, his arms tight around her. She felt him press a kiss on the top of her head, and then he said softly, his voice thick with emotion, "God, I love you."

Sam felt her eyes begin to leak. "Oh, Jesus, Joe."

"What?" he said in concern. "Is it your arm?"

She shook her head and tried to stop blubbering. She was partially successful. "No, you moron. It's my heart. Your timing really sucks. After everything I've been through today—couldn't you have told me this morning, or tomorrow? Damn, I need a handkerchief."

"Use the sheet. I'm not getting up unless it's to call the doctor. You said I shouldn't say it until I couldn't help myself."

"Well, I know, but . . ."

"Want me to take it back?"

She was using her left hand to wipe her eyes and nose with a corner of the sheet, so she had to punch his chest with her right. Pain immediately flared in her arm.

"Ow! Damn it."

"Serves you right," Joe murmured, but he laid a tender kiss on her arm, just above the bandage. "I was only bluffing. I wouldn't have taken it back."

"I wouldn't have let you."

"You always have to have the last word, don't you?"

"Yes." She flashed a mischievous grin. "I love you, too."

He laughed and kissed her. When her tears had stopped and her face was dry, he said, "In case you hadn't noticed, Colonel Herrick's murder has been solved, Valerie's name has been cleared, the

German agent has been caught . . . and you're still here."

Sam rubbed her cheek against his shoulder. "Mmmm, I'd noticed."

"Assuming you don't disappear into thin air— or 1995— before morning, would you be willing to marry me? As soon as possible?"

"Oh, God. That does it, Joseph. Yes, I'll marry you, but you're gonna *have* to get up and get me a hankie."

He did, but not right away.

Lucas had thought he was prepared. He was wrong. When the tall, slender, white-haired woman opened the door of the luxurious hotel suite, his knees almost buckled.

It was the eyes. The skin around them might be sprinkled with age spots and creased with a hundred fine lines, but those incredible eyes hadn't changed in 54 years.

"Dear God," he muttered.

"Goodness, Lucas," she said, and the voice was almost the same, too. "You look like you've seen a ghost. Come in and sit down before you faint."

He felt her hand on his arm, urging him through the door, but he couldn't take his eyes off her face.

"Joe, pour Lucas a stiff drink," she called as she closed the door and gave him a surprisingly strong push toward the living room. "Jack Daniels, if there's any in the bar."

As Lucas's legs propelled him across the thick carpet, he heard her say behind him, "You must be Valerie. I've been looking forward to meeting you for more than half a century. Obviously Lucas isn't in any shape to introduce us. I'm Samantha Mercer, Joe's wife."

Four hours later Lucas was still feeling dazed. Of course, he realized that could be partly because of the three whiskeys he'd had.

"I'd love to hear more about the OSS," Val said to Sam. "Especially the things the two of you did during the war."

Sam patted her hand affectionately. "And you will, dear. We've collected a lot of fascinating stories over the years."

"Every one of which she'll repeat in meticulous detail if you give her the least encouragement," Joe remarked.

Lucas roused himself to say, "I'd like to hear about my mother."

Samantha smiled at him. "Good. I hope you'll want to meet her too, when you're both ready."

"I assume you named her Josephine for her father," Val commented.

Sam nodded. "That's right, but we call her Josie. She was always something of a free spirit, very independent."

"Just like her mother," Joe said.

"Good grief, Joe, I was never as headstrong and rebellious as Josie," Sam protested, then frowned at his laugh of disbelief. "Well, I wasn't!

"Josie dropped out of school and ended up in San Francisco in the early '60s," she said to Lucas. "Lived in a commune for a while, reclaimed the original family name of Mirkovic. Sometimes we wouldn't hear from her for months on end. I guess she was only trying to 'find herself,' but it was a very worrisome time for us. Especially when we learned that she'd had a child and placed him for adoption without even letting us know."

"But it all worked out in the end," Val said softly. "Didn't it?"

"I'd say it worked out wonderfully," Joe replied. He smiled into Sam's eyes. "But then my opinion could be just a little biased."

Lucas shook his head. "It's all so . . . incredible. Not just that it even happened— though God knows I still sometimes wonder if I'm dreaming the whole thing— but the *connections*. How do you explain it to yourselves?"

"We don't," Joe said. "It can't be explained. I'd have gone crazy years ago if I'd let myself become obsessed with trying to figure out the whys and hows."

"So instead he let me drive him crazy," Sam said. Sobering, she leaned forward to lay a hand on Lucas's arm.

"Some things we'll never understand, Lucas. My connection to Ernst Reiner, for example. I *think* my mother was his granddaughter— or would have been, if events had followed their original course. But now . . . who knows? I'll never be able to prove, to myself or anyone else, that we were related. It doesn't matter. We know, Joe and I. And, as he said, it all worked out wonderfully for us. We've had 54 years together, and I wouldn't give up a day of that time for all the money— or all the answers— in the world. I only hope that you and Valerie will be half as happy together as we've been, and still are."

Something else that hadn't changed, Lucas thought— her no-holds-barred honesty. He laid his hand over hers.

"We will be," he said huskily, then grinned and added a teasing, "Grandma."

Val excused herself to use the restroom and Joe

got up to make a call. Lucas was eagerly pumping Sam for more information about his mother, when he suddenly stopped in mid-sentence and turned pale.

"Oh, Jesus."

"What?" she said anxiously.

He stared at her with something like horror. "I don't know why it didn't hit me till now. . . ."

"Lucas, it isn't nice to frighten an old lady. What is it, for heaven's sake?"

"You." He lowered his voice to a whisper and darted a guilty look at Joe, who was still on the phone. "Me. *Us*, for God's sake!

"Oh, that." She waved her hand in dismissal. "That happened years ago."

"Not for me, it didn't!"

"I suppose that's right," Sam murmured. "Oh well, however long ago it was, it's in the past."

"The past," he muttered as Joe hung up the phone. "Right. Six whole weeks ago."

Either Sam didn't hear him or pretended she hadn't. Joe and Val rejoined them at the same time, and Joe announced that he'd confirmed their reservation for dinner and asked the front desk to get them a cab.

"After dinner we can come back here," Sam said as she pulled on her coat. "Since the curfew's still in effect you won't be able to drive back tonight anyway, and we have an extra bedroom."

Val agreed eagerly, not bothering to consult Lucas. "And you can tell us some of those stories I'm dying to hear."

"Of course!" Sam said as the four of them left the suite and headed for the elevator. "Though you have to understand, dear— " She glanced over her shoulder, looked straight at Lucas, and

winked. "— some of them are classified top secret."

After a moment's stunned surprise, he laughed.

Dear Reader:

Sometimes, or so I've been told, an entire story will erupt from a writer's imagination full-blown. Everything is suddenly and miraculously *there*— plot, characters, conflict, settings, theme, transformational arcs, black moment(s), climax(es), resolution, and all the other stuff works of fiction are supposed to contain— playing out on the screen of the writer's mind like a movie, complete with a soundtrack and special effects. The only effort the writer has to expend, I assume, is to type like crazy to get everything down on paper or disk before the final credits start rolling. This must be a truly wondrous, even transcendental, experience. Someday, if I remember to pick up my toys and eat all my vegetables, maybe it'll happen that way for me. But I'm not holding my breath.

I'd flirted with the idea of writing a time travel story for quite a while, but I could never settle on a specific period I'd like to send a character back to, or— equally important— a *reason* for zapping some poor unsuspecting soul through time and space. (For me, a story has to demonstrate cause and effect, a logical progression of events and their consequences or results, or it isn't worth writing.) Also, I knew that if I ever did undertake such a story, I'd want to deal not only with the character who travels through time, but also with those people she or he leaves behind. After all, their lives would also be thrown into chaos, and it wouldn't be fair to just abandon them to fend for themselves.

I played around with several possibilities, but none of them caught and held my interest. Until one day near the end of 1991, when I happened to wander into the living room while the television was on. There were President and Mrs. Bush, visiting the USS *Arizona Memorial* to commemorate the 50th anniversary of the surprise attack on Pearl Harbor that propelled the United States into WWII.

The tiniest germ of an idea lodged itself in my brain. Pearl Harbor . . . World War II . . . Hmmm, what if there was *another* surprise attack, on the same day, at virtually the same time, many years later? And what if this event somehow caused two people to switch places and times? Okay, I thought, it has some potential, but who *are* these two people? *Why* would they switch places and times— why them, and not two other people? What happens to them afterward?

You get the idea. It took a gazillion more "what if" sessions and the better part of two years, but I finally figured out what was going to happen, to whom, and why. And *then* I had to research and write the book! I suspect Denise Little wondered at times if I'd ever finish it; I *know* I did. Every writer should be blessed with such a patient, supportive editor.

Now that it's done and in your hands, I hope you'll enjoy it. (Sorry, you'll have to supply your own soundtrack and popcorn.) I'm taking a few days off, then I think I'll start playing "what if"